passive intruder

passive intruder

a novel • **Michael Upchurch**
W. W. Norton & Company
New York   London

Copyright © 1995 by Michael Upchurch

The text of this book is composed in Optima with the display set in Retrospecta.
Composition by Crane Typesetting Service, Inc.
Manufacturing by Courier Companies.
Book design by Guenet Abraham

Library of Congress Cataloging-in-Publication Data

Upchurch, Michael, 1954–
Passive intruder : a novel / Michael Upchurch.
    p.   cm.
I. Title.
PS3571.P375P37   1995
813'.54—dc20   95-5393

ISBN 0-393-03865-3

W. W. Norton & Company, Inc.,
500 Fifth Avenue, New York, N.Y. 10110

W. W. Norton & Company Ltd.,
10 Coptic Street, London WC1A 1PU

1   2   3   4   5   6   7   8   9   0

for John

contents

part one

wherever you go

Just when Susan started feeling old, Walker made her feel young again.

She was twenty-four and he was thirty-nine; it was absurd for her to worry about her age. But it came as a relief when Walker, a photographer at one of the Seattle daily papers, dismissed it as an issue.

Susan worked for the newspaper, too, as a receptionist, a job she performed with the same brisk disinterest she had brought to waitressing, being a bicycle messenger and acting as publicist for a film festival—occupations which scattered her energies and offered her a pleasantly makeshift social life, with everything temporary, everything insecure.

Her romances had been just as haphazard: a procession of quivery young men with slicked-back hair and restless eyes who were attracted to her calmness, but didn't know what to do with it.

Walker knew, even if it did take over a month for him to notice her at her telephone switchboard right outside the photo lab: "Joan isn't back from vacation yet?"

This got him a dirty look: "She isn't on vacation. She quit. In June."

Far from being put off, he melted at this.

His accuser shifted uncomfortably behind the name plaque on her desk, which read "S. POND."

"What does the 'S' stand for?" he asked.

She told him.

He tried it out: "*Susan Pond. . . .* I like that."

"Good for you."

He stared at her brightly.

She bared her teeth at him.

He winked and left.

From that moment he took her over, smoothing his way past her as if he had subjected her to some bland enchantment, a spell more ordinary than any in myth or legend but just as effective. By continuing to meditate aloud upon her name and her thankless role as office dogsbody ("So how are the underlings doing today?"), he managed to get a rise out of her. She knew he was being obnoxious, but there was something so genially perverse about his banter that it made her want to banter back.

A few weeks later, while taking a break from the newsroom videomonitors' broadcast of the Iraqi invasion of Kuwait—the highlight, so far, of an unsettling new decade—he discovered her doodling pictures of fleeing sheiks on a memo pad. When he asked her about them, she admitted she had done a little life drawing in college before she dropped out.

He immediately adopted this as his cause. A skilled draftsman, he fiddled with her efforts and made the sheiks more lively. She watched what he did, and admired the results cautiously. It took some more nerve—and several drinks—for her to dig out and show him a few of her college sketches.

His verdict: "The human figure's what you have a talent for, so that's what you should work on most. You need to follow your strength."

With this, another hurdle was jumped. She trusted him. And increasingly he held her attention by expanding on that trust.

He seduced her more deviously—by offering to be her model.

They met at her apartment on the Saturday after this informal drawing conference. With some minimal chitchat he disrobed, and she found herself staring at him, not strictly in a spirit of study. He treated his nudity with such nonchalance, however, that she felt honor bound to try to do the same. It would have felt like cheating to admit to an erotic interest in her model.

She took up her sketchpad and pencil—only to set them down again.

"You want me to pull the shades?"

"You'll need the light."

"We're sort of high up," she assured him. "I don't think anyone can see you."

"Just as long as you can."

She started to draw.

He was smooth-shaped, solid, self-conscious not in an inhibited way but as though his body were an instrument and he its virtuosic player. His posture was studiedly relaxed, casually observant. His brown hair was thinning slightly at the crown of his head, but this sign of age translated only as a kind of vigor. About thirty minutes into the session, his feet began kicking small kicks, restlessly, of their own accord, and he apologized.

"Don't worry," she said. "It's a movement I can work with."

He invited her to take a closer look—"Let's leave the feet out of it. . . . "—and she proceeded to isolate the various sections of his body, observing them as she would a form of wildlife: the deltoid slope from shoulder to breastbone; the swelling path from back to buttocks; the length of his throat as he leaned back and swallowed; a firm but thickish waist; a crowded, muddled groin.

Each of these places, as she studied them, suggested a progress toward tenderness. They also triggered in her a surge of nervous energy. She came up close to him—too close—and then found herself yielding to an urge she had been trying to suppress for the last half hour.

He drew her toward him and they kissed. His breath had been sweetened by a mint, and his breasts—when she traced her finger across them—turned out to be ticklish. She squatted lower on her haunches. His arousal, by this time, was obvious. A cavernous sensation opened up beneath her which needed to be filled, and she shifted her center of gravity. She had no questions about this. . . .

Afterwards, she wondered if the whole life-drawing business might only have been a scheme for getting her into bed. If so, it was dismaying how easily it had worked.

Still later in the week, it occurred to her that these feelings were like nothing she had ever experienced. It astonished her that workaday life had room enough to accommodate them!

He kept on posing and she didn't get tired of it, so they set a wedding date for September.

Walker, in earnest—wanting the marriage to be ironclad, un-threatened—took an HIV test, the implication being that this would help in assessing all inner and outer threats to their union. And his test results were negative, just as Susan's had been a few months earlier when she applied for medical coverage under the newspaper's group policy.

From there the engagement proceeded smoothly, apart from Susan's parents' quiet expressions of concern, bordering on dis-approval, at her marrying an older man she had known for a mere two months; a man who turned out—as Walker disclosed during his second modeling session—to have been divorced only in May. (The reason for his distraction in June?)

Susan thought it wise not to inquire too closely into this failed marriage, but was suggestible to doubt where doubt was planted—and her mother planted it as tactfully as she could. Maybe Walker was "bad husband material." Maybe there was a "problem" Susan ought to find out about. Thus, at her mother's prompting and with Walker's approval, Susan contacted her fiancé's ex-wife, Eleanor—a blond Southerner not strident but breezily loud in her contempt for soft things.

"You'll have a good time with Walker," she declared. "You'll see him through. Or maybe you'll see through him?"

Susan, understandably intimidated, made no answer to this.

"Either way," Eleanor continued, "I think you've both made a reasonable choice." She gave a flat laugh. "And I'm *fond* of Walker," she insisted, leaning close. "I think the world of him! But you'll find ways of sneaking around that, I'm sure."

Susan was too shy to ask about the choice Eleanor had made in abandoning a marriage to someone she seemed to hold so dearly—or was it Walker who had done the abandoning? When Susan put this question to her husband-to-be, the details stayed vague but the tone was enthusiastic. Walker discussed Eleanor as he might a child he had raised and shaped until she was strong enough to choose her own path out into the world and stick to it. He even called her on the telephone several times in Susan's presence, airing his sanguine feelings about his impending marriage.

"There's nothing secretive or shameful about it," Susan tried telling her parents. "A divorce can be a daylight affair—not like Aunt Ginny's. It can end in friendship."

They weren't convinced. Or perhaps they understood that their daughter, while comfortable with her fiancé's friendship with his former wife, was less than comfortable with the wife herself. They remained polite whenever they met with Walker, but their feelings toward him were guarded.

As for Walker's parents, they were old and frail, lived way off in Montana, and apparently felt no need to get acquainted with the bride before the wedding. His sister, Mary, would not be attending the ceremony at all. When Susan asked him why not, he told her, "She's out of touch right now. She can't be tracked down."

He wasn't nearly as disturbed by this as Susan was—but, sensing her discomfort, he made a point of explaining about his family and how little they had to do with his life. It was pure chance, he elaborated, that his parents had given him the name of one of his idols, that of James Agee's behind-the-camera collaborator. He had toyed, at an early stage, with changing his last name to "Evans" in homage to his hero; his family name—*Popman*—had such a silly jack-in-the-box ring to it. But then he had dismissed the idea: "A man should stick with the name he's given."

To Susan the notion of a name change wasn't such a weighty matter. How far, after all, could it be from "Pond" to "Popman"? Her willingness to accept the change struck her as something flexible in her which was flexible in all women, and which, in the end, made them stronger than men. As she lay enwrapped in Walker's arms at night in the months that followed their honeymoon, she would even thrill at the thought of the transformation that a name change implied—and at the way a legal metamorphosis, with its simple trick of paperwork, might become a real one. . . .

Even a fairy-tale marriage requires a trial by exile or separation—a time when the nuptial couple abandon each other or the world of their origin and succumb to the flux of travel in order to remake themselves, dig in deeper, discover the intricacy of what they are.

Over the summer Walker had sold some of his artier photographs in a group show at a gallery in Pioneer Square, and for their one-year anniversary he proposed spending the money on a three-week rail journey across the country and back—down to San Francisco for a day or two; along the coast to Los Angeles; across the desert to New Orleans; up the eastern seaboard to Boston where Mary, his incommunicative sister, lived; then a straight shot back across the continent, with a layover in Chicago. It would be their first real vacation together.

The time since their wedding had passed quickly and yet, in retrospect, seemed of lengthy duration because the year had been so extraordinary—wars in the Persian Gulf and Yugoslavia, a coup and then a countercoup in the Soviet Union, the world ushered through one fly-by-night era after another. The weeks had passed rapidly, speeded by surprises, but when scrutinized were so incident-filled that it was difficult to see how their every event—the oscillations in public feeling, the unpredictable flare-ups of global threat—had fit into a twelve-month period.

"No telephones, no television, no headlines," Walker chortled. "It'll be perfect."

Susan restrained herself from pointing out how easy it would be to pick up a newspaper on a station platform. Instead, she let his dangled lure entice her as much as it enticed him. Her job was nothing but switchboard gridlock, newsroom videomonitors, afternoon and evening editions, and she had no objection to abandoning them all for a while. . . .

In San Francisco—a city of pastel houses, waxy evergreens and out-of-season flowers—Walker revealed himself to be an ardent urban hiker, jackrabbiting up the hills as if under deadline. Susan could hardly keep up with him. The only rest she got was when he stopped to take pictures with his Polaroid—his source of "instant gratification," as he called it. Away from work and the newspaper's photo lab, he enjoyed an orgy of carelessness, pointing his lens at random, not caring what it caught.

At first she perused each snapshot, no matter how blurry or haphazard, eager to enter what seemed to be a game for him. But after a hike to the summit of Buena Vista Park where he went through a whole roll of film (Walker was drawn to summits), she was too tired and sweaty to look at his results. It was late October and the day was blazing. Besides there were the joy-boys to spy on as they tried out their lust with a glance and followed it into the bushes.

Looking at Walker, wishing he would pay her a little more attention, she wondered if lust might be the thing to go for. But then, approaching Castro Street, her eyes met a wraith on his way to old haunts, threading a wasted face past the sidewalk's healthier specimens, and the flame immediately died in her. It was something she had seen in Seattle—and thought of as an exception. Glimpsed here, it felt more like a prediction or a law. She couldn't keep her eyes on the pain, the enfeebling threat of it. And the victim preferred not to be studied.

When, at length, he had passed out of sight, she took Walker's hand—chastely but firmly—and urged him on his way.

They caught a bus and did the tourist thing over at Fisherman's Wharf, where they cooled down with two waffle cones. There, with the water view and sharp light mesmerizing her body into neutral, she put death out of mind, thinking she was safe from it for now (safe, especially, from any slow or wasting death), and remarked to her husband, "Sometimes I think it's just a matter of luck, don't you? Nothing to do with will or personality at all."

He wasn't sure what she meant by this; asked her to re-phrase it.

"Doesn't everything—" she knocked on the wood beneath them, "—just feel lucky?"

His glance made it clear he still had no idea what she was talking about: "You mean the bench?—that it hasn't been hacked to bits by vandals?"

"No, no. You and me. Sitting here together where we've never been before."

"There're a lot of places we haven't been."

"You're right, there are," she said thoughtfully.

She mused on this for a moment, then suggested, "So maybe neither of us has any?"

"Any what?"

"Any will. Any personality."

"Sure we do."

"How do you know?"

"How could we *not* have any?"

"Well, if we do, they never seem to come into conflict." She wasn't teasing but in earnest, pressing him, "Well, do they?"

He smiled at her.

"You know what I think?"

She opened her eyes wide, waiting to hear.

"I think you're in need, in very serious need—"

"Of what?"

"Another ice cream cone."

"Oh no. Not ice cream. Chinese food!"

He gave her a stern look.

She begged him: "Please? Pretty please?"

"But we just ate."

"So we'll get fat. And besides, we could just order vegetables. . . ."

On the bus from North Beach into Chinatown an angelic-looking five-year-old boy across the aisle from them frantically kissed the man accompanying him (his father? his uncle?) on his cheeks and all over his face. The recipient of these kisses looked worried and embarrassed, especially after getting a wet smack right on the lips. Kisses, it seemed, were part of a shrill attention-getting game, and they were contagious, prompting Susan to give Walker a lingering peck on the cheek—which he returned, the purring of his lips suggesting contact elsewhere.

Thus distracted, they missed their stop. The bus had gone underground, emerging near Union Square, and in order to reach the restaurant they'd chosen from their guidebook, they had to walk the length of the Stockton Street tunnel, a subterranean corridor which brought memories of the '89 quake—or its televised broadcast—fresh to mind. It seemed pure chance that the earth didn't grumble and heave as it had two years ago, the concrete caving in on them as they wandered in search of food. This whole *area* was under a variety of threats, as the massive wildfire across the bay in Oakland had shown only the week before. And Chinatown, when they reached it, felt more like a sooty, pedestrian-choked underworld than prime gourmet territory.

At dinner, buoyed by a fair amount of sake, Susan speculated once more on the nature of their luck.

"Some people just wear their fate on their faces, don't they?"

Walker wasn't listening: "Hmmn?"

"Like that woman over there. You can see what she's been through—"

"Over where?"

Susan squinted but couldn't quite locate her: "That's funny—"

"Well, what about her?"

"You can tell—You can just tell—Well, take me for instance. I've got a bland face."

"No you don't. I like your face. I *love* your face. And your eyes. And these other bits—"

"Hey—cut it out."

He drew back.

"It's bland," she continued. "And I can sense I'll have a bland fate. I'll just be—bland! Don't you sense anything?"

"A great desire to gobble you up. But otherwise, no."

She pouted at this dramatically, to make a joke of it, and he held up his Polaroid, the flashlamp popping out its little cyclops eye at her, square and solemn.

"Say 'cheese.' "

"Don't!" she objected.

"Then say 'cold sesame noodles'!"

He went ahead and blinded her. Finding her drink by feel, she waited for her vision to return, then grew restless.

"What is it?"

"That woman—" She looked around the dining room. "I wonder where she got to. . . . "

She didn't notice anything else out of the ordinary until they were back in their hotel room—where, flopping down on the bed, she let the dusty sweat cool on her, idly shuffled through Walker's photographs, then sat right up and said: "But here she is!"

"Who?"

"The woman at the restaurant." She flipped to another snapshot. "And this is her in the park!"

The restaurant's Chinese reds and the glow of its lanterns; the park's winding paths and dark tunnels of rhododendron—both served as delectable backdrops to uncertain subject matter.

"How can you tell it's the same person?" he asked. "Or even that it's a woman?"

The face was obscured in every picture. And the only thing to suggest it was the same figure from shot to shot—and that this figure might be female—was the strangely contoured overcoat she was wearing, fluid and viscous, like a wrinkling lava flow. Why wear something so heavy in such hot weather? And could there really be two people so similarly overdressed in two different parts of town?

"My god! This is her on the bus, too. She was looking straight at us!"

Walker peered over his wife's shoulder at a shadowy outline from which a smile emerged, a smile as intense as the loopy grin on the face of the kiss-crazy kid. Apart from the smile, however, nothing about this figure—age, sex, hair color—was readable. Even its race seemed indistinct.

Susan was anxious: "Why would she be following us?"

"It's a fluke," Walker said. "They all just look alike." And then with evident pleasure he added, "It's a weird picture, isn't it? You might try drawing from it. I bet you could really get somewhere with it."

With this, he dismissed the matter, as if there were no point in making a fuss over something he didn't understand. San Francisco felt like more of a city than Seattle. Maybe a coincidence like this wasn't surprising when the given amphitheater was so vast. The city, perched on its hills, *was* strangely like a stage, a grand proscenium on which odd performances and unlikely connections could be expected.

She saw it that way too—as a kind of floodlit diorama viewed from on high—and, taking her cue from Walker, let its warm and tawny colors soothe her to sleep.

For Walker the wedding had been almost a side effect of what he was after. He talked of it as though the only logical form it could take would be a civil ceremony witnessed by strangers solicited off the street outside the King County Courthouse. But when Susan made clear that her parents and her sister, Celia, would be hurt if the wedding didn't include them, he readily agreed to a more elaborate celebration as if this were no sacrifice at all—simply a matter of arranging more stage scenery.

He called his parents in Havre with the news, and the elder Popmans "agreed to attend," as he put it. As for his sister, Mary, he had no explanation as to why she wouldn't make it to the wedding, beyond the fact that she was "out of touch." When Susan pressed him on this a day or two later, he assured her there was no hostility between himself and his sister. They were reasonably close, even if they did live thousands of miles apart: "It's just she doesn't have the energy to communicate some-times."

His parents, when they arrived, turned out to be a good twenty years older than Susan's. They stood stiffly, as though braced for a fall, and gave off a waxy radiance, holding their future daughter-in-law with a luminous gaze that suggested some stern brand of common sense—but whether this was the real thing or simply the pallor of old age made impressive by some trick of the light was difficult to say. Susan couldn't help thinking they embodied an ancient authority, a line of expectations, a pattern that imposed itself on generation after generation, and it dawned on her how far Walker must have fallen from that pattern. This made her all the more curious about his childhood and youth, which he rarely discussed.

After his parents retired for the evening, she asked him what he had been like at fifteen.

"I felt grown-up," he said firmly, "more sensible than anyone around me. But I didn't want to be a man."

"Why not?"

"Being a man was dangerous," he explained. "All that Dad and the government wanted to do was send you to the jungle to die. I could see it coming. That was back when they had the lottery for the draft. And even if the draft didn't get you, they'd keep you at home, trap you in a job you didn't like so you could support a wife who resented you and kids who thought you were an antique. It looked like a no-win proposition."

"I guess so. . . ."

She said this doubtfully. A *bitter* Walker? And so young? She couldn't envisage it. But in matters like this, the fifteen years between them could feel impenetrable at times. They had grown up in different eras and neither could quite credit what the other's young experience had been like.

He continued: "Canada was—what? Thirty miles away? But I wouldn't have dreamed of going there. The thought was taboo."

"So what changed things for you?" she asked, realizing he was describing hell itself, if of a quiet variety.

"A nice lady down the street the summer I was seventeen. And then a college deferment that was sheer luck. After that I met Eleanor in Boulder and began to realize you can make up the rules yourself. You could in Boulder, anyway—and Seattle, too, I guess. Choose your place carefully enough and you can choose your own reality . . . choose your own drug as well."

Walker, it turned out, had been something of a pothead.

"Just be courteous and kind," he concluded, "and you can smile away what's alien around you, get along nicely."

"And what about Mary?"

"What about her?"

"Did she make a choice too?"

He couldn't say; he wasn't sure what it had been like for her. Except he knew that she, too, had felt that life was elsewhere: "She got out—but I have no idea how much the place followed her."

With a sinking feeling, Susan began to realize what an effort it would take to embrace the full *scope* of Walker. Marriage would help. Their time together was bound to shed some light on him. But it would be on only a fraction of him—and not even the formative fraction at that.

The average American male's life span was, what, seventy or so?

That put Walker more than half the way there. She would need a shorthand, a quicker way through. She had hoped that what he revealed about his sister might give away as much about him as it did about her. But not if his knowledge was so limited; not if he drew such a blank when it came to Mary.

She changed her tactics, asked about his photography—and did slightly better, got a few results. . . .

At the wedding, the two sets of parents had faced each other like species from different planets. Walker's father was a granary manager—"mostly spring wheat"—while Susan's was part of a Seattle investment firm that had recently been absorbed by a Californian institution, which was all he could talk about at the moment. The newlyweds' mothers exchanged more general pleasantries, but when the nuptials were done with, they parted as if never expecting to see each other again.

Celia, accompanied by her new friend Martha, chided her sister: "Well now that the courtship's over, maybe we'll be seeing more of you?"

"After we get back. I'll give you a call."

"Promise?"

"I promise," she said, and did her best to keep the words from sounding empty. But with each passing day of their honeymoon on a San Juan Island hideaway, Walker's "spell" grew stronger and something in her felt a little more hollowed out. The feeling was blissfully relaxing. Being with Walker was as pleasant, as undemanding, as being on her own. Their moods, their whims, their banter seemed a perfect match, with no friction to them at all, except a delectable sexual friction, the grazing of skin upon skin.

Walker would sprawl back naked in bed like a perfectly shaped doll—a *stocky* doll with a roguish grin and a chubby erection. She would straddle him, brush against him, feel him lift toward her ticklishly. His tongue would taste her. His mouth would open wide for her. And his Polaroid camera would document this unraveling, the pictures sliding out, their focus less important than the gist of the movement they caught. . . .

This camera activity came as something of a surprise to her, but seemed only a fair exchange: his making a subject matter of their coupling just as she, with her pad and pencil, had made a subject matter of him.

Afterwards they would retire to the Jacuzzi that came with the place.

There was nothing they couldn't say to each other.

"My problem," Walker declared, "is that I like making love with the same woman over and over again."

"That's a problem?"

"In some situations, yes." He snorkeled toward her. "But maybe not this one?"

She shimmied up to him.

"Maybe not," she agreed.

Their honeymoon, if one discounted its Polaroid sessions, was the most conventional thing they had done together—three nights' luxury accommodation, lounging and gamboling in a vast oval tub, rejoicing in the slippery shapes of each other. It was like a parody of itself, and they warmed to it. A magnum of champagne they had purchased in Friday Harbor sat by the faucets. Two tall, fluted glasses nested in the shampoo rack and gathered mist like perspiration on a lover's brow. Her breasts and Walker's genitals bobbed in the water: frivolous trinkets they had thought to bring with them.

With towels on the floor and clothes hanging from the sink, they made love once more, not caring what got soaked this time. The champagne bottle fell but failed to smash while she angled down on him. And the tickling thread of him entering her found no outcome: her contraceptive pill had seen to that. But just the thought of his possibilities dying within her—all that genetic coding going to waste!—was stirring, exciting.

She surfaced from jets of swiveling water, dunking his head and holding him under until he reared up in protest. Then she dodged back and fell, both of them laughing, exploding with wetness. When they finally simmered down, they couldn't stop gazing at each other.

Back in Seattle, over the next month or two, she lost touch with friends; couldn't even stir herself to call Celia, who accused her, "You're sex-dazed. You're slick with it. It's in your voice. I can hear it."

"Well maybe. And I feel like I'm getting stupider!" she confessed.

"You're sure this is healthy?"

Celia, with her rapid turnover in girlfriends, seemed unlikely to understand, but Susan put it as best she could, trying to keep all mention of enchantment out of it.

"Maybe not—but the feeling just gets larger. . . . "

By the time of their train trip a year later, she had no desire for anyone's company but Walker's. Visits to her parents' house in Issaquah; dinners with Celia and her girlfriend Martha (who was proving to have surprising staying power); lunches with colleagues from the newspaper—all were a distraction from what she wanted most.

With Walker she felt anesthetized, devoid of tension, immune—a *good* feeling. With everyone else she felt restless and alone.

As the train pulled out of Seattle's King Street Station on the first day of their trip, she had leaned into him and asked, "What do you think? Can you give me a guesstimate? Readers want to know. Are we way too happy?"

"Of course."

No doubt about it. This was serious.

On their second day in San Francisco they followed a lazy agenda of urban strolls and window-shopping; did some bookstore browsing in Haight-Ashbury; took a bus out to Fort Sutro to watch the Pacific blindly crash and roil against the rocks below; and then, in the evening, went out for an Indian meal—after which Walker, worried that he had tired her with all their wandering, suggested an early night.

At the hotel reception desk they asked for their room keys, along with two heavyset middle-aged men who, in a fog of alcohol, accompanied them into the elevator and got off at the fifth floor with them. Susan worried for an instant that these two, like her lady from the bus and park and Chinese restaurant, might be "pursuing" her. But with a murmured good night they moved further down the hallway and entered their own room next door.

Walker was all care and consideration. He opened a window which let in a breeze from the airwell. Undressing, he mockingly posed for her, offering her an opportunity to study him—but she felt too lethargic to dig out her sketchpad. As she slipped her clothes off, he asked if she wanted a back rub and she took him up on this, not making a fuss when she noticed their position on the bed gave him a view of their activity in the dresser mirror. His attentions soon moved from the small of her back to the swell of her hips, until he turned her over and nosed his way up her inner thigh to inhale her small forest of smells.

Her armpits proved his only other distraction.

Their bed began to sing, and its song found a counterpart in the amplifying airwell. The men next door, it turned out, were a couple—as she should perhaps have guessed they were—and both songs became more bouncy.

Walker, hearing their noise, stretched out to dim the lights, then bent down to her again, tongue racing. Her smells were in his nostrils and on his lips; she tasted them there. His hips—as inevitable as surf unrolling—guided him upward and inward, against her and into her, while his shoulders arched away from her. Reaching for his Polaroid, he had her take pictures of *him* this time, so he could see what it was like: this moment when he lost himself, wasn't himself, surpassed himself. Feeling foolish, she did her best, while the couple next door yelled to the ceiling.

Things came to a halt. Thighs clung but weren't pumping. Sleep filtered out of flesh-heaviness. Her hands let go of the camera. Her hips slid into the photos it had spat on the bed. . . .

When she saw what those photos were the next morning, before Walker awoke, she kept her fears to herself, dismissing the eyes as an illusion, although she did check the airwell to see if there was a fire escape or, unlikely though it seemed, a five-story-high ladder propped up there. She even leaned out to see if the aging lovebirds in the next room could have spied on them—but this was unfair because the eyes belonged to a face that was feminine and round, not masculine and square.

When she offered the photographs she thought most damning to Walker as they finished breakfast in bed together, he made no comment except to say that with his cheeks puffing out like that, he looked even fatter than usual.

She spent the next half hour cheerfully protesting that she *liked* the solid feel of him—all the more so, now that they were far from home, away from familiar surroundings. . . .

And then they entered unstable land: a tumult of hills sutured in rawhide.

South of San Luis Obispo, the train met the coast and didn't head back inland until after Santa Barbara. The mountains were as pointed as pyramids and the views were magnificent—a wind-swept celebration of continental plates in collision.

In Los Angeles, where they had scheduled an overnight layover with a package tour of Disneyland the following day, they stayed in a glass-and-concrete monolith patronized mostly by business-men. Walker, as she might have expected, was excited by the view: a floor-to-ceiling vista of lights spreading out like a neon-threaded carpet two hundred feet below. As with San Francisco, it was her first time in the city, but she couldn't summon any enthusiasm for exploring it at night. What she saw from the windows looked full of fatigue, empty of content. She asked if they could just stay put and relax, watch TV, ''—or I could sketch you, if you like.''

Walker, agreeing to this, undressed, and soon her pencil was reveling in the contrast of sumptuous lover and sterile surroundings. When, however, she noticed his attention stray-ing toward the bag that held his Polaroid—the immaculate sheen of their accommodation challenging him as much as it challenged her—she stopped what she was doing and asked, "Do you have to?"

Her voice was calm, but she couldn't conceal from herself her worry that even here, some twenty stories up, she might see a face *out there* beyond the glass—or, worse, intuit a figure inside their room that was neither herself nor her husband but something in between.

Walker replied: "Not if you don't want me to."

But clearly he was up for it.

She relented, told him to go ahead, hoping that the way to beat a fear or superstition was by refusing to acknowledge it.

He stepped into the bathroom to load his camera, then emerged with a sterner-than-usual look on his face. This time, he announced, he was going to do it carefully. But he had trouble phrasing what "it" was. Something that would capture the lilt of her, he suggested.

"Okay if I keep on sketching?"

"Yeah, sure, carry on."

She was drawing a face from imagination: something she occasionally attempted when she didn't feel like discipline. And it wasn't another of her sheiks (under Walker's tutelage she had ended up making a series of them), but some sort of gypsy woman with a smirk on her face.

Susan found herself smirking back at her.

Walker asked if she could look a little less cheerful.

Putting the sketch aside, she rose from her chair. More in protest than cooperation, she tried all manner of poses: parodies of magazine clothing ads, perfume ads, car ads. Anything that required a lissome, drooping female figure to flounce in wind-swept clothing around a room or in a street or on a rocky precipice.

"No," he told her, "not a spoof. Something a little more intense."

She stopped twirling—and stared at him directly.

"Sorry," he said. "Not quite as intense as that."

She looked down at her discarded sketch, thought of picking it up, but didn't. She didn't know what to do.

"Maybe if we turn on the TV," he suggested.

"If you like."

CNN was broadcasting the continuing chaos in former Yugoslavia. On a picturesque rampart in Dubrovnik, citizens were ducking missile fire, scurrying along narrow streets, creeping with particular stealth past places where stone walls had given way to bomb sites.

"And maybe if you say something," Walker advised her.

"Say what?"

"Doesn't matter," he told her. "Try talking to yourself."

"Like I'm crazy? I can do crazy, if you like."

He already knew her "crazy": a goofy sendup.

"No, no. Something more ordinary, nondescript."

He guided her into the position he wanted: a head shot, close-up. His shutter clicked as she told him her mind had gone blank. He suggested that she try making vowel sounds.

She obliged him, all the time keeping her eye on the television screen, where a reporter was interviewing people who were struggling with battle-zone conditions.

"You still have to go to your job," one said through a translator. "You still have to eat."

Another interviewee, a woman, looked strange to Susan; was wearing some kind of national costume, brought out of the closet only for folk festivals, one would think, or as a sop to tourists hungry for local color—except these clothes appeared to be this woman's daily wear. The television announcer was saying: "Four days ago this woman lost her husband and her home when Serbian missiles destroyed their encampment outside the village of—"

Susan sat up. The woman on TV was a gypsy, a real one, and she was identical, or close enough, to the gypsy Susan had just drawn. And the eerie thing, as she recited her woes to the translator, was the smile on her face—an expression one might take at first to be beatific but which, upon closer examination, was nothing but endurance. Not a smirk, but a curling of the lips and a squint against whatever cruelty—the glaring sun's, the dispassionate camera's, the airborne bombs'—was out there.

"Hey—!"

"That's good."

"No—on TV."

But she had vanished.

She grabbed the sketch to show Walker: "It's the same woman!"

"You drew her from TV?"

"No, I drew her—and *then* she was on TV."

It wasn't the first time she had gotten the natural sequence of things—a subject to be observed and then the observation being made—mixed up. On occasion her sketches became almost clairvoyant: a face she invented on paper would turn up on-screen or in the flesh a short time later. But she had never felt comfortable telling anyone about this.

She tried telling Walker now: "I wasn't even trying. I mean, it's strange."

"Coincidence?" he suggested—which only made her wonder if the sketch was too cartoonish to look like a portrait to anyone but herself. What could be more clichéd than an amateur artist's notions of a gypsy woman?

But, then, why draw a gypsy woman in the first place?

"We can turn it off if it's bothering you."

"Not 'bothering' me—"

She searched for a more appropriate word, but had so little idea of what it might be that she gave it up.

He hit the remote control and darkened the screen.

After a while, with reluctance, she conceded, "Well maybe it *is* just a coincidence."

"Yeah, that's it."

"But what does it mean?"

"Probably nothing. Coincidence is just . . . coincidence. It makes you more alert, perhaps? But it's nothing you're supposed to understand."

With these words, he lifted a weight from her. A feeling as tidy as her name change, as quieting as defeat, encompassed her.

And now the pose he had requested and the phrases he was after mutely emerged from her: *She's always walking with me. She never leaves my side.*

The syllables were like images, tricks of time taking her off somewhere, deep down and beyond, toward a realm where depth didn't matter. . . .

Eventually she surfaced.

Walker looked at her dubiously: "Boy, you were gone there."

She agreed. She had been out of it, miles away. And at the same time she had been right here.

It all felt make-believe, as her marriage did sometimes—too good to be true. Even the coincidence of the sketch began to seem doubtful. At any rate there were no means of verifying it; the woman wasn't likely to be on TV again.

Her thoughts turned, with sudden concern, to Walker.

"Did you get the shot you wanted?"

"Oh, yeah—I think I did. I think I got the perfect shot."

"Good."

He looked at her curiously.

"So where were you? What were you thinking? Or can you tell me?"

She tried to answer—but, confusing the television image now with those from San Francisco, she couldn't begin to say who "she" was.

By day the hotel-room windows were suffused with brightness. They framed dim skyscrapers, beyond which was only a limbo wisped by palm trees. Mild smog diffused all light to a lurid pallor—whitish lemon, milky ocher—in which any apparition would find it difficult to survive.

After breakfast, they boarded the tour bus to Anaheim and took the freeway passage out to Orange County. Gray-green hedgerows blocked the view to either side. The hiss of tires on tar was a bland continuum. And the parking lot they entered an hour later was a fathomless blacktop sea, the glimmering roofs of automobiles serving as its whitecaps.

Quarter of a mile away, the theme park rose like a fantasy stronghold. The peak of a scale-reduced Matterhorn loomed over eucalyptus trees. Once past the ticket barriers, they headed down the pristine brick sidewalks and clean cast-iron latticework of an artificial Bourbon Street. An old-fashioned cinema was playing a Mickey Mouse cartoon. A clothing boutique offered perennial summer fashions. Souvenir stands sold T-shirts by the dozen.

A seven-foot-tall rabbit crossed their path and waved hi.

Susan asked doubtfully, "Why are we here?"

Around her, people looked bent on serious pilgrimage. It felt almost like sacrilege to pass through here as an unbeliever.

"At least it's pedestrian-friendly," Walker consoled her. And then: "Should have taken the earlier tour. Look at these crowds!"

They settled in to wait for their first ride: Space Mountain. With the line at a halt, Susan asked her husband again about her sister-in-law. She was still a little nervous at meeting Mary.

"What does she do in Boston?"

"She's a sort of perpetual student."

"Still? How old is she?"

"Thirty-three? Thirty-four?"

He thought about it, and settled on thirty-four: "She's taken a year off here and there—why it's taking her so long. Now she gets paid to do research. Not much, but enough to live on. She's working on her Ph.D."

"That sounds impressive."

"Oh it is, it is."

"And in Boston? Where?"

"Cambridge, actually. M.I.T."

"Good grief!"

"Yeah, she's got the brains in the family. I'm just the entertainment."

"What's she researching?"

"The minds of rodents."

This gave Susan pause.

"Does she have to touch them?"

"Oh, I'm sure she does. But she's always liked animals. When she was twelve—"

He started in on what he called one of Mary's "animal epi-sodes," something to do with a dozen chicks she brought home from a hatching experiment in science class. But his words were drowned out. A family behind them erupted into chaos, the baby starting to howl and all the other kids joining in. Conversation became impossible.

Twenty minutes later the squawling simmered down enough for Susan to ask, "So what happened to all those chickens in the end?"

Walker couldn't remember: "Gave them to a farm, maybe . . .?"

Susan wondered what it would be like to have so distant a sibling, especially one who found it so difficult to keep in touch. Before her marriage (which she still sometimes saw as a sublime interference, a diverting aberration from all that was normal in her life), she and Celia had both had apartments on Seattle's Capitol Hill, a ten-minute walk from each other. They got together at least once a week—or had done, until the advent of Walker. If Celia had been on the other side of the continent, Susan was sure they would both have been pained by the physical gap between them. Or else, she fantasized, she might be tempted to think of Celia as a twin, a protean counterpart, doing all the things she didn't dare do, living out an agenda that she couldn't even formulate to herself.

The real Celia, by contrast, was a constant reminder that a sister could be more matter-of-factly different. Susan might have had a "secret friend" throughout her childhood (a friend she seemed lately to have reacquired!), but Celia, the older of them by two years, had never been it. She was there merely to be loved, not understood.

The line coiled from the sunny glare of the theme park's pedes-trian thoroughfares to the inner dimness of a noisy arcade filled with lighting effects and famous chattering robots from block-buster movies. Twenty minutes later Susan and Walker were plunging and screaming in a roller-coaster car, dropping through darkness while galaxies flew around them and the rings of Saturn spun overhead. They enjoyed a full three minutes of vertigo and blasting sound, then stumbled back into daylight.

Walker was pleased. Susan still was dubious. As the afternoon progressed, they spent five more hours in three more lines to go on three more rides, the purpose of each being to obliterate all conventional notions of space-time. To Susan there was one comfort in this: it felt as though no one could follow them here because it wasn't a real place. It was already so populated with ghoulish or saccharine goblins and specters that it left no room for apparitions of one's own.

The last ride they took involved ascending in gondolas along rising canals to a labyrinth of caves where chirping automatons— rabbits, chipmunks, ravens, roadrunners—sang jolly songs and chuckled warnings about the plunge to come. The creatures were friendly and the atmosphere insane. The climax of the trip was a vertical passage down a roaring waterfall where you could see nothing ahead of you. It made Susan think of bad visibility on a highway in a rainsquall where all you want to do is pull off the road and wait for the storm to pass. Afterwards, when she mentioned this to Walker, he agreed that he could use something a little gentler in the way of rides: "I'm having trouble keeping down my Tiki Burger. And feel my heart!"

She put her hand to his chest where a small insistent creature throbbed percussively beneath his padded flesh. She whisked her fingers away. He smiled at her questioningly. She tried smiling back, then looked around to see if there were any less violent distractions.

Cruising in a cable car through a hole in the miniature Matterhorn seemed just the ticket. The line wasn't long and the sign was alluring: ONE WAY TO TOMORROWLAND. The grounds looked lovely in the sunset, but the ride was over quickly. At a loss, they took an inadequate trip to Mars, then wondered how to kill the remaining two hours before their bus returned to Los Angeles. It was getting dark. The restaurants and shops were closing down, and the crowd was getting more raggedy, aggressive, unpredictable.

Sometime later, a histrionic choral version of "The Star Spangled Banner" began to play, the music changing key as it soared, accompanied by the crackle and thud of fireworks. Alice in Wonderland and the Mad Hatter appeared and disappeared. Goofy, Donald Duck, Snow White and a bunch of dwarfs were caught by an erratic dazzle that lit their costumes in a strobelike flicker while the air filled up with the scent of gunpowder.

Walker leaned over and whispered, "The message seems to be: Drop acid and vote Republican."

The fireworks, apparently, were a signal to the crowd to go home, and Walker voiced a worry that with everyone leaving at once it might take a while to work their way over to the parking lot where their bus was waiting.

Susan, noticing the dwarfs scurrying down a side path, nudged him and suggested, "Maybe that's a quicker way out?"

They followed.

A door opened onto a changing room where Alice was nervously smoking a cigarette and Sleepy, removing his head, turned out to be a young black man with a radiant smile. The door then closed and the only way to go forward was down an alley that led to a glow of ground lanterns which illuminated steam-railway tracks. Walker and Susan followed these, trying to keep sticky eucalyptus branches out of their faces, until they at last reached the main train station and the ticket barriers, now opened to release the flowing hordes.

Outside the theme-park entrance, the air grew chilly and she kept tight hold of her husband's hand. In the dark, the threat of that face which might pull her toward its world and snare her with its smile grew real again. All the way back to Los Angeles she stared down at her lap, not wanting to have contact with her fellow passengers, avoiding any eye that might be trying to catch hers. She prayed that Walker wouldn't take any pictures, and he didn't. He hadn't all day—as though it discouraged him to be met with sights so meticulously calculated to invite a camera's lens.

At the hotel they had a quick dinner, and then it was time to go. A doorman hailed them a cab. Again she looked at nothing for fear of what she might see. She didn't relax until they were actually in the station—where, standing on the platform, she allowed herself one glance back; then sighed with relief as they boarded the Sunset Limited for New Orleans.

It was amazing the confidence that came with secret knowledge of a person!

At work, upon her return from their San Juan Island honeymoon, Susan had faced the people whose needs she tended—reporters, editors, artists, researchers, lowly freelancers—with a new self-assurance. Reporters, she had always felt, held secrets that they might or might not divulge in print, and these secrets animated them, giving them an easy manner she once had envied. But no more.

With marriage, even her dullest routines seemed enlivened by her own harbored images of Walker naked, Walker in the throes of orgasm, Walker stretched out on his sofa for her to study minutely, a sketchpad on her knee. With these languid poses and blurry ecstasies of her husband constantly in mind, she had such a sense of authority on a subject of interest to everyone around her (Walker was something of a newsroom heartthrob) that it was all she could do not to flaunt it.

Reporters would ask if there had been any messages for them while they were out; celebrities would arrive at her desk for interview appointments; a senior editor would tell her to tell his wife that he was breaking his lunch date with her—and it took an increasingly conscious effort on her part to answer them intelligibly. Her foremost thought was: "I'm your equal. I have a life. And you don't know it."

She wondered if other women felt so rocketed up by their marriages. It seemed to her that her marriage wasn't like anyone else's: the husband offering himself night after night, the wife getting it all down on paper. It even struck her that Walker's first nuptial entanglement—like her own desultory romances—had been an incompetent affair at best, a poor imitation of what was to come, merely a rehearsal, a sketchy counterfeit.

She saw herself, as he tacitly encouraged her to, as the point toward which he had been heading all along. And she agreed with him: she felt they had always somehow known about each other, as destinations if not as personalities. Now they were living for each other, and their mutual devotion made her almost flamboyant.

Her growing sense of love-borne weightlessness had been rendered more giddy by that winter's atmosphere of imminent war and antigovernment protest. Circling helicopters, visible from the newspaper offices, monitored a freeway peace march that stopped traffic in hopes of stemming hostilities in the Persian Gulf. Peace had soon caved in. Ground war followed air war. Television screens were filled with missiles and rumors, and her dizziness approached elation. Fear and abandon became indistinguishable, producing a marvelous imbalance on her spine. There must be solid facts somewhere—"Why are people wearing gas masks in Jerusalem?"—but none of them touched her.

It didn't surprise her that her good luck came framed by the world's downward spiral, for there was something incendiary about both kinds of fortune. Her feeling of vertigo was a summons to recklessness. She looked away from the world, deliberately failing it, because she knew that when her own casualties hit her, as they inevitably must, the world in its bitterness would fail her in turn, take no account of her. It might even seem a peaceful place.

Happiness made her heedless. There was something almost virtuous, she felt, in dwelling on her joy in the midst of the crisis. She carried on drawing her sheiks as if they were strictly personal in inspiration, had no connection with reality at all. And it was marriage that gave her the nerve, the strength, the callousness she needed in order to do this.

Other aspects of her new situation were less straightforwardly emboldening.

Walker's house, which he had owned with Eleanor for a number of years, was on a cul-de-sac in Seattle's North End. A two-story affair made mostly of plate glass, or so it seemed, it sat deep in its wooded lot surrounded by tall nodding fir trees. In the shadow of these, Susan immediately understood why the early European settlers had felt compelled to clear the land and reduce susurrant cathedral spires to stumps, hollows, truncations. There were too many whispers, too many damp presences.

Her Capitol Hill apartment, by contrast, seemed to belong to another country at another latitude with another climate. Its windows had a western exposure and its views were of the Space Needle, the Olympic Mountains and a smooth lead sliver of Puget Sound. High on its hillside overlooking neighboring roofs, it resembled a princess's tower from which Walker had rescued or abducted her—it was difficult to say which. With its casual

snagging of any passing light, it had a quasi-Mediterranean qual-
ity . . . an impression compounded by the flourishing windmill
palm trees outside her windows, planted long ago, and now,
years later, almost twenty feet tall.

At Walker's house there were no such hints of gentle seasons.
The lofty firs brought a caution to his wife's movements, a wariness that sprang from her sense of isolation. But to Walker's eye
this note of stealth resembled an increase in grace, a radiant
outcome of solid bliss. He hadn't questioned it; while Susan kept
the question—*What am I afraid of?*—to herself.

And of course there was a pedestrian side to their life together,
foibles and quirks for them both to get used to, the things that
always surprised you about a person—mostly sleeping and bathroom habits.

There was also a marked increase in their moviegoing and
their museum and gallery visits. Once they stopped shuttling
between his place and hers, they seemed to have more time to
do these things, and with each of these activities she saw another
side of Walker unveiled or suggested.

With films, it became clear, he was more concerned with
technique than content: "He wasn't even *thinking* about color!"
He objected to anything schematic, no matter how competent:
"You need a bit of anarchy. Only the arbitrary can feel just right."
But when Susan objected to some fantastic coincidence in the
same movie's story line, Walker to her amusement would seemingly reverse himself: "I have no problem with that. In life there's
no pattern, but there's plenty of coincidence."

This sentiment, distilled to *No pattern—but coincidence*, became a phrase they shared between them like a talisman.

Walker, she began to realize, cherished anything that showed
something familiar from an unfamiliar angle. At a downtown
gallery, he grew excited over a series of paintings, giant-sized,
depicting the interiors of airliners: the half-glimpsed heads of
passengers . . . the slight, meticulous curve in rows of seats . . .

the streamlined repetition of meal trays, shoeless feet and carry-on baggage. He also had a passion for teased-out information, for characters who threw everything around them into doubt, for stories that seemed to be about one thing and then were about another. And he had a weakness for tales of psychic possession, outer-space aliens who skipped vampirically from person to person, multiple personalities competing for a venue in a single body, futuristic shapeshifters who met one piece of mayhem after another with the cunning of a modern-day Proteus.

Under Walker's tutelage, Susan began to gain an appreciation for horror films and ghost stories—or at least for those, like Cronenberg's and few select others', of a more sophisticated variety. And when Walker asked for her response to some of the screen hauntings and psychic parisitisms he persuaded her to see, she had the peculiar feeling he was talking about things he would never fully understand himself, but which, mysteriously, were finding fertile ground in her.

Similarly, on weekends when he photographed her (after they had taken to bartering their services as models for each other), she sensed that his shots of her were telling him something small about himself that he was unable to comprehend. A blind spot, as annoying as someone's unconscious habit of slovenliness or absentminded whistling, prevented him from doing so. But this only made her feel more tenderly toward him.

The feeling grew stronger, too, of there being something or someone other than herself whom he was addressing as he directed his lens at her—possibly Eleanor? Or was it some kind of *ur*-woman, a recurring archetype, whom he imagined both his wives to be?

Maybe when she posed for him, he stopped seeing her altogether—saw only some abstract, feminine side of himself.

Whatever the case, the feeling didn't go away. And in growing more durable, it offered a sort of companionship, soothed a loneliness out of her that had arisen from finding herself so closely bound to this new man in her life. Would she have felt as lonely with a woman?

She asked her sister about this. And Celia's answer was that loneliness was unpredictable, slipped out of seemingly benign moments, could open its abyss with just a word or two: "The important thing is to have someone to sleep with. Not just sex— but a body to hold while you're dreaming. I know that sounds awful."

Susan had laughed and agreed that it did.

Still, the thought merited consideration. She put her own peculiar twist on it, acknowledging that the body, in her case, was obviously Walker's. But whose was the companionship?

The question, she decided after a while, didn't bear thinking about—or, more accurately, bore no answers.

New Orleans: the town demanded tourists and they sheepishly played the role.

They had woken to the desert, Arizona and New Mexico—a vast and tan expanse where the eye could play confidently. Encompassing rings of wrinkled blue mountains, fancy as pastry, were cast in a precision glaze. And the flat-packed sands beneath the welded track felt equally firm, equally exact.

On entering east Texas the next afternoon, however, that steadfast feeling began to go. By the time they were deep into bayou country, careening through swamps and shack-filled villages, there was little telling where black lagoon ended and solid land began. The very railbed seemed a fragile, improvised sandbar, and it was with some anxiety, as night fell and they neared their destination, that Susan studied the arrangements of dank levee and flat city presenting themselves by the flare-lit glare of oil refineries. If you didn't tread lightly, watching every step you took, you might be sucked down. Or so it seemed.

From the train's parched coolness, they emerged into a mildewed, tepid atmosphere. Walker looked queasy. When she asked him if he felt all right, he muttered something about the catfish they had dined on aboard the train a few hours earlier.

"It's bothering you?"

"It was a little greasy. But I'm fine."

A cab took them to their hotel—floodlit, pink and, as it turned out, on the wrong side of Rampart Street. After unpacking they went for a stroll at funeral pace, to keep from getting drenched with sweat, and soon found the main drag of the French Quarter. This Bourbon Street, however, was disconcerting after the one at Disneyland. It tried desperately to replicate the theme park's fantasy of good times and high spirits, but it couldn't keep out the surrounding city's air of sullen menace.

A con artist cornered Walker, boasting that he could tell him where he got his shoes: "The place, city and state."

Walker fell for it.

"You got them on your feet, buddy—and you're in New Orleans, Louisiana."

The price for this information was twenty dollars, and it was hinted that things could get ugly if no payment was forthcoming.

Walker gave him ten, then said to Susan, "Let's get out of here."

Policemen mounted on horseback roamed the lighted thoroughfare as if in expectation of trouble at any minute. And away from the lights and hustle, the neighborhood was unreadable. They paced uncertainly along the iron arcades of Decatur Street, then retreated up the length of Ursulines to their room, where the air conditioner took the night's steamy atmosphere and laced it with a chemical chill.

Walker—who, unlike Susan, had always been curious about the city—admitted, "This may have been a mistake."

"You really think so?"

She wanted to give him the benefit of the doubt.

"Well, maybe not. . . ."

The following day, Halloween, they set out with umbrellas in hand to confirm or refute this. Their hotelier warned them vigorously not to stray from the tourist route. He alluded to crack deals and muggings, an atmosphere of chronic mayhem. But by daylight the place seemed more benign in its decay. Walker took both his cameras: "The costumes should be great!"

Together they wandered from Jackson Square, with its grand old French cathedral, to Canal Street's swarming gray corridor of Radio Shacks, fast-food outlets and triple-X-rated film theaters. Susan commented on the unusual number of patent-leather-goods stores, and Walker fantasized aloud about her terrorizing the town from on high in a pair of shiny stiletto heels.

On the other side of Canal was a business district where white men in Italian suits sidled coolly through the swelter. Then office buildings gave way to nondescript warehouses and a shelter for the homeless. When an elevated expressway came into view with a no-man's-land beyond it, Susan's wariness got the better of her. She asked Walker to put his camera aside for a moment and retreat with her toward more populated thoroughfares.

He took a picture of her requesting this, then obliged her.

His enthusiasm for all he saw only increased as the afternoon progressed. They boarded the St. Charles streetcar and rode through the Garden District, where mansions rose up like confectioners' dreams. Alongside their elaborate whitewashed shapes, dark trees umbrellaed out of lime-green lawns. The sky got so heavy that warm showers spilled out of it, and through these downpours odd figures strayed. One derelict, with a fresh urine stain spreading down his frayed trousers, came aboard the streetcar pleading for funds, but the driver turned him away without much argument.

Down side streets there lay more modest, low-roofed dwellings. And the mansions, too, now that Susan looked more closely, were really just apartments—some swanky, some makeshift, but each telling of the city's decline, its history of balkanized opulence.

At Washington Street a boisterous herd of schoolchildren—all of them in uniform, most of them black—came aboard and Walker switched to his Polaroid. As the ancient car screeched along its rails, a party commenced.

The rails ran down the avenue's grassy median and at every intersection automobiles engaged the streetcar in a game of derring-do, trying to make turns across its path. The schoolchildren whooped derision or encouragement at the car drivers, then turned back to Walker—who was on a roll, passing out Polaroids, reloading the camera and handing Susan the occasional odd shot he wanted to keep. The kids were having a grand time, too, but a few of them frightened her with their shouts.

"Check out his camera!"

"Check out his *wife*!"

In the melee of dark faces—as the kids raced up and down or rang the bell to get off—Susan failed at first to notice the figure sitting a few rows ahead of her. Neither old nor young, dressed in subdued colors, the woman was positioned outside Walker's general line of fire; and when Walker poked his viewer in her direction to snap a gaudy cypress palace, she curled up like a possum until she was hardly there at all. Yet she appeared to be taking careful note of the jubilance he inspired—and using it, perhaps, to time her exit.

The window glass darkened. An impending cloudburst passed by. The heads of trees swayed thickly on their boughs. The sticklebacked air was as close as ever. Any rain would have been a relief, but none fell beyond a few scalding drops.

When Susan looked across the aisle again, the woman was gone.

The streetcar came to a halt at a broad intersection surrounded by shopping plazas: its terminus. And it felt as though they had been in a foreign country and now were back in America. When they disembarked with the few remaining passengers, Walker proposed returning on foot to Rampart Street, but Susan vetoed this. He meant the whole four miles—probably more with sight-seeing detours—and she didn't feel up to it: "Walking. Sweating. It'd be miserable."

He looked up at overhanging live-oak branches, as if to pinpoint where the heat was coming from.

"You're sure?" he asked.

"We could ride back, take a nap, be ready for tonight," she suggested.

So far, they had seen no signs of Halloween revelry.

He gave it some thought, then conceded: "Okay."

The car, with much racket, switched tracks to make its return journey, and then the driver got up and slalomed down its length, knocking the wooden seats into their alternate position so they would face forward on the trip back into town.

"Get back on now?" Walker asked. "Or look around here a little?"

She weighed their surroundings.

The car's whirring motor made a sound of departure.

"Get back on," she said—and smiled, to let him know "a nap" could mean all sorts of things. . . .

In their hotel room, the air conditioner issued such a musty odor that Walker shut it off. Warm damp immediately gathered, baking out of the walls and filling the drawn curtains, its luke-warm languor making her skin come alive as she peeled off her clothes. Walker stayed a step or two behind her—until he noticed her eyes' invitation and footed softly toward the bed to join her, shucking aside one item of clothing after another.

His limbs had an agenda of their own now and she tried to lose herself in this, taking refuge in the solid bulk of him. But to her annoyance the indeterminate face of the woman on the street-car kept coming back to her. Darkness spread. Outside, some thunder rumbled. Soon a siege of rain slapped down at the pavement as if to reprimand their union. Walker slowed his rhythm a bit, and the face grew more elusive. When Susan attempted to speed him back up, she found him so slick with sweat that she couldn't keep hold of him. The face stared fully at her and seemed to view her problem with amusement. It was almost tender in its gaze.

Afterwards, with the door between bathroom and bedroom open, she watched him from the tub and realized that her ploy hadn't worked. He didn't want to nap, and he didn't mind being grimy. He was panthering around the room, half-dressed, clearly restless. He had turned the television on, and the big news was of an early winter storm that had swept across the Plains. There was snow in Minneapolis and Chicago. The cold front was headed for the Gulf as well. Tomorrow would be crisp, clear, dry.

With the change in humidity, Walker suggested, they might find themselves in a different city. He wanted to document this one while it lasted, and he assumed she would prefer to doze for a bit.

Putting on his slacks and grabbing his camera, he called into the bathroom, "Back in an hour or two. You get some rest."

He was out the door before she could raise a protest, his withdrawal so abrupt it drew a gasp from her.

She lay back in the water, baffled for a moment; then rose from the tub, feeling clean and new, weak and abandoned. With all tension banished from the room, she returned to bed.

Walker was right. Sleep was what she wanted.

She let it take her over.

When she was with him he fit her perfectly. But when he was away, he grew distant as a phantom.

She had tremendous difficulty describing him to those who didn't know him. It was just as difficult specifying what made their interaction so smooth. And wouldn't someone see a coldness in her calling it "interaction"?

Yet that was how it felt—as if they were part of some expertly handled traffic pattern.

It sometimes struck her that they were two ciphers. Notions passed through them. Their ingredients were constantly changing, being replenished. There was always something fresh for them to find in each other. But underlying this busy surface was something strangely indistinct, a force that laid gentle waste to the boundaries between them.

This seemed a central, guiding truth to her, but she didn't dare express it to Walker. She was too nervous of his reaction to it. Instead, to her own surprise, she sometimes found herself inquiring about Eleanor, as though Eleanor were bound to be less disconcerting subject matter.

"What *was* she to you?"

She wondered how a brand-new person—herself—could have stepped so easily into Eleanor's vacated role in Walker's life.

" 'Is,' " he had insisted. "Still is."

At the back of his mind, he confessed, he felt as close to his ex-wife as ever. There were even ways in which his marriage to her, by some measures, had never ended!

When Susan got over her alarm at this—this had been only a month after their honeymoon—she challenged him, "I'm just a follow-up, then? A second-best?"

"You're—You're like nothing that ever happened to me before—"

Had he gotten this line from one of his movies?

"I mean," he continued, "imagine me being able to tell you that!"

She withdrew from him a little.

"Eleanor and I met too young," he said, seeing her fear and wanting to reassure her. "And when you're as young as that, you tend to see your partner as representing the whole of the opposite sex—"

"That's if you marry for the wrong reasons," she corrected him.

He granted that she might be right; that it was probably a foolish way of seeing things. "But it's one that surrounds you! You've never been in this deep before! At least I hadn't. In someone—and going for the heart of her. Then one day you realize that *everyone* fits this way together," he sighed, "and maybe in other ways, too."

Susan assumed it would have been Eleanor who disclosed to

him a few of these "other ways." A vision came to her of Walker sitting back in bed, about to be lured into some unusual sexual practice, and saying in measured tones: "Okay, I'll try it. But if it hurts too much, can we stop?"

His imagination could expand to savor most things. There was little you could say that would shock him. But in his behavior he was, as he freely admitted, absurdly consistent. He didn't mind what he ate at breakfast as long as it was the same thing every day. His morning menu, he informed her, changed only once every decade or so. In 1987, for instance, on an impulse he had substituted lime marmalade for orange on his English muffin—and had stuck with it ever since. Similarly, he had gone the same way to work each day for years until some prolonged road construction near his house made this impossible. It took him weeks to grow accustomed to the designated detour—but once he had, he never returned to his earlier route.

In bed, she knew the exact progress his caresses would take. Any new move she tried out, recalled from an earlier lover or from something she had read, always surprised him.

She tried framing questions as to how varied his carnal experience had been before he met her. When she implied that his moderate good looks must have opened up some doors for him before AIDS fears made bedhopping a no-no, he grew mildly alarmed and said he had never even been in a singles bar: "It's been straight from Havre to Eleanor to you."

"What about that high school teacher? Didn't she count?"

"She was married. And it only lasted a few months. We were too afraid of being found out. And after that there was really only Eleanor."

His "really only" suggested that there might have been other women whom he now discounted, women whose names meant nothing in comparison with Eleanor's or hers. And as for their faces—

But Susan preferred to let the thought go.

"Like I said," he went on, "I'm happiest doing it with the same woman over and over again. I can't seem to get it up for anyone else."

This was news to her: "Why not?"

"It's—Well, it's partly just a wariness of strangers."

His answer was unexpected, if only because he had never shown the slightest wariness of her.

When challenged on this, he said, "But you didn't feel like a stranger to me! I met you at work. I knew where you were eight hours a day. And then, when I found out what your interests were. . ."

She gave him a look of patient skepticism.

"Of course," he added, sensing her surprise at his relative chastity and worrying that she might want something more, "there've been fantasies. All types."

"We'll get to those later," she said, convinced by now, but unable to believe her luck. She had had her fair share of boyfriends, from high school on, and had always been careful of them, aware of the limited ways in which they saw her and she saw them. With them there was an awkwardness, an uneasy sense of exposure to someone she didn't feel safe with, someone she hardly registered as real—until reality inevitably prevailed and she would realize what a target she presented to someone she didn't particularly like, let alone respect; someone whose carelessness, matched with hers, could only lead to hapless misery.

With Walker sleeping by her side, she could see that a treacherous part of her life was over. Maybe this was due to their age difference, his advantage of years over her—in effect, his "maturity." Or maybe it had to do with his growing up in a freer, less inhibited time. Those fabled 'sixties!

Whatever the case, in his company her barriers went down and an unfamiliar breeze played on some suddenly nude aspect of her, as she saw it. She felt a pleasant shock of candor. She had never realized how enclosed, how thickly enwrapped in herself she had been before. This new sensation was ticklish, invigorating—yet it also prompted her to keep something in reserve. It seemed advisable to cherish her luck, to mount any means for its defense that she could. Walker was trustworthy. She had more faith in him than she had in herself. But there was no knowing what lay beyond Walker.

And then she would have the dream where it happened; where all reference points were lost; where walls weren't walls and time wasn't time; where lines of ghosts—all drab, all shapeless— were following her, and the person she had been tangled with in her sleep groaned but couldn't hear her. . . .

It was no distance at all from that sleep to this sleep. A sound awoke her and Walker, entering the room, dragged his fingers across his forehead to wipe off the sweat. His eyes were soft as candle wax. He met her gaze and advised her: "It's turning into a zoo out there."

"A zoo?"

"You know—Halloween."

"Does that mean you want to go back out?"

"You don't want to?"

"I don't want to get dressed, is the thing."

He looked at her questioningly.

"It's too warm for clothes," she explained.

"Not everyone is wearing them," he told her.

She sat up: "What? People are just strolling around naked?"

"Well, no. But some don't have much on. . . ."

Disguises made the streets feel safer. Even down the darkest stretch of Ursulines, the shadows that took shape were playacting, not menacing. One man, dressed as a sultan, walked accompanied by his scantily clad galley slave: G-string, acanthus leaf, nipple ring, silken headdress . . . that was all. A woman masquerading as a witch smiled at Susan as she stepped off a sunken curb and onto cobblestone. Affable vampires headed into bars for a drink.

Walker's Polaroid was slung by its strap around his neck, bouncing on his chest where—security-conscious—he protected it with his arm.

He was saying, "—these crumbling old buildings. Feels like I'm in Colombia . . . or Cuba somewhere. A Caribbean port at any rate—"

"We're on the Caribbean, aren't we?"

"Not really. The Gulf of Mexico. And would the Caribbean smell as sulfurous as this?"

A man in the garb of a priest, but with devil's horns rising from his head, passed them by. Around the corner, they were met by a klieg light's hot and blinding brightness: the lamps of a television camera crew. Late-night news teams were gathered on the corner of Bourbon and Dumaine to broadcast the bacchanalia to the city at large. The galley slave had reappeared and was playing to the cameras. The devil-priest, right behind him, was shouting to the microphones, "What determines the size of a raindrop? What are we in for from the skies tonight? And what can we do to protect ourselves . . .?"

The fluid movement of the near-naked slave was complemented by the tufted stiffness of his headdress and the studded frippery of his choke collar, which Susan hadn't noticed before. This collar and the cinquefoil pattern of his body hair—up his thighs, out of his groin, across his narrow chest—seemed like encoded instructions on how to feast upon him most delectably. And in the brighter light it was possible to see that his "owner"— a light-skinned black who had the rein of the choke collar in his grip—was enjoying this game of tugging and controlling as much as his white "slave" was.

Two pairs of lips swerved. Devil-priest and slave flicked their tongues at each other until the latter was yanked away with a "Down, boy" reprimand.

The slave writhed in response to this, shimmying from the groin. The devil-priest lifted his skirts to display remarkably hirsute thighs. He taunted slave and master alike. A television cameraman came over to talk to the trio, either to tell them to simmer down or to make suggestions on how they could camp it up further. Or was he arranging a date for later in the evening?

Walker's Polaroid caught it all.

There were open-air restaurants where guitar players sang pandering versions of old protest tunes. There were dim, low-ceilinged bars that seemed lit by oil lamp rather than electricity. There was a flurry of plaques enumerating which writer—Faulkner or Williams—had written which book, and when, on what particular floor of which particular house. And then there was a house where no book had been written at all, whose residents had invented an occasion of their own. In a window case piled a foot or so deep in wine-bottle corks, they had left this memento:

July 4, 1976
On this site, nothing happened!
So we had a party!!!

"They've been there fifteen years?" Susan asked.

"I guess so."

"Everyone seems forced to have a good time here," she murmured.

"Either that or they're going out of their way to achieve states of mind that can only lead to anticlimax."

They passed an open doorway that gave onto a brightly lit room. In an armchair facing the entryway, a hefty young man dressed only in ragged jeans kept track of passersby. The room was a mess. Was he trying to ventilate the place? Or was he offering himself for sale?

They cast a glimpse at him, which he returned with a blunt appraising stare. And then a shutter rattled; a telephone wire hummed. A palm tree whispered and stopped them with its rattling sound. Its dry fronds hissed and thrashed. The spell of warm flesh was broken. A frigid wind was scraping the city clean, twisting down its streets as if to reclaim it. They hurried back to their hotel room, where they put on the heat rather than the air conditioning—the chill had penetrated that quickly.

With a careless flourish, Walker emptied his pockets of Polaroids. On the counterpane were a dozen square snapshots of muggy warmth and festivity in streets where there now was only a sculpting chill, increasing emptiness.

While he showered, she perused them to see what he had captured.

And there she was again!

From behind the galley slave, whose skin was tawny in some shots and albino-white in others (his master stayed permanently in shadow), the woman stared out, no body evident, only a face. Or was that her overcoat—the same as in San Francisco—blending in with the background darkness, reduced to indistinction by a flashlamp explosion's unnatural chiaroscuro?

She was in half a dozen shots at least. And when Susan studied those in which she seemed at first to be absent, she soon came forward. With close examination, she could be found on the outer perimeter or in the window reflections of every picture Walker had taken.

Susan began to turn the most obvious of these facedown—until, losing her nerve, reluctant even to touch them, she left them as they were and backed away from the bed.

"Walker?"

The sound of the shower being noisily wrenched off was followed by the sound of him toweling himself off vigorously.

She called his name again.

The bathroom door opened and he emerged with the hotel's terry-cloth robe wrapped tightly around him to keep his shoulders warm: "Does the water here taste strange to you? Kind of muddy?"

He hadn't heard her.

"Come here—look at these."

"Any of them any good?"

"Just take a look."

"I am, I am."

Curious, he began to flip over some of the facedown ones.

She joined him at the bedside and placed the photographs that bothered her most in a row to make it obvious.

His eyes grew distant.

"Well, they aren't all great—" he began to admit; then stopped short, started to laugh. "But you're right. That *is* a little strange. I didn't mean to."

"Mean to what?"

"Get these guys in every shot."

He was indicating the slave/master/devil-priest trio.

"They're not in every shot," she contradicted him.

"But in most of them. I was trying for them here, with the camera crews . . . but not in these."

He mused on this for a moment, then tossed the coincidence aside: "Maybe we were on a guided tour and didn't know it?"

She looked at him seriously.

He stared at her blankly, removed the terry-cloth robe and finished drying himself. Then he gathered the pictures together and put them in his shoulder bag.

She decided she wouldn't say anything if he didn't say anything.

Before he turned the lights out, he asked, "Do you think they have any brandy? My stomach's nagging me. Maybe room service—?"

"Brandy settles a stomach?"

"You're right. Never mind."

With the covers pulled over them and the thermostat turned up, they retired for the evening. Walker nodded off instantly. But Susan stayed awake—staring at the darkness, answering its shapes as if *she* were the camera, zooming in on a face that wouldn't oblige her; a face that knew her tricks, saw what she was after, declined to be caught. . . .

Walker's hunch turned out to be correct.

In a brighter, drier atmosphere it wasn't the same city. There were no phantom women; there were hardly any shadows! And her fears, which had held such sway the night before, receded like a nightmare you recognize as ridiculous upon waking. Why, after all, would someone have trailed them here all the way from San Francisco?

The thought flitted through her mind that Eleanor might have hired a private eye to spy on them. But she immediately dismissed it for reasons that would have perturbed her had she considered them more closely: Surely Eleanor had no need of information. Surely it was safe to assume that Walker's ex-wife could divine for herself any information she needed, even from a distance of two thousand miles.

They had a late breakfast in the French Quarter, then made their way across town. For the first time, she put on the long army-green raincoat she had brought with her: a budget version of a London Fog affair. It had been too warm and muggy to wear it before. Now it served as a neck-to-shins windbreaker against the freshening day. Walker, by contrast, looked strangely under-dressed with no cameras strapped around his neck. She had persuaded him to leave them at the hotel.

Wandering in the brightness, they marveled at the overnight change in the city's atmosphere. This blue, this sharpness, was like a brisk aunt entering a habitually slovenly household, her acerbic perfume cutting its way through a potpourri of silt. Tingling gusts of wind were a reminder of the solid continent to their north and prompted in Susan a desire to gaze in that direction. Walker went along with this, as enthusiastic about trying out the city's conventional public transportation as he was about riding its touristy streetcars. So on Canal Street they caught a bus which ferried them up to the northern end of town—and southern shore of Lake Pontchartrain.

The lake, in turmoil, was a curious sight. The weather system that had snowed in Chicago was stirring a crashing surf against low breakwaters, and though the day was radiant, the stiff on-shore breeze left the lakeside park close to deserted. Little traffic cruised the winding boulevard; few walkers trod the springy turf. Palm trees and pines blew in unaccustomed directions, like luxuriant fur being ruffled the wrong way.

"Race you to the levee top?"

"Deal!"

She beat him to it and was pleased to see she was considerably less winded by the exercise than he was. As they strolled along the man-made barrier, they had the churning waters on their right and a line of bulky brick mansions on their left, looking vulnerable from this angle. The broad earthen wall underfoot felt too crumbly, too soft, to protect anything.

They came to a bridge over a drainage canal, then headed up another grass embankment, where Walker flopped down, the exertion of the climb too much for him.

"I'm seeing stars," he said.

She looked up at the sky, then out toward the horizon, and countered: "*I'm* seeing optical illusions."

This perked him up: "Where?"

"Look—the bridges."

The transition from water to land was an indistinct affair, and the trestles of the bridges spanning the choppy waves seemed to float on a clear lacquer of their own. They had a spectral caprice, appeared anchored to nothing at all. Susan squinted to see them more clearly.

"Is it all just in the eye? Or is it a physical phenomenon? You'd need a camera to decide, wouldn't you? Something to record the evidence."

He smiled at her.

"What?"

He clambered up to sitting position, announced: "One of the guys at work—he gave everyone these last Christmas. Got them at Woolworth's. Said they only cost a dollar or two. I've been wanting to try it out."

From his sport-coat pocket he produced a toylike contraption, tiny, disposable, almost a joke—except that with its load of film and its little black lens, it had the serious unblinking look of any of its larger cousins.

"Does it really work?"

"It ought to."

She told him what she wanted: snapshots of the elusive bridges, from the top, bottom and midway up the levee; snapshots of herself against the smooth grass embankment's angled incline to give an idea of the scale involved; and, finally, snapshots of the waves frustrated by the piled rock barriers "—especially over there, at the canal entrance. There's a whole elaborate rigmarole to keep them from surging through."

She skipped back down, posed, moved forward, posed again. At every point, Walker snapped the shutter twice.

This happily occupied them for an hour. Water and land in such precarious balance with each other fascinated her, as did the mingling of an artificial landscape (levee, rock barrier) with natural elements (blue-funneled sky, agitated whitecaps). This was something new: doing a kind of nature study and making her model—herself—insignificant. The outdoor setting produced a riskier, more exposed feeling than did being cloistered with Walker, naked and safe, in a heated room.

Their trip back into town coincided with the end of maids' working days, and she and Walker were the only white people on the bus. Sounds of Creole and round-syllabled Black English too thick to understand in detail filled the rumbling vehicle.

They passed a famous cemetery lined with elevated tombs and thought of getting off. But Walker's guidebook warned against entering the place on your own—too many muggings.

While strolling down Rampart Street, they overheard a conference among derelicts that also served as evidence of a fraying social contract. A husky-voiced woman declared with an orator's vigor: "We'll take their money one way or another. If they want to give us somewhere to live, fine. If they want to keep us homeless, it don't matter. But we'll get it, I'm tellin' you, even if we have to take it . . . !"

At the hotel reception desk, the porter asked if they were enjoying the town. He listed the tourist attractions he hoped they hadn't missed.

They had been to none of them.

Back in their room she cozied up to Walker, found his ear and murmured, "I'm glad we're getting out of here."

"Me, too."

His hands, when she took them, felt chilly. And he wasn't sure, when she asked him, if he wanted any dinner.

In the unfamiliar bed that third night, they stayed in smooth embrace and she thought of how strangely limbs and faces fit together; sometimes awkwardly—too many elbows!—and sometimes with pillowed snugness.

Yes, yes, it was possible to lose yourself; to be warmed by marriage, steeped in happiness.

For reasons that had less to do with nostalgia than thoroughness, Eleanor Popman kept and filed every postcard she got—those from her ex-husband, or from anyone who happened to drop her a line.

A name would appear on the back of a *carte postale* of the Eiffel Tower or some temple in India, and she would have trouble placing the sender at first. Who was Antoine? Who, she tried to remember, was Peter—or was it Patel? (The handwriting was terrible.) It often took effort, a suspenseful moment or two, until— yes, of course!—the syllables blossomed and some marvelous specifics of flesh would play in her mind.

She kept all photographs, too, or at least those she had been able to wile away from Walker. In her studio apartment—spartan, spotless, yet suggestive of certain luxuries—were albums of black-and-white glossies, some taken by her former husband, some by mere strangers. Indexed and in order, they occupied a whole shelf of her bookcase and told a tale of ravishments and decay, triumphs and travesties, conquests and defeats. Nothing was ever rejected; everything went into the archive. Since her college days—when she had come to appreciate her erotic power and how, eventually, it was bound to fail her—she had kept this record of her trysts, her vagaries, her outermost spirals. She didn't want to lose a single piece of evidence.

This was what she relished, this was what enlarged her— weaving a fugue of couplings, confidences, memories, updates. She had never understood how people could fail to experiment, how anyone with half a heart or the tiniest vestige of a questing spirit could refrain from asking, "Those two, standing over there, against the railing, smoking the cigarettes . . . what do you suppose they taste like?"

All her life she had been eager for the answer; had wanted, in a sporting way, the goods on everyone. Her one regret was that promiscuity was sometimes impractical if you wanted to keep your job, your sanity or, in recent years, your health. To her there was an innocence to sex, something sweetly social in the way skin greeted skin. She likened it to exercise: sailing, aerobics, swimming . . . activities that left you glowing with exertion. The only kind of contact she feared—and the fear stemmed not from the prospect of being hurt but from an utter impatience with the limits of the world around her—was one which insisted that skin-to-skin greetings inevitably led to gravity-bound entanglement. She hated situations where she was forced to show her hand, act dismissively, deny emotion or insist that sex for her was a kind of game.

Surely that could go unstated. Surely it need not be spelled out.

She took pride in "doing it, not talking about it"; a pride she had confidence in, which was why the feelings triggered by

Walker's postcards were catching her so off-guard. Of course she still "loved" him. She loved a lot of people: for the nourishment they provided her, for the entry they gave her into their hidden lives. But the formalities, the domestic routines, the possessiveness of marriage—these were unimportant, weren't they?

So she had thought. But when she looked again at the chirpy messages Walker sent her, she felt the same twinge of jealousy that any jilted housewife would have felt. A milder version, perhaps, but still unmistakable—because Susan went unstated in them, Susan wasn't spelled out.

It was a soft blow, an unexpected sign that her connection with her ex-husband was as visceral as ever. It also suggested that she was a good deal more curious about her successor than she cared to admit.

Susan seemed a distressingly conservative choice for Walker to have made—a deliberate retrenchment, worrisome if only for the hints she embodied of compromise on his part. She was someone Eleanor would never have picked out for him. In their one meeting, Eleanor had acted on instinct, attempting to confuse her—a feat she had accomplished with such ease she felt almost ashamed of herself. She couldn't imagine Walker settling for anyone so guileless. If that was what he wanted, why leave Montana? Why not simply stay in a place where everyone knew more or less everything about you?

There was almost a scorn in his choice of Susan, too, an all-too-casual disowning of his first marriage. Or maybe not scorn. He was too sweet for that. But regret, yes—and disconcerting clues that he had wanted something this uncomplicated, this legible, from the very beginning. It all came back to the question of limits, of how much a person could take.

Eleanor couldn't let him know she saw this; would never have revealed how deeply she had pondered the matter, let alone how much it disturbed her to acknowledge any new phase in his life to which she had no access. She was too afraid of alarming him, estranging him further. The best tactic was to feign acceptance of everything that had occurred, all the losses she had instigated.

She picked up the first of his train-trip postcards, from San Francisco, and read it again:

> Dearest El,
>
> Getting lots of fresh air and exercise (the hills are every bit as steep as they look). No fog surprisingly— Alcatraz, Sausalito and the Golden Gate all super-bright. Train trip was "wunnerful, yust wunnerful." See you in November.
>
> Your loving "X"

No hint of hostility there, even though she would have welcomed such a hint, if only to have a message addressed specifically to *her*. Instead there was a generic geniality that he doubtlessly dispensed to all his friends and acquaintances. It wouldn't have surprised her to find the same message scrawled on each of the postcards he sent.

Discouraged, she went into the bathroom and rolled up her sleeves to examine certain bruises and fading welt marks.

She had been overdoing it lately, dabbling in new territory, some of it rather painful, none of it very satisfying. Maybe it was time for "bland" to make a comeback? Bland, at least, didn't need medical attention. And bland had found bland in this business of Walker's marriage! Susan, from all appearances, was a kind a soapstone, soft and characterless, waiting to be carved. . . .

Well, she was young, that was all. There wasn't much you could know at twenty-five, was there?—no real way to see what shape your life would take; what sensations or appetites would be yours.

Eleanor considered this, tried to persuade herself it was true— until, rolling her sleeves back down, she looked in the mirror and drawled: "What crap."

She had known more or less *everything* at twenty-five. She had even wearied of it and looked forward to her present decay, the detailed ripening of her flesh from soft to softer to (one day) softest. She would have to call on Susan again, sound her out when she got back from her trip. Maybe the girl had hidden depths. Maybe she could be taught a thing or two. Walker might appreciate it. Or would it just alienate him further, disrupting what little surface cordiality Eleanor had managed to bring to their rift?

She turned away from the mirror, annoyed by the notion that she would have to behave now, rein herself in, refrain from interfering, simply because of the power of marriage. Another avenue of satisfaction—and she liked to keep as many open as possible—had been closed off to her.

What to do?

Her short-term solution was to make a phone call, arrange a meeting with an interim lover who lived downtown, and vent a little steam that way. She did this, then returned home a few hours later and leafed through one of the photograph albums; spent a long while comparing her present self to her past incarnations. An interesting process: flesh sweetly paling, coming loose. Why tamper with it? She surely wasn't the only one to find it less interesting when muscles were defined than when they were indeterminate.

Image spurred memory. Memory spurred a shape. And shape spurred a liveliness: a place where she put her fingers, stirred herself up, reaching with her other hand under her blouse to tamp down a yearning there, too.

There were never enough hands, never enough answering pressures.

Was she just a device? The bane of her ex-husband's life? She wondered how he described her to his wife: "Always fun at a party—and good in a crisis, too!" Or was it "Great in bed—but impossible to live with"?

At any rate he kept her in mind, stayed in touch, called her up from time to time, sent postcards. . . .

She had become what she was with him; had merely wanted to go a little farther; not to *leave* Walker—who, more than anyone else, was her reference point—but to give in to the urge to disintegrate a little and see what else was out there, what hidden reserves of personality might be lurking in the gloom.

Again she scanned the mirror for clues—and discovered an appearance that was purringly quiet. No sign of agitation. More like a predator whose actions are undramatic to itself, surprising only to the prey it captures with a sting of its tail or a flick of its tongue. Not that she was destructive, necessarily. She simply wanted there to be no boundaries, no restrictions. After all, a body was a world that could be revisited. She insisted on this— and hated being cut off from any world she had known.

Turning off the bathroom light, she moved to the kitchen where she poured herself a drink and, in a careful hand, marked the date of Walker and Susan's November return on her wall calendar. Then, before retiring for the night, she glanced again at the second postcard Walker had sent her which seemed more encouraging than his first, especially in its sign-off:

Yo, El!
  Greetings from Disneyland. The Tiki Burgers are fantastic—and so are the rides! Can't think why we never came here. Minnie and Mickey say, "Hi!" Next stop: New Orleans. Hope it's not too steamy. . . .

                              XXX and OOO from your only
                              —"Mr. X"

In Washington, D.C., where they made a day of it, Walker dropped the Lake Pontchartrain shots by a one-hour photo place, eager to see how they had turned out, and then crossed over to the Mall with Susan, to take in the sights and breathe in the city's stale late-autumn warmth. Before boarding the Night Owl for Boston, they picked up the pictures and examined them over dinner in Union Station. Walker was the first to comment.

"Strange. It must be a double exposure."

"What?"

"This one here."

He handed it to her while continuing to leaf through the others. Then he dropped them all on the table, looking badly undermined: "Every one of them's screwy. Could it have been the camera?"

She reached for them cautiously, as if they might burn her. When she saw what he meant, she was almost as irate as she was perturbed.

"It's her again!"

"Who?"

"She must be a real sicko. She's been shadowing us the whole time!"

"Where?"

"She was on the streetcar with us, too, only I didn't want to say. And she's in all those pictures of San Francisco. You still have them?"

"I mailed them home already."

"It's the same woman," she repeated.

"It can't be. Why would anyone follow us clear across the country?"

"Well, it's not a double exposure. It looks like me from a distance—but that's not my coat."

He studied the photographs more closely: "It could be you, you know. That blur? If you moved slightly? And the coat might look darker if it was double-exposed. They *all* look like they have some kind of filter on them."

But while he shuffled through the shots again, another change of expression came over him. As if in disgust at having been conned, though he hadn't made the purchase himself, he said: "Thing must have been a piece of junk."

"What?" she asked.

"The camera."

She didn't reply to this.

He gathered the photographs back into their envelope and consoled her: "Still, some of these are interesting. . . ."

"Throw them away."

He looked up in surprise. She was glaring at him from across the table.

"But you might be able to use them, don't you think?"

"Get rid of them," she repeated.

He asked her: "Even these ones of the waves?"

"All of them."

It was a matter of necessity—a message, almost, to this presence that was vague; this specter that was shrouded and mute; this prankster who, even now, might be listening in on them. Susan had gone through all the photographs quickly but attentively. Each had etched its outline on her mind. There would be no forgetting them. If she wanted to use them as "models," she had only to close her eyes. But she was frightened of them. And her fear wasn't merely for herself.

"Toss them," she insisted.

"You might change your mind. They're eerie. You may want to use them for something else."

Walker never threw out pictures. He had files and files of them in his basement archives.

"It's happened to me before," he said. "When I came out to Seattle I got rid of a lot of stuff, and then I was kicking myself."

She had no reply to this. He could be right. She didn't care if he was. Whether or not they were double exposures, the photographs were clues to something she would rather not know. But Walker was immovable.

He chided her: "Admit it. You hate throwing things away."

She shrugged at the truth of this, felt her will collapsing.

"Besides," he continued, "some mistakes can tell you as much as the things you do on purpose."

She wondered if this could be the voice of failure speaking. He had confessed to her more than once that he had ambitions outside photography; that he wanted to be a painter. But his drawing skills had not translated into a gift for composition. The drama, the tension, apparent in his news photos occurred mostly by chance—a matter of choosing the one, out of dozens taken, that looked just right. The painstaking decision process that a painting required, the conscious attempt to shape a vision on canvas over a stretch of time, was somehow beyond him. Little wonder, then, that he wanted to hang on to these pictures which had an undeniable power, no matter what, specifically, one saw in them.

They reached a compromise—or, rather, he strong-armed her toward one.

"I'll send them back home," he said, the offer sounding more like an order. "And then they'll be waiting for you, if you want them."

She let him do as he pleased; told herself they were more his shots than hers. After all, he had been the one to take them. And it would be easy enough to dispose of them, if they still bothered her, once she was back in Seattle.

He sealed them in their envelope, went off to find a stamp machine, came back empty-handed: "Mission accomplished."

They boarded the train shortly before ten o'clock. And the minute they pulled out of the station, she knew she had made a mistake. She wanted to find the mailbox, reach inside, retrieve the vital evidence. She wanted to ensure that those images existed nowhere except in her mind.

But there was nothing she could do about it. In a rash moment (they were still in the railyard) she started to try the doors of the slowly moving train when the conductor wasn't looking, then lost her nerve. People could get killed that way. The car attendant on the Sunset Limited had told her so.

Back in their coach, she couldn't sleep. Her own agitation, along with the train's, kept her awake, shifting from one position to another as she tried for comfort, for stillness.

She lay next to a lightly snoring Walker with her eyes wide open; saw the envelope en route from Washington, D.C., to Washington state. She pictured it floating in a cavernous space where anyone could use it, like a bomb, against her. And the images that stared back from its sealed-in contents were like passive companions, silent intruders. Think of them, and they yielded no meaning. Speak to them, and they wouldn't answer.

They were only images, after all—and they seemed to be waiting to be acted upon rather than about to take any action of their own. There was no real distinguishing the point at which they made sleep impossible from the point at which they found in sleep their dream-solution.

Susan dealt with them as best she could—and then, losing consciousness, allowed them to deal with her.

Boston was dark. The air spat cold. The streets were being lashed by a fresh Atlantic storm, in raw wet contrast to Washington, D.C.

Here, she thought, figures swaddled in overcoats would at least belong. If they turned up in photographs, there would be nothing remarkable about them at all.

Walker's sister, Mary, lived in a garden floor apartment on the north side of Beacon Hill where, through a quirk of acoustics, she got tremendous traffic noise from the expressway bridges over the Charles. "Garden floor" meant two or three levered windows at shoulder level: the only interruptions in curved and sunken brick. The place was cool as a dungeon, and its proprietress solemn and slim. Her dress hung straight and tuniclike, her owl-calm eyes had a knowing look, and her salutation of her sister-in-law, after Walker's introduction, was more an apology than a warm welcome: "Sorry. Was in Africa. Couldn't make it to the wedding."

This was the first Susan had heard of the trip.

"Oh, we wouldn't have expected you to come so far!"

"Nevertheless—bad timing."

"Well, you're right," Susan said, "it was last-minute. And Walker's idea of a small wedding is practically nonexistent."

"Got the invitation," Mary assured her. "Came too late. Forwarded in the mail. One week's notice—no telephone nearby. Walker not much on formalities."

"I'd done weddings before," he excused himself, but with a doubtful look at his sister.

"Well, I hadn't!" Susan objected.

"Pay no attention to him," Mary advised. "Out to rankle."

The two women turned their gaze on him.

He laughed in submission: "Whoa, okay! You want a wedding? Then bring on the cake and the rivers of satin—and bring the divorce papers while you're at it."

"Hmmn."

This clownish version of her husband seemed more like something trotted out for Mary's benefit than her own.

Mary said: "Never change, do you? Be nice."

Susan asked: "What were you doing in Africa?"

"Visiting a friend. Peace Corps."

"Which country?"

"Rwanda."

"What was it like?"

"Interesting," she enthused. "Tiny, crowded, friendly. 'The Switzerland of Africa' they call it. What tourist brochures say. Not entirely accurate."

"I've only barely heard of it," Susan confessed.

Mary, adopting a sober tone, gave a dry synopsis: "Agrarian economy. Population explosion leading to rampant deforestation. Deforestation leading to erosion. Erosion ruining farmland. Ruined land leading farmers to clear more forest." She paused for breath, then continued: "Population consists of various tribes with history of hostility, on hold for the moment: squat Hutu, willowy Tutsi, tiny Pygmies. Could all blow sky high—especially if they lose tourist income. Gorillas big business. But gorillas need forest."

Susan nodded dumbly at this.

"Rampant HIV infection in the picture, too," Mary added as an afterthought, "but no official figures."

"It sounds horrible," Susan responded cautiously.

Mary shrugged her shoulders. "More civilized than here." She gestured around her. "Slower pace. Quieter. Schoolgirls in blue uniforms. Pleasant, well-mannered people. The part where we were anyway."

"How long were you there?"

"One month."

Mary's shorthand style of speech became more expansive: "Of course it was hardly like getting to know real people at all. More like something you read in a book. Elaborate protocol, oblique manners. *Things you're just supposed to know*! Hugging a man a no-no. Suggests adultery. Better to shake hands."

Susan narrowed her eyes as if vowing to remember this the next time she was there.

Walker, impatient, changed the topic: "So how's the experiment going?"

Mary lit up: "Disaster! I almost drowned Edgar Allan last week."

Susan looked at her: "Who?"

"One of my rats."

"Mary's research is on memory," Walker reminded Susan.

"*Drugs* and memory," Mary corrected him, "with possible application toward Alzheimer's. Been using a water maze."

"What's that?" Susan asked.

"Small swimming pool filled with water."

"How does it work?"

She smiled and told them: "Insert a transparent plastic platform. Insert rat. Let it find platform. Videotape search pattern from overhead. Some swim a circular path. Others zigzag. You wait till they learn location, go straight there. Then you scoop up rat, move platform, drop rat in again. Goes to the old place. Platform's not there! Takes a while to find it. A minute, usually. You create patterns in platform movement. How quickly are these learned? Depends on rat. You breed for best pattern-memory ability. Came very close to breeding Super Rat. Only problem was: dropped genius rat in pool, went to look through viewfinder. Something not right. Edgar Allan swimming furiously, heading straight for platform. But wasn't keeping head above water. Accidentally bred out self-preservation instinct. So—back to the drawing board."

She gave them a mischievous look.

"Drinks, anyone?" she asked. "Nice bar nearby."

Her movement reflected her speech: arms like loosened clock hands, loopily swinging up or down as she switched off lights and locked up the apartment. Staccato action.

She was relaxing with Susan now. And the more relaxed she was, the more expressive her elliptical syntax became.

"Never can tell the weather," she announced. "One night, thought it was pouring rain. Sudden squall. Drainpipe hits window, see. Grabbed umbrella, went in street. Dry. Turned out old drunk was relieving himself against windowpane. Didn't think anyone lived there. Apologized."

She stood up smartly. The overcoat she put on to go out in the bluster was as straight as her dress—a vertical soft-wool tube. No wind could catch it. The dark coat made her vanish in the night air and fooled each breeze into taking her for its own.

At the bar, a streamlined camouflage of another sort manifested itself in her. In ordering their drinks, she assumed a flawless Boston accent.

Then, abruptly, and strictly to Walker, she announced: "Ansel Adams. Museum of Fine Arts. I have to work tomorrow, but you'll want to go."

This mention of more photographs was met with a silence which Mary gauged before dropping the matter and asking them about their travels.

"So—New Orleans. Fun?"

"We had a supernatural experience there, didn't we, honey?" Walker offered.

Susan said nothing.

Mary, lighting up a cigarette, waited for the story. Susan started telling it, with Walker demurring on certain details until he took over completely. The San Francisco pictures, he said, hadn't bothered him the way they had bothered Susan. Just some indistinct, thin-blooded tourist who happened to have taken the same path through town that they had.

"But in New Orleans—down by the water anyway—" He shook his head. "Of course it was probably just the camera. Messed up winding mechanism. Or—"

"—or Eleanor?" Mary suggested.

The mention of her name startled them both.

"What do you mean?" Walker asked.

"A case of projection," Mary theorized. "Fear of the old wife. Paranoia at what changing wives means. Becomes a kind of ghost between you. What a psychiatrist might say, at any rate. At *high* rates. But—" She stabbed her burning cigarette into an ashtray, then looked up with a confidential grin. "—I despise psychiatrists."

Susan, at a loss, asked, "So you don't believe what you just said?"

"I'm a scientist," Mary proclaimed stoutly. "Mysteries remain mysteries until explanations are found. At least in my book. This grasping for reasons. Pah!"

"And 'projection'—?"

"Everything's projection! Animus, anima—call it what you like. Doesn't help. Not with what you're talking about."

"What would?"

"Nothing . . . yet. Answers surface."

"Dirt on the lens, maybe," Walker suggested.

Mary gave him a look of regal disdain: "All evidence now in Seattle?"

They nodded their heads in affirmation.

"Sounds to me," she airily declared, "like a great excuse not to go home."

"I'm beginning to think I'd love to go home," Susan protested. "I'd fly there tomorrow if I could."

"But we've got our train reservations!" Walker said.

They moved on to less touchy subject matter.

Brother and sister exchanged inquiries about distant relatives; expressed a mutual distaste for Havre and a grudging admiration for the physical spectacle of Montana. This was a topic Walker rarely discussed with his wife, and Susan, who had never been there, asked them what the place was like.

"Practically tundra," he dismissed it.

"Exaggerating," Mary leaned forward to tell Susan; then sat back. "But please continue."

Havre, Walker explained, was a railroad town set in a hollow, a breadth of dry valley, a sort of shallow river canyon carved from the Plains. To get any sort of view you had to climb the bluffs that hemmed in the south end of town. And even then there wasn't much to see. Only a tease of mountains—the Sweetgrass Hills up by the border, strange lumps; the Bearpaw Mountains to the south. They might be called "mountains" but that wasn't what they were. They were just big foothills, cut adrift from their range.

"Our folks took us to the Rockies one summer," Walker said. "Glacier National Park. And that ruined them for me."

"Big sky," Mary chimed in. "Astonishing at night. Fewer satellites back then. The stars, moving slowly—a heaven-full, a galaxy of them. And, underneath, tiny lights. Oh, it was tiny. Hated it there. Had to get away. Always wanted a city."

"And you did get away," Walker reminded her.

She acknowledged this with a sniff, indicating she still had a bone to pick with the past. Or rather with the name her parents had given her.

"All the way through school: 'Mary Poppins' this, 'Mary Poppins' that! 'Where's your umbrella? When are you going to fly away to Lon-don?' Got sick of it."

"Parents couldn't help the name," Walker pointed out, lapsing into his sister's shorthand style. "Never heard of the book."

"Think not?"

"Definitely. Way before the movie came out."

"Well, at least still have umbrella."

She saluted Susan with this.

"You had it back then, too? The same umbrella?"

"No, no. Montana dry as a bone. Inebriated. Sorry."

Her head wobbled slightly, like a puppet's. She was on her third or fourth gin. Lifting her chin in a jerk of bravado, she explained, "Alcohol. Clears the mind. So answers *can* surface." And then: "Popman—ridiculous name!"

Toward midnight, they walked back up the hill to the basement apartment. A drizzly mist—there was less wind now—uncurled itself from cobblestones, sidewalks and townhouses. It wrapped around the cast-iron streetlamps that lit their way. There was no taking shelter from it. It was soft and mobile, heedless of the laws of gravity. It slipped under fabric and seeped into bones, in the winding streets.

"Brr-rrr!"

Mary's folded umbrella was forthright and undaunted as her

precision-work limbs. She had a staccato stride to match her voice. She held her head high, her feet instinctively avoiding dog turds on the sidewalk, her profile cutting a path through chilled vapor. It was as if she had bred herself as intensively as she had her rats for optimal glitch-free movement through a labyrinthine environment.

Inside, she offered them a choice of brandy or port as a nightcap, then readied the foldout couch where they would sleep.

The drizzle stepped up its intensity; became an icy, bitter sleet for a minute or two, then receded. The motor traffic on the river bridges roared monotonously; sometimes whined as intimately as someone clearing his throat in the next room.

Susan and Walker lay awake in bed, Walker wondering aloud what it was about his sister that exhausted him.

"And my guts are restless," he added.

"My stomach's bothering me, too."

"Gas pains," he elaborated in Mary's telegraphic style.

"Mmm-mn."

She caressed him experimentally. Did he want to? Maybe it would soothe him.

He turned over, away from her: "Mary might hear. Such a small place."

She drew back her hand, caressed herself a little, then didn't know where to go with it.

Take the plunge?

No. Not with Walker right beside her. She heard him sigh.

When the rain came back, they both went to sleep.

"Have I ever told you about my greatest moments as a projection-ist?"

"Um, no. . . ."

Susan thought at first that he meant "projection" in Mary's sense of the word. But he didn't.

He puffed up as he launched into the story: "Well, in high school I sort of established a monopoly, somehow convinced the right people I was the only one who could operate a film projector without running into problems. I even got out of classes that way."

He grinned as they walked briskly through Back Bay, toward the museum.

"Anyway," he carried on, "we had a civics teacher, Mrs. Fitkin, who was supposed to be teaching us health education too. She was just fine on the evils of smoking and drinking and what happens to Grandpa's dentures if you drop them in a glass of Coca-Cola and leave them there for a year. But when it came to sex education and venereal disease, she couldn't handle it. No one else could either, apparently. I guess it was a pretty common problem at the time, because there was this film they would ship up to us from Helena—*The Beginnings of Life*, something like that. Or maybe it was *Life's Sacred Beginnings*—with all these line drawings of erections and vaginas and wombs and fetuses. . . ."

His eyes grew dreamy at the memory.

"Mrs. Fitkin had no confidence in her mechanical abilities," he continued, "so from the tenth grade on, once a year, she had me show it to all her classes. I'd get most of the afternoon off, setting up the film and running the projector. She was ridiculously grateful—and embarrassed, of course. Her husband was a policeman, and she really just wanted to teach everyone how to be good citizens. She was afraid of him—he got a little violent with her sometimes, I think—and she wanted to keep him from getting all riled up. She was from Oregon originally. I don't think she liked it in Montana. Later she asked me to take the photographs at her brother-in-law's wedding. I still think of that as my first big break."

He gazed into space for a moment, then said: "It's funny. She's the one I had the affair with the next summer—both of us wrecks. But her husband wasn't interested in her at all. He never found out about it."

Susan waited for more—an adolescent seduction, the cop's wife stimulated by the film to try her hand with a ready and willing seventeen-year-old. There must be details.

But Walker didn't offer any.

"So what about your other 'greatest moments'?" she asked.

"Oh, there was really just one," he confessed, "when I was working at the Crest, right after they broke it up into four theaters.

They'd installed a platter system where you get the whole film on one huge lazy Susan affair instead of using two projectors and changing reels. We were opening something big—*Close Encounters*, I think—and we were supposed to be showing it on two of our screens, but they'd only sent one print. So there we were, stuck—until I got this idea. All the old equipment was still lying around: projectors and pickup reels that hadn't been thrown out yet. And the hallway just happened to allow for a fairly direct route between two of the projection booths. So I rigged up this cable-and-pulley affair. We had film going out the door, into the hallway and into the projector next door. It was kind of crazy but it worked. And it was neat—racing back and forth, looking into the theater and seeing Richard Dreyfuss build this mudpile replica of Devil's Tower on one screen, then seeing the same thing on another screen, a moment or two later, only he wouldn't be quite as far along. It was like playing with time or something."

He looked straight at her, not seeing her.

"Yeah, it was neat," he repeated; then took note of his surroundings.

A large, square edifice of cream-pillared marble—the museum—promised shelter and escape from the chilly day. The temperature had dropped off after last night's drizzle, and the sky's pinkish gray imposed an absence of color on all that lay beneath it.

Walker paid their way in, checked their coats, found a floor plan and investigated what there was to see. Along with the Ansel Adams, there was a special exhibit of early Picasso and Matisse. Some nineteenth-century Romantic landscapes and the museum's permanent collection were also possibilities.

It was too much. They hadn't given themselves enough time for it.

They started straightaway with the Adams, Walker alighting on one photograph after another, his eyes intent as talons. He processed each image efficiently—until slowed down by one particular sequence.

He murmured: "Ah . . . wave action."

The photographer, from a California clifftop, had aimed his lens down at the Pacific and been caught in a trance of chaotic repetition—never the same, always the same; a rhythmic lack of pattern. How to tell if a coincidence had occurred? You would have to stay there with camera in hand for months, maybe years, to establish that a wave had hit a stretch of rocky beach in a duplicate way, prompting identical ricochets of spray. And by then the coast itself would have changed.

So, really, there was no proving anything. One had to settle instead for affinities: mere suggestions of a fluid continuity.

Susan left Walker studying these clifftop shots and visited a neighboring gallery that offered an exhibit of musical instruments, all of them mute, some of them glass-encased as though exiled from their purpose of existence. When she had her fill of silent trumpets, dumb fiddles and tongue-tied oboes, she joined her husband, who was poring over a display of correspondence between Adams and one of his associates.

"You almost done?"

"Hmmn?"

"Can we try something else?"

They made short work of Picasso and Matisse, then moved at random along marble-floored corridors into a dark gallery on a lower floor where they were surprised by Gilbert Stuart's portrait of George Washington with its patches of canvas left bare—a sign of deference to what couldn't be known about the man?

Retracing their steps, they basked in the silken surfaces and tensions of Cassatt and Sargent, Homer and Chase—recognizable human faces floating against oddly abstract backgrounds—until, pressed for time, they headed upstairs where they found several rooms of Impressionists and their successors, including a Gauguin that dominated the south end of the gallery.

"I had no idea this was here," Walker marveled. "I thought it would be in Europe somewhere."

It was more mural than painting, and less a group portrait than an unfolding pageant: "Where Do We Come From? What Are We? Where Are We Going?"

All the figures were Polynesian and female. One figure bathed where there was no water. Another reached for fruit from the trees. Several were gathered as if waiting for an announcement they would respond to skeptically. An old woman held her hands against her face, knowing nothing could be done about her condition. She had suffered every sort of loss there was, and now awaited only the final loss: of herself. Nearby a young woman leaned toward her, reclining in the sand but with eyes averted, oblivious of death.

These were the obvious layers of the painting's activities. Just below them, one could detect the figures' deep puzzlement at these roles they had been assigned, their sense of imprisonment in them. Susan felt the painting had coerced her into a role as well. Her eyes wouldn't focus.

And now there came voices and a light susurration; the hollow sound of waves or a bamboo whisper; a sibilance of palm fronds trembling on high as treetop predators schemed to spoil this idyll.

A coconut landed with a thud in the sand.

No, no, it was only a woman dropping her purse at the other end of the gallery.

Susan tried standing up. She felt chilly and faint. She sat back down, glanced at Monet haystacks, poplar rows and cathedral facades that were off to the right. Someone was telling her to stay as she was, *where* she was. It was Walker, quiet but alarmed, asking: "You all right?"

"Did you hear them? I mean, do you see—?"

She looked again at the Gauguin. But it had gathered itself into itself. It refused to speak.

"See what?"

The painting made no movement, no sound.

"Nothing. I must've—I need a soda or something. The cafeteria's downstairs?"

Walker consulted his floor plan. It was.

"Want me to come with you?"

"It's okay. You stay here. You want to look more, right?"

"Well—"

"So stay."

"It's just that this is our only chance."

She looked at him sharply: "For what?"

"For seeing these. We don't know when we'll be through here again, do we?—or if they'll even be on display." He gestured around at the walls. "I wouldn't have wanted to miss it."

"And you haven't."

He peered at her: "You're sure you're okay?"

She tried to reassure him: "Just thirsty. Really. I'll be all right as soon as I have a drink."

She didn't look back as she left—but could sense, without turning around, the anxious expression on his face.

In the cafeteria line, two floors below, she grew still more impatient; couldn't understand why the people ahead of her were dithering so prolongedly over their choice of food. She mumbled, "Something. Anything. Just grab it. Life's too short."

She poured herself a large-size lemonade—a waxen canister of icy pink sweetness—and then, as she got to the cash register, slid an enormous slice of pecan pie topped with synthetic whipped cream onto her tray.

Following an overhead arrow that pointed the way to a NO SMOKING section, she took a seat where, hunched over her plate, she saw only the table's surface. She concentrated on her snack, broke apart the morsels of pie with difficulty, using a plastic fork.

The gooey nuts adhered to her teeth. Where they stuck against a molar's enamel or the roof of her mouth, she poked at them with her tongue until her jaws ached from trying to dissolve the tacky syrup. Everything—what she ate, how she felt, where she was—was making her irritable and uncomfortable. She sucked up her drink through a plastic straw, then regretted it as her temples throbbed in icy pain.

And now there came the final annoyance: harsh cigarette smoke blowing at her, from right here at her table.

She looked up. . . .

It was a face of untold distress. It was a face that needed a cigarette to calm it. The woman wore a long dark overcoat even though it was downright steamy in this basement cafeteria. She was mouthing words, but only smoke came out. The cigarette flew and flew, leaving a trail of fumes behind it. Susan attempted to look past its haze and into the woman's eyes. Crow's-feet fanned out from them in a radius of lines that dissolved in vague features. And the eyes themselves held no detail—as if they were holes to dive through. There was no reading the thoughts they were expressing. There was no deciphering the words she was mouthing.

The woman gestured to show she was going to try sign language. But her hands—which like her face were neither old nor young, yet somehow filled with too much experience—made one indistinct shape after another, all nonsense. The burning cigarette interfered at every stage. Susan knew no Ameslan, but she could tell this wasn't going well. The woman's face writhed in frustration; she shivered as if at a blast of Arctic air.

Susan began to feel a chill, too, coming through the sweatiness. She looked around to see if anyone else had noticed this soul in torment, but no one had. The patrons of this cafeteria carried on eating and chattering, their packages at their side. Their complaints, what Susan could hear of them, were predictably petty. They wouldn't know what bad luck was until it hit them.

When she turned back to rescue this freezing woman from whatever crisis she was going through, all she caught was a glimpse of an O-shape on her lips—a frantic hello-ing—and then the dark wool specter was superseded by a tan-colored mass that slid brutally into its place: Walker.

"What is it? Jeez, Susan, what're you looking at?"

It took her a full moment to recover. The cafeteria was stickily hot again. She needed a cooler place.

She asked him, "Are you hungry? Are you thirsty?"

He wasn't.

"Then let's get out of here."

Over dinner in a North End restaurant, Walker's sister offered *her* hypothesis.

"Flu that's going around," she said. "Had it myself. Comes and goes. Hour on, hour off. Rats were bothered by it, too. . . ."

Back at the apartment, Susan waited until Mary had gone to bed, then whispered to her husband, "I don't have what a rat had! And I don't think it's the flu."

"Mary's the scientist. She'd know if the flu was going around."

"It probably is. You wouldn't have to be a scientist to know that."

He looked at her, fearful of what she would say next, expecting to be accused of something.

"If you could only have *seen* this woman," she insisted. "It was the same woman. She was dressed exactly the same as in New Orleans, San Francisco. But she's never been this close before."

"Two more days," he consoled her, "then we'll be on the train."

"That's not going to help."

"How do you know?"

"She's followed us every step of the way!"

"Honey, you've got to calm down. You've really got to."

"I can't calm down."

They coasted along in silence for a moment.

Susan turned away from him, overcome by a certain thought; then turned back, almost pleading with him.

"It's just that it's more than I bargained for."

"What is?"

"I don't know. This—This—"

"This what?"

But even as she came up with the word, she sensed some undesirable pun in it which made her wish she had held it back.

"This . . . *vacation*," she told him.

It was their last day visiting Walker's sister and each of them agreed that a jaunt along the North Shore might be just the thing to soothe their nerves. Susan, after a good night's rest, had tried to make light of her "hallucinations." But by now they all believed in them.

"Short drive out of town," Mary said. "That'll do it."

She floored it along Route 1, a riotous commercial strip. Acting as tour guide, she pointed out a roadside restaurant in the shape of an eighteenth-century sailing ship and commented, "Good seafood there."

"Really?"

Walker was dubious.

"Not to mention fabulous decor. . . ."

They briefly followed a six-lane boulevard flanked by industrial parks and shopping malls, then left it for a two-lane thoroughfare through old New England towns that had grown up so fast you couldn't tell where one ended and the next began. Saltbox cottages, august mansions, instant condominiums, gas stations, church spires, graveyards—all made a patchwork pattern of the landscape.

Along a stretch that reeked more of car exhaust and harbor fumes than autumn lawns and burning leaves, Walker spied a sign that said:

WITCH CITY AUTO BODY

"Um—where are we?"

"Salem."

"Salem where the witch trials were?"

"Just passing through. Shortest route."

Beyond Salem, the road followed the coast and they could see a bank of whiteness hovering a few hundred yards offshore. Susan, alone in the backseat, looked at it dubiously. Mary, at the steering wheel, announced that these waters were often fogbound this time of year. Walker, in the front passenger seat, kept his Polaroid ready in case any mist-enshrouded wraiths should make their presence known. Fog seemed a likely venue for them.

But he was disappointed. Fog merely limited sight.

At Gloucester Harbor, they entered the white wall as you would a special effect: a truncated orb of visibility, shifting and luminous, its brightness hurting their eyes. Up near Rockport they went for a stroll on a beach, taking pictures of one another as they stepped into or out of the earthbound cloud. But fog, instead of introducing new and impossible figures into Walker's snapshots, served only to obscure the camera's most overt subjects. In one close-up that Mary took of her brother, Walker wasn't there at all.

Susan studied the picture warily, until a chill set in.

"You don't feel it at first, do you?" she said. "And then—"
She indicated the car: "Anyone want to get back into sunlight?"

Their reentry into the crisp scarlet and lantern-orange of autumn was as precipitate as their vanishing from it had been. In Manchester they took a walk and did some window-shopping. In Beverly they stopped for another stroll, followed by dinner at a restaurant that once had been a railway station. All the staff were dressed as nineteenth-century engineers in striped overalls, bright neckerchiefs and floppy hats.

"Thought this would be appropriate," Mary murmured.

Mary, evidently, was a connoisseur of the Boston metropolitan area's offerings in restaurant kitsch.

Walker was in his element. But the restaurant's railway theme appeared to have no special appeal to the young woman who waited on them. When Walker mentioned his and Susan's cross-country trip to her, telling her how long it took and the variety of scenery you saw while in transit, she only wrinkled her nose and turned to Susan to ask if it didn't get boring—the implication being that while Walker seemed the type to savor seventy-two hours of tedium, Susan looked as if she had more sense.

Susan's reply: "Not on this trip. No."

"Only the East Coast is boring," Walker said pointedly. "Too flat. And the trees all get in the way."

But the waitress had gone.

He expanded on his statement for the benefit of his companions: "Fog, trees . . . they close your mind down. They wipe out sights."

Susan, in a joking tone, asked: "But I *like* all the trees. At least when they're changing color like this. So what does that say about me?"

Mary, more seriously, argued: "I don't consider the East Coast boring."

   Walker merely looked at his Polaroids, unable to conceal his disappointment.

   Back on Beacon Hill that night, he and Susan—as if to smooth out an imbalance arising between them—made necessary love; were spun close together; found a path that was open; didn't care whether Mary heard them or not.

South Station was the end of the line—a place where, on Amtrak at least, you could only turn back. And their send-off from its New England terminus was a blend of dank salt-harbor smells and vivid images of Rwanda, courtesy of Mary, who was telling Susan: "Lake Kivu, Ruhengeri . . . the names are like names in a dream—a dream that women stare out of, burdened but indifferent. They're *used* to their load. So take care of yourself."

Susan couldn't think of any reply to this, so made none.

Walker was quiet, too, studying the air as if it were a musical score indicating an unusually long pause.

The boarding call sounded and they joined the slow-moving crowd. Seating themselves in cramped quarters, they looked through tinted glass at Mary, who kept vigil on the platform—a comically precise silhouette.

Susan felt oddly free to talk about her while staring at her outline.

"Has she ever had a boyfriend?"

"Oh, I'm sure she has. Or maybe not. She's so thorough, it's a moot point. Even if she *hasn't* done something, she's usually re-searched it from top to bottom. With her the results would be about the same, don't you think? I get the feeling there's nothing that would surprise her. Some people just know it all from the start."

With a shudder, the train began its heavy glide.

Walker's sister stood rooted to her spot, slender as the pillars that held up the platform roof. She gave them a parting salute.

Susan pressed a hand flat to the windowpane in answer, then sat back and said: "I like her. She's comforting. In a brisk kind of way."

A long while later—after they had passed through Back Bay Station and were paralleling a six-lane highway headed west— Walker answered, "Yeah, she's a card, all right. Eccentric. Even a little crazy. 'A month in Africa.' Ha!"

This came as a shock to Susan: "You mean you don't think she went there?"

"I'm sure she didn't."

"But she seemed to know all about it."

"Pile of library books on her dressing stand. Basil Davidson, Thurston Clarke. I had a look. She's been taking notes. Everything she told you—all rehearsed." He seemed on the verge of saying something more, but then thought better of it. "Probably just couldn't afford the flight," he concluded.

"To Rwanda?"

"No, no—to the wedding. And didn't want to borrow. Has her pride."

"You can stop talking like her now," Susan reminded him gently.

He snapped a little more awake at this: "Oh, that's right, I can, can't I?"

An intercom announced that dinner would be served at five o'clock. Already November darkness was blotting out whatever there was to see of Boston's western suburbs. They had a table to themselves in the dining car and afterwards went for drinks in the lounge, where they met a man who said he was the heir to the Honey Bucket fortune and a woman who insisted the best place to raise children was Guam.

The drinks were supposed to help them sleep, but the train's jostling route through the Berkshires transformed alcohol from sedative to stimulant. Also, this was the one stretch of the trip where they'd indulged in a private compartment—and Walker, after growing up on movies where rail travel held an erotic allure, wanted to try out sex on the train . . . a mixed success, made somewhat heartless by the necessity of retiring to their separate narrow bunks afterward. He took the lower, she took the upper, a few miles past Albany.

The train's motion was an evolving contradiction—it rocked you to sleep, then shook you awake; rocked you, then shook you.

It was, Susan decided as she drifted off, a way of taking note of each step of the night; a way of marking off miles like moments. . . .

Dreams slip softly by. There's the one where she's sliding past the Sweetgrass Hills. At the sound of Walker's voice, the horizon starts to contract, the mountains rear up, the dryness tingles, the grasses enclose you in their lap—

With a jolting *thunk* she was shaken awake.

The train was proceeding at a clip over a rough section of railbed. And there had been some other disturbance.

Walker was quiet. The dark was absolute. At midnight they had drawn the vinyl window shade down before turning out the light. Now, while feeling for the window shade's handle, she listened more closely for Walker's telltale snore: a gentle sound, a rhythmic rustling. . . .

The shade flipped up.

Dim light shone from a rippled sky. Tigerstripe clouds were made readable by moonlight. Through rows and furrows of cloud, as the train cruised past a silvery river, the lunar disc became a mutable etching—a full moon, a *skunky* moon, black and white, changing its shapes and stripes as it moved along.

The door to the compartment opened, and she gasped a small scream.

"It's me. It's me."

The voice was Walker's. But the words were spoken less in reassurance than in a quiet horror. Shirtless and shivering, sweating and pale, he closed the compartment door and switched on the light.

"I saw this woman with a rearranged face—"

"In the corridor?"

"I wanted to find it but there wasn't any door. And this woman, she just scared me, really scared me—"

"What do you mean: 'rearranged face'?"

"Off to the left. I can't explain, I don't want to explain. Like something you see in the future, a place where you lose all your confidence—"

He started to talk at random. He mentioned a doctor—"Dr. Bloom" or "Dr. Broom" was it?—and then began to get angry, as if at something she had said.

It occurred to her that he might be sleeptalking.

"Walker?"

"—no matter what—"

She looked down from her bunk. He wasn't just shirtless—he was naked, with his cock semierect. In the limited space, she clambered down to join him.

"Walker, it's me."

She had put on a nightgown earlier, but the atmosphere was stuffy. The thermostat wasn't working and it was too warm under the covers. She had taken it off before its smooth nylon itch turned to sweat.

And now her body split to surround his, meeting it skin to skin. A breast found a hand whose palm cupped a nipple. A shoulder found a shoulder, a thigh found a thigh. She held him gently while she tried to wake him. He shuddered. The train creaked like crazy: a thousand restless spinsters in a thousand wicker armchairs.

"Walker?"

"—and she's listening to my closest heart. . . ."

When he finally woke, he reached for her not in a carnal way but as if to ascertain her existence. He remembered his dream when she asked him about it, but didn't want to discuss it with her: "You'll just think I'm paranoid—"

Still he needed to be comforted. She tended to him, let him touch her, her solidity coming back to him.

Dream or nightmare—whichever it was—withdrew for the moment. And they found that, with a bit of maneuvering, the tiny lower bunk could accommodate them both after all.

They lucked into a knot where closeness lulled them.

A snug fit—precious.

Emerging into daylight was like slipping out from under a thick industrial cloud. It brought a euphoria with it which she suspected Walker felt too. All darkness, literal and metaphorical, receded away from them. Even Ohio, with its silvery warehouses and its cornstalks reduced to stubble and its fallow fields blighted by a night's hard frost, looked reassuring. Against this pale background a cloaked figure in grim, implacable pursuit could easily be eluded, couldn't it?

At breakfast they were seated with a nun and a rustic-looking character who had a camera with zoom lens and a bolo emblazoned with a "Colorado Railway Association" logo around his neck—a hard-core rail aficionado.

He and Walker immediately started in on camera-talk.

Susan smiled at the nun, letting the two men jabber on until breakfast arrived. Then she interrupted them to ask if the railway buff would be visiting Chicago, too. It turned out he would.

He was a data processor from Los Angeles, planning a stopover in the "Windy City," as he put it, to get further acquainted with a woman he had met through his telephone dealings at work.

Susan asked what he knew about her.

It didn't sound like much: "—but her name is Oriental and she *sounds* Oriental, so I'll be real surprised if she's something else."

Apparently he had something more than friendship in mind. He mentioned a case where a wedding and three children had resulted from a telephone courtship: "—and that marriage is as happy as anything else you see."

The nun, anxious to change the topic, threw in cheerfully, "They say you'll have to wear a gas mask soon, to breathe in Los Angeles."

Walker took her up on this, asked what her destination was.

"Lancaster, California."

The railway buff announced that he was originally from that part of the state.

"You know Lancaster?"

"In the desert. Hot," he said.

"But cool at night."

"Well," he conceded, "cooler."

Then he added that it was in high desert, so it might be cooler than—

He went on to name a few places.

After the nun left, Walker asked him how well he knew Chicago: "We've only got three hours. That enough time to walk to Lake Michigan and back?"

The man looked doubtful and said it was six or seven blocks— maybe more.

Walker turned to Susan: "I think we can manage that, don't you?"

"Sure. No problem."

"Let's plan on it."

But after the railway buff departed, he added: "Just a matter of my stomach settling down."

"It's still bothering you?"

He nodded solemnly, as if having to concentrate on untangling his guts. Then, indicating the passing view, he said, "See? I was right about the trees."

Some were leafed in burnt sienna. Many were bare. To Walker's mind they were present in the appropriate amount—as dividers to fields, not a claustrophobic wall hemming in the railbed. Even the diesel smells and industrial landscape of Gary, Indiana—where the train stopped a few hours later—seemed to him a welcome sight, a topographical curiosity. And once they crossed the state line into Illinois, entering an endless expanse of railyard and derelict factory, he perked right up and started taking snapshots as the bulgy, blocky Chicago skyline rose on the horizon, wrapped in a fumy haze.

Fifteen minutes later, the train backed into the station.

They had arrived in midafternoon. Lunchtime restaurants, catering to office workers, were already closing down. But Walker didn't want to take time out for a meal: "Maybe after the lake—"

He consulted his map, which indicated they should cross the bridge to Adams Street, a thronging corridor with a marble gleam at the end of it.

"Is the pollution bad?" he asked. "I can't seem to get a deep enough breath. Or is it the river?"

He peered over the railing at the green, opaque water.

"The river has a smell," she confirmed. "The air does, too. Is it bothering you? Don't walk so fast!"

He glanced suspiciously from pavement to skyscraper to the end of the busy thoroughfare, then heeded her advice, broke his stride, settled into a saunter.

Trains rattled overhead. Sickly popcorn and pretzel aromas

filled State Street. Sidewalk vendors sold powerful brands of sausage, using silvery tongs to extract them from steaming carts. The air was a crystal-powder breakdown of chemical shards. On crowded sidewalks, a restless horde drank this mixture down. No one paid attention to traffic lights. People were in shadow. No sunlight hit these streets. Everyone was pale. But Walker's greenish pallor—more like an allergic reaction than a lack of tan—concerned her. Clearly he hadn't slept well, even after she'd gotten him back to bed.

They came to Michigan Avenue: a borderline between landscaped park and urban grid. Across the street, the swollen Greek temple of the Art Institute rose up, massive in scale. Above its portals, a rippling banner announced:

AN EXHIBIT OF FRAMES

Walker talked Susan into "framing" the museum with her fingers while he took a picture; then suggested they visit it after seeing the lake.

The avenue leading to the lakeshore was enormous. And the tree-lined paths of Grant Park, to the right, formed infinite vistas. The park, sealed off by steady streams of traffic, was nearly devoid of human commerce. Its only patrons were the derelicts who lived in it, wrapped in overcoats, huddling against the cold. The place spoke of bankruptcy as much as elegance. Its bare trees were widows reaching out for what they missed.

Susan sensed her pursuer might be among them. But apart from one distant figure who was scavenging the garbage cans, all these park-dwellers were in a dormant state, motionless, reclining on vandalized benches. . . .

A nudge of breath came in close to her. She whirled around to catch it: a dust devil, as tall as she was, dragging candy wrappers in its wake, moving out from the pavement into oncoming traffic.

Walker said, "Yeah, it's good to get a break from the train, a bit of fresh air, isn't it?"

The air *was* marginally fresher here. Gusts of it came off the water, and she breathed more easily for her husband's sake. But when it came to the shoreline itself, she felt only disappointment. From where she and Walker stood waiting for a signal to let them cross eight lanes of traffic, she could see their goal: another flat lake.

She said something to this effect.

"Lakes usually are flat," Walker smiled.

"No, what I mean is—"

In the pit of her stomach she felt something spiral inward and collapse: the dust devil returning and swiveling down through her.

"—flat, and surrounded by nothing."

He gestured in disagreement back toward the skyline of the Loop: "Supposed to be a glory!"

"Oh sure," she granted him, "but this—"

She turned toward indistinctions of lakeshore, horizon, marina: "I'm not even interested."

"You getting cold?" he asked.

"It's what a *highway* needs," she objected. "It's not on a human scale at all. We'd have to be cruising by at sixty miles an hour to appreciate it properly."

The traffic light still hadn't given them a walk signal, and it looked as though it might be some time before it did. She suggested they head back to the Art Institute.

Walker seemed unsteady on his feet. She slowed her pace to match his, while trying to fathom what had chilled her. The museum, when they reached it, was a mob of tourists, schoolchildren and frantic docents. Everyone appeared to be as interested in picture frames as in the pictures themselves. The line to the featured exhibit twisted round and round. At Walker's suggestion, they skirted it and headed for the modern art galleries instead. A black wool feeling threaded up her insides.

In a quiet gallery they found some Georgia O'Keeffes. Susan lingered by these while Walker disappeared into the next room.

He was back an instant later, wild for her to follow him: "Be still my thumping heart. Forty years old and I can still be smitten! You've got to have a look. She's beautiful, she's hilarious!"

She went to see what had caught his fancy.

The woman was a placid ruin—mirror and compact in hand, cottage-cheese thighs like something set in mottled concrete. Her hopes, her discontent, ran vaguely in her face, which was mildly woeful.

Certainly the painting had its wit. But it felt cruel to laugh at it—or at *her*, anyway. She was what she was. On her dressing stand were cut-glass jars for facial powder, a vase of drying blossoms, a hat, a change purse, a comb. And there was the wicker chair! She was sitting on it.

"Albright. Ivan Albright. Ever heard of him? *I* haven't—"

Susan craned closer to read the painting's title. It was elaborate: "Into the World There Came a Soul Called Ida (The Lord in His Heaven and I in My Room Below)."

"Some boudoir!" said Walker.

Susan shrank back from it. It was a vision of people as carbuncles—not horrifying, but as sad and piercing a thing as she had ever come across.

Walker was whispering, confiding in her, "—might not have a postcard, a book on this guy, you know? Never even heard of him! I have the camera with me. If I sit there, maybe I can get a shot. You want to stand by the door, cough if anyone's coming? Make sure the guard—They usually don't like you taking photographs. . . ."

She was moving off anyway, embarrassed by what the picture exposed and by her husband's behavior. She retreated to the O'Keeffes, which were more detached, less disturbing. The gallery was crowded, the pictures difficult to see. She tried pressing in closer until, as if at a signal, a constellation of people fragmented around her, prompting her to stand aside with them, make herself small.

She soon saw why.

The woman seemed at first to have suffered a stroke. But, no, it was just that sorrow and a subsequent absentmindedness had gotten the better of her. Her cheeks and chin were like putty, drooping in a hangdog expression. Her eyes, half shut, had soft dark circles beneath them, and her lips were pursed into a taste of something sour, "rearranged" in a shape that allowed for only the smallest pleasures. She didn't look at any of the paintings. It was more as though this were a constitutional she took every day, a stroll that happened to lead through an art museum. Her skin was as chalky as that of Albright's Ida. Her bowed head spoke of a hard determination.

She passed through and, as she did, exchanged a glance with Susan that showed she was as surprised to see Susan as Susan was to see her—at this time, in this place and by this altered light. There was no mistaking the heavy-hanging winter coat she was wearing; no misunderstanding her good sense in wearing it. It was cold out there!—as cold as the clattering noise that came to Susan now . . . a sound of hard plastic hitting the marble floor at a random angle.

Is there order? Is order glorious?

The gallery was empty. All visitors had drifted out of it but one.

Ida was puffed out with a looseness of flesh. Despite this, she evinced a strong sense of self-possession. She lured Susan on in an ancient direction; put a stutter in her walk because she knew what happened next; positioned her on the bench so she could be next to Walker—whose head was bent down to examine his lens.

Together, they called his name.

He saw nothing, heard nothing. The camera was out of his hands.

With a scolding smile, a museum guard approached and knelt to scoop it up—so took the brunt of the body as it slid onto the floor.

Yanked by the shock, Susan joined them there.

The guard skittered away, stood swaying in alarm, until he thought to go for help, leaving her alone with her husband.

"Walker. . . ?"

She could hold him, she could touch him—but solidity didn't matter anymore. The ghost had gone out of him.

A rumor went rippling at the news.

A crowd started to gather.

The *absurdity* of being cast in this role—

That was her first thought, a thought that surfaced with startling clarity out of the commotion in the museum gallery. For there was no doubt about it: the role was hers.

Beyond the shock, there was the incongruity of it, as if she had leapfrogged generations in a matter of moments. A widow at twenty-five? How was she going to play *that* part convincingly?

From a great distance, from the very periphery of her mind, she saw there was no need to worry. Something was guiding her. Her body was telling her what to do. It was making huge dry sobs, as stiff as they were convulsive, tensing her up and snapping her apart like kindling. She watched herself in amazement as her shoulders and back were racked with shivers strong enough to pull a muscle. All her companions, an endless succession of them in their long dark overcoats, were watching her too. . . .

And then they were gone.

Certain bright details—the useless ambulance; the phone calls to be made; the rail brochure informing her that "Amtrak Express offers station-to-station transfer of human remains to over 85 cities"—joined a random pool of moments which, once they had registered, remanifested themselves vividly but with no regard to sequence. And the gaps between these moments were as blank as words wiped clean from a chalkboard. She kept vague, ghostly traces of them in mind, but none of their content. She performed all necessary tasks from a strength she invented.

The phone calls were the worst part of it. It was late Friday afternoon in Chicago: midafternoon in Seattle. After reaching the hotel room that the hospital receptionist had arranged for her, she locked herself in and pulled all the drapes closed, as if to ward off the calamity around her.

She tried her mother at home first.

There was no reply—and her parents had no answering machine. Even if they had had one, what message could she have left on it that would have conveyed what needed to be conveyed?

She dialed her father at work. His secretary told her he had departed early for the weekend.

"With your mother," she added.

"They were going away somewhere?"

"Oregon, I think. Yes, I'm sure. That spot where they usually go."

Susan knew the place—and knew that it had no telephone.

She dialed Celia's number and got Celia's latest message: no words, but some prerecorded yodeling or a parody of yodeling by a musical satirist . . . the latest in a series of jokey machine-greetings.

Susan tried, but, after being yodeled at, could not bring herself to say what she had to say. And the beep was unusually long, suggesting a backlog of messages. Maybe Celia was gone, too, down to Oregon with her parents, or off with her girlfriend Martha somewhere.

She could try Celia at work—or, no, she couldn't.

Of her two address books, she realized, she had brought along only the older one that needed updating, which meant she didn't have Celia's latest work number.

She looked through the addresses and phone numbers she *did* have, and had trouble reading them. Something was in the way. An image of her more current address book waved brightly before her—in the place where it belonged, by the kitchen telephone at home—but a molten glassiness, a liquid heat streaming across her eyes, was distorting it. This failure to find the right numbers, this inability to connect with the voices she needed, was wearing away a barrier, releasing a flood in her.

She was weeping. But weeping wasn't practical. She should try again. Where was Walker's wallet? In it was a tiny address book, always kept up to date. It would have his parents' and sister's numbers, which she was also missing. No one had given her his things yet. She had come straight from the hospital to this hotel. Should she now go back to retrieve his belongings?

The receptionist who had booked her here—what was her name? And had she told Susan to sit tight until contacted or to return to the hospital in an hour or two?

Susan couldn't remember.

Someone knew where she was, at any rate: the receptionist and perhaps the coroner. And she knew where they were, even if she couldn't recall their names. She had *asked* for their names and they had given them, but now they were gone from memory. No names, no names. . . . What if there was a shift change? She didn't even have the name of the hospital: "But I know where it is. I've got to be practical."

She wiped her eyes, again went through her address book, saw the names of colleagues at work, supervisors, friends she hadn't seen in months. What could they do? Nothing. She was not connected to them.

There were loose papers in her purse. She found grocery-store coupons, a dry cleaner's receipt, two business cards for people whose identities were a mystery to her. At the bottom was a crumpled sheet of paper with a phone number and an hour for a rendezvous that at first didn't mean anything to her. And then it did: *Last summer. Her meeting with Eleanor. A number for Eleanor.*

Who else was there? Not Aunt Ginny—she would be worse than useless.

As she dialed the number, a part of her stretched over the wires, riding their gentle static and losing itself in sounds that suggested some methodical erasure.

"Yes?"

It was Eleanor's voice, husky and distrustful. But perhaps she answered all her calls this way.

It was even more difficult talking to a live voice than to a tape recorder, but Susan managed to get out the name that went with the voice.

The voice said, "Yes, this is Eleanor, who is this?"

She wasn't able to say. Instead she began, "Walker—It's Walker—"

His name felt terribly thick to her. It seemed to stick feebly at the base of her throat. In attempting to utter it, she felt she was having to learn to speak all over again.

"Susan?"

"Yes."

"You're back from vacation already?"

"No."

"Then where are you?"

"Chicago."

"With Walker?"

"No."

"Where's Walker?"

"Walker's—gone."

There was no need to expand on this. The silence at the other end of the line indicated it had been understood perfectly. For a moment this comprehension teetered back and forth, one way, then another, in a strange precarious balancing act, before toppling into further understandings:

"But it's too soon. It's just—too soon."

Susan was silent.

"And you're where?"

This meant which hotel. Susan told her. Eleanor coaxed the room and phone numbers out of her, asking, "You're sure of that? You've got them there in front of you?"

She said she did.

Eleanor asked: "You haven't been able to reach anyone else, have you?"

Susan, saying nothing, nodded no.

But Eleanor understood this too; instructed her to hang up and wait in her hotel room.

"I'm flying out there, but I'll need to make arrangements. I'll call you back to let you know when I'll get there. Do you understand?"

She nodded wordlessly again, then said aloud that she did—though the way that she said it was riddled with doubt.

Eleanor asked: "What? Is there something else?"

"Can you—Can you call his parents? I've lost their number. It's at home, I mean."

"I've got it. I can phone them. Is that all?"

The brusqueness of her voice was oddly soothing.

"Can you—? Can you call—?"

Eleanor waited.

But no other names emerged. She had been going to say "Walker."

Eleanor smoothed the moment over: "That's okay, it's all right. We can make more phone calls later."

Susan said nothing.

Eleanor proceeded, "Just stay where you are, and I'll get back to you as soon as I know what's what."

In twenty minutes, as promised, she telephoned with an esti- mated time of arrival and repeated assurances that she had the matter in hand: "Don't worry. Don't think. Stay calm. I'll help see you through this."

Susan took the information down, then replaced the receiver.

She stepped to the window, stared at the street below. The city around her was a fathomless gray sea she didn't want to enter.

She hung on in the hotel room, retreated to the bed, stayed hunched up tight until Eleanor arrived, a little after midnight. Then she allowed her weakness to show. It was Eleanor who oversaw the body being loaded on the freight car while Susan stood at a distance from the train. And it was Eleanor who sug- gested they get a sleeping compartment instead of riding with the crowd in Coach Class, as Walker and Susan had planned.

Darkness fell, and they passed through a landscape that was neither city nor countryside. The heavy sliding glass door of their "roomette," firmly latched, was covered in a rough blue synthetic material, isolating them from the rest of the train.

Eleanor said: "We're lucky you're traveling in November. Any other time of year, they're all booked up. That's what the agent told me."

They used their isolation to sleep and think.

When it grew light again, they were in North Dakota. Barbed wire made the land into a face harassed by scars. Where fences gave way, the Plains' shallow slopes unfurled low-flying sculp- tures—rolling grimaces of sandstone, where bedrock was ex- posed by a river's hunger for soil to carry. What towns there were were mostly mobile homes and weathered clapboard, with occasional fast-food logos blaring from highway intersections seen from miles away.

Havre was as Walker had described it—a fantasy of tidy habitation set in the cleft of a landscape that was arid and vast. The mountains he had mentioned were even smaller than she had imagined. She could see now why they wouldn't have been enough for a boy. And they were too far away.

The town was a service stop for the train and passengers were encouraged to stretch their legs. It was late afternoon and bitterly cold. A wind scoured every section of the platform. Walker's parents came out of the waiting room and, with a few words, consoled Susan while Eleanor stood at a discreet distance. The elder Popmans didn't attempt to bridge this distance from their ex-daughter-in-law, but took silent note of her. Susan couldn't help feeling that the behavioral protocol she had been raised with wasn't adequate to the occasion. In polygamous societies, in Africa or Utah, how did widows act who had lost the same husband? She was sure there must be a book on this. But there seemed no way to inquire about it just now.

Instead she kept making observations—or, rather, details kept emerging from nowhere, as if an unknown force were foisting them on her.

The first was that the stiffness in the elder Popmans' gait had less to do with age than environment: it was simply a reflex reaction to the unceasing wind. They braced themselves for it whether it was there or not, because in this place its absence would have been the exception. Everyone on the platform, even Eleanor, who was making a purchase at the snack stand, walked uncertain of their balance. There were slicks of ice on the pavement to take into account, but wind was the overriding factor.

Back aboard the train, during the long pauses in conversation with her in-laws—seated in a compartment across the narrow corridor—Susan studied the landscape and made her second observation. Seeing bluish humps to the north, she asked, "Are those the Sweetgrass Hills?"

Her father-in-law confirmed they were. Like giant slumbering beasts embedded in the Plains, they invited the eye to follow their ridgebacks: spinal curvatures that pushed at the land's tough surface. She gazed at them until they seemed a way of stepping off into the sky.

Finally, more trivially, there were the postcards that had been for sale on the station platform. It had soothed her to buy a few, though she at first didn't know why. She looked at them now.

One showed a woman clad in a fur jacket, sunglasses, gaudy earrings, a silk scarf and Capri pants. She was walking a pig on a leash. "Montana Poodle" was the caption. The others, including one where a small group of spectators was cheering on a bear as it chased joggers down the street, were similarly jokey. It struck Susan that Walker, however alone he had thought he was while growing up here, would now have kindred souls roughly his age somewhere nearby if he were to return.

She wondered if he knew this, and if knowing it should make any difference in his place of burial. As the train wound its way through the Rockies, she couldn't help wondering—as though wondering, *concentrating* on the question, would give her an answer she needed—if, enclosed as he was in a box for shipment, he could be said to "know" anything at all.

At the funeral, she saw the images of what was happening, but was numb to the substance behind them—Eleanor standing up straight, as though *she* were the widow stricken into sorrow; Mary nearby, her umbrella planted firmly in the bright green turf; Susan's parents, with Celia not far off, grouped closely around their daughter, wanting to enfold and protect her but not quite knowing how; Walker's parents, at the end of the service, retreating from the grave like weakened monuments shuffling along. . . .

The burial was in one of Seattle's hilltop cemeteries. And again there was a feeling of teetering comprehension, like that she had sensed in Eleanor when calling her from Chicago, only this time it was comprehension of a bigger extinction all around. Everything was fragile. She felt she was straddling an enormous landscape which might drop abruptly in any direction at any moment, and this seemed appropriate—for Walker had taken lively note of each rumor and revelation of the city's latent seismic instability whenever an article about it appeared in the newspaper.

Now, buried, he would be a part of it.

In Seattle that year, winter never came. A soft monsoon moved in and wrapped the city in drizzle and mist, but there wasn't any snow. Even frosts were rare. In early January a wide space of blue opened in the sky—an overhead crevasse of light, uncommon for the season. The sun was blazing. But the fir trees around Walker's house, acting on penumbral agendas of their own, absorbed and extinguished its radiance.

Time turned to dullness, a colorless continuum threatened by memory. And she had been right. Now that her life had imploded, the world was serene in its response, as though bent, in the greater scheme of things, on an equable distribution of local and terrestial anguish. Oh, there were various minor wars, endless famines, spreading epidemics and a sense of global economic doom on the TV network news each night. But there wasn't the feeling of overriding crisis that had marked the Gulf War and made her feel so anomalous in her happiness at the time. She had trouble now keeping track of any news reports; could barely bring herself to read the paper for fear that she would be undone by a "people piece" about some smiling photographed couple or, equally, a back-page item about some hateful instance of needless cruelty. The immediacy of her shock at Walker's loss had spread out, over the passing weeks, to a throbbing ache— less specific each day, but more all-encompassing. And the shadows she navigated were potent, necessitating care in everything she did if they weren't to be released and envelop her. It took all her wit, all her intuition, to keep from steering herself straight back into a wilderness of grief.

Not long after the funeral, Eleanor, as if acting on rights ceded to her by her rescue of Susan in Chicago, came to visit—and she continued to do so, sparingly at first and then with increasing frequency: an unexpected antidote to grief. She was a disturbing antidote, however, implying as she sometimes did that Susan's brief marriage had been merely a prelude to this newfound intimacy between the two women; an intimacy in which, apparently, almost anything could be said.

"I wanted out of the rut," Eleanor admitted late one night, after a bottle or two of wine. "And Walker, I guess, needed a nemesis."

Susan protested that Eleanor hardly struck her as a nemesis: "Some marriages just don't work. Everyone knows that."

Eleanor, disregarding her, continued: "Most women want it the other way around, you know. Any lawyer would tell you: if your husband is dead instead of divorced from you, you're at least eligible for his social security. . . ."

"You mean—you knew he was going to die?"

"We're *all* going to die. It's in the cards. But the timing, I admit, was unexpected—"

Under the living room's track lighting, Eleanor appeared sculpted by her wardrobe into mute, plush colors that offered a warmth, yet said "professional woman." Her dress was part smoking jacket, part formal gown. Its very softness looked tailored to emerge from marble—from the lobby, say, of one of the fancier skyscrapers downtown.

Susan, in jeans and one of Walker's old shirts, felt dowdy by comparison. In the last several weeks, she had taken to changing into this shirt as soon as she came home from work. She slept in it as well. It was one she had rescued from the laundry basket upon her return and not washed since—the only thing that gave her a smell she needed. . . .

She also left Walker's greeting on the answering machine intact—would sometimes call home from the office just to hear his words on the tape. She had an endless bounty of images of him on hand, but this was the limit of his sound.

Her conversations with Eleanor were conducted over the herbal teas Walker had been fond of, which Susan now found had certain tonic properties. Their aroma seemed to slip into her bones, venting them, aerating them, making them soothingly smooth. She waited for tea's warmth to rise in her brain or slip down her spine and out to her extremities: a substitute for something. She knew the path it would take, and most nights its progress made her placid.

On other occasions, when rainstorms spread their arcs and drummed fingertip patterns on the house's walls of glass, the two women would go below to raid Walker's wine cellar. Susan knew nothing of vintages, vintners, what should be consumed now, what should be left in the dark for a few more years. Her only purpose was to create a bole of heat, of floppy revelations and slurred gazes that could hold their own against the sodden chill of muddy driveway, mossy lawn and cloud-skimmed trees.

Within these revelations, there was an ongoing feeling of Eleanor as "mother"—or at least "instructor"—who had somehow read the whole story beforehand and knew what was coming next. On evenings when Eleanor drank too much to drive back to her apartment, Susan would invite her to stay the night. By December this invitation was implicit in Susan's first offering of a glass of wine, and by January it was being made several times a week.

The bedroom, with its king-size bed, was the one room in the house that had more walls than windows. It was a large and gracious secret chamber, and for both women the sharing of it became a kind of subterfuge. Susan knew what her own conspiratorial aim was. In sleep, and even in the semiwaking fissures between dreams, it was possible to believe—with the way Eleanor's nightgown rode up her hips and bunched at the crotch—that it was Walker who held her, the soft nub of his cock nestling up between her buttocks. But Eleanor's aim remained unclear.

Susan kept quiet about this sleeping arrangement, deeming that, as long as it wasn't frankly sexual, it wasn't the business of her friends or family. She found herself thinking resentfully that neither her mother nor father, nor even her sister, would have slept with her if she had asked them to—and then she would pull back in surprise from her bitterness at this.

What was she hoping for? Possession? Obliteration? A kind of amnesiac enchantment?

It was all these things, apparently. And increasingly Eleanor obliged her by providing them, inhabiting all her sleeping and waking hours, supplanting Walker at the same time that she served as an extension, a continual reminder of him. There was nothing overtly carnal in Eleanor's attentions, but there was something disturbingly coddling about them. Where was solitude in all this? She had thought she would be *alone* with Walker's death.

Eleanor's solicitous interest in her led Susan to make damaging admissions: "I think I'm beginning to need you."

"And I'm growing fond of you," Eleanor would reply.

What kind of exchange was that?

Still it was a comfort, as Celia would have been the first to point out, to have a warm body on hand when you twitched up out of nightmare. Eleanor, in the dark, was an easeful ridge, a welcoming landscape at her side. And in her mind's eye Susan would see this landscape's contours as the clue to where an enormous body lay buried, a rugged region she could call her own.

By now she knew her role as widow inside out—but she was losing sight of who was playing it. She stayed shut up in the language of her body. Sometimes it was enough to pretend to be starting over, taking stock, as she paced from room to room. At other times this was no comfort at all.

She found herself murmuring phrases aloud in the supermarket or while driving to work. She began to worry that she was entering a realm so private that only she could decipher its syntax. She followed routines that were in equal part noble and automaton. People who didn't know her well—and that seemed like almost everyone—commented on how valiantly she was "holding up," and it took considerable restraint on her part to keep from lashing out and telling them how wrong they were.

She had so much to think about! Bereavement, as she now understood it, was a kind of directionless vertigo. It made her distrust her choice of distractions. She never wanted to go to movies anymore because the silliest scenes might make her cry. And she didn't want to listen to music because a certain cluster of notes might break her down completely.

That left only Eleanor, and even with Eleanor she found herself smiling out careful answers where she meant only a fraction of what she said: "Yes, I'm fine. Work's busy. They're installing a new voice-mail system. No one's too happy with it. But a guy at the copy desk says it's easier than it looks—"

She was uncertain of where her allegiance lay: to life or death. Her gestures—spun integers—were coming from somewhere else. At times she feigned good cheer so well she felt she had mastered it. On other occasions she lost all trust in herself. She was constantly surprised at how solid some people seemed to think she was. Only Eleanor was inside her situation, with open eyes.

Susan would tell her how Walker was the one man she had ever met who made her feel she had no annoying habits. She revealed how their marriage had been "a perfect match of blanknesses" which there seemed no way of repeating, no way of duplicating. And Eleanor would nod at this, in seeming appreciation of the fact that most people are too strange a shape—too much themselves—to be anyone else's "blankness."

It was always Eleanor going to Walker's house and never Susan going to Eleanor's. But did Eleanor think of this house as Walker's? For Susan, the car, the video collection, the lawn and the trees were all his. She still thought of her body as his, too— or at any rate no one else's.

In a moment of quiet reflection, after the two women came back from a birthday dinner for Susan at a seafood place on Shilshole Bay (she had turned twenty-six with the new year), Susan glanced up at his possessions all around her, took his ex-wife's hand, and spelled it out: "We've both had him inside us. And now we're seeing things he doesn't see? Is that it?"

Only Eleanor could be the auditor of these thoughts. Only Eleanor could siphon them off, direct them to where they would do least damage.

Susan opened up to her.

part two

whatever you've been

Dr. Sidney Jerome Plume, a silver-haired psychiatrist in his late forties, had bent his world to his will. He had his own schedule, his own peculiar taboos and his own little rules concerning funerals and photographs, mementos and reflections.

His manner was strict. He would not discuss sex outside his hours of consultation, and with certain patients he prohibited the use of the phrase "unresolved feelings." With friends—that is, with those few of his friends who were left—he liked to argue that all duplication of the human image, whether on film, television, or even in a magazine ad, was a decoy, a distraction, a serious impediment to the inner reflection that could render a psyche whole. The same, he insisted, was true of more personal visual records. Snapshots, home movies, a bathroom medicine cabinet's fleeting mirroring of oneself in the morning—all were a threat to peace of mind. It was inner reflection that counted, he would declare. Everything else was a false front, a mere veneer: a tourist attraction.

He met his friends only at breakfast, and he preferred that they come to him. (Among his diminishing circle of acquaintance, his blueberry pancakes and homemade sausage were legendary.) All other times of day were reserved for his clients, and his evenings were heavily packed, especially in winter. When asked why he arranged his appointments so as to exclude most possibility of a social life, he would explain that there were things people would say only at twilight when the world had gone dim on them and the ghosts could slip out. Seattle's notoriously gray climate, he theorized, was a fertile breeding ground for the imprints the mind casts up when encouraged by an absence of light, and it would be a pity not to take advantage of it.

He rarely took weekends off—although his lover Bill, a lanky Californian who affected a sleepy laid-back style, chided him about this—and he would leave his house only when intensely pressured to do so. He had grown up in this house, and now that he was lucky enough to live in it again, he hated to abandon it even on some casual chore or leisure outing. It was a beautiful house, a complete house, inherited from his parents (both now dead), so why *should* he leave it?

Of late, there had been no need to. One of the local supermarket chains had started a home-delivery service, and when Bill was away on a business trip or camping expedition—as he frequently was—Plume had his groceries delivered to his door, happy to pay the ten-dollar surcharge rather than go out shopping himself.

The house was a small but exquisite brick bungalow in Laurelhurst, placed on a hillside that sloped down to thirty feet of frontage on Lake Washington. His neighbors to the north and south had boats, but Plume preferred not to clutter up his sliver of lakeshore with a dock or a boathouse. He enjoyed looking at other people's sails on the water—his mind took flight at the sight—but the urge to acquisitive ownership was one he understood only abstractly. True, he now owned this house, but he had not altered or added a thing to it. All the valuables within—hi-fi, furniture, Chinese lithographs and drawings—were, like the house itself, inherited from his parents, and he accepted their arrangement of these belongings in a careless, unthinking way.

Even if he didn't take conscious pride in his role as curator of his parents' past, he placed greater stake in it than either he or Bill realized at first. When Bill, shortly after their move from Queen Anne Hill to Laurelhurst, suggested junking Plume's father's La-Z-Boy armchair as an opening gambit in redecorating the living room, Plume had gone numb with shock. Surely these things were immutable. Surely, if you could change them, then you could change anything in the world, entirely according to whim, for no good reason at all.

No, it could not be done.

Bill dutifully absorbed this lesson, and thereafter either moved with more tact—or didn't move at all.

On its verdant spit of land, surrounded by similarly attractive residences, the cottagelike house appeared immune to the world's catastrophes. The winding street that led to it had the smell of a country lane, although it was wide enough to accommodate the Metro bus which left every half hour for Wallingford and Magnolia. Plume, on his rare sorties, always took this bus rather than Bill's Mazda or his father's ancient Plymouth station wagon—not out of nervousness over driving, but because from the bus, especially from the high seat over the wheels, he had an excuse to peer down and scrutinize his neighbors' homes and yards . . . his preferred form of contact with them.

The illusion of immunity extended to Plume's garden. Set so close to the water, it existed in its own modified temperate zone. Within this zone, ornamental kale grew to preposterous heights, and forsythia and miniature cherries came into bloom before they did anywhere else. Even his mother's "subtropical" contributions flourished: a thicket of bamboo and a trio of windmill palms, clustered against a fence with a southern exposure. A neighbor's towering monkey-puzzle tree added a final exotic note to the landscape.

The garden funneled toward sun. The lawn, which stayed green throughout the winter, lapped up light. The entire arrangement— brick walks, radiant turf, garden beds—was toylike. Patients, when they approached the front door, were immediately drawn into the playfulness of this environment and would relax some- what. Plume's level voice would suggest that a mind, like a garden or a room, is a game to be learned. He would give a thing its name, but from a distance. He hated his own given names—since college he had gone by his last—and in his thera- peutic sessions he focused more on a person's role than on his or her identity.

In keeping with this, he referred to Mount Rainier—framed in a kitchen picture window that his father had designed—as "the volcano," never merely "the mountain," and he would smile as if keeping back information whenever his neighbor to the north chimed across her laurel hedge on sunny mornings, "Isn't it lovely? The mountain's out!"

It was out now; and the settled weight of it loomed beyond the strand of the Evergreen Floating Bridge like an ice planet squatting down on the horizon while plotting out its next course of action. Its frozen radiance belied its threat of spewing fire. But the threat was there: climbers told of steam caves melting labyrinths in the ice at its summit.

Friends of Plume and Bill had climbed the mountain and skied its higher trails. They had gone skin diving, skydiving and hang gliding. Several of them had left the sheltered waters of Puget Sound to circumnavigate Vancouver Island. And they did these things with an obstinate gusto, as though they could never get enough of the natural spectacle around them.

Or, rather, they had once done these things.

Being generally well-to-do and free of responsibility, they had made frequent trips to San Francisco and New York as well, while locally they had enrolled in one of the gyms or sex clubs—it was often difficult to tell which was which—off Seattle's own Pike Street.

They had trusted their world. They had swallowed down as much of it as they could. And that world had swallowed them in turn.

Those lucky ones who had survived—having escaped, as Plume and his lover so far had, contamination—were sufficiently sobered by the deaths around them not to seek out risks that once had appealed to them. Cross-country skiing and day hikes in the Cascades; an afternoon's sail across Lake Washington and a single partner at night—these were more their style now.

Both men belonged to a group that organized these outdoor activities, but Plume rarely attended its events. His schedule didn't allow for it. And he derived as much pleasure, during the ten-minute intervals he alloted himself between appointments, from glimpsing the snow-capped terrain above Kirkland and Bellevue through the telescope on his deck as he ever would have from clambering on the slopes themselves.

As for funerals, his rationale was that in working to help others find their way through life, it would put him at a professional disadvantage to be saturated in death. He let Bill represent him when it came to comforting the bereaved—Bill's circle of friends, at first, had been the harder hit with losses—and he wrote sizable checks to the appropriate organizations. But he did no volunteer work and partook in no marches. He kept his visits to the sick to a minimum, with the excuse that he didn't want to exhaust them. And though increasingly housebound, he thought of himself as representing the norm, deeming that it was natural, with age, to lose the desire for all company except a handful of intimates.

Those around him—especially the few who had known him

twenty or more years ago—saw him as curious, shrewd and considerably more perverse than he himself acknowledged. They were fascinated by the change in him and frustrated by their diminishing opportunities to gauge it. The blame for that change had gone at first to Bill. When the two had met, over a decade ago, Plume had been the gregarious one and his new partner shy. But in less than a year they had exchanged roles. It was almost as if, having found a surrogate whom he could train to take over his social life, Plume had been freed to pursue his true introspective nature. Or it may simply have been that, as his practice flourished, he had no need to seek out intimacy elsewhere since right here, in his own home, he had people willing to pay him to receive and shape their confidences. The compliant Bill had long since mastered the requisite excuse for his lover— "He has all those sick psyches to tend to"—and when their friends spoke of the couple these days, it was Bill's visage that came more readily to mind.

Slow deaths had been a part of the two men's existence for almost as long as they'd been together—a low-level hum with moments of intense predation. After the first few years of shock and helpless anger, they succumbed to a dispirited acceptance: of death arriving now rather than later, of big eyes staring out of gaunt faces of friends who would soon just be names in an address book.

There were periodic twinges at particular losses, inevitable doubts as to what the doctors knew. To bridge these losses and doubts, Plume and Bill would withdraw on occasion into acts out-of-bounds to any two strangers these days. The whole instinct of their middle age was geared toward safety through detachment, both physical and emotional. But death sometimes worked like an aphrodisiac—as if only sex could fill the gap where life had been. Their mutual trust consisted of directing these outbursts toward each other.

In another era, they might have parted after a year or two.

Instead they held on to this marriage where they led their separate lives by day and reconnoitered shortly before midnight to find release—a sort of cathartic contentment—in the dark.

Just now they were in a lull, a moment of reprieve. A certain brunt of deaths had peaked and passed. If pressed, Plume would have admitted to being relieved at having fewer people to keep track of. In contrast, Bill—who had brought a vast social acquaintance with him when he met Plume—found the house too quiet. Hence his absences.

The quiet of the house, to Plume's mind, was its greatest asset—so much so that he had long since dispensed with having a secretary. As soon as reliable answering machines had come on the market, he had invested in one and, with the help of this contraption, taken over the booking of appointments himself. Always nervous at talking on the phone, he found himself growing more confident and fluent as an increasing number of his patients acquired answering machines of their own. Machine could talk to machine, arranging real-life encounters, and it was cleaner, more efficient, that way. What disturbed him nowadays was when seven coded digits drew a live response.

This was the case with Walker Popman, who had canceled his appointments (down to one a month) for October and November, and then failed to turn up on the designated date in December. The December appointment fell two days after Christmas, so might be deemed a holiday cancel. But when the usually reliable Popman missed his end-of-January appointment as well, there was no such excuse. Plume dialed his number to investigate—and a woman's voice answered the phone: "Yes?"

"Could I speak to Walker Popman, please?"

"Who is this?"

The voice was more weary than suspicious. Plume had difficulty answering.

"I'm—I'm only calling because he's missed his appointment."

"He made an appointment with you?"

"For yesterday. And for earlier, in December."

"That's impossible," the voice said.

"I'm afraid it's true."

"No, really—it's impossible."

There was a weighted silence, both parties having no idea where to go next.

Plume broke the impasse, explaining, "We had a standing arrangement. He canceled two appointments last fall, but I thought we were to resume, you see."

"Oh."

There was another long pause.

"You're his wife, I take it?"

"Yes. And you—you're his doctor? You knew he was sick?"

"Psychiatrist, actually. Dr. Plume. Is he sick? He hadn't mentioned it. Is he there?"

Again there was hesitation.

And then: "My husband is dead. He died in November. While we were on our trip."

"Ah, well—Ah."

He could not find the words with which to meet this. It left everything feeling unsafe. His only response was panic. And panic, he felt, needed to be disguised.

Again he attempted to speak—and this time words came. He only hoped they sounded as heartfelt as he intended them to be.

"I'm—I'm really so sorry. I had no idea—about his passing on."

He started to say something more elaborate, more revealing of his fondness for Walker, then thought better of it, simply adding, "You have my condolences."

Her voice sounded deadened: "It was his heart."

He went in the direction this suggested: "So it was—sudden?"

"Yes. It was."

"I'm sorry," he said again.

Her words became bitter: "They had a big thing in the paper. They ran his photographs. You didn't see it?"

"I don't always read the paper."

"They did a nice job. A nice job—but it felt like something make-believe. It was like reading about your own funeral."

"Yes, well—it would."

"It's still a shock. My friends don't understand that. They say they do, but they don't. They have their protection. They're not feeling this. They're not *inside* this."

"Friends can't enter—"

"One minute we were looking at a painting. The next minute he was gone, just gone."

"I'm sorry to—"

"You're a psychologist?"

"A psychiatrist."

"That's what? More qualifications?"

He answered her vaguely, wary of mentioning medical prescriptions. But his answer didn't satisfy her.

"What was he seeing you for?" she demanded. "His divorce? How *long* had he been seeing you?"

"I'm afraid I can't—"

"I've changed. Something about him changed me. At home, at work. My sister thinks so, too."

She left these statements hanging, waiting to see if they put him off. Then she went on: "You say Walker had a standing appointment?"

"Yes, he did."

"When's the next one?"

He gave her the date in late February.

"Could you see me? And could you fit me in sooner than that?"

"Ah—"

"I'm over the worst of it. I'm not crying anymore. But I've got to talk to someone. There's something going on, I don't know what exactly. It's like—not a dream, but some kind of optical illusion? Or optical reality, maybe . . .?"

She was unable to put it more coherently into words.

"We could arrange an interview," he suggested.

"To do what?"

"Decide on a therapy . . . ?"

She asked him what his rates were. He told her and said if she had the same medical coverage as her husband, the policy would pick up a good portion of the tab: "Especially in the case of bereavement."

This, as if it were a relief to have an obvious outward trauma to put down in the paperwork, instead of some dim interior malady.

There was a crackle of static on the line, before she answered in a voice that had no doubts at all: "Let's do it, then."

Her tone was conspiratorial. Together, it suggested, they could cheat someone out of something that was rightfully theirs.

Her aggression disconcerted him. He spoke slowly, became more businesslike, letting his voice act as her sedative.

This had the desired effect.

Their exchange resumed its tone of professional distance.

"I see most of my patients in the evening," he informed her, "to accommodate their work schedules. Is a week from Monday at five o'clock good for you?"

It was.

She hung up.

He penciled it in.

It is a commonplace that young children attribute to their parents a gift for control of the world that exceeds anyone else's—or not a "gift," exactly, but a *given*.

Parents are the pillars that keep worlds strong.

In Plume—or "Jerry," as he was then—the illustration of this commonplace went well beyond the norm, and his mother and father often found themselves in the awkward position of having to debunk, as gently as possible, their godlike status in his eyes.

Among his earliest memories (impossible to say whether it was the genuine article or taken, instead, from his parents' much-repeated accounts of the incident) was one of walking with his mother toward the bus stop late on an April morning when he was four years old. They were on their way downtown to buy him a new pair of shoes. Early for the bus, they had lingered over neighbors' gardens, carefully noting what was in bloom from one yard to the next. She held his hand and had started swinging it in time to a nursery rhyme when the rumble sounded and the sidewalks swayed and the bushes trembled. Not knowing what else to do, she froze against the movement, squeezing her son's wrist so hard that it hurt, and braced herself like a surfer on his board against a literal groundswell.

When it was over, her son, ecstatic, tugged at her arm and begged her, "Do it again, Mommy! Do it again!"

In his parents' social circle, this was the best account of the 1949 earthquake—7.1 on the Richter scale and centered some sixty-odd miles from Laurelhurst—that anyone had to offer.

Similarly, though not as dramatically, the boy attributed to his father a power over landscape that was absolute . . . until a third-grade geography textbook suggested possibilities to the contrary. Up to then, Plume had seen the "volcano"—symmetrically framed by the kitchen picture window when one sat at the head of the table—as having been positioned there *after* the Laurelhurst house was built, expressly for the man of the house to gaze upon. His father, an architect, regularly referred to Mount Rainier as "one of the newest places on earth," and his tone was such that it struck his son as a pride in accomplishment, rather than mere awe at the powers of nature.

The story that father read to son about an even newer place—Paricutín, in Mexico, where a farmer had gone out one day to find a baby volcano sprouting in his cornfields—somehow reinforced this impression. The boy was enchanted by it and subsequently checked all neighborhood lawns closely for beckoning plumes of smoke that might expand from twisting wisps to stentorian clouds. He prayed for an eruption that would force a change in the landscape. And he counted it as his first lost illusion when he one day came to realize that his parents' kitchen had been custom-designed with an already existing Mount Rainier in mind.

In retrospect he wondered if these grandiose notions of parental power had something to do with his being an only child, solemn in temperament, somewhat isolated and with few corrective influences on his thinking. Fearing ridicule, he rarely questioned his parents or teachers or schoolmates about any of the phenomenological and etymological puzzlers that presented themselves to him. Where others his age had a sense of humor or an eye for the absurd, he was somehow lacking in these and so stayed mired in such quandaries as the mysterious connection—for surely there had to be one—between "penicillin" and "peninsula." Did the antibiotic only grow on narrow fingers of land? And why, in old movies on television, were so many remarks made, at certain crisis points, about "winding up in Bellevue"? The Seattle suburb across Lake Washington was, admittedly, a poky place—but hardly a destination with which to threaten someone.

Misconceptions took root, engendering private visions of the world which were not dispelled until surprisingly late in childhood. It wasn't a matter of being hoodwinked. It was just that he had never dared tell anyone what he was thinking—so no one had thought to set him straight.

On the sexual front, as adolescence approached, a similar state of affairs existed. There were adorations: Fabian, Elvis, Dion. All the boys loved them! When he asked his mother which singer she thought more beautiful, she answered him with an odd look and an admission that none was to her taste: "Think of the greasemark they'd leave on the pillow, dear."

He thought of it—and loved them even more.

There was a boy in his eighth-grade class who *looked* a little like Elvis—dark eyes, smooth skin, lazy eyelashes—whom he rather aggressively pursued. Soon they were best friends, staying overnight at each other's houses, feeling each other up under the covers, sometimes even kissing—until summer came and the boy went away to Boy Scout camp. After he returned, he would have nothing to do with Jerry . . . only looked at him from a distance as though he had learned something appalling about him.

What Jerry learned was: Not everyone liked Elvis in quite the same way he did.

In ninth grade he got religion—a brand of faith distinguished not by any recognition of the transcendence of the spirit, but by a denunciation of the foulness of the flesh, with its pustules and appetites, its droolings and ejaculations. A heavyset and homely girl with extraordinary spelling abilities had led him along this path, and the detour lasted a whole month—long enough for him, in a moment of hysteria, to take his entire Elvis collection out to the barbecue pit and melt it down. Elvis—with his creamy flesh and ambiguous lips—was temptation itself and, even after Jerry had destroyed his LPs, Elvis would come to him in his dreams, not even dressed sometimes, and ask to be kissed, ask to be comforted: "They burned my records, man."

By the end of that same year he had reversed himself again, and on his Christmas wish list put in a request for new copies of the phonograph albums he had destroyed.

"But don't you have those already, hon?" his mother asked.

"I do—but they're scratched."

He had made two discoveries. The first, in the fiction stacks of the undergraduate library of the University of Washington, was Gore Vidal's *The City and the Pillar*. He consumed it on the spot, taking breaks from it only to alleviate the excitement it induced in him with sessions in the rest room. And it was in the rest room that he made his second discovery.

There, on the walls of the stall, despite a janitor's efforts to keep them clean, were messages and inquiries suggesting there were other boys, college boys, on this very campus who loved Elvis—or perhaps some other singer or film star or even a fellow student—in exactly the way that Jerry did.

In his reading he soon moved on from Vidal to Tennessee

Williams: the stories in *One Arm* and (it embarrassed him even to think of the title) *Hard Candy*. He purchased the books at a store along the seedier stretches of First Avenue downtown and kept them under his mattress, extracting them at night to puzzle endlessly over the sometimes careful, sometimes explicit wording of "Desire and the Black Masseur" or "The Mysteries of the Joy Rio." Both Vidal and Williams made it clear that the shameful behavior of sailors and military men was akin to the urges Jerry himself felt toward Elvis and toward several of his classmates, and at the end of his senior year in high school he decided to ask his father—always a genial and approachable soul—about it. The reason he thought this might be a likely path toward explanation was that his father had been in the navy *and* he played guitar (in the Spanish style, granted—but, then, Elvis looked sort of Spanish).

He approached the topic obliquely: "What I don't get is the big deal about breasts. Are you really supposed to like them? Why do guys want them so big? They make me kind of sick. And they're messy, aren't they? Don't they leak? I wish they were small—or not there at all."

With a few questions and answers, the existence of a problem was confirmed. And for the next several weeks, on Thursday afternoons, young Jerry visited a psychiatrist with the ambiguous name of Bolter (did he clasp things shut or shy away from them?) in his offices on First Hill just a few blocks up from the Greyhound station with *its* toilet stalls, where the man-to-man messages were far more graphic. . . .

Housed in an elaborately gloomy apartment building of ivy-covered brick and stone, Dr. Bolter's office was richly paneled and carpeted, with dark and glossy bookcases encircling the heavy desk and overstuffed armchair where his consultations took place. A fussy, many-paned window looked onto an airwell which let in hardly any light and effectively insulated the room from the bustle of downtown commerce several blocks away.

Set on precarious slopes with wooded ravines twisting up at
unlikely angles toward street corners, the psychiatrist's building
was one of several grandiose affairs in the area that seemed an
architectural homage of sorts—to a vertiginous Manhattan of the
mind, perhaps. Both inside and out, it reminded Jerry of certain
Hollywood renditions of city life: urban dwellings and meeting
places where the tongue's first duty was to be glib and the heart's
first order of business was to stalk and be stalked.

Dr. Bolter himself felt as exotic to Jerry as the building he
occupied. Dressed in a suit that looked vaguely "European," and
with a face that was babyish though creased by age (Jerry guessed
him to be in his mid-forties), he sported a severe buzz cut, salt-
and-pepper in color, imposing on his rounded scalp a militaristic
discipline—intended, no doubt, as compensation for the pudgi-
ness of his features. These features were lit by a Tiffany desk
lamp which was the room's sole source of illumination, shedding
limited pools of brightness on the desk's broad surface and catching the psychiatrist himself most luminously on his plump cheeks,
naked chin and chattering mouth. His eyes and forehead remained in shadow, for the most part.

Still, there was hope of insight to be had here; a possibility
that Dr. Bolter, in the same way that he added unfamiliar accents
to Jerry's notions of his native city, might also illuminate the
workings of a sexual self the boy had grown up with but taken
a while to recognize as deviating from the norm. This office, with
its closeting closeness, seemed the perfect sanctuary from which
to emerge with a new and more malleable version of oneself,
and even its difficult access held a promise of sorts. It was approached by steep sidewalks, a settling heap of stairways, glass
doors housed in a grottolike entryway, a corridor so thickly carpeted it swallowed all sound—and, finally, an elevator ride *down*
one floor (the building dropping below street level in its rear
northwest quadrant, as a result of the erratic terrain it occupied).

The psychiatrist, it seemed, lived as well as worked at this address, for there were two BOLTER doorbells to choose from, one of them marked OFFICE. Corridors and elevator were mute and luxurious, sleepily lit as in a dream, with always a hint of a lost soul or fellow wanderer moseying down the hall or around the corner: a door just closing, a light just turned out. Or maybe it was the chubby bas-relief gargoyles above the building's entranceway, with their grimacing smiles of pain (the developer's original plan had been to fill the ground floor with dental suites), that made all visitors feel they were about to encounter company from another dimension.

Whatever the case, Jerry persistently sensed he was not alone here—which, of course, he was not—and he soon came to savor the building's offering of a compact urbanity, a world within a world.

The one drawback was Dr. Bolter himself, whose ongoing monologue had nothing to do with the young man's reasons for being here. Jerry could only assume, after twenty minutes of therapy, that any success this brand of treatment had resulted from patients realizing they would have to learn to help themselves, since the therapist clearly had others things on his mind.

"Thermal energy . . . yes, tap the resource. Tap the—geysers or whatever. No geysers? Then tap—Tap the hot springs! Various places. Up and down the Cascades. Underutilized resource. If Iceland can do it, why can't we?"

He growled the question out.

"Has to be an answer!" he insisted. "Waterpower not enough. You've thought about it, yes? They're teaching it in school?"

"Well, not exactly."

"Never been to Iceland?"

"No. . . ."

Dr. Bolter addressed his patient over the rims of smudged bifocals: "What we have here—resources, geothermal—just like what they have there, eh? Hot springs! In a number of places. Kind of sexual, Nordic, sexual. So, Jerry, you were saying 'sexual.' "

Plume from behind his own large lenses, and with too much feeling at the center of him, answered, mortified at having to repeat the word, "I was saying 'homosexual.' Except I haven't really done anything about it yet."

The doctor sat back: "Oh well, that. Never mind that. Never mind, later for that. 'Homosexual'—that can come later. First we look at your parents. Your mother, now, is that the trouble?"

"I get on fine with my mother."

"Your father, then—a little hostility, eh? Perfectly normal."

"No, no. He was the one who sent me here. He was worried."

"About what?"

"Not 'worried,' I guess. But shouldn't I be talking to someone?"

"About what?"

"—if I want to go with guys instead of girls."

"I said later for that, but if you want to talk about it now—"

"What else is there to talk about?"

"So, this is it. You're not making this up. You're—You're—Not some ruse, eh? Something for the draft board? This is what you want to talk about."

"My father—"

"You hate your father!"

"I like my father, I love my father."

"But how *much* do you love your father. Giving him this worry. A little too much, eh? A man—A man—An architect! A man with a plan. Building those buildings! That kind of thing."

"He doesn't build the buildings. He just designs them."

Dr. Bolter took this and went with it: "Makes them up but doesn't follow through . . . not the practical sort . . . just makes it up . . . matter of laying the pipes . . . steam can travel, but what about cooling? . . . Don't want water pipes, waterpower, plenty of that already, don't want. . . . Dig down deeper!—closer to the magma—tap the source—"

Plume stared at him blankly.

Dr. Bolter rallied and addressed him: "Now, then, this—this 'homosexual.' What is it, exactly?"

"What do you mean, what is it?"

"What form is it taking, who's involved."

"Well, no one so far—"

Before he could explain he had lacked the opportunity, the psychiatrist cut him off: "But you got the idea somewhere? Someone's been talking to you?"

"No, no, I've just always wanted to. I thought *everyone* did—"

"Despite all the evidence."

"What evidence?"

"Your mother, your father—opposite sexes, attracting, procreating. . . ."

"Well, aside from them."

"Precisely."

"Precisely 'what'?"

"You never saw them as sexual?"

"Well, no, of course not. Who—?"

"Then maybe it's time you did. See them that way. Get the thought processes started. The sex process: get it started. And then break away! Detach yourself. Cut the cord. Go somewhere. Summer in Alaska. My own son. Worked in the canneries there. Got over it. Worked wonders. There in Alaska. In Juneau. Hikes above the town, up to the tundra. Made new friends there. Ten minutes flat. Up in the tundra. Just wonderful up there."

"Yes?"

"This obsession—this 'homosexual'—take it outdoors, dissipate it, see the bigger picture: or even right here, outdoors here too! North of the Olympics, south of the Olympics. Fronts coming through, above, below. Up and down the Sound! Where they'll meet is anyone's guess. Convergence zones, eh? Unpredictable."

Plume, lost, waited for more.

But there was no more: "So. Put those thoughts on hold—and we'll pick them up next week. Same time, same place. Iceland, Alaska, thermal energy. Got to keep it outdoors. Keep outdoors safe."

The man clapped him on the back, slapping the breath out of him, inducing a sort of shock. He wasn't to be taken seriously— but Jerry saw him two more times, to satisfy his father.

The second session went much as the first had, except that Jerry had the distinct feeling, as he made his way from vestibule to psychiatrist's office, that he *was* being followed or observed: a different sensation from being aware, while treading past oaken-doored apartment entrances, of his close proximity to other people's lives.

The third and final session was still more of the same: Alaskan tundra, Icelandic geothermal power, the Puget Sound convergence zone ("—absolute hell for meteorologists!"), only Dr. Bolter couldn't locate his file on Jerry or remember, exactly, what their consultations had been about, so they had to start over again from scratch. When they had finished and Jerry stepped out of the elevator, eager to hit the Greyhound station, a clownish but familiar figure came cavorting toward him on tiptoe, intercepting his path before he could get past the grimacing gargoyles—a boyish man, from another dimension indeed, maybe a year or two older than Jerry, and unshaven, with Elvis-y lips and sex in his eyes and a barely containable bounce in his limbs.

This figure addressed him with a smile and said, "Oh boy, oh boy, you're the one who's been seeing my father!"

"I am?"

"I've been looking through his files. I know all about your 'problem'!"

"You do?"

His "familiarity," in fact, was a family resemblance. And Dr. Bolter's aging baby features, when elongated and restored to youth, were sublime in his son, if somewhat hectic in their anima-tion: "Hey, hey, you shouldn't listen to him! He doesn't know what he's talking about."

"Well, I figured that."

"How could he? He hasn't even tried it."

"I assumed not."

"Come on, come on, let's go upstairs. My mother's dead, and there's lots to eat. My dad's got three more appointments. He'll be hours, yet. We can do anything you like: in his bed, under his sheets. . . ."

Jerry hesitated. Here was his opportunity, materializing before his eyes, as if merely wishing had made it so.

The question came: "You want to—don't you?"

He did.

So they went.

The kid's name was Campbell, Campbell Bolter, and he illustrated a commonplace of another kind—that the children of psychiatrists, like those of clergymen, are almost always more deeply
troubled than the troubled souls who consult their parents. The
difference is they *exult* in their trouble.

Campbell ("It's like a prime minister's name or something, I
don't know what Mom was thinking of") was twenty to Plume's
eighteen, had already gone to college and dropped out, and had
evaded military service by sporting a bobbing erection at his
army physical and drawing everyone's attention to it. When he
was twelve, his mother had died of an asthma attack in the bath—
all that splashing hadn't been the usual frolic with a gentleman
friend but a solitary cry for help—and Campbell reportedly got
his reckless spirit and bewitching looks from her. He knew his

way around town. He shoplifted. Once or twice he had exchanged sex for cash, the pinnacle of his "escort" career being when he picked up a priest, attended to his needs, then forced the poor man to write a check for his services, remarking to him with a wink, "You'll go to hell for this, you know."

When Plume objected to such cruelty, Campbell explained it as an act of revenge: "A friend of mine—a very close friend—became an alcoholic because his mother put beer in his bottle to keep him quiet during mass. He was only a baby! But he was a Catholic baby, so he never had a chance."

Plume refrained from asking a chance for what, and did not inquire which "very close friend" this might be. Campbell, in conversation, alluded to *multitudes* of very close friends, none of whom Plume ever met—including a certain "Man from Juneau" who wasn't at all what Dr. Bolter had in mind when referring to the friends his son had made in the Alaskan capital.

Plume grew especially curious about this Man from Juneau: "What did he do up there? Was he in government?"

"Honey, I don't know!"

"What, you never knew what his job was?"

"All I know is he was hot, ouch!—sizzling. His mother lived in Ketchikan. And he had money. Got me out of that cannery so I wouldn't smell like fish. That was Daddy's idea, me working there. Crazy, like all his ideas. . . ."

Campbell also had a large anonymous acquaintance, knowing, as he did, every trysting spot in every public toilet in every damp corner of downtown and the University District. His sexual hijinks even extended to the workplace, where he had twice been fired for fucking on company time—on one occasion with the boss's son.

Sometimes he looked like an Arab, sometimes he looked vaguely Celtic. When undressed, there was no small attention his body didn't invite. It seemed to arch in all directions in search of response, and Plume had only to speak to arouse him: "Oh honey, your voice—it's so soft, so feathery. . . ."

Both Campbell and Dr. Bolter seemed equally obsessed, equally unhinged, the difference being that Campbell's sexual drive, unlike the psychiatrist's thermal energy concerns, was something Plume could understand and reciprocate even if he was too new to some of the acts themselves to perform them with any sense of confidence or comfort.

"Are you sure we should be—?"

"No guilt! No guilt!"

"But—"

Campbell would put a mock-dramatic hand to his forehead, look away, then turn sharply back: "Please, if you're going to bring guilt into the picture, I'll have to ask you to fuck me even harder. I'm a martyr, you know."

These antics made Plume squirm, were a little too fey for his taste. But the sex—any sex—was difficult to resist. On the strength of it, he decided not to go away to college but to live at home and attend the University of Washington. In order to instill some sense of a break between his high school and college years, however, he converted the basement of the Laurelhurst house to what his mother called a "bachelor's pad" and moved down there. With its separate lakeside entrance it gave him privacy for studying, meditating, sleeping late—whatever. His mother's one condition: no girls were to stay after midnight. She didn't want to condone a standard of behavior not her own. And her husband, protective of his son, had not seen fit to spell out to her the reasons for the visits to Dr. Bolter. . . .

Another change: It was at this point that Plume became "Plume" instead of "Jerry." He hated the latter name, appreciated the monosyllabic efficiency of the former (as did Campbell), an efficiency that held a suggestion of disguise, a feathery masking of what had been embarrassingly naked in him up to now. Disguise was persuasive, and it wasn't long before the affectation felt natural, especially after he made new friends who knew him by no other name.

In changing his name and (in however small a way) his living arrangements, Plume unknowingly led Campbell into a situation of unprecedented stability which relaxed him and made him, for the time being, easier to deal with. Once they had desecrated Dr. Bolter's bed with their revels, Campbell expressed a preference for staying overnight at Plume's basement digs with their greater sense of privacy. Plume's mother had no objection to her son keeping male company at all hours, and soon the two were, for all practical purposes, living together. Living together—and living it up as well.

Four in the morning, five in the morning, light as the air, they swam naked in the lake, then shivered and found games to play— the games that get you warmer. The summer lingered well into September, and on full-moon nights, in silver circles of water, Campbell had a halo around him, looked like a Blake figure: ecstatic, inside rings of mist and moonlight.

The only suprise was that the Plumes' elderly widowed next-door neighbor, Mrs. Andersen, sometimes chose this hour, too, for her dip, and went as naked as the boys, emerging from the lake with her ancient breasts pointed floppily down.

Campbell, slipping his hand into the water, trying to stir something up there, would say: "It's enough to make you go limp, isn't it?"

But not for long.

Women were remote to Plume, left him inert. Men were somehow his opposites—at least Campbell was—and he went straight toward them.

Several months passed. Campbell's dark eyes stayed nervous, alive. But with Plume he no longer put on his maximum show, his full array of histrionics. Instead he looked at Plume intently— at his now-longer hair, fuller body, glistening limbs, beginnings of a mustache—and found there a presence that was shy and timid, but also more solid and peaceful than any he had ever known. Was Plume a beneficiary of his own placid nature? And how, exactly, did the mischief creep out of him—as it did from time to time—without disturbing his essential sobriety? Under that calm, it was clear, there was something slightly haywire, a strange willingness to be shattered.

These were contradictions in his lover that Campbell found difficult to grasp, difficult to explain. To Campbell it seemed miraculous that Plume, with his settled temperament, had ever agreed to take up with him in the first place: "Oh you're beautiful—a kind of shapeshifter. Who knows *what* you are?"

But Plume could never say.

So the following week after stealing a Super-8 movie camera, and off and on during the next few years, Campbell—with his lens on his lover at all times—attempted to find out.

Plume's nineteen-sixties were a festive affair with a nightmare component, a decade as jittery as the images captured on his lover's camera.

The light exposure was uneven. Some sequences were bright, some sequences were dark. And all were entangled in the now-you-see-it-now-you-don't charm of the mercurial Campbell.

Campbell introduced him to good food, fine wine, foreign movies, raucous music. When Campbell entered a room or a bar or a music store or a theater lobby, he seemed always intent on tracking something down—a drink or a record, or merely a good position from which to observe and be observed.

He arranged things for Plume: a visit to a second psychiatrist to confirm Plume's homosexuality for draft evasion purposes; a meeting with an elegant cross-dresser, now a University of

Washington administrator, for consultation about Plume's career possibilities; a marijuana cigarette with which Plume could alternately numb and enhance the televised news reports of race riots in Los Angeles and various East Coast cities. (Up to then Plume had only dimly heard of the drug—and he hadn't been aware of racial discontent at all.)

With Campbell as his guide, a world which Plume since childhood had assumed must reflect his own staid temperament came to seem more topsy-turvy, especially as he paid greater attention to its public events. During their second year together, this world lost still more of its sense of stability when another earthquake struck the city, again in April, but later in the month and earlier in the morning. The 6.5 temblor found Plume in bed, gripping his lover's hard cock instead of his mother's hand—but after an initial ballooning of primordial fear, the liquid shocks yielded equally satisfactory results.

There were new and nervous-making titillations with every season. In winter on his days off, when a chill from the lake penetrated the basement apartment, Campbell liked to wrap himself in a woman's ankle-length fur he had "borrowed" from a downtown wholesaler's outlet where he managed to stay employed for over a year. Plume would leave for classes in the morning in a mild state of alarm, sure that his mother was bound sooner or later to enter his "bachelor pad" unannounced—she had a key—and discern the true nature of the two young men's relationship as she stumbled across Campbell lounging in his furs and little else ("It's the sexiest way to keep warm, sweetie"). His father, he supposed, had figured it out already.

When Plume asked his lover to maintain a lower profile and keep the noise down while he was gone, Campbell would chide him, "Oh, what's the fuss? You need some excitement in your life and I'm the one who can provide it. You might at least admit it to yourself—" he opened the fur coat, "—seeing as how you act on it often enough."

The smile got bigger. The window shades were open. It was midmorning. His mother might turn up outside at any moment to work in her garden. But Plume could not resist what was beckoning. He swaddled himself in scents of flesh and fur.

Later, succumbing to what Campbell would have called a "uniquely Plume-like" brand of rational shame, and what Plume himself felt as dismay at his inability to lose himself in the spirit of the moment, he went secretly to a psychiatrist—his third—at the university for a consultation. When asked his reasons for making the visit, he replied with an evasive summary of his love life, referring to Campbell only as "this person" of unspecified gender, and concluding, "The thing is: I think I'm kind of inhibited."

"Well, now, a little inhibition isn't necessarily a bad thing."

"But I can never relax—with him, or with anyone."

The man looked at him more closely, as if the pronoun had tipped him off. He said nothing for a moment and then pronounced: "Yes, it's a good thing you came to me. I can tell just by looking at you that you're a deeply disturbed young man."

This, Plume felt. was not at all the case. Who did this guy think he was? Violating his own resolve to keep the consultation to himself, he reported it directly back to Campbell, saying: "He was joking, right? But what if I'd *really* had a problem?"

Campbell, standing up in his furs, stalked the room and held forth: "Not a joke, dear. Just incompetence. Anyone can see: you're as sane as I am."

This was not entirely reassuring.

Campbell continued, "They don't understand about appetites, these guys. Can you imagine—a therapist who doesn't understand about appetites? They should all be taken out and shot!"

"Even your father?"

"Especially my father—if only for personal reasons."

"Actually he's beginning to look like the best of a bad lot. . . ."

This launched Campbell into elaborate theories about his father, himself, his family. He speculated on the meaning of his father's obsession with thermal energy and blamed his own lack of money sense—a lack which was beginning to dizzy Plume— on the timing of his mother's death: "There I was, just starting to figure it out. You save up your allowance for the things you want—a beautiful shirt, a copy of *West Side Story*—and then she dies, so what's the point?"

Campbell stole shirts. He lifted LPs. He was skilled enough so that no one noticed. Only once had he been caught, when he was fourteen, and on that occasion his father, after returning the stolen goods, had a long conciliatory talk with the store manager, making Mrs. Bolter's death sound more recent and directly troubling to the boy than, by that point, it was. The manager didn't press charges. And within the month Campbell—without any trouble this time—shoplifted there again. In recent years he had become more selective in his thievery—and more generous too, showering his lover with ties, cufflinks, fancy scarves, sturdy socks and choice shirtwear.

Plume wasn't happy about this.

"I wish you wouldn't, I can't accept these."

"All right, all right, I'll wear them—but can I keep them here? My father will wonder where they come from."

In spite of his steady job and weekly regimen of shoplifting, Campbell could not, at twenty-five, afford to move into an apartment of his own.

"No, that's not all right."

"Honeybun! You need these things! They're necessary. Here, at least help me out with this wine. You've never tasted anything like it."

"My god, did you steal that too?"

He had—and he was right. Plume had never tasted anything like it.

Ongoing worry became routine. When Plume voiced these worries, Campbell responded with a sort of cha-cha dance-embrace and an off-key rendition of "Don't Get Caught, That's a Crime." In retrospect it would amaze Plume how long the two of them had stayed together—over eight years!—like a marriage almost, minus any sense of security or good faith. Instead there was a constant blending of anxiety and enchantment, an agonizing choice between jumping ship and cruising ever more deeply into turbulent waters.

In some ways they belonged together. By certain lights, they brought the best out in each other. It was Campbell who encouraged Plume in his choice of psychiatry as a profession, Plume's idea being that there clearly was a need for therapists more sensible and sympathetic than any of the three *he* had consulted, or any of the half-dozen his lover had seen.

Campbell agreed: "I think it's a great idea, sweetie. You'll be wonderful! I mean, who else understands me the way you do? That, to my mind, is a whole qualification unto itself. There ought to be a special degree awarded."

In other ways Campbell's constant rebellion against the status quo had taken them to the end of their possibilities together. Their "appetites," as Campbell called them, were out of sync: Plume's were modest, Campbell's insatiable. All the sex and rushing around could be exhausting, Plume found, making you vulnerable to head colds and impairing your judgment of people, places, situations.

In the summer of 1969 they had traipsed around local rock festivals—Gold Creek, Sky River—Campbell with Super-8 camera in hand, lovingly documenting naked hippies dancing in acres of muck, while Plume followed along.

On the first occasion, this was passable fun. On the second occasion, the field was a mess and the music awful. Rain began to pour and they scrambled in the mud. When they finally found the car it was blocked by a dozen others with no prospect of having a way clear in the next twenty-four hours. Dusk was approaching: they decided to hitchhike back to Seattle.

After walking a mile or so they were picked up on the outskirts of Enumclaw by a clean-cut man in his forties, trim for his age, who concentrated on Campbell, the better-looking of the two, and plied him with questions: "Been to the festival, eh? Play the guitar? No? Never played it myself either!" He snickered as if this were a witticism, then offered, "Look, I can give you boys door-to-door service. But wouldn't you like a shower first? We could stop at my place. It's on the way."

Campbell, with Plume kicking him in protest, agreed to this. And the moment they entered the little suburban house, the man started closing all the drapes and plying them with liquor: "Let's see, let's see, there's vodka and there's whiskey and there's bourbon and there's cognac." He touched Campbell whenever the opportunity presented itself, at the shoulder or hip, then let his hand glide down in more rewarding directions.

The two undressed. Plume kept his clothes on and merely viewed the proceedings—despite Campbell's imploring looks that he join in.

Their host said, "Why's your friend so shy? I *like* all this mud, don't you? You're my filthy boy—beautiful and filthy. My wife, now: she'd clean you up, she'd scrub behind your ears. But we'll have our fun first."

Plume drank the vodka. Plume drank the whiskey. He saw the smoke of burning cigarettes rising from an ashtray and wished he could *be* smoke: evaporate, disappear.

His last memory of the evening, before passing out, was of their host, between one round of sex and another, striding naked to a record cabinet, pulling out an LP, putting it on the turntable— and it was the same tune Plume and Campbell had heard hours earlier, played live and so badly *out* of tune that, along with the rain, it had prompted them to leave the festival: something about getting together and smiling on your brother.

Campbell was certainly smiling now.

Plume, shuffling off to one of the bedrooms, lay down with a child's flimsy mobile revolving above his head and had never felt so depressed. New Year's Day 1970 was another four months away, but he had a sharp sense that the decade—and more than just the decade—was drawing sourly to a close.

If this was where Campbell was heading, it would pull him to pieces to follow.

"We should go to New York, man. Or at least San Francisco."

"You mean move there?"

Campbell, it seemed, was restless: "Why not? Ditch this town. Do something different, go someplace else."

Plume objected. He liked it where he was.

"What about Europe, then, just for a vacation?"

"How could we afford that?"

"Once we're over there, we can peddle ourselves."

Plume laughed.

Campbell, it turned out, was serious. He and Plume were still young enough, he said. And Europeans weren't like Americans. They didn't draw as many distinctions between boys and girls: "You saw *Satyricon*. . . ."

On another occasion Campbell, wanting to give Plume a little hands-on practice in his chosen profession, invited him: "Okay, then, analyze me."

"I don't want to analyze you."

"We can't all choose what we analyze."

"But you haven't come to me with a problem!"

"Suppose someone sent me to you and said I had one."

Plume had no difficulty envisaging this—but still didn't want to mess with it.

"I'd refer you to someone else," he said grandly. "You can't analyze your friends."

Campbell was astonished: "Of course you can! My god, what else are they for?"

Plume would not be drawn.

"Come on, come on," Campbell said. "Look, I'll make it easy. How would you *describe* me? To another person?"

"Just casually?"

"Just casually."

Plume was hesitant, did not want to comply; then couched his answer in terms and tones as nonjudgmental as possible: "I'd say you have a certain headlong charm—and an occasional mild tendency toward self-destruction."

Campbell lit up, ready to pounce, ready to disprove something: "That's a cop-out, man. The whole human race has a certain charm and tendency toward self-destruction! You're dealing in platitudes."

"You really think the human race has charm?"

"They're nice to fuck, anyway."

Breakup, Plume began to think, was inevitable. And the end, when it came, came suddenly.

Plume agreed to a visit but not a move to New York (this was in the fall of 1971), and on their second night there, in a bar on Greenwich Avenue, he somehow lost track of Campbell. The place was packed and the music loud.

He searched—but his search was fruitless. The crowd, with

much complication of dance and sweat, reconfigured itself every five minutes. He returned to the hotel alone, feeling more mournful than angry. He had wanted it to end, but in a more orderly fashion and without this worry that something awful had happened to Campbell, who gave no signs of life over the next twenty-four hours.

It wasn't until the evening of the next day that Campbell at last called the hotel and said he wouldn't be returning home: "I've met someone."

"You've what?"

"I've met someone. He's rich, he's a concept sculptor: body paint, the living flesh. He's an actor at the—" Here, the description degenerated into mumbles enhanced by static on the line, before concluding in a clear statement: "—and I think I'm going to try it for a while."

"You're staying here for good, you mean?"

"Uh, yeah—with this guy. For now, anyway."

"Just like that?"

"Honeybun, don't be angry. You'd like him! I'm sure you would, once you've—once you've—"

The word was garbled; sounded like "maladjusted."

"I just wanted you to know," Campbell continued. "I didn't want to do anything behind your back. Don't be upset. We're still honest with each other, right? Are you crying? Honey, don't—please don't cry. Tell you what, I can call you back later. Later tonight, would that be good? Or maybe in the morning, before you get the plane."

"But I might not be here."

"What do you mean?"

"I might go out—"

"Go where?"

"—and stay out all night. Just like you did."

"Honey, no, don't do it. Don't do anything rash. That's not you, that's me. Like you said: self-destructive. It's my nature.

Distant father, broken home, all that stuff? It's true! No real stability. It's my fault. You tried. You don't have to tell me, I know, you really tried. And this guy's nice! I would have called earlier, but it's just that—Well, we—'' There was a sucking in of breath. ''Well, actually, I wasn't going to say—'' Another sucking in of breath. ''—but we've been in bed all day. We're in bed—um—now, and haven't been out of it. . . .''

''I see.''

''You should meet him, you should come over. He's from Montreal. You could practice your French. Or hang on, wait a minute—''

There was a brief consultation with a background voice: ''Well, maybe not tonight. But the next time you're in New York . . .?''

Twenty-four hours later, stepping out into the parking lot at Sea-Tac Airport after the long flight home, Plume smelled the pleasant night chill spiced with woodsmoke, felt the dust-thin rain on his face and found it was already impossible, on reflection, to imagine Campbell staying in this town forever. It was too tempered a place, without extremes. Someone like Campbell was bound to try somewhere else. The surprising thing was that he had put off his escape until now. It might even indicate how closely he held Plume—in mind, in heart—that he had stayed as long as he did.

Still, their link had been severed, or at least badly mutilated. It might eventually scar over into friendship, Plume supposed. But not just yet.

So what did that leave him with?

Only the ''archive,'' apparently: the Super-8 films that Campbell had shot over the last eight years and not taken with him. Warm images, watery and overexposed or dark and full of violent movement, played against Plume's basement wall in chilly silence, with naked hippie boys and girls trying a little too hard for saturnalia, their figures alternating tediously with Plume's own—and, less often, Campbell's.

The images of Campbell were the true, covert reason for looking at each reel over and over again, but those lasted for only seconds at a time. Campbell had made a point of keeping the camera in his own hands, rarely entrusting it to his lover, and so, more often, it was his own meager likeness that Plume was compelled to observe.

He balked at this at first . . . until one night, staring at a sequence of images he had seen over a dozen times, it took him ten minutes before he could interpret a certain figure's features— and recognize them as his own. His transformations over the years became a source of morbid fascination for him, showing, as they did, the continual influence of Campbell and his own susceptibility to it. There he was with a buzz cut and thick eyeglasses on the beach at Alki in 1964; or with short-back-and-sides, and Adam's apple trapped beneath a turtleneck dickie, on a trip to Mount Rainier in 1965; or with hair slightly longer and Beatle-esque sideburns anchoring his narrow cheeks, on the sand bluffs at Discovery Park in 1967; or angrily objecting to Campbell filming him while further assassinations were televised in 1968. The last reels showed him stepping gamely into the water at Spirit Lake, its shallows reflecting nearby Mount St. Helens in 1969.

In short, there were dozens of Plumes to choose from. Too much of him had been captured. And each shot was annoyingly proprietary, prompting imaginary conversational standoffs that he couldn't get out of his mind:

—*This is my version of you.*

—*But who wants to know this much about himself?*

After overdosing on these images and gaining from them a "perfect knowledge" of himself of a strictly external sort, he banished them, renounced them. He studied photographs of other people, instead, and saw how misleading these were too. Here was one of a man who, in sickness, had the appearance of health. Here was one of a woman who, in mild contentment, presented a fair facsimile of glum lethargy. (Plume's father, who as he pushed seventy suffered increasingly from a chronic heart ailment—and his mother, whose doctor believed she would live forever.)

Film, either moving or still, Plume came to believe, was equal parts exposure and disguise. And it could break you apart, as it flaunted its power over memory.

His own sense of his time with Campbell was of following a mischievous, libidinal force out into the world. But the Super-8 films denied this, unpersuasively at first—and then, with the tyranny of repetition, all too effectively, suggesting that the two of them had merely taken the imprint of their time passively, unimaginatively, and not done much with it.

Unnerved by this thought, trying to convince himself that images were only decoys and not true evidence, he hid the films away. And though he stayed in irregular touch with Campbell, he never offered to send the films on to him, nor did Campbell ask for them. They had been shot as a kind of joke, really, something done—as Campbell did almost everything—without method or intention.

Plume kept them in the dark. And there they stayed, out of sight, canceled from mind, perhaps for someone else to come across eventually—by which time, he hoped, his camouflage would be complete. He would no longer be whatever he had been. He would have slipped beyond anyone's finding, without access, without entry, not even of himself to himself. He would have feathered his past away and given it pattern, with a folding of wings.

In the meantime there was sex to be had.

Feeling more wanton and agitated than ever—feeling, in fact, more like Campbell than he'd ever imagined he would feel—he went ahead and had it.

For Plume, politeness always came first—which perhaps was an advantage in putting clients at ease as they entered his premises, but had its drawbacks in eliciting from them the candor intrinsic to investigations of the psyche.

Not that politeness amounted to concealment. On the contrary, Plume in his own life moved deliberately, according to a guileless agenda, taking pains to ensure that outward action reflected inward state of mind with a low-key concision. A change of perception, he felt, demanded a change of circumstance—one as streamlined and considerate of others' feelings as possible.

It was for this reason that in the spring of 1972, amid the continuing hoopla of antiwar protests all across the country, he made a move into rental apartment and office accommodations on Queen Anne Hill—not its southern or western sides with their panopticon views of mountains, bay and Sound, but its steep enshadowed northern bluff, looking down on the Lake Washington Ship Canal. The completion of his postgraduate studies and the conclusion of his years-long affair with Campbell were the inspirations behind the move—a move which, as he stared down at waterborne traffic sliding at a stately pace between precise embankments, satisfied his sense of order and soothed some more reckless itch in him as well. Having a brand-new vantage point in a long-familiar town felt, to his cautious mind, oddly and winningly like subversion.

Still, there was something about the gesture of the move that spoke more loudly than he intended—if not to his friends, then to his mother and father. The relinquishing of his ground-floor bedroom in the Laurelhurst house for the basement "bachelor pad" had been a natural progression, an almost "organic" development. But his abandonment of Laurelhurst altogether, he feared, would strike his parents as a betrayal—or, at least, a needless extravagance, an ungrounded sort of whimsy.

His worry at their perceiving it in this light led him to act more secretively and severely than he had wished. He made all the arrangements without informing them of his going until two days before he went—and then, once gone from home, he avoided home as if it were forbidden to him.

In his mind a wall had been built across the city, at points equidistant from Laurelhurst and Queen Anne. To breach it required a special occasion, the kind of holiday (Christmas, Easter) that in other divided cities allowed citizens, through special dispensation, to meet and celebrate on a stringent timetable and under watchful eyes.

On the rare occasions when he *did* visit the Laurelhurst house, he avoided going to the basement or even down to the lakeside garden, shunning the reminders of Campbell there. Instead he would position himself before the view that, by now, interested him most: the kitchen window's, with its front-and-center framing of the rising volcano.

In these and other circumscribings of his own movements and behavior, he was—he dimly realized—attempting to bring to his life the same gift of control he had attributed to his parents as a child. For the more he ventured out into the world, the more he saw his life as bordering on chaos—and the more each fluid facet of it became a candidate for compartmentalization.

At his gym on Capitol Hill, he was a quietly affable figure—still angular, with his large bespectacled eyes as solemn as ever and his hair cut shorter now in wisps that were already graying. Without pursuing them aggressively, he was a partaker in certain sauna activities—usually in a circle of three or four that had a friendly, comradely atmosphere to it. There were also less fleeting encounters, taken beyond the sauna although they might be initiated there. These lasted several hours, or even several days, instead of a mere twenty minutes, but they still served more a purgative function than anything else. Most were anonymous: into an apartment and out again. In Plume, they induced a welcome shedding of skin, a longed-for moment of transformation which came not as he removed his clothes—although that was part of it—but when he removed his glasses and let his myopia take over. Only when he saw it out of focus did the world, for as long as an hour or two, became an engrossing facsimile of what he wanted it to be.

There was nothing that (and no one who) had Campbell's impact, and this was what he had expected—although as he reached and then passed thirty, an obsession with a younger man's looks could sometimes inspire in him an intensity of response that was agonizing. The surprising thing was that the younger man sometimes responded as well. Plume's graying appearance and still youthful face were an alluring combination, making him seem both lithe and steady. And it was steadiness that some of these sauna contacts were after—at least for a while.

Some were intrigued, others put off, if they learned he was a psychiatrist; and this gave rise to complications. He felt it was his duty to leave his job out of the picture when entangled with someone—an attitude that didn't necessarily go down well when it became clear he was unwilling to analyze a lover for free or to gossip about his clients. ("I don't need their names!—I just want to hear about weird stuff they do!") Most of the time he kept his profession to himself.

In bed he was sweet, affectionate and only occasionally distracted. Out of bed he was perceived as someone you could ask to your dinner party, confident that he would enliven your table's conversation. ("So tell us—what made you become a psychiatrist?" "Thermal energy had a lot to do with it.")

In this way—with various pairings, breakups, realignments, grand passions and utilitarian fucks—Plume became a man about town, a notable figure in a social circle consisting mostly of the numerous ex-lovers of current boyfriends. He enjoyed a "dalliance" (as he thought of it) with a crime reporter at one of the Seattle daily papers and intermittent "trysts" with a U.W. English professor who bored him with lectures on neglected novelists (Christina Stead, Wright Morris) but was otherwise entertaining. There was also an assistant press secretary at the mayor's office who faded in and out of his life at regular intervals with tidelike serenity.

One entanglement led to another. There was little sense of the rules changing and no sense at all of years going by—as long as youthful appearance could be mustered as proof against their passage. Even bitterness was rare, a dry and lighter waspishness being the preferred mode of expression for romantic disappointment. Plume's was a circle, a shadow-milieu, that spiraled back endlessly on itself, occasionally replenished by new and perturbingly attractive recruits (eager volunteers, actually), and all partakers knew they were better off tolerating one another than fussing and sniping. Feuds merely served as entertainment, prolonged until their participants got tired of them, which in some cases turned out to be a lifetime—a very short lifetime.

It was into this picture that Bill, fresh from Fresno by way of San Francisco, arrived—and quickly established himself. His second year in town, he crossed paths with Plume—and then kept crossing them . . . not a soul mate by any means, but a reasonable match in temperament: guarded, rational, polite, even courtly. At thirty, he was five years younger than Plume, but oddly older in manner. With his mustache, long face and lanky build, he had the looks of a matinee idol—distortedly so, as if in parody of himself or transported from another decade. He had moved to Seattle in connection with a job so boring—in some tier of management with an office-supply firm intent on expanding up and down the coast—that Plume had to write it down in order not to forget it. He was moderate in all his tastes: enjoyed hiking, disco dancing, classical music, movies, reading, basketball tournaments, but with no special emphasis on anything in particular. And he had come at an opportune moment, after the departure from Plume's life of a moody, sexual dynamo with the unlikely name of Trigger Wright: the closest thing Plume had experienced, so far, to a recapitulation of Campbell.

Trigger (or "Trigg") was a high-speed romantic, feverishly celebrating anniversaries with his lovers—one-week anniversaries, two-week anniversaries—then dropping them shortly afterwards. He was twenty-five and seemed never to have heard of staying put. Born in Maryland, he had come to Seattle after several years in Washington, D.C., six months in New York, two months in Los Angeles and eighteen in San Francisco (where it had taken him longer than usual to work his way through the town). He had a cartoon brightness, a nervous cough and a recurrence of rashes that appeared, he said, whenever he was under pressure— which, given the way he treated people and goofed off on the job, was often. His domestic life was always in turmoil and he was frequently about to be fired. He was the kind of guy other guys slept with against their better judgment—if only to be able, later, to include his image in their nightly masturbatory regimen when they were between lovers. Trigg was in splendid shape, but had worried until recently about being fat. (His slight cushioning of flesh—in the face, around the lips—was more like lingering baby fat than impending middle age.) In the few weeks Plume knew him—"Hey! It's our third anniversary!"—he was in an ecstatic mood because he'd lost five pounds without even trying. Trimmer than usual and in high spirits because of it, he became convinced this was the moment to make his move. Ditching Plume, he returned to the gym in search of better things.

It was at the gym, only three months later, toward the end of 1980, and several weeks after the arrival of Bill, that Plume heard the news: Trigg, on a visit to his parents in the western hills of Maryland, had taken to his bed and mysteriously died—of pneumonia, it seemed.

This was not just alarming. It was also puzzling.

Had his cough suddenly gotten worse? But his cough had always seemed an affectation. What *kind* of pneumonia was it? True, people died of pneumonia every day—usually when they were old and every other part of them had worn out. But someone still in his twenties?

It didn't make sense.

Feeling prematurely mortal at thirty-five, Plume contemplated this death more closely and more anxiously than did most of his peers. Beyond the sudden shock of it and the embarrassing triumph of having outlived someone who had treated him badly, he sensed something amiss in the bigger picture. He would often think back to this moment when, for him and his circle of friends, the new decade had begun in earnest—even if they could not know it yet.

In the meantime he persuaded Bill to give up his house-share in Ravenna (too close to Laurelhurst) and move in with him, for reasons that went beyond simple companionship.

The house on Queen Anne was good-sized, handsomely situated, open to the light—but it needed something that Plume himself could not provide. It was oddly lacking in personality. Its rooms were large but had no distinctive pulse to them. Its furnishings were like the furnishings in hotels, attracting as little attention as possible. Even after eight years, few details had accumulated within these walls to give a clue as to Plume's tastes, predilections or occupation. ("Vocation" was too strong a word for a profession Plume had chosen less out of passion than in reaction to others' shortcomings.)

In failing to imprint his accommodations with his presence, Plume illustrated a commonplace of another sort: that the children of stable marriages, who have the fortune to grow up in households richly appointed in both feeling and goods, often lack furnishing and emotional skills of their own. The years-long process by which their parents attained a plateau-harmony of understanding eludes the younger generation, appearing simply as a *fait accompli*. Like a cathedral's imposing facade, such marriages can seem more natural phenomena than collaborative endeavors, thus distracting outside observers (and children, in these instances, are always outsiders) from the intricacy of their parts and the effort that went into them.

In Plume's parents' modest case, domestic bliss and its attendant material furnishings were simply a matter of ensuring that a living-room couch was comfortable or a breakfast nook convivial. But until he moved out, it had never occurred to Plume that a couch could be lumpy or a breakfast table dull.

It was here that Bill, who came from a poorer background which he was determined to transcend, made his influence felt. Under his regime, stark rooms acquired inviting details and the broad sea-deck plainness of an upstairs balcony was transformed into a hanging-gardens delight as blossoms and greenery were conjured from redwood planters and hanging baskets.

Plume saw comfort emerging from around him and was

pleased with it. Even if he didn't know quite how it had been managed, he was content to help pay for it—and so, on the strength of this, he and Bill withdrew more confidently into coupledom. Instead of an anxious flux of bars and discotheques, their life became a string of once-a-week dinner parties and an occasional movie. For Plume, after years of public circulation, there was something pleasant, almost illicit in the privacy of this new routine and its tacit refutation of the past. The past couldn't be denied entirely, of course—for, however dinner guests were placed around the table, there was no avoiding seating ex-lover by ex-lover. And though earlier liaisons and conquests would go unspoken during the meal, afterwards, during the car ride home or while loading the dishwasher, the topic would be opened up for discussion:

"I forget—did you sleep with him?"

"No, I wanted to. But I never got the chance."

This was during the interim, the time when little was known about the plague. Nine months after Trigg died, a possible explanation appeared in the back pages of the *New York Times* with an article about a "gay cancer" that was going around. No cause had been determined as yet. Poppers might be to blame, or some other drug. An excessive number of sexual partners—four hundred, five hundred, even a thousand a year ("My god," Plume laughed, "who has the time?")—seemed also to be a factor. But the disease appeared not to be "communicable" in the usual sense of the term. Both men assured themselves they had little to worry about.

Still, toying with science-fiction-like scenarios of doom, they pondered what the explanation of these deaths might be. Suppose, Bill hypothesized, that humans turned to homosexuality as rats did (in certain widely reported experiments) when overcrowding became a problem; and suppose, too, there was something genetic encoded within you that brought on a wasting of population when overcrowding continued to be a problem.

As a theory, this was close to superstition. Surely such a "wasting" would affect heterosexuals too, Plume argued. But it wasn't as close, both men agreed, as some of the wrath-of-God theories that were going around: "A lot of these guys—they're crazy. And with Reagan, who knows how much he listens to them? Do you think they'll put us in quarantine? Do you think they'll put us in camps?"

Plume doubted it, but felt unpleasantly at the center of something in flux that might show its outline in retrospect ("It started like this—then grew into that"), but which the present moment kept shapeless, full of change and menace.

Within the year, Bill's "genetic" theory had to stretch to cover Haitians. And both theories—"genetic" and "wrath-of-God"— quickly broke down when newborn babies, hemophiliacs and drug addicts (needle users) came into the picture.

Then the news broke that the "wasting" *was* communicable; that there was a virus spread through sex, though what kind of sex remained uncertain, and through blood transfusions. It was also suggested that this virus had a dormancy period of as much as a year.

There followed an era of less than nine months (but where crucial perceptions are involved, an era can last for as little as five minutes) when an uneasy sense of amnesty reigned. Bill and Plume and their immediate circle of male couples had all been together for a year or more, living in relative monogamy, the opportunities for "extramarital" adventures diminishing somewhat as one pushed forty. With six months being the agreed-upon safety margin, they had a wary hope of being home free. It violated common sense that any virus could lie dormant even *that* long—and if you came down sick as much as a year after exposure to it, well, then, it could only be bad luck. It helped too, reportedly, that they were in Seattle rather than New York or San Francisco, where contagion was more widespread. They preferred not to remember that, when visiting these cities, they had cut loose in a way they rarely did closer to home.

In Plume and Bill's case, the visits to those cities continued— but were made together and with a sense of playing it safe, even if others were not doing so.

Campbell was not doing so.

On a weeklong vacation in New York, they had stayed with him in Brooklyn and discovered this. Late on their second night there, after everyone had gone to bed, Plume heard a ruckus in the living room that roused him from sketchy sleep. With every cliché about the city coming to mind, he crept toward the dimly lit room with an umbrella in hand as his only weapon, there to find and be mortifyingly thrilled by the sight of Campbell in motion, looking as delectable as ever as he enthusiastically fucked a Hispanic kid who was draped over his couch.

Bill's voice, startling Plume, called out from behind him and said, "I hope we're practicing safe sex there."

And Campbell, grinning up at Bill, whom he had despised from the moment they met, replied, "I don't know—are we?"

Clearly they were not.

The guests retreated to the guest room, leaving their host to his pleasures. And it seemed, in the worst way, not to matter. Whoever was going to get it appeared already to have it. Every year the virus's dormancy period was pushed farther back in time: preposterously far. And even though a blood test was devised to detect its presence, its workings continued to be protean and enigmatic. It was spread more easily through some sexual acts than others, but there was no exact borderline between safe and unsafe. Certain people could live with it in their blood, it now was said, for three years, four years, perhaps even longer, without showing any ill effect. And then a fever, an aching, a constriction in the chest or discoloration of skin would indicate the illness had surfaced. A wasting and unraveling of resistance set in on every front, sometimes drawn out for a year or more, until everything that could be used in a body had been used and only a skeletal husk was left.

With the exception of Trigg (and Trigg had died out of sight, making his death oddly abstract), that husk was, for Plume, only a rumor as yet and that skeleton, sometimes still talking, was a skeleton on TV.

He was, he decided, more scared of rumor than of fact—and he could, he liked to tell himself, perhaps have risen to fact.

But when fact finally reached him and friends started to die, he did not rise to it. Instead he sank from it, shunned it and withdrew.

He had his reasons for this. He deemed himself, as people sometimes do, "constitutionally unsuited" to making hospital visits, even to friends who dated back to his college days. These friends were visited by Bill instead, while Plume *in absentia* gave money to the ad hoc organizations that sprang up around the crisis.

He went further: finagled his consulting hours so that, more and more, for him and Bill, a social life became impossible— or, rather, two *separate* social lives were ensured. In his work he grew increasingly dependent on losing himself in the problems of others, as long as those problems were not medical problems. And although he didn't put it this way (he didn't put it any way at all), he engaged in a vanishing act. Few people saw him. Few had news of him, except through Bill, and Plume quickly came to prefer this arrangement.

He also began half-consciously to turn down new gay clients. He understood their situation and the threats to it too well, he felt, and he had, as he saw it, nothing more to contribute to the discussion. All too often their problems were real, desperately so in some cases, and admitting of no solution.

What intrigued him more were problems he saw as willful or imaginary. ("Come on now—why *can't* you be friends with your ex-wife?'') Most straights, it struck him, lived their lives on strange and impossible terms, presenting him with a challenge to which, he told himself, he was better suited. Here he could be "objective." And in taking up this challenge, he could also be a maverick, bucking a constrictive trend within his milieu by being gay, but not a "gay psychiatrist."

In less honorable moments he convinced himself that avoiding gay clients made "good business sense." What if the contagion was more general than anyone admitted? What if the blood test was no good, or only partially accurate, and a person could be a carrier of the disease for years and years without showing any signs of it, latent or apparent, in the meantime spreading it more widely, unchecked, than anyone dared imagine?

Occasionally Bill would tell him of newcomers who, in an attempt to leave the past behind, had moved to Seattle from New York or San Francisco after their entire social circle had been wiped out—a phenomenon which was beginning to manifest itself here as well. Clearly there was no place where one could escape the sense of depredation for long, and Plume told himself he was making the smarter bet by staying where he was and varying his clientele as much as possible so as to ensure *having* a clientele in the future. This was not an act of discrimination or fear, he convinced himself, but one of pragmatism. How could he donate money to charities that needed it if he had no business?

Yet even as he became "pragmatic" in focus and listened with puzzlement to the uncertainties of nervous young college girls whose parents footed their bills, or to slightly older men whose marriages to creatures so unlike themselves were leading them toward violent impulse or apathetic misery, Plume had a sense of having gone off-track. It hit him especially in the evening, when his working day was done and his last client gone. He grew aware of Bill in the living room next door, waiting for him— but the life Bill was living had somehow grown alien to him. A subject matter filled him that could not be translated or shared.

There was patient confidence to be considered, of course, but there was also a feeling of being possessed by lives laughably remote from the slow horrors Bill and his circle of friends were experiencing. Plume had abandoned that circle, or at least maintained his distance from it—with odd result.

Idle erotic notions would play within this maintained distance and a strange emancipation emerged from it. At the gym which he continued to attend, the same hanky-panky went on that had always gone on, despite prominently posted signs forbidding all sexual activity, and he found himself drawn into these activities once again after having spurned them for several years. The fact of sexual danger made no difference. This splendid creature over here and that portly graying one over there were both vigorous with life and shaped to be supped upon. That they might nurture within them their own layer-by-layer destruction simply did not compute, despite all the evidence. A body was meant to be greeted; a cock, however furtively, was meant to be kissed; and from time to time it was impossible not to be seduced by the appearance of health, ignoring whatever threat was hidden.

"If they've got it, then I've probably got it too." He still had not been tested. "I'll pretend it doesn't exist."

The ease with which this delusion could be maintained, and the infractions of the rules it led to, threw him off-balance and into paranoia. Who was safe? What was there to say that Bill wasn't tempted this way too? If Plume couldn't trust himself, how could he trust his partner, or anyone?

He felt he ought to have a talk with Bill.

He did not dare have a talk with Bill.

His own behavior, he felt, was inexcusable—even if his infractions had been (medically speaking) mostly harmless and even if Bill was doing exactly the same. Every time he stepped into the sauna, he felt he was about to betray someone. And every time he entered his consulting rooms, letting himself become absorbed in worlds not his own, he had the same feeling of two-faced treachery.

It was under these circumstances, in this state of disintegrating trust in himself and those around him, that the sudden death of his father—from a stroke—threw him and flattened him. It freed him into a vacuum, a forlorn sense of detachment, with nothing to struggle against, and nothing to cling to.

One month to the day after his father's death, as if in loving mimicry of her husband, his mother suffered a stroke too, a milder one—and needed someone to look after her. The walls Plume had constructed in his mind—between "then" and "now," between Queen Anne and Laurelhurst—had crumbled. Some kind of war was over.

After much persuasion, Bill agreed to move with his lover to Laurelhurst, where they had the freedom of the house by day and the privacy of the basement "bachelor pad" to retreat to at night. For Plume the sense of return was symphonic, overwhelming. This, he realized, would one day be his house. It was furnished the way he liked it, with embellishments more subtle than those Bill had lavished upon the house on Queen Anne. It now grew evident to Plume that Bill's notions of comfort and luxury stemmed from the movie-and-magazine fantasies of his childhood, and this felt less like something to be affectionately mocked in his lover than something to be tolerated.

Bill was uneasy, but to Plume the new situation was practical. They saved on rent. They also saved on the expense of the twenty-four-hour nursing care which would have been necessary if his mother had been living alone. Instead, from the basement at night, the couple could hear any "thump" from above and immediately go upstairs to ensure everything was all right.

They moved about quietly, anticipating such sounds. Too quietly perhaps: Plume's mother was wary of Bill. And quiet anticipation could sound too much like eagerness.

In late summer of 1990, when events in Kuwait were making it feel as though the whole world might blow at any moment, the situation again changed. Plume's mother suffered another stroke, more serious than the first. After several weeks it was clear that it would be necessary either to hire live-in nursing care or move her into a rest home with the appropriate medical facilities. At Bill's insistence, the latter option was taken. But no sooner had the plans been made and put into motion than the invalid died—expiring with a long and erratic wheeze while her son, across the room, packed her suitcase in readiness for the move.

It was a blunt end, but kind in its way. She had hated the idea of the nursing home as much as she had hated the alternative of having two strangers—the nurse and Bill—living in her house. Perhaps, after all, she had the gift for control that her son had attributed to her so long ago.

Within the month, Plume moved himself and his lover upstairs, and the Queen Anne office was abandoned for the one in the basement below.

But by that time Walker Popman had been seeing him for almost a year.

To Plume, there *was* such a thing as a perfect patient—a person as absorbing as a well-wrought play; someone who allowed him to forget himself.

Certain patients achieved this by being vivid monologuists who would suffer no interruptions. Others, like Walker, achieved the same effect more subtly—by drawing back, playing hard to get, voicing skepticism about the whole process, but allowing it to continue nonetheless.

The pleasure in a mind like Walker's was its willingness to spar and its determination to focus on specific problems, keeping all emotional fuss to a minimum. Plume always felt gladly confirmed in his own common sense whenever he met with clients as spare in their personal dealings as he was, and Walker's *curriculum vitae* was as spare as could be.

Born in 1951. Thirty-eight years old, at the time of his first visit. Grew up in Montana. Both parents still living, and now in their seventies. He saw them "maybe once, twice a year." There was a younger sister, too, whom he didn't see as often, "—but we talk on the phone, if I'm the one calling. She doesn't like to run up her bill."

He had been married three years, although the relationship dated back almost twenty years to 1970. His wife, he said, was from Georgia.

"Ah," joked Plume. "A Southern belle."

Walker objected, "No, not at all. No nonsense about her—though she has two brothers who might qualify. Well, I shouldn't say that. One of them's a drunk, incredibly fussy, never amounted to much. Other one's married, living in South Carolina, has two children. I met him once and he seemed awfully dull to me—"

"What about you? Any children?"

"No. We both agreed. That wasn't what the relationship was about."

"How old is—?"

"Eleanor? My age, almost. About to turn thirty-seven."

"And does she have a career?"

"Different things at different times. Right now she works in publicity at—" He named a local repertory theater.

"What interests does she have besides theater?"

"Gardening. Clothes. The tarot."

"The tarot?"

"She's jokey about it, but partly serious. I just go along with it."

"She gives readings?"

"At parties and things. It's popular, I guess—"

Plume, sensing a note of evasion, jotted it down, then continued his inquiry: "If you could give me some idea of your marital relations. . ."

Walker seemed amused: "You mean sex life?"

" 'Sex life,' if you like. Or anything else you care to mention."

"How much detail do you want?"

Again this was asked with a smile.

Plume fumbled: "Whatever—Whatever you're comfortable with."

"Well," Walker drawled, teasing the moment out, "we're not exactly in our first supernova . . . but we get along. We enjoy each other."

"So it's comfortable."

"You could say that."

"And there's trust between you, you're faithful to each other?"

"Well," he drawled again, "maybe not in the usual sense."

"You're saying you've had an affair outside your marriage? Or earlier? Outside your relationship?"

"Me? No, never. Or not successfully."

Plume asked what he meant by this.

"It didn't work. It wasn't 'fully consummated,' I guess you might say."

Plume stopped writing, looked up to see how this had been offered—but Walker was elusive. Plume made a special note on his legal pad, then continued: "And what about Eleanor?"

"Oh, she's fooled around."

"How do you know?"

"Because she tells me about it."

"And this is a source of anxiety to you?"

"No, no, it's not. Or it wasn't. There isn't as much of it these days. . . ."

"But you've had disagreements over it in the past?"

"No, never."

"It hasn't made things tense between you?"

"Not tense exactly."

"You've sensed there's a problem and you've asked her about it."

"We haven't really discussed it. Not as a problem, anyway."

There was a pause here, an invitation perhaps, on Walker's part, for Plume to dig past obstacles planted, half deliberately, in his path. Walker, it seemed, was beginning to rise to Plume's challenge, however cagily.

The questioning resumed: "So it's an 'open relationship'?"

"I guess."

"And what's Eleanor's attitude toward that?"

"It was mostly her idea."

"And her attitude toward you?"

"Toward me? Well lately, I suppose, it's been more affection-ate—"

"More affectionate."

"—and a little more distant, too."

"*Distant*, you say?"

"I know that doesn't make much sense—"

But Plume forged on as though it made perfect sense: "So what you're telling me is there's been a change in her feeling for you and this is what concerns you, this is what brought you to me."

Walker, taking fair measure of the accuracy of Plume's guess-work, grew more serious: "The thing is there's no actual evidence for—for the feeling I'm having. But I know, I just know in my heart—"

"What do you know?" Plume smiled, in expectation of another wry twist or turn, another teasing obfuscation.

"—that she's getting ready to leave me," Walker said soberly.

The answer drew a chill into the room. This was a twist, all right, but not the kind he had expected. Concealing his surprise, he inquired: "You mean for good?"

"Well . . . I assume so. At least that's what it feels like."

"You say that rather calmly."

"Maybe because it doesn't feel real yet?"

"She hasn't said anything? You're just intuiting this?"

"Actually, it's this whole card business."

"What about it?"

Walker appeared reluctant to tell him: "It was a while ago . . . she gave me a reading. It's only a game, but she seemed pretty serious about it."

"What did it say?"

"That there'd be three women in my life. And since Eleanor only counts as Number Two, that meant—" But he cut himself off in midsentence: "Hell, I'm not sure *what* it meant. But I've thought about it and assume she has too."

"You haven't been tempted to discuss it with her?"

"Oh, sure! Except I know she'd just laugh it off—unless I caught her in the right mood. She has her moods, you know. . . ."

Plume had heard this before—the wife as alien creature, unpredictable, full of whims—and it always annoyed him. Usually it indicated the existence of peculiarly masculine blinders in a marital situation, and he could never believe the man was so stupid as not to be able to see this for himself.

They wrangled around this. And the picture grew more elaborately clouded with their every exchange—as though Walker, far from describing his situation in terms of cliché, was offering something more intricate and offbeat. Two Eleanors began to emerge: one who was woven into him, another who seemed to be dismantling him piece by piece. Both, in the account he gave, operated with a similar smile and a similar enticement. In order to keep track of them, Plume suggested, it might make sense to allow these sessions to be tape-recorded: "This way you can listen, *hear* what you're saying—and pick out what's fact-based and what might be fantasy . . . or just exaggeration."

"Ah . . . playback as mirror, you mean?"

Plume said uncomfortably: "If you like."

Walker leaned back and chuckled. "I don't think I have the patience to sit and listen to myself droning on and on."

"That's not quite doing yourself justice—"

"But I know myself. I don't."

"Don't what?"

"Have the patience."

"Would you object if I recorded the sessions just for my own use?"

Walker didn't mind—and didn't take it seriously.

Plume found a tape, slipped it into the machine, began recording—and then spent the next ten minutes with Walker debating Eleanor's role in the marriage. He asked how demonstrative a partner she was: "You say she doesn't always show it, but she cares for you. It's more than just a habit. You're sure of that?"

"I'm sure of it."

"Then why not ask her about this card business if it's bothering you?"

"Because even if it's true, it's not true yet."

"Why not?"

"Because it isn't going to happen till it happens."

"You make it sound inevitable."

"Kind of . . . that's sort of what it feels like."

"You don't seem the type to go in for mysticism. And yet—"

"I know, I know."

"So in the meantime all you're doing is bottling it up?"

"Yeah, well. That's why I wanted to talk to someone. . . ."

They went back and forth on this for another quarter of an hour, until Plume, giving up, said, "That isn't much to go on. And we don't have time to dig any deeper right now. But maybe we can arrange a schedule—?"

"I sort of thought it might take more than one visit."

"Would a weekly meeting be possible?"

"Once a week? That seems—"

"It's what we'll need if we're going to establish details."

"What kind of details?"

Plume explained that he liked to obtain as full a background as possible, then whittle it down to something that offered practical measures: a "hit-and-miss process," perhaps, but one that allowed client and consultant to stay open to surprises. Juggle the pieces, he said, rearrange them with care, and the most casual detail could attain a surprising amount of weight.

"And you think that'll work?"

Walker sounded uncharacteristically earnest.

"Well . . . there's no guarantee."

Walker pondered this, then said, "I guess that's how I'd do it—in my job, I mean. Sometimes it's like you don't even know what you have, until you shuffle through and look at it. Then suddenly you find exactly what you're after, or something you weren't expecting at all—"

"I'm sorry: your job is—?"

"Oh, I thought you knew. I'm a photographer—"

Popman named his newspaper and the gallery that represented him.

Then the two men shook hands, postponing further investigation until the following week.

That same night in bed, while drifting off and making the usual rounds through his pantheon of fantasy men and lost loves (the jester's prance of Campbell, the more sultry come-hither slither of Trigg), he glimpsed a new arrival among his dozen odd regulars and dreamed of Walker strolling like a satyr down the walkways of sleep, bestowing loving favors on creatures of his own sex in shadowed recesses along a winding corridor that led—the dreamer somehow knew—to a "ball" where all was permitted.

This had happened before with clients—their slipping into his dreams and sometimes his nightmares—but never so quickly, never so frankly. Even with Campbell and Trigg there had been a delay of a week or two before they turned up playing significant roles in his dreamlife. Walker's instant appearance was unprecedented and surprising. It called for explanation.

During his first session with Walker, Plume had—in a diligent way—enjoyed himself, but registered no special attraction to his client. With their second encounter, however, he grew more self-conscious as he addressed Walker from behind his desk. His dream had shown him a Walker naked and aroused, and now he had a hankering to compare the burly, eroticized image of his dream-memory with the actual man in his office. Walker's careless attire—flannel shirt and baggy khaki pants—made him appear slacker and baggier in build than in the dream, but still hinted at the appeal of a body type that Plume had not previously considered in a sexual light. It occurred to him to wonder if, as one aged, almost every body type became an object of interest; if age in fact helped one become an epicure of physiques. Or did tastes simply, and always, change to suit the occasion?

Whatever the case, it made this second session more awkward, inspiring in Plume a nervousness that communicated itself all too clearly, he feared. But if Walker registered it, he also dismissed it as casually as he would any of his wife's less agreeable moods, unaware that he might be the cause of them—and therefore confident that they weren't worth examining.

After a stilted fifteen minutes or so, they found themselves trying to determine when, exactly, Walker's fear of Eleanor's leaving had originated. Was it with the tarot reading? Or had there been some less obvious but more telling clue preceding it? Walker, as though searching out the solution to a math problem, said this was what made life interesting, wasn't it?—figuring out where a change might have occurred, where something began to end.

Plume was gentle but firm. He turned the discussion toward a consideration of Walker's earliest sexual experience for whatever clues might lie there: "Maybe if we get back to Grace."

"Who?"

"I'm sorry. Your high school teacher? Mrs. Fitkin?"

"Oh. Gloria. Her name was Gloria."

"Did you have an idea of what you wanted with her? And did she conform to it?"

Walker laughed and said she would have conformed to anything anyone asked of her: "She was a total doormat for her husband—so I tried to be a bit of one for her."

"In what way?"

"Nothing serious. No S&M, or anything like that."

"What, then?"

He had simply indulged her, he said, and been indulged *himself* in the pleasurable sensations of being a kind of toy for her to play with.

"So she made you do things you didn't really want to do?"

"Not at all, not at all. I enjoyed it. Who wouldn't?"

Plume didn't comment on this. His own tastes, he felt, had no application here. Instead, he moved on to Eleanor: How had she and Walker met? And what had she been like?

It was at the University of Colorado, Walker said, in Boulder—his second year there. And she was, he remembered, pretty much the same as now: completely straightforward, a little reckless. There had been a party where Eleanor was hostess and Walker a guest. And it was Eleanor who had taken the initiative.

"What happened?"

"What she said was, 'You want to come upstairs and we'll investigate this situation?' Those were her exact words."

"And what was the situation?"

Walker took a moment to find a tactful way to phrase it—and then, giving up, explained that he had been wearing "kind of skimpy" hiking shorts which made his arousal obvious.

Plume took note of this mention of hiking shorts—and drew his chair in closer to his desk to keep his own reaction to it from being a factor in their exchange.

"So you went with her," he said blandly.

"It was her Southern accent! I couldn't resist it!"

"Why not?"

Walker looked at him oddly: "Well, why should I? We both just knew what our bodies wanted us to do."

This was lightly offered, but threaded, as well, with a memory of awe at the abruptness with which desire had overcome them. He continued in a more sober tone, giving his account of their love affair.

They had moved in together soon afterwards, in a group house with shared kitchen and with mattresses on the floor: "That whole scene . . . we saved on rent." They stayed there all through college, then came out to Seattle where the setup was much the same, in a commune in Fremont where things could get pretty wild sometimes. There was a motorcycle gang next door, which was a nuisance—revving engines and breaking glass at three in the morning—but it was also where Eleanor got some of her men: "Or 'boys,' I should say. A lot of them were still in their teens."

Plume inquired: "And while she was with these, ahem, motorcycle boys, you weren't doing anything similar?"

Only once, Walker said. And there was a time in college too, he remembered, with a professor there. But in both cases Eleanor had "precipitated" the encounters.

"You mean these were encounters between you and another man?"

Walker shrugged. "What can I say? It was the 'seventies."

Plume drew his chair in still closer to his desk and asked if Walker had had any other homosexual experience.

Walker said he had not. He didn't care for it much. Any early curiosity, he confessed, had soon evaporated with the episodes themselves: "I don't even think of them as counting, really. I'd almost forgotten about them."

"What about other women?"

"Oh she was into that too."

By now Plume was getting quite a picture of Eleanor—and

feeling annoyed at the way she kept drifting back into the lime-light. He explained that he meant *Walker* and other women. And Walker revealed that there had been one, early on, at an alternative weekly where he worked: bright, young, in the adver-tising department. But the affair didn't get far: "I couldn't even keep it up. And the newspaper didn't last long either. . . ."

This was met with a ponderous silence.

Walker called out: "Hello? That was supposed to be a joke."

Plume, snapping to, said he was aware of this—and wondered what the humor was trying to conceal. Had impotence been a problem at other times?

Walker said it had not.

Not even with Eleanor?

Never with Eleanor.

Plume asked if this wasn't a little out of the ordinary. Usually it was the familiar that fails to be stimulating . . .?

Walker said: "Not if you know Eleanor."

Plume, deeply puzzled, attempted to summarize, "So, for the most part, you've felt—you *feel*—sexually functional, fulfilled, relaxed with Eleanor. She's pretty much the most comfortable partner you've ever had."

Walker confessed he'd never really had anyone *except* Eleanor. Mrs. Fitkin was so long ago—and their affair, such as it was, mostly consisted of his feeling sorry for her: "Really it's all just been Eleanor." Her extramarital flourishes, in his view, were simply one more aspect of their mutual marital devotion.

Plume pronounced, "I'm all in favor of marital devotion—but I'm having difficulty understanding what makes yours work."

"I wish *I* knew!"

"I'm also surprised that it's now, when Eleanor appears to have abandoned her extramarital activities, that you think the relationship is in danger."

"Yeah, well—"

"It was better when she was seeing other people?"

"I guess that kind of thing's supposed to make you miserable. But somehow it didn't—not with her telling me about it."

"And you're sure she's told you everything?"

"I assume so. If there's more, I wouldn't mind hearing about it. . . ."

"Would you say there was a physical resemblance between Eleanor and Grace? I mean Gloria, Mrs. Fitkin—"

Walker's answer was confident: "Not at all. None whatsoever."

"—or similarity of temperament?"

"Not that I can think of. . . ."

Their second session ended on an unresolved note.

The following week, Plume came up with some preliminary questions to run by Walker as a sort of exercise. "To get things started," he explained.

Walker was amenable to this.

First question: When he looked at himself in the mirror, what exactly did he see?

Walker pressed his hands together, drew them to his chin, and gave it some thought before answering, "A guy, in early middleage I guess, who's maybe not in the greatest of shape, but still, well, semi-attractive—"

"What about with Eleanor? When you look at *her*, what do you see?"

"It's hard to say," Walker offered after another long pause. "We've grown so close, she feels almost a part of me."

Plume wanted to know if this feeling was stifling in any way.

Walker said it wasn't, not at all. It was a good feeling, a solid feeling—"like she shapes me, makes me firmer."

Did he, then, recognize some feminine side of himself in Eleanor?

Walker denied this, insisting simply that she was his best friend and his most trusted confidante.

"But lately you don't feel that way!" Plume countered. "And it's as if you've been thrown out of your private paradise."

Walker thought this was overstating it. Things weren't that bad.

"They may not be that bad," Plume commented, "but they can't be all that good either if you're coming to me. I think you're holding back. I think you feel you've strayed from the path somewhere and you're trying to keep calm about it—but all the time you're worrying that you've lost your way. There's been no indication from Eleanor that there's a problem, apart from this one episode, this tarot card reading, which hasn't been mentioned since. And yet that one incident has triggered doubts about your whole relationship. It seems to me there must be other factors involved which you're simply repressing. You're denying your real problem."

Walker maintained he wasn't denying anything: "I *admit* I have a problem. That's why I came to you."

"But everything you've told me is strictly on the surface."

"That's all I know!—what's on the surface."

"But maybe that surface is a decoy, a diversion of sorts. Maybe what's vital is underneath. Maybe that's where the answers are."

"I don't see it that way. It's surfaces that count. They're the one thing you have a real chance of seeing or changing. The rest is bullshit, if you ask me."

"So what steps would you take if you wanted to see your surface directly?"

"Exactly what I'm doing now—finding out what *you* see. Maybe there's a pattern I repeat without knowing it."

"I wish I could tell you. But you're not really opening up with me."

"You want me to make something up?"

"No, no, of course not. But I need something more to go on than what you're giving me. Isn't there anything beside the cards. . .?"

There was no reply from Walker.

After a moment, Plume ventured: "Let's get back to the photographs, which to my mind raise a number of questions. I'm wondering if there's something a frozen image gives you that you don't get out of a live presence or memory?"

"I'm not sure I can answer that. I mean, I would hate to start thinking about it that way."

"Why?"

"What if I get so self-conscious that I can't do my job anymore?"

"You're serious?"

"Partly, yes."

"I think it's something we have to consider."

"You do, huh?"

Plume nodded.

There was a longish silence, an exasperated sigh, and finally: "Well, then, go ahead if you like. Consider it."

Plume took note of the unvoiced sentiment—*Hey, why not? Let's see what this guy comes up with next!*—and carried on in an even tone: "Granted, it's a craft. And it gives the satisfaction of a craft. You make your living from it. But there's more to it than that. My sense is that you use what you shoot, especially the private photos, in a therapeutic way to achieve control over situations that are otherwise inescapably fluid. Eleanor is loose. Eleanor is chaotic. But with these photos in hand—of Eleanor, of these lovers of hers, even of yourself—you can hold on to something and be assured that it's yours, that it's *you*. Am I right? Am I close? Surely this is a direction worth following, if only for the facts it might turn up along the way. Will you follow it?"

There was another long silence. And then Walker, mildly intrigued, his note of skepticism abating somewhat, agreed: "Okay. If you want to, let's follow it."

Plume, with new confidence, inquired when Walker had first

made a connection between his erotic fantasies and his photographic obsessions.

Walker vaguely supposed it had been in college.

"Not any earlier? No magazines? *Playboy? Penthouse?*"

"I thought you meant *my* photographs."

Plume clarified the question—but still Walker had no specific answer.

In high school, he confirmed, there had been skin magazines, but they were so remote! He couldn't connect them with any actual females he knew. Looking back on it, he *seemed* to have been sex-obsessed: he talked about it and had lots of crushes. But at the same time he was yearning for something more ethereal, with no anatomical details involved: "Just a sort of massive melting into heavenly cream cheese. That was how I pictured it."

Plume was dubious: "Into . . . cream cheese?"

Walker expanded on this, extolled the notion of souls communing without the bother of bodies, imagined a gentle blending of male and female spirits with the universe itself; and then confessed to the shock he had received, in an age of airbrushed centerfolds, upon encountering female pubic hair: "I mean, up until Mrs. Fitkin, I was pretty damn naive."

Plume, pushing back from his desk, kept his thoughts about female pubic hair to himself and returned again to the question of cameras and college. What had happened in Boulder?

"That's where I bought my first Polaroid."

"Expressly for these sessions?"

"Isn't that the whole point of a Polaroid?—or ninety percent of it?"

Plume was tempted to take issue with this, but continued: "You had no difficulty persuading Eleanor to join in? It provided you with stimulation?"

"We were hardly in need of more stimulation."

"Then what was the point?"

"It was just . . . fun, I guess. Exhibitionism and voyeurism, all in the privacy of your home. Other couples must do it. You're saying you never—?"

"I can understand wanting pictures of Eleanor. But this business with yourself—"

"I just wanted to see what it was like."

"What what was like?"

"What *I* was like—when I succumbed to that kind of oblivion."

"Yourself, alone on the bed, brightly lit, at the moment of sexual climax? Using the automatic timer?"

"Okay: exhibitionism, voyeurism and narcissism. But doesn't that just make me an all-around guy?"

"Why not collect pornography?"

"It's not the same thing. It's not as personal."

Plume leaned in toward his desk again: "Did Eleanor ever suggest skin magazines, videos?"

"Oh yeah, she's picked some up sometimes. Videos, I mean. I'm a little embarrassed to rent them. But she's cool about it."

"What sort? Women? Men? Both together?"

"All sorts. But frankly, there aren't too many good ones. They all look synthetic—or else they're mean-spirited, not playful enough. And the *camerawork* is so bad! I don't get turned on by them. They're not what interests me."

"When did you last have a Polaroid session together?"

"Months ago. Maybe even a year."

"Is it possible that at this stage in your marriage, you've fully explored the 'surface' of yourself, as you put it, and this is making the marriage go stale?"

"Oh no, the surface keeps expanding."

"What do you mean?"

"Well for one thing we both got fatter." He said this with great good humor. "Or I did, anyway."

"And?"

"That's why we did it last time."

"Did what?"

"Took the pictures! We were going on a diet. But before we did, we wanted to document it. Keep a record of how fat we were. . . ."

With this second mention of "fat," Plume floundered. Sooner than planned, he brought the session to a close. It seemed to him disconcertingly obvious that he was more intent on unraveling Walker than Walker was on unraveling himself. But he didn't want Walker to find this out. All he wanted was to keep on digging. He longed to go deeper and deeper. He was anxious to learn *just how fat* Walker was. And he was ready for as much of Walker's voice as he could get, no matter what it was saying.

Walker's problem might be exquisitely precise—"Why, for no good reason, do I think my wife's about to leave me?"—but Plume's reaction to it was an increasingly unwieldy amalgam of frustration, impatience and (he knew) groundless hope. He felt stricken by a caprice that plucked at every corner of him, disrupting his concentration on anything but a narrow spectrum of interest—an interest that, from an ethical standpoint, he disapproved of in himself entirely.

It happened, he knew, to everyone in the "miz biz," as some of his colleagues called it ("I'm in the miz biz—I shrink heads"). It had even happened to *him* on several occasions—but never so pronouncedly as this, and never at speeds so ecstatic.

This was it: the big no-no.

He had fallen—headlong, abysmally—for his client.

From this point on, the mood of their encounters grew erratic: sometimes friendly, sometimes guarded, occasionally hostile. Plume, nervous with desire, resorted more than ever to gym sauna liaisons to purge himself of the twangy tensions that his "crush" (as he now dismissed it) induced, since he could not, for some reason, vent this crush as he had vented past crushes—on Bill. Even with the lights out and his eyes closed, there was no fooling himself about where he was or whom he was with.

In his sauna encounters he tried to keep within certain bounds of conduct, but this was difficult. Kissing, it was clear, would constitute betrayal—not of Walker but of Bill—and so far he had managed to refrain from this. Other kinds of contact, however, were less easily averted, especially once one yielded to the momentum of the act. With a wordless gesture, a stranger would indicate his readiness—and Plume would not resist. Afterwards, however, recalling how far he had gone, he would be frightened, thinking: "I didn't want to be that close . . . but was I *really* all that close?"

His weekly sessions with Walker were almost a relief by contrast, even if they meant going back repeatedly to the original source of titillation. At least they weren't physical, for it was out of the question that Plume would put the moves on Walker. Walker, instead, was his fantasy, and if he ever tried to make him more than that, Walker (he trusted) would rebuff him. It was only a crush, only a crush, he told himself: a spiraling eruption of feeling which Walker, thankfully, seemed entirely unaware of. After all, Plume had the perfect camouflage. In any other situation where one person concentrated so fiercely on another, the recipient of these attentions would naturally regard the offerer of them as desperately infatuated. But with it being Plume's task to probe, infatuation went unnoticed.

Walker seemed not even particularly to like him. And though Walker's indifference to him, along with his own semi-invisibility within his role as therapist, toppled Plume into a sort of hell, it was a heavenly kind of hell, allowing him undreamed-of access to his man. This was all that he asked—an opportunity to study his client for a limited time each week—and the longer it went on, the more he came to depend on it. In an odd way this was less threatening than any of his affairs of the heart had ever been because it was arranged according to a strict schedule to which both parties dutifully adhered. Bill had a tendency to run late. But Walker, like Plume, was punctual, appearing exactly when he said he would.

Every detail about him was a detail that counted. Sometimes his voice was hectic. Sometimes it was sweet. Sometimes it was irritable, for instance when Plume pursued him with questions about his photography or the volatile nature of his dealings with Eleanor. But this didn't matter—just as long as the voice was Walker's, and the mouth, and the eyes.

It was Walker's marriage to Eleanor they were discussing now.

And Walker was frank, Walker was forthcoming, as he observed that the taking of vows had induced a sense of settling down between them, even if the vows themselves had been inspired not by any sense of a new phase in their relationship but by a need to obtain medical coverage for Eleanor: "I mean, it's getting rough out there, with all the insurance companies tighteningup. . . ."

Plume, reacting to the protective tenderness he heard in his client's voice, became as determined to save the marriage as if it were his own. Even if Walker was off limits, he could at least help him to be happy.

He began to pour on his standard brand of common sense.

Surely, he said, there was much for the couple to be pleased about. Both, he pointed out, were satisfied with their jobs, and money was not a problem. Eleanor's extramarital activity had dwindled down almost to nothing to the best of Walker's knowledge, and with formal marriage they had taken measures to ensure the security of their life together. Yet Walker was convinced that Eleanor was about to take off at any moment. Why? She must have given him some reason, apart from this tarot card reading.

As always, Walker was evasive—or simply slow in answering.

It was nothing she said or did, he replied. It was just the way she was. He was sure she was going to do it. He couldn't put it any more clearly.

To Plume this was not nearly clear enough. He grew more brutal, more direct, and derived a mild thrill from this.

"And how do you feel about that?" he asked.

"How do I feel?" Walker echoed. "Like I'm watching my life in a movie. There I am, on-screen, going through the motions— but I have no control over the plot."

Plume disagreed with this, insisted Walker did have control and should put that control to use. There must be some simple concrete thing that had put him on his guard concerning Eleanor and made him think what he was thinking. First he had to identify it. Then he could act upon it.

"But I tell you, there's nothing."

"Try. Please just try."

The imploration forced Walker to take a minute or two to troll for an answer—until he finally came up with an unlikely one.

"Well, for one thing, she's gotten more considerate, as if she wants to do the right thing by me."

"I would have thought that was a good sign."

"Not with her. With her it's a bad sign."

"Have you asked why she's doing it?"

"There's no real way to talk with her about it. She'd tune it out, pretend she didn't understand."

"You think she may still be having affairs on the side?"

"Oh that wouldn't worry me."

"What sort of thing are we talking about? One-night stands? Ongoing relationships? What type of man is she attracted to?"

"Always younger, in their twenties. One kid was nineteen. But like I said, that was a while ago."

"Still, the possibility of it recurring must pose a bit of a threat."

"Well I'd rather it was her having the adventures and telling me about them than me going out and getting them for myself.

I just don't have the time, for one thing. And hey, I admit, I'm a voyeur. If she leaves me, her stories will be one of the things I miss."

"So you really believe this is a viable arrangement?"

He insisted it was. In their own peculiar way, he said, they were happy. On the surface there was no reason to worry at all. When Plume began to ask once more why, if she had said nothing and there was no other issue at stake, etc., Walker interrupted him: "Because it's in the cards. Literally. She read it there, and I know she took it seriously."

Plume took a different tack: "Does she have an interest in the occult outside of the tarot?"

"Oh yeah—palm-reading, tea leaves. The whole shebang."

"This is a recent development?"

"Relatively recent. The last few years. But there's always been something. Sufism, the *I Ching*. Nothing that ever ruled out dope and martinis."

"Now *there's* something we haven't really covered yet: this substance abuse, this drug usage. . . ."

"It's only marijuana."

"And you're fairly heavy in your use of it?"

"Not anymore. We don't know where to get any. And we were never all that heavily into it. Otherwise I'm sure we'd be more resourceful, track some down. . . ."

Walker's answer rose and collapsed without any rewarding insight. There was a long pause. Plume reverted to his earlier line of inquiry: "In her . . . relationships, with these . . . young men—"

"We're back to that again. Can't we talk about something else?"

"Were these just—flirtations? Or were they fully consummated?"

"No, I guess we can't."

"In a moment. But first if you could tell me—"

"Oh, she went all the way with them, I'm sure."

"And this happened within the last five years?"

"She's kind of slowed down. But yes."

"Were they practicing safe sex? That could be a source of considerable anxiety—and rightly so."

"I assume that at some point they must have made the switch. I don't feel comfortable asking her about it. I just take it for granted she has some common sense."

"Do the two of *you* practice safe sex?"

"Not all the time. She's on the pill—"

"But you assume she does when she's with other men?"

"Well, yes."

"You don't sound too sure of it."

"Maybe I am, maybe I'm not."

"You seem a little exasperated by the question."

"I *am* exasperated. I don't know why we always get on this, when it's the other thing that worries me!"

"What other thing?"

"The thing I can't put into words. The thing I have no evidence for. The thing that makes no sense to me."

"But it sounds to me like you're denying factors in your marriage that pose a threat to it, that would pose a threat to any relationship."

"No. The problem is: you're harping on your own concerns more than what's concerning me."

Plume, in cool tones, not wanting to concede any truth in this, went back to Walker's fear of Eleanor's leaving him: "But you have absolutely nothing to back up your concern apart from a tarot card reading by someone who, if we're to give any credence to the process at all, is by her own admission an amateur. Otherwise there's nothing in your marriage to indicate it's in a state of unrest, let alone crisis."

"Well that's the thing. If you can't put it into words, then it doesn't have much weight as evidence. But it can still be a factor, can't it?"

"I don't see how we can get to the bottom of this unless you specify the exact nature of your worry. The source of it, I mean."

"I don't *want* to say what it is. I don't *want* to give it any more weight than it has already. If I don't talk about it, there's still a chance it will just go away, stay indefinite."

"We're going in circles here. You've already said what it was. You're afraid—for no apparent reason—that your wife is going to leave you."

"Okay, I said that. Now what?"

Plume, damping down impatience, pulled back from the conversation, chided himself for getting so worked up. He must not shout at Walker. He must not get angry with Walker. He wanted to deal with Walker calmly. He wanted to be Walker's friend! And maybe Walker was right. Maybe he *was* "harping" on his own specific concerns about sex and betrayal, to the exclusion of the more enigmatic concerns at hand.

He wanted to . . . kiss Walker? No, no, that would be unproductive, that would be unprofessional. And yet he wanted to *be* unprofessional, right now—take Walker in his arms and give him a gentle, brotherly kiss, from one punctual person to another. He wanted to climb across his desk and embrace Walker the only way you *can* embrace a person: in the flesh, skin to skin, heart to heart. He wanted to beg forgiveness of Walker and call on his sympathy. He longed to confess to it all—his fantasies, his yearnings—and receive absolution, make some sort of penance. (Campbell had often asked: "Are you *sure* you're not a Catholic?") He would give up jerking off in the sauna. He would vow not to lose control of his dreams again. He would be true to Walker in as unsexual a way as possible. He would even lower his fees, give Walker a discount, in apology for any mishandling of their sessions resulting from his lust for him: "I realize I haven't been 'all there' lately. . . ." He would invite Walker upstairs, introduce him to Bill, and they could *all* be friends. He would erase these roles of client and consultant and put in their place something more intimate, more affectionate, that would include Bill as well—for he'd like to stay true to Bill, but how? With a little threesome, maybe. . . . No, no—

Walker's question—"Now what?"—still hung in the air, waiting to be answered. And Plume, regaining some control over himself, reached for glib lines of encouragement that would disguise his thoughts. Whatever happened, Walker mustn't know, Walker mustn't guess—that he saw him in this light, that he felt this ballooning desire for him.

In a voice that verged on accusation, he echoed, " 'Now what?' "—then offered, "The only rational step *I* can see taking is persuading Eleanor to come in with you and have the two of you try a little marriage counseling. No psychobabble, I promise. Just a straightforward but monitored situation where you could both try to be honest. And you've virtually stonewalled on that possibility."

"I haven't: it's just that I know *she* would."

For a full twenty minutes they went back and forth on this—until the session sputtered to a close. Walker left. And Plume, calmer once his client had gone, still had hope; could still envisage, at the edges of his mind, a happy ending, the promise of some breakthrough.

The following week, however, and for the remainder of January 1990, Walker canceled every one of his appointments.

This had happened before—a client walking out, either temporarily or permanently. But it had never left Plume so despondent. He wondered where he'd gone wrong, what he could do to make it right. He was tempted to contact Walker, but counseled himself to wait. If Walker wanted to come back to him, he would do it in his own good time. And when, on a weekend in early February, Walker did exactly that, returning unexpectedly, it seemed to

Plume that he'd been rewarded for his patience. He was delighted at first, even a little triumphant—until he registered the agitated state his client was in.

It did not take long to discover the cause of Walker's agitation.

"It's Eleanor," he said.

"Eleanor?" Plume asked.

Eleanor had gone. Eleanor had left.

She was now, as Walker half plaintively, half derisively put it, "out of the picture."

Plume, all sympathy, prescribed his client a powerful brand of tranquilizer so he could sleep at night. He also advised him that regular physical exercise was often a help, if not a cure-all, in dealing with psychological grief. Finally, and almost in passing, he suggested that they resume their regimen of weekly consultations, starting immediately.

Walker agreed—and they were back in business.

Machines in the kitchen buzzed as Bill breakfasted. The coffee grinder whirred and the teakettle wailed—until he moved out of the kitchen and down a dim hallway, the light fixtures rattling as he searched for his keys.

His lover dozed lightly through this. There were always several false starts before each morning's final exit. Tranquillity came only when Bill had gone: the front door latching, the deadbolt clicking, the motor in the driveway revving and then vanishing.

With his house restored to him, Plume fell back to sleep.

Half an hour later he blinked himself awake, threw on his bathrobe, stepped to the window and investigated his garden. It pleased him that the forsythia was budding. Usually it waited until later in the month. Crocuses poked up and split towards color too, and several determined roses offered soggy signs of bloom. Each plant on the shallow slope from house to lakefront gave him comfort and company—and, at the same time, anxiety.

There were patches of lawn where nothing grew. And his fear was of killing what his mother had raised. Her palm trees, in particular, were marginal to this climate. And the advice he got from friends about them was troublingly vague: "It could be too much water—or else not enough."

No one would be pinned to measurable quantities.

He pictured his mother, straw hat on her head, watering can in hand, her very image containing a shorthand of gardening tips. But the exact nature of her plant care, the tricks with which she conjured her summertime beads and banners of color, never came clear. Under his eye, fuchsia and azalea and brittle Klondike potentilla remained hopeful mysteries, verdant but not flowering. As for the bulbs, the squirrels had gotten every one of them. They dug up his flowerbeds and upset his order. He had made an inquiry: it was illegal to kill them, even if they were in your house. They were a protected species, he was told, in danger of extinction.

Well, they certainly flourished here! Their vigor knew no bounds. They were glossy and oversized, sleek and undefeatable—but was anybody keeping track of this? Probably not.

He sighed, came indoors, showered, had a bite to eat; then walked down to the lakeside. It was astonishing how balmy the last three days had been. If this was global warming, he liked it. The lake was quiet and he liked that too. In summer the sound of motorboats bounced off the hills and plagued the air with tension.

After locking up, he caught the bus to the University District, where he roamed through secondhand bookstores, searching for a gardening manual that would meet his needs: one that demystified watering. This was an eternal quest and as usual he had no luck. He also looked for a book on squirrels, but could not find one sufficiently critical of them.

Lunch was in a coffee shop run by an Asian family who turned out a delicious soup and sandwich, as tasty as his mother used to make: corn chowder, homemade bread. There was even an outdoor deck with small picnic tables where, on pleasant days, one could sit.

This day was pleasant—but not as pleasant as that.

On the bus trip back, sighting the volcano's icy cone, he made his salute. The mountain anchored the far end of the lake, while the university playing fields that served as its foreground were quiet and deserted, as if evacuated for eruption. The bus dropped him off in his usual spot, leaving an exhaust-filled silence in its wake. He savored his sense of removal from the city. Across Union Bay was the floating bridge to Bellevue—but its hum of traffic was like the hum of the sea.

Late in the afternoon he withdrew to his office to review his patient files and listen to Walker's tapes. With a strangely sexual regret and woe, he realized they contained the most he would ever have of Walker: of his words, his fears, his impatience and skepticism. A life had reached its limits. The tapes, however, still had their possibilities, or so this visit from Walker's second wife seemed to suggest—though what these possibilities were, precisely, was difficult to say. Should he tell her of the tapes' existence, or should he conceal it?

It would all depend on who she was, and what she wanted.

In his file drawers, he looked for a recording which dated from the time when their sessions were murkiest—exactly two years ago, February 1990, after Eleanor had deserted Walker. In retrospect, Plume wished he had been more understanding, more overt in showing his sympathy. This was the point in their sessions when he had stopped being merely a sounding board for his client and become something like Walker's only point of reference.

On tape, the awkward opening of the two men's conversation

spelled out the tension between them. There was another tension too for Plume to contend with, deriving from the mechanical confidence with which the cassette player, as it spooled out its sounds, contradicted the fact of death: for Walker's recorded voice was every bit as alive as it was angry.

Plume spoke first.

"So what would you like to start with?"

"Start with? Start . . .?"

"Or—just sum up? Maybe you should tell me what's happened since last week."

"Since last week? She's started divorce proceedings, got herself a lawyer. But we can still be good friends, she says. I went along with it. I didn't know what else to do. I can't fight her."

"Why not?"

"Because we never fight."

"But there's obviously been a disagreement here."

"Oh has there? Look, let's just get this over with, settle the bill, fill out the insurance form, whatever needs to be done. That's all I came here for. No point carrying on with it. I don't think you're doing me a damn bit of—"

Plume cringed to hear himself rake back over the same tired ground:

"But there must have been a warning sign, a clue you misread or couldn't see. Something."

"The warning sign was exactly what I told you: there wasn't any warning sign."

"It makes no sense to me."

"Yeah, well, that makes two of—"

A harsh glitch on the tape announced the start of their next session. Walker's fury had abated only marginally—and his sarcasm was fully intact.

Again, Plume spoke first:

"Any better . . .? I know how hard this is."

"Oh things are fine. Things are just dandy. Except she keeps calling me."

"Calling you?"

"Every day. Sometimes twice a day. At home. At work."

"Why?"

"To tell me she misses me, to tell me she 'needs' me."

"Then she's—regretting her move, opening the way toward a reconciliation."

"Not a chance. Her missing me and her going through with the divorce are two entirely separate—"

"But does she say *why* she's going through with it?"

"To get out of my way."

"Even though she needs you, even though she's feeling—"

"You don't understand. She's going to go ahead with it, no matter what she 'needs' or what I say. It just helps her to make out like she's doing this *for* me instead of *to* me."

"But what's her rationale?"

"It's in the cards. It's in the fucking cards. I tell you, I'd like to burn those cards."

"Maybe—Maybe this is an overreaction. On both your parts. To let your lives be ruled by a party game—"

"You know those cards? You know what they are?

They're not just a game. They're what makes her seem unreachable. They're what makes it feel like someone's stolen her."

"What about—?"

"But no one's stolen her. That's just the way she is. It's all just arbitary. It's all in her mind."

"You have her number? You can call her if you like?"

"Oh sure."

"Where has she moved?"

"Queen Anne—she's got an apartment there."

"Has she told her family? What do they say?"

"She's told her parents, yeah. And her mother called me from Georgia. Her mother thinks she's crazy. But then she always did. Thought she was crazy for marrying me, too. No money."

"How does money come into it?"

"Her mother's idea is: If you have to work to get it, then you can't be said properly to have any. *You'd* meet with her approval, I'm sure. Or do you call this work?"

There was a brittle, contemptuous silence on the tape. And then his own uncertain voice:

"Maybe we need to—change our focus?"

"Ha!"

"I can see what you're doing here. What you're doing is venting your—"

"I know what I'm doing. And I don't need you to tell me."

"Let's—Let's get back to—another question? It may seem a bit—"

Plume pressed STOP to escape his own blundering. He fast-forwarded, hit PLAY, then heard Walker mockingly ask:

> "—running the newspaper how much? Fifty bucks an
> hour? A hundred? There's the deductible, of course.
> Lucky she left me: a legitimate 'emotional trauma.'
> Makes it easier to fill out the paperwork—"

He couldn't bear to listen, sped through the tape for another full minute. When he hit PLAY again all he got was gentle magnetic static waiting to absorb its appointed sounds. But there were no sounds.

He checked his file notes and was reminded that, for the rest of February and into the next month, Walker had failed to show. On March 15, he finally turned up, only to apologize for his behavior during his previous visit and to ask to have his tranquilizer prescription refilled. He hadn't stayed long enough for a session to be recorded.

On the 22nd, he returned to announce that all his problems had been solved. No, Eleanor had not come back to him. The divorce was proceeding at full pace. But he had had a "vision." When Plume asked what sort of vision, Walker said that was his business, and his alone. Again he wanted to end therapy, but was matter-of-fact about it, not accusatory.

One month later—in late April—treatment resumed. Plume found the appropriate tape, put it on, and had to turn up the volume. Both voices seemed to have dimmed as if with age in the interim. Doctor and patient weren't as confident as they had been in their earlier anger and frustration.

Plume remembered the reason for his own loss of confidence: he and Bill had just had news that a close friend of theirs was in the hospital again, this time with pneumocystis pneumonia. Their circle was quite literally closing—being extinguished, shutting down. (Almost two years later, as he listened to the tape,

this same pneumonia-stricken friend was dead and his lover seriously ill. Of all the wild ones Plume had known, only Campbell
had escaped untouched, seemingly refuting the disease's reality,
and how long could that last?)

The reasons for Walker's subdued manner emerged more gradually. He described his "vision." But as Plume's notes indicated,
this vision was nebulous. It was of a woman, but no particular
woman; a familiar figure, yet not quite real; someone distant,
but who listened to his "closest heart."

Walker had met her, or imagined meeting her; he seemed
oddly unable to distinguish between the two. And his voice was
a blend of evasion and stupefaction—monotone in character,
possibly drugged. This "someone," this woman, was "blank" to
begin with, but lately had acquired a characteristic or two. She
kept on changing: "Whatever she's been, she's not that now."

Plume struggled against the chill, the tingling sensation these
words produced—then as now—of his mind having been read,
his own prognosis anticipated. On the tape, he challenged
Walker:

> "I find it odd that she keeps altering her appearance
> like that. Can you go back? Can you describe her for
> me again, the way you first saw her?"
>
> "The way she used to look? But she doesn't look
> that way anymore!"
>
> "Is it just the way she looks? Or is it the way she
> behaves?"
>
> "I don't know . . . I'm not sure. *Something's*
> changed. Maybe her makeup. Or her hairdo. Some-
> thing for sure. And it's like she's more relaxed in her
> job, instead of always nervous about it."
>
> "Her job? This is new. Can you tell me what her
> job is? What it involves?"
>
> "No. Not really. It's just a . . . job."

There followed a silence, less tense than wan from an exhaustion of possibilities. Plume, losing himself in the auditory illusion of the tape, scribbled a note to cut down the dosage of the tranquilizer Walker was taking; then came up sharp against the realization that, in this case, any dosage was a moot point.

This "vision" session ended. And the next week, when Plume attempted to pick up where they had left off, Walker was vague and irritable. With no further details on his "vision" forthcoming, their talk turned to more concrete matters:

"So what have you heard from Eleanor? Does she keep calling?"

"All the time lately. Day and night. If the phone rings at three in the morning, it has to be Eleanor."

"Now why would she call you at that hour?"

"Oh . . . to tell me she knows."

"Knows what?"

"Good things are going to happen to me!"

"Ah, well. That's cheering, isn't it?"

"A nutcase . . . I'm beginning to think I spent half my life with nutcase. And she wants to help me choose her successor."

"So you don't think it's her successor you're seeing, then?"

" 'Seeing'?"

"This woman who keeps changing. The one who now seems not as nervous in her job as she once was."

"You mean at the newspaper? Who are you talking about?"

"What we started with—that 'vision' you had."

"I don't remember—"

"I could rewind the tape."

"I tell you I don't remember. Why *should* I remember?"

"I could play it back for you. See . . .? This might be where it's useful to—"

But it wasn't useful. When Plume had played him the recording of the relevant session, Walker irritably dismissed it.

"I was stoned, that was all."

"You were?"

"Yeah, I was stoned when I said that."

"You mean on marijuana."

"Marijuana, the stuff you're giving me . . . whatever."

"So you found some."

"Eleanor did. She brought it over and we smoked it together. And then I came over here . . . was it last week?"

"Yes, it was last week. And did she stay over?"

"No, no, nothing like that—just wanted to get high withsomeone. . . ."

Despite inquiries, Walker revealed nothing more about this renewed drug usage. And he had nothing to say, either, about his first face-to-face meeting with Eleanor in almost three months.

Plume moved on to a recording from July 1990, just before they'd gone from weekly to monthly consultations. It found his client still sleepy-sounding, but with no suggestion of a lapse in memory.

". . . actually have a confession to make. Something I just figured out."

"Yes. . .?"

"It's a little embarrassing."

"About the woman at work?"

"Yeah—her."

"You said you were going to find out more about her?"

"Well I did. I did. And I realized when I went up to her desk: it *is* my mistake. She's a different person entirely. Even the name plaque is different.

"I'm not sure I understand."

"The other one? She left in June, just after the divorce came through. And now this new one . . .?"

"Yes?"

"Well, she's angry at me. I can tell."

"I'm—I'm not surprised."

"But in a nice way. And it looks like she'll give me a chance. She even says she'll go out with me."

"You're saying you—"

"She's angry at me, but she's forgiving too—and I guess I'm a little in love with her. . . ."

The voice was both doubtful and wistful. It trailed off on the tape—as though, like a ghost, it had nowhere definite to go. And then the office clock struck five, the doorbell rang and the tape clicked to a stop.

Plume ejected it, filed it—and stepped off to greet his late client's wife.

part three

whoever you are

"Honey—? Susan? Is that you?"

"It's me."

"It didn't *sound* like you! Is it the flu?"

"It's just me, Mom."

"And you're seeing this doctor when?"

"A little over a week—but not for the flu. He's a shrink. A psychiatrist."

"Oh honey I hope he's a good one, after all you've been through—"

"Mom—"

"With everyone else it's the flu. Even if you had the shots. Your father had the shots, and still—"

"Daddy's sick?"

"He's been sick but he's better now. Of course he wouldn't

admit to being sick. If you want my opinion it's because of this merger."

"I thought that was over with."

"Oh it is! It's final. Only now there's all this restructuring."

"Which means?"

"Your father might lose his job. Or says he might. Have you noticed how everyone thinks they're going to lose their job lately?"

"Well, the economy's not so great."

"That's true. That's certainly true. And what about you? If you're seeing this psychiatrist you must be—"

"I'm doing okay. I try not to think about it. It's just this guy, he's someone Walker used to see, which is why—*ah-hrrem*—which is—"

"Susan?"

"—which is one of the reasons—"

"What was that? It sounded bronchial!"

"I was clearing my throat. I just swallowed some saliva."

"Saliva? Honey, are you eating right? Are you looking after yourself?"

"I don't know—maybe not completely. . . ."

"You ought to take care, you're all worn out."

"No, I'm not. Well maybe I am. But it's from work as much as—"

"Why? What's happening at the paper?"

"It just seems so pointless, it really does, without him there coming up to tease. No one's teasing. Everything's so gloomy. Two other people just died. It's been a bad week."

"Oh yes, I saw. They did those stories. You knew them?"

"No. Or only by sight. They weren't in my department."

"That woman was brave, I thought."

"Mmmn."

"And that young man?—he was brave, too, of course. Terrible."

"Mmmn?"

"AIDS and cancer. AIDS and cancer."

"It'll get better. It's just this week. It has to get better before it can get worse."

"Terrible. . . ."

"So what have *you* been up to lately? What's your latest acquisition?"

"You mean my lady down at the Market?"

"Sure. What's new from her?"

"Well, she showed me these *windmill* salt-and-pepper shakers. I was thinking: maybe for Celia. But then there's Martha to consider—I'm just not sure about her tastes."

"If they seem like Celia, you should give them to her. I'm sure they'd both think it was sweet."

"Or you could have them."

"No, Mom, really. Let Celia have them. And besides I'd feel weird bringing anything new into the house."

"You'll have to get over that."

"I know."

"You'll have to make it *your* house."

"I know, I know."

"You need to get out more!"

"I do get out—to work. But it's still so dark after five, I don't feel like going anywhere. Anyway, Eleanor comes over most nights."

"Is that really such a good idea?"

"It's okay. Sometimes she stays over. I'm not too crazy about sleeping here by myself."

"You could stay with us."

"No, I couldn't. Not for any length of time. Besides, I need to get used to it."

"At least it's not a divorce. At least it's not like Aunt Ginny. She's driving your father crazy. She's so bitter. And she thinks your father can do something for her. An annulment! A divorce isn't good enough for her. She wants it all to be annulled. After twenty years! It's a good thing he's only a corporate lawyer. He can refer her. Three years since Frank left, and she's still all twisted up. So maybe you're lucky in some ways.''

"Lucky?''

"You're right. I should stop talking. I should hang up.''

"No, Mom. That wasn't what I meant. I—''

"I'll call you next weekend if we don't hear from you before then.''

"No, Mom, really—''

"I'll go. I'm going. Say hello to Eleanor.''

"Okay, I will.''

"And take *care* of yourself, you hear?''

"I will, I will. Mom—?''

"Susan?''

"Dad?''

"Your mother just talked to you, did she?''

"Yes, she did.''

"So how are you?''

"Fine, Dad, just fine.''

"That wasn't what she seemed to think.''

"Well, I'm not exactly ecstatic.''

"No. I wasn't thinking that, I wouldn't expect that. It's only been—what? Three months?''

"Almost. But I still have trouble believing it. I mean it feels as if he's still here, or nearby—or as if *something* is nearby. The way you said you felt when Grandmommy died? But it's getting better. Really it is.''

"It was nice seeing you at Christmas—and last week, too.''

"It was nice being there.''

"We—*hrmphh*—We—*kha-a-aghh!*—''

"Dad? Is that the flu? Mom said—''

"No, no. Over it now. Just a frog in my throat. Thing is, we thought you might be coming out here more often, after all of this—*hmmn, hr-r-r-mn!*—business. Only half an hour drive, you know."

"I know, I know. It's just that I'm—I'm not sure what it is. Like I'm having trouble leaving the house or something."

"Or we could come to you."

"Oh no, not yet. Not just yet. If you can wait—"

"Susie?"

"I'm sorry. It's not that I don't want to see you."

"No need to apologize, honey."

"I guess I still just need it to myself for a bit. To get used to it."

"Mom says you're uncomfortable there?"

"Not uncomfortable exactly."

"Well if you're unhappy—"

"Not unhappy. But it all still feels like it's *his* somehow—"

"Can't expect that to change overnight, I guess."

"—inherently his, forever, I mean, and I'm some sort of long-term guest. But that's sort of the way it felt the whole time anyway. . . ."

"Ginny could come out. She might have some redecorating ideas. Get her out of my hair for a while. Be doing me a favor."

"I don't think so, Dad."

"She needs some sort of distraction. And you know that's the one thing she's good at."

"Spending other people's money?"

"Making a place look nice. You've heard about this annulment nonsense?"

"It's wild, Dad. Even for Ginny."

"I've tried explaining. But she won't listen. My own goddamn sister—"

"I could try, if you want. But it's probably hopeless."

"It is. It is. She got a good deal out of Frank. She got the house, the car, reasonable alimony. Not a huge sum, but he was clearly willing to pay to get rid of her. Can't say I blame him. An annulment—sheesh!''

"I know."

"It's a question of honor, she says. She wants never to have been associated with the man. After twenty years. As if you can snap your fingers and change a thing like that. A name change would make more sense to me, but she's worried how it will affect her credit rating. She should take the energy she's putting into all this nonsense and start looking for a job. I'm afraid she'll start hitting us up soon."

"What about your job? Mom says you're worried?"

"It's your mother who's worried. She reads the paper and thinks—I don't know what she thinks. Anyway, I'm not too concerned about it. Yet."

"But you're a little bit concerned?"

"They should know what I'm worth to them, but with these new guys from California coming in . . . with these . . . guys . . .?''

"Dad?"

". . ."

"Dad? You still there?"

"Now—*hrmphh*—Now here's an idea. I was going to ask you—I was going to ask—Now you don't have to feel pressured by this, and I know it's still early, awfully early, but while the chance is there—One of these guys, he's from Los Angeles, moving up here, and he's really a very impressive young fellow, unattached as far as I can tell, maybe still in his twenties, the most competent of the lot—"

"Dad . . .? Thanks, but no. Not yet. I appreciate the thought. But I'm just not ready for it yet."

"And you're sure you don't need help? Money?"

"Really. I'm in good shape."

"All the—er—arrangements. They're working out? Insurance, and so forth?"

"It's going to take a while, but I think it'll be okay. I'm fine for now. And I've got Walker's accountant to help me with the taxes. It's not any of that. It's just the strangeness of it. This feeling of being watched over, sort of spied upon even. Sometimes it's a nice feeling, sometimes it's a little creepy."

"I understand."

"Actually, Eleanor stays here quite a bit, so I'm not *entirely* on my own."

"Eleanor?"

"Walker's other wife. His first wife, I mean."

"Oh right, that's right, your mother was saying. I wasn't going to mention. . . . That's not—*hmmn*—awkward?"

"It's strange. But it's nice, too."

"She coming over this weekend?"

"Tonight. We might rent a video or something."

"Got any plans for this afternoon?"

"Not really but—it's difficult, Dad. Not difficult, but hard to explain. I wake up, and if I don't have to go to work, I'm happy just to stay where I am. Really, Dad."

"You know we're concerned about you."

"I know. But I think I'm all right."

"You're sure?"

"Not entirely. But staying put seems to help. I'm seeing everything from a distance, you know what I mean? If I went somewhere else, I'm not sure—who I'd *be*, exactly. The context is important. I know that sounds stupid."

"You'll call? You'll be sure to call us if you need anything? Anything at all. No matter how silly it seems."

"Yes, Dad."

"We hear from your Aunt Ginny all the time. We certainly wouldn't mind hearing more from you."

"Oh Dad—"

"Anytime at all. Three, four, five o'clock in the morning. We'll be here."

"Really, Dad—"

"We're trusting you. We're trusting your good judgment when it comes to asking for help. None of us has been through something like this."

"You're sweet, Dad, really sweet, both of you. I promise I'll call, and come see you, and you can come over here. Soon. I'll try to snap out of it. It's like it's this dream I'm in, staying in the house all day, on a weekend. It's not all that unpleasant. Really. And Dad—?"

"Hmmn?"

"Tell Mom to give the windmill salt-and-pepper shakers to Celia and Martha. I think they'd appreciate it."

"Will do."

"Bye, Dad."

"Bye, Susie. Take care."

"You too."

"Hi, it's me."

"Celia?"

"Dad says you need to get out of the house. He just called."

"Oh, Celia. Not today. Really. I—"

"He said not to take no for an answer."

"I can't. Eleanor's coming over and—"

"What time's she coming?"

"Somewhere around six."

"Plenty of time. I'll be there in half an hour."

"But Celia—"

"It's sunny. It's nice out. We haven't even really been alone since this whole thing happened. I was thinking Discovery Park."

"Celia—?"

"Quick, before the weather changes. Grab this chance."

"First I'll have to—"

"Later. Get ready. I'm on my way."

The first time she saw them it wasn't in a dream but in a pleasant waking reverie—of a corridor in a railway compartment, dimly lit, moving and swaying. She was with them somehow and seeing what they saw, feeling what they felt for each other.

Now, a week later, here they were again.

They were a young couple. He was tall, bright-eyed, dark-haired, well into his twenties, but with the build and carriage of a teenager—a slightly coarsened teenager. The prominent Adam's apple, the look of sexual surprise . . . there was no real telling when he would thicken to accommodate them. He was still years away from a swagger.

His companion—his wife?—had a Pre-Raphaelite beauty, with pale skin and a halo of red-frizzed hair shot through with the tawny gold of the light surrounding her. And yes she *was* his wife, Susan now deduced, noting the gleam of their wedding bands. She was tiny compared to him. And the place where they walked—not quite ocean and not quite sheltered bay—looked familiar to Susan . . . something about the clarity of the air, the intensity of the sunshine.

If only she could turn her head to *see*.

But her ability to maneuver depended partly on these two. There seemed to be a trick to it, like learning to parallel park. Her range of vision was restricted to what she could glimpse through them: a situation so odd that she felt it imperative to call it to their attention.

With effort she placed her image in the woman's line of sight, and they made eye contact. The woman seemed startled by this. She smiled at Susan uncertainly, with a flicker of pity for her.

But that was all that was needed. Susan withdrew from sight and was able to decipher where they were.

It was San Francisco: that unreal landscape of sandy beach and city sidewalk not far from the Palace of Fine Arts. And the view was inspiring. There was a backdrop of woods which must be the Presidio. Across the water was the rocky pyramid of Angel Island and, closer by, the smaller but more formidable citadel of Alcatraz. To the west, the welded arc of the Golden Gate Bridge spanned the gap between unstable headlands.

The halo-haired woman was lagging behind by a short distance, trying to catch up with her husband, who appeared distracted—as impractical as he was beautiful. No wonder she had fallen for him. And he was carrying something in his hands: the reason for his distraction. His wife, drawing close to him, complained that she felt too tired to continue this walk. Their conversation wasn't audible, but Susan was able to intuit it. She had almost seen what he held, caught the gist of his reply, when she was jarringly interrupted.

"Susan? Hey, Susan! You still with us?"

In front of her, her sister's face swam closely into focus, filled with concern: "You all right? You look pale! You're not going to faint, are you?"

Other people moving along the sandy path took polite notice of these two women in possible trouble; then hurried on, Celia's casual stance assuring them that all was well now.

Celia awaited Susan's explanation, which was slow in coming.

"I was seeing—I don't know what I was seeing."

"Stars, maybe?"

"Not stars—"

"Little birdies?"

Susan was quiet for a moment, then asked: "It looked like I was going to faint? I'm sorry. Maybe I'm not ready. Maybe I should just go back, stay at home, until—"

"No, please, feel free, go ahead, faint! It's coming back, you know. There's this one guy's films where even the men get to faint. I'm so glad it's coming back. It's the sort of statement that had no real equivalent, no viable successor, you know? A blameless opting out: there aren't too many ways of doing that."

"It didn't feel like fainting exactly—"

"Have you ever fainted before?"

"No."

"Then how can you tell?"

"But I didn't fall. I kept on standing."

"You could just be hot. Why don't you take that thing off?"

"Hmmn?"

"Your coat. It may be the first of February, but today's like spring."

"I thought it would be chilly out here. A breeze or something. This makes a good windbreaker."

"You're probably burning up."

"You're right—I am."

The raincoat came off, and in an instant she was able to see with better focus, walk with surer balance.

The sky was peach-yellow and soft azure. The madrona trees—

with their red bark peeling and dark leaves clustered in clumps of green shadow—looped out at precarious angles over the sandy bluff, lending the scene a carnival air with their suggestion of derring-do. Birds drew busy parabolas in the undergrowth. Picnickers spread out their feasts in the unusual sunlight. Kite fliers took advantage of the gently stirring air.

The two sisters walked in silence for a while, then resumed their earlier conversation.

"That's what Dad told me, anyway," Celia said, "—that it's Mom who's having job worries on his behalf."

"That's what he said to me, too."

"So what do you think?" Celia asked.

"I think they're probably both worried. They've *always* worried." This was said with a hint of sober mockery. "They've worried about you for years, and now they're worrying about me. I'm their new excuse. They have no hope for the world in general. Maybe it's even a source of satisfaction to them that Dad's job is in danger? Or maybe it's something to distract them from making too much fuss over me."

Celia had the sturdier build, the greater stamina of the two sisters. She was resistant to, and subtly energized by, regular low dosages of pessimistic outlook. Her persistent quest for an all-fulfilling romance was the result of an optimism and dissatisfaction so contradictorily entwined that they made her company as tiring as it was invigorating, and she was trying now, with mixed success, to rein herself in. She said that there was always hope; that Mom and Dad were simply too comfortably situated to know about it. They looked out from their coziness—at derelicts panhandling downtown, at news reports about imminent food shortages in the former Soviet Union—and understood that, if thrown into the fray, they would never make it: "But, then, what chance is there they'll be thrown into the fray—any fray?"

She was about to go on, but stopped herself. She wanted to give Susan an opportunity to lead the conversation. And Susan, sensing this offer, took it gratefully; steered their talk toward the subject of her "widowhood." The word still sounded ridiculous, almost taboo. There was something about it that she hadn't been able to pin down yet; a crucial aspect of it that she wanted to articulate.

"I think Mom's more depressed about it than I am," she hazarded. "There's just too much action in it for me to feel depressed yet. I'm still being buffeted. I'm numb, but full of adrenaline. And I cry, but I'm crying at the stupidest things. Like I was eating some crackers the other day—Triscuits, which I hardly ever eat, it was Walker who ate them—and I started thinking how he must have been the one who opened the package, because it was old. I was going to throw them out before we left on our trip, but never got around to it. They were stale, there were just a few left. But I was so glad I hadn't thrown them out!"

She calmly wept as she continued in an analytical voice: "It's like I'm not feeling what I'm crying, I'm only taking some of the pressure off. Does that make any sense? I think Mom wanted things to be complete for me—and I keep being amazed that for a short time they were! Whenever I can forget about what happened, it's as if they still *are* complete. They're complete in my head. It's just that reality fails to take notice."

"I can imagine."

"Just now—" she hesitated mentioning this, "—back on the path, I was there again—"

"Where?"

"Not with Walker, but with this young couple—"

"Sweetheart, it's not as if you're middle-aged."

"—on this beach in San Francisco. I recognized it. And I recognized *them*. I'd seen them before. On the train. Not on our trip, but in that sort of waking dream I had . . . the one I was telling you about?"

As Celia slowed her walking pace, Susan grew aware that any statement she made would be reported back to her parents.

Resentment of this welled up in her. She tried, without success, to keep the note of paranoia out of her voice.

"Everyone's concerned about me, aren't they? Everyone's wanting to warn me about things. Mom and Dad thought it was a mistake, me marrying so quickly. And now they probably think the whole thing is a disaster—"

"They don't say that," Celia advised her. "They don't even hint at it."

"—but it wasn't a mistake. It was the best thing I ever did. I'm glad we went for it. We needed every bit of time we had. And we never even argued."

"Not ever? You didn't fight with him about just some stupid thing?"

"Not really, no. We didn't."

As she said this she realized it was less a defense of her marriage than a way of keeping something from Celia's scrutiny. She didn't want any light sardonic comments—her sister's specialty—being made. That wasn't, to her mind, a way of lifting a person's spirits. But Celia made one anyway.

"Well in that case," she joked, "you're doing better than Martha and me"—and instantly regretted it.

Susan, however, didn't react to this; was resigned to living in a limbo where tenses were uncertain and Celia's "doing" made as much sense as "did."

They came to a spot which drew Sunday strollers and bicyclists from all over the city: the park's outer bluff, a hundred or more feet above the water, a lofty perching place from which to view a spacious diorama of Sound and landscape. Mount Rainier—suspended like a hologram above a discoloring haze of smog—dominated the view to the south. It might have been a mass hallucination, its glacial gleams and ripples of ice resisting all connection to the planet below.

Further west, the Sound spread out in a miles-wide multiform highway, paved and rolled in matted metals, the low winter sun searing a reflective strip down the length of it—a light that winked and wavered, giving the whole sight, even the sharp serrated edges of the Olympics on the water's far shore, a spectral serenity.

This was a ritual. The small crowd at this vantage point would be drawn into the view's hush—and then would murmur a suggestion to leave, as Celia did now, making way for new spectators.

They headed back toward the car, Susan dawdling slightly, reluctant to follow.

"You should come see me and Martha," Celia said. "We could have you over to dinner sometime. We could go back now if you like. I'll cook something up."

"Or we could go up to Walker's. You could call Martha."

Celia stopped short—and Susan collided with her. They were back on the path where she had had her "fainting spell."

"Maybe Mom does have a point," Celia said curtly.

"About what?"

"Maybe this isn't the way to get over it."

"What's not?"

"It was bad enough to be so much his when he was alive. I hardly saw you! For a whole year, you were out there, hidden away—"

"It was what I wanted. Somehow I knew. It was what we both wanted."

"—but to stay so much his after he's gone—"

"That's changing. Slowly but surely."

"I don't see it."

"It's not a thing you can 'see' exactly."

"Isn't it?"

"I can feel it from inside. It seems like nothing's changing. And then I'll notice it's slightly better. At least the ground's not giving way anymore."

She said this as much to convince herself as persuade her sister. And in fact most of her lingering doubts as to its truth were gone, even if the ground did give way a little as she uttered it. But she now had a new doubt in mind—to do with this San Francisco beach and its drifting, dreamy couple, caught in sharp sunlight.

Celia was dubious.

"I guess I can't imagine it. I wish I could. Or no, I don't—I guess I really don't. . . ." She sighed. "It's impossible, isn't it?"

"Pretty much—yes."

"If I say something stupid, just slap me, okay?"

Susan brought the palm of her hand tenderly to her sister's cheek:"Like this?"

Celia feinted impact: "Yeah, that's it."

They went on to discuss Aunt Ginny. Celia recounted a recent visit she and Martha had made where Ginny—"plastered out of her mind"—had warned them never to trust a man, never to place their hope in a husband.

"I don't think she's cottoned on to us yet," Celia lamented.

Susan, smiling, consoled her: "And I suspect she never will. . . ."

It was only with the third "reverie" that she noticed what the young man was carrying—and realized she had known it all along.

This was on Sunday of the following weekend, the day before her appointment with Plume. Acting upon the advice of Celia and her parents to "get out and do something, break up your routine," she had made a brunch date with a woman from work. She didn't tell Eleanor about these plans. The idea was to open up some unfamiliar territory in her life, with no past connections encumbering it. A new friendship, a fresh start, might be a chance at a new normality.

She had met Terry in the newspaper cafeteria when they shared a table during the lunch-hour rush. Terry had the angst-filled humor of someone from a Woody Allen film and Susan kept

having to remind herself that this was a real person, not a character actress, she was chatting with. Their conversation, friendly
but smart-alecky, felt more like lines from a script for a sitcom
pilot that would never get produced: the timing was all wrong.

Still, she felt the acquaintance worth pursuing, if only because
Terry was exactly the kind of exotic whom Susan would have
been unlikely to befriend a few months earlier. Terry was new
to the paper and had moved to Seattle from New York after
leaving her husband for reasons she preferred to hint at rather
than disclose. She worked in the accounting department, talked
mostly about herself and, from what Susan could tell, rarely read
the newspaper. It seemed a safe bet that she knew nothing about
Walker. As a precaution, however, Susan gave only her maiden
name when they exchanged phone numbers. This was an experiment.

They chose West Seattle as their spot because Terry hadn't
been there before. On Alki they found a pleasant breakfast place
with a view up the Sound. All went well until they decided to
take a stroll along the seawall. The tide was low, the meager
beach exposed, and when Terry suggested a walk on the pebbly
sand, Susan gladly joined her. The weather had broken—was
now all squalls and sunbreaks—and as they stepped down to
the water, a soaring fissure in the clouds made for a change of
focus, a manic brightening of color. Then, with the sun going in
again, the beach turned into a shaded path while the broad
searoads that led to the Strait of Juan de Fuca became masked
in fanciful rock formations, flower-decked walkways, jungle
fronds. . . .

Susan looked to her side—and there they were: husband and
wife.

She was walking parallel with them, although they weren't
aware of her yet. Wherever this was, the climate was dry, despite
the luxuriant foliage. Branches spread overhead in a lacy umbrella. Thatched huts nearby appeared ageless, constructed along

ancient lines, but in good condition, and were part of an open-
air café where patrons quietly lingered over their beverages. No
automobiles were in sight (there wouldn't have been room for
any), but a surflike roar of traffic and commerce, children's cries
and megaphoned announcements, was emanating from all
around.

There was a change in atmospheric pressure, and Susan knew
at once that the young woman had recognized her—or, if not
"recognized," then sensed her presence. Husband and wife were
keeping to the dimmer side of the café where thatch-roofed umbrellas spread out to offer shade. The woman's awareness of
Susan was strangely reluctant, as though she felt she would have
only herself to blame for what she might see. Her husband
seemed oblivious to this; was looking at his watch. When he
glanced back up, his question fluttered and spread like a banner
across the smells and light and warm temperature of the whole
scene:

DO WE HAVE TIME FOR COFFEE?

They went into slow motion. Jungle vines and sounds of water-
falls began to wheel above the couple and pull them in closer
to Susan. They waved for a waiter—a strapping blond teenager
dressed in festive colors who took their order, then disappeared.
The young woman was letting her husband know that she hadn't
slept well last night. Her husband muttered a sympathetic reply.
The waiter returned with their drinks, and then amplified luau
music started up. On a stage area in the midst of the chiming
water, four young Polynesian women appeared and began to do
a grass-skirt dance. The husband investigated something in his
lap. This was somehow a warning to Susan. When he lifted the
object of his attention above the table rim and aimed it in her
direction, she had only a moment to duck to the right in order
to evade his lens-range. She barely made it. And the violence of

her movement splintered the moment, landing her back on the beach at Alki . . . where she almost had to laugh.

The mind plays tricks. But what purpose could it have in offering a logic so tidy? If she hadn't been caught off-guard by what her brain conjured up, she would have taken herself to task for her lack of imagination.

But it was creepy, too, to have "seen"—all during her cross-country trip with Walker—a woman who halfheartedly evaded a camera's lens; and then, back in Seattle, to half-consciously *become* a version of that woman by indulging in one teleprojectory daydream after another. What would Walker have said to this? Here was pattern to spare—pattern that had nothing to do with coincidence. Still, there was something unnerving in the way these "reveries" came unbidden, the way they gripped her in their embrace even while letting her pinpoint their meaning. And there was something panic-making too in the way that she, while fleeing her dream-man's camera, slammed into her brunch companion, almost knocking her down on the dirty sand.

The elements of her real surroundings rapidly reconstituted themselves. Sight, sound and sensation slipped their way back into plausibility. Her feet were wet. While absently studying the Winslow ferry making its way from the city to Bainbridge Island, she hadn't noticed the sizable wake that a freighter closer by had stirred up.

Terry was spluttering: "Oh my god, I'll get salt on these shoes! Salt water! It ruins them!"

Susan stared down at her companion's footwear in bewilderment. Beneath their patent leather, two enormous shoes curling up at the toe began to come into focus. Lifting her eyes, she saw they belonged to a seven-foot-tall rabbit of recent screen fame. He was ogling the South Seas dancers and winking at the crowd, while the camera-man's wife sat grim-faced, grudgingly amused, a little disgusted. . . .

"—six hundred dollars! That's right—six hundred dollars! So

I ask him, 'Was it *good* for you? Did you finally manage to get off?' And then I ask him where the hell he thinks he's going to get six hundred dollars."

"I'm sorry—what?"

"And the bastard thinks he's going to get it from me! Thinks I'm going to go into my savings, and bail him out. Like it was the first time. He's promising me he won't do it again, he really promises. Like if it worked on me once, it'll work on me twice. So I tell him, 'Promises don't mean a thing—you've seen to that.' And that's when I called my cousin who's a lawyer and he says the first thing to do is switch my savings to another bank and don't tell Ritchie, don't give him a clue. I mean, this is just after I put them in this joint account because I think things are going better? Like I want to show him some trust or something?"

"I'm sorry—He got the shoes for you? They were that expensive?"

"You're kidding."

"I must have missed—"

"First you tackle me like we're playing football. Now you're telling me you're not listening to a word I'm saying?"

"I'm sorry—"

"It was phone sex! It's got nothing to do with the shoes! It was one of those goddamn 976 numbers. The whole time I'm at work, he's at home jerking off to this business when he's supposed to be looking for a job. And you know what he tells me? 'Sex is all over the place these days—why get it from just one person?' That's what he says. 'It's in the air around us.' That's his theory. I can't believe I'm telling you all this and you're just drifting off. It's that boring? If you think it's that boring, then why did you—"

"I don't think it's boring. Really, I don't."

"I don't get you people out here. At first it seems like you're just standoffish, dreamy. Okay. But this! This is rude."

"There's a reason."

"They told me. They said, 'It's not just Californians they don't like—' "

"It's my fault. I've made a mistake. I've used poor judgment."

"In asking me out? 'Poor judgment'?"

"No, no. But there's something I should have told you."

"Oh yeah? What's that?"

"It's my husband—"

"You got a husband?"

"I—Well I had—"

"Either you got one or you don't."

There was no getting around it.

"I did. But he died. In November."

Terry's drop-jawed reaction made it difficult to continue. It would have been tempting to laugh if it hadn't been necessary to launch an immediate mop-up operation. She mustered all the sincerity she could and insisted: "It's okay, really it is. It's all right. I was just hoping that if I went out with someone who didn't know him, who'd never met him, someone completely unconnected, maybe I could forget, or just take a break—"

"Oh jeez."

"I shouldn't have. I really shouldn't have sprung this on you."

"It's just that no one told me—"

"I was trying not to—"

"You should've said. You really should've said something."

"We'll try it again. When I'm more . . . up to it? I'm sorry. It's like I'm still having trouble concentrating on anything around me. I didn't mean to drag you into this."

"You don't have to apologize. Honest you don't. I should be the one—"

Susan violently shook her head in disagreement.

"You want to leave?" Terry asked. "You think you should go home?"

"Yes."

But she had tears in her eyes.

"You can see to drive okay?"
"Oh, yes."

Eleanor was standing at the window in stern expectation. Susan attempted a smile at her as she turned into the driveway.

The crunching gravel quieted into red brick. The nodding fir trees, with their dark interiors and silvery outskirts, shed their facades and revealed the cast-iron balconies of Bourbon Street in their Disneyland incarnation, pristine and clear.

The beautiful pair in their summer array started to cross.

Susan honked at them. The woman eyed her warily, her husband looked merely impatient. They let her pass by. As she pulled up to the house, she caught another glimpse of them in the rearview mirror.

There they were, after standing so long in line, about to embark on the devastating ride.

"Did you see them?" she asked as she burst through the door. "They were right there! Did you get a look?"

"At what?" Eleanor asked.

The safety bar went down. The roller coaster jolted into action. It sailed past a copper mine, a waterfall, a Wild West saloon.

That was when the alarms went off. That was when the ever-diminishing part of her that still felt like herself advised the increasingly alien whole to steer a cautious course, to follow up, to get to the bottom of this before it got to the bottom of her.

The phone call from Dr. Plume, a week and a half ago, had been her serendipitous invitation. His office was her opportunity—an opportunity she had looked upon dubiously at first . . . before seizing it, placing her hope in it, clasping it to her. It surprised her that Walker had resorted to someone like this. But it also relieved her that, as his last bequest to her, he had put this particular "someone" in her path.

After the episode with Terry at Alki, she wanted to be told if she was sane or crazy. If crazy, she wanted advice on which drug to take. This sense of *becoming* a hallucination was confusing to her. True, there was a shameful kind of power in it. But with it came a danger of disintegrating, of being rattled to pieces from seeing too much. These vapors of mind—how else to define them?—were a freedom or illusion impossible to live with on a day-to-day basis, entrapping her in too much awareness. They were too vivid, like colors whose brightest component is pain.

A drug might dull or erase them. Less creditably, an extensive verbal analysis might reveal them for what they were.

She doubted that an appointment with Plume would offer all the answers. But it seemed her only alternative now—her one chance, perhaps, to regain control of herself, recover Walker, and anchor whatever it was within her that was so perilously drifting.

Knee-level lanterns lit a brick-lined path where the air grew damper with the murmur of water. A sign saying OFFICE led past rustling bamboo toward a basement-level entrance that was lit from within.

She thought of turning back: *This is morbid. This is ridiculous.*

Then her finger pressed the buzzer and a door swung open, exhaling its warmth toward her. "Doctor" and "patient" (there was reassuring artifice in assuming these roles) effected mutual introductions before moving inside.

No need to take this seriously. I can always walk out.

She noted her surroundings: wood-panel veneer and acoustic-tile ceiling; an office of intimate dimensions, yet far from cozy in appearance. It was too well ordered, too regulated, to be cozy. And its occupant loomed larger than the space at hand; stood six feet tall, was conservatively dressed, had thick white hair and a charcoal-gray mustache.

Susan looked at his forehead as if to read his thoughts there. She mused uneasily on his vast store of secrets. More than anything, he resembled a sad, intelligent dog. As he had on the phone, he offered his condolences. He hoped she was over her first shock, and suggested that she call on him for whatever "support" he could offer.

She immediately took him up on this, asking how long Walker had been a patient of his—and when, exactly.

He smiled defensively: "You understand there's a limit to what I can tell you?"

She didn't back down: "I do. But still, as his wife—"

"He came to me in late 1989."

"Why?"

"He had worries about his marriage."

"His marriage to Eleanor—?"

"Yes, he was afraid she was going to leave him."

"And did she?"

"But you know she did!"

He seemed as surprised by her revelation of ignorance as she was by his of unadorned fact.

She lost her bearings for a moment. She hadn't expected him to be so forthcoming. Also, the information was more straightforward than any she had ever had from Walker or Eleanor. She pushed forward, perhaps more aggressively than necessary.

"That," she conceded, "was never clear to me. I had the impression it was more mutual."

"No, no. Your husband was quite unambiguous about it."

"What did he tell you? Was there a reason—"

"I'm sorry, you've caught me a little off-guard. I'm really not sure what's appropriate under these circumstances. I assumed he would have—"

"But I know Eleanor. I could ask her."

"Then why don't you?"

She glanced at him sharply.

"Have you given it a try?" he asked.

There was a degree of sympathy in his voice—and a note of curiosity too. She wasn't sure how far to be drawn by either of them.

"Wouldn't that be the shortest route?" he went on. "After all, she's bound to know more than I do."

Her air of confrontation, of near-boastfulness—*I know Eleanor, I could ask her*—hollowed out and crumbled. She grew subdued. She called to mind the nature of her friendship with her late husband's ex-wife and then was forced to admit, "It's just that it's difficult talking to her sometimes . . . about things like that, anyway."

"She sets up barriers?"

"In a way. Yes."

"And that's why you're here."

"Well, no, not exactly."

"But it's one of the reasons?"

This was too sudden. This was going too fast. She wondered how they had gotten in so deep, so quickly. She peered at him to see. But the room was annoyingly dim, like a dream lit with insufficient wattage.

She replied uncomfortably: "Well, yes, it's one of them. . . ."

He let her answer hang incomplete—an admission, almost, of defeat; a confession of how helpless she was before this ex-wife. And then he became more brisk and businesslike: "But you're here about yourself as well."

His reluctance to linger on the topic of Eleanor, after zeroing in on it so quickly, aggravated Susan. It was a profession she didn't understand: making your living by prying into other people's business. Still, there were things she wanted to know and information she could learn, presumably, only from him.

"It's me I'm here about," she confirmed, "and Walker, too. I'm not sure it's possible to figure out Eleanor."

"Why not?"

"She seems to operate by rules unlike anyone else's."

Plume's tone was almost professorial: "And you're not sure what those rules are exactly?"

"No, I guess not."

He regarded her more closely, as if about to offer useful advice or demystify something for her.

"You may be seeing complications where there are none," he said. "My understanding was that Eleanor doesn't follow any rules at all."

Susan felt this wasn't entirely accurate. Eleanor, it seemed to her, *did* behave according to certain rules: disarming rules, discomforting rules, rules that took down the barriers in people. But there was something too formal in the manner of her late husband's therapist for her to feel she could talk him into an appreciation of this.

She told him, instead, that he might be right.

He smiled, only half convinced, sensing her reservations, and proceeded with his questions.

He wanted "first things first," and dug for details of her family history. He asked about her relationship with her parents, her friendship with her sister, the circumstances of her husband's arrival in her life, the sequence of her love affairs before her marriage.

His voice was both invasive and inviting. At every point, he seemed to know too much, as if he had diagnosed her "type" already and was proceeding accordingly; or as though he'd been through this whole business before—which she supposed he had with Walker, though not from this particular angle.

They established the various facts of her background, before he asked about the dream she had mentioned on the phone: "How much do you remember of it? Anything significant?"

She told him it was more than one dream, now, and that

actually, more than anything else, it was the real reason she'd wanted to see him.

"You're having trouble sleeping?

"No, no, I'm sleeping okay."

"But there've been nightmares?"

"Not 'nightmares' exactly."

"What, then?"

"More like . . . recurring instances—?"

She didn't know how else to put it.

"—and I'm not asleep when I have them," she added.

"Instances of—"

"It's difficult to say. All I know is I'm seeing things."

"What sorts of things?"

"Like memories—altered memories of places I've been."

"Can you give me more detail?"

She complied, starting off with her first dim apprehension of her couple in their shuddering train compartment, then going on to describe their beach walk in San Francisco. Finally, there were her glimpses of them in Disneyland, surrounded by fake jungle scenery, strolling along a bright synthetic Bourbon Street, about to board a spine-jolting ride: "It was so vivid! I even slammed on the brakes. Eleanor was there, too, and didn't see a thing. But the woman glared at me."

"This 'dream' woman?"

"Yes."

"So she was aware of you."

"Oh, yes. It's a two-way thing. Except sometimes I have to work to get her attention."

"What if you didn't? Wouldn't she just go away?"

"It—It doesn't seem to work like that."

"Why not?"

"I'm not sure. It's a little creepy. It's like I want to see her, in spite of myself."

"Is it always apparent where these visions are taking place?"

"In San Francisco and Disneyland it was. On the train it wasn't. I mean, it's definitely Amtrak, but I couldn't tell where."

"These places in the dreams—you saw them all for the first time last fall?"

"That's what doesn't make sense!"

"What doesn't?"

"Why can't I see them the way I remember them? The places are the same but the light isn't, and the weather isn't. Or maybe not the weather. Maybe the angle I'm seeing them from? Somehow they're different. And why is it this couple taking my place, *our* place, if it's all coming out of memory? It was horrible. In Chicago, it was horrible—"

"What was?"

She wanted to cage the words, hold them back; then found herself releasing them in a mumbled rush: "—where Walker—where Walker had his—"

"Pardon me?"

She spoke up: "Where he died. Where he had his heart attack."

Her eyes fell to her lap as if she were ashamed of the pain the words involved. Then she looked back up at him earnestly.

"If it was Walker," she said, "it would make sense. I'd love to see him. But these two—this couple. I have no idea who they are."

"Could they have caught your eye during your trip, maybe only for a moment, and you've halfway forgotten them?"

"I guess so. But I have a good memory for faces."

"Out of all the faces you must have seen, how many could you possibly recall? Consciously, at any rate? Wouldn't it be natural to forget them, with all that happened afterward?"

"It doesn't feel like that. I've had dreams, just regular dreams about people I don't recognize at first, then remember who they are when I wake up. Or where it's supposed to be my mother, and the person looks nothing like her, and then turns out to have been someone else entirely—my old school-bus driver, a third-grade teacher, people from years ago—by the time the dream's over. But this is different."

"What's different about it? Just that you're awake when it happens?"

"Isn't that enough?"

Apparently it wasn't. He sat there, almost gnomelike—an awkwardly long-limbed gnome—waiting for more.

"Somehow I don't think they're coming out of memory," she said at last. "Somehow they're . . . stranger than that. Like something being imposed on me."

"What are your feelings when you see this couple? Not your feelings afterward, but your feelings within the situation—what *you're* doing there, what *they're* doing there."

She offered the possibilities reluctantly, or with a semblance of reluctance, not wanting him to know how much thought she had given this already: "It's like they're—real people? And I'm being 'sent out' to them, or getting these reports on them, whether I want them or not? It just seems to happen. Nothing logical triggers it off."

"Are you sure?"

"Well, no, I'm *not* sure."

"Is there something else? Maybe something that happened on your trip?"

She grew a little defensive: "Well, maybe. Something connected. . . . I don't know, it's just so crazy."

"What is?"

She wasn't able to read him accurately enough to tell whether he was reading *her* accurately. Even if he was asking the right questions, there was a possibility that his questions were simply a performance, a routine run-through of a standard interview format instead of a genuine ad lib reaction to the answers she was giving him. There seemed no way of discovering which it was. He was like an actor who is playing "sincere." Nothing he said seemed genuine—though he did, for the most part, seem considerate and capable. And he was tactful, too, as if he'd given her an unspoken promise that he wouldn't laugh at her, whatever she said. Any private doubts he had about the information she offered he would keep to himself.

She supposed this unreadability—this appearance of being meticulously unaligned—was a sign of his professionalism, or perhaps a hazard of it. Whichever it was, it left her feeling peculiarly protective of him: to the point where she was willing, after contemplating the consequences, to answer him. He needed something from her, it seemed, and this was all she had to give him.

"Well, there was this woman—"

"This woman in your couple."

"No, no, on our train trip. There was this woman—always by herself, alone—who I kept seeing and Walker didn't see."

"Where did you see her?"

"Everywhere."

"What city, I mean."

"Every city—San Francisco, New Orleans, Boston—"

Plume waited for more.

"Even in Los Angeles," she resumed. "It was weird. She wasn't there, exactly—but she was on television. I mean it wasn't her. It was a gypsy, in Yugoslavia, a refugee. But it was a version of her. Or an echo of her."

"And your husband *didn't* see her?"

"I had the feeling he was humoring me about her."

"You told him about her?"

"I tried to."

"And again you were awake when you saw this?"

"Oh yes."

"Was there any reason why you would see her and your husband wouldn't?"

"Well, he was always busy with his camera, changing film, things like that—"

"Every time she appeared?"

"No, not really. That's the thing, you see—"

"And you think she may have something to do with your dream-couple?"

"Well, maybe. Except the experiences are so different."

"How so?"

"When I saw her, I would just see her. I mean, everything else didn't go away the way it does with this couple. She'd just be in the crowd, hard to catch sight of, maybe, but definitely there. Well, sometimes I didn't *want* to catch sight of her—"

"Why not?"

"She was—a little scary, I guess. In Boston she was right in front of me. And in Chicago—in Chicago I almost touched her. It was just before Walker collapsed. But that was when she looked scariest of all—like she was too much in focus."

"And have you seen her since Walker—since your husband died?"

She took note of this: how, for the first time, he used Walker's name—casually, easily—instead of saying "your husband"; and then, as if in fear of being too presumptuous, withdrew his use of it.

She answered, "No. No, I haven't."

"What about these dreams of your couple? When did they start?"

She considered this: "Maybe a month ago? But it's like I've had hints leading up to them."

"And are they scary, these two?"

"No, they're not. Not at all. When I see them, I feel . . . I almost feel warmly toward them. But it's like I'm a little bit scary to them."

"Do you—Do you have any interest in the occult?"

The question startled her: "No, not really."

"But you're familiar with what some people call an out-of-the-body experience?"

"You mean where you leave your body in bed and your spirit just does—whatever it wants? Flies across the Sound? Does a loop around Winslow?"

Plume smiled: "It doesn't have to be that elaborate. It could just be a sense of stepping outside yourself or being at one remove from a situation you're in: a sports event, a dinner party, a walk with friends."

"I thought that was normal."

"Oh, it is, it is. Now what are the differences between that feeling and your feeling with this couple?"

"With this couple it's . . . more radical? More complete? I have no control of it. I don't even feel it coming on. And I lose sight of where I really am."

"What about with the woman on your train trip?"

"That was more normal, like I said—like spotting someone in a crowd, only you lose sight of them. With this new thing, this couple, it's different, really different. Almost like I'm being taken somewhere."

"You say your sister thought you were going to faint?"

"I don't know—I didn't feel sick or anything. I didn't feel dizzy."

She looked down at her lap. There was something pent up in her. Plume gave her time to bring it out. He glanced at his watch under his desk: ten minutes left.

"I know what the problem is," she finally said.

"What is it?"

"It's that I'm still depressed and it's making me imagine things."

"Well if so, you're doing it somewhat more graphically—" He could feel his phrasing grow unintentionally flippant, and started over again: "I mean, most people would call it more than 'imagination,' what you're describing. You think it's more than that, don't you?"

"Maybe—Maybe I'm just indulging myself. Maybe if I try, they'll go away. Maybe if I put my mind to it, I can will them off somewhere, away from me, out of sight—"

"But you haven't been able to so far."

Again she looked into her lap.

"Or have you?" he pressed her.

She said nothing.

"You don't even know when to be on your guard against them."

She glanced his way and nodded miserably, but didn't speak.

Gently he encouraged her, "Go on. There's something else . . .?"

Clearly there was—for even in her misery, she looked busily impatient, as though dealing with a problem of logistics as much as one of bruised and baffled feeling.

He waited for her to address this.

And it was an outburst, a protest she wanted to make: "What I really don't get is: why are they going to all the places Walker and I went?"

"But it's not all the places. You've only mentioned San Francisco and Los Angeles. And the train, that first time."

"But what if they keep going? What if New Orleans is next? And if it's all just memory, why is it teasing like this?—the place but not the person. It should be more straightforward. If it's Walker trying to tell me something, he should at least let me get a glimpse of him. He should at least come all the way through—talk to me—let me *feel*—"

She stopped in midsentence, could not continue. Her words had clogged on "feel." Her voice was stuck. And then a cluster of sobs punched the air around her. They lodged in her chest, her throat—only gradually abating, and leaving in their place a residual ache and tension.

He gave her time to recover—a minute, maybe two—before suggesting in a low voice, "Perhaps you've had enough for today."

She turned away, couldn't answer him; was powerful with her loss.

He tried, as delicately as he could, to defuse that power: "There's a lot to discuss. We may have taken on too much at once. What would you say to a weekly appointment?"

She turned back quickly toward him: "It's like I'm crazy, isn't it? It's like I'm a crazy person. You think so, don't you?"

"I don't think you're crazy—I don't think you're crazy at all. But that's not the main thing," he counseled her. "If *you're* thinking that you're crazy—well, then you're probably not being fair to yourself. Especially after what you've been through."

She made no reply to this, stared at the floor.

"I think I could do you some good—help you sort it out."

He could not get her to meet his eyes.

"And maybe it helps that I knew your husband," he added.

Again there was no reply.

He ventured, "I think you should know that I liked Walker, very much. I was *fond* of Walker—" Where had she heard that before? "—and I like to think I helped him: with Eleanor, I mean. So maybe I can help you too, more than another therapist could— *because* I knew him. It's a little unorthodox, but I'm willing to give it a shot if you are."

With this freer use of Walker's name, he seemed to be referring to something she did not understand.

"How often did you see Walker?" she asked, as if this would clarify a certain matter.

His voice was as balanced as a diplomat's: "Once a week until late last summer. And then once a month. Sometimes not even that."

She took this information in and turned it over.

He gave her time to reflect on it, then implored her once more: "I think we should keep on going, don't you? Let's give it a try."

There was the beginning of a response, and a delay of response. He experienced a ticklish sensation while waiting for her to make up her mind—then assumed a look of level satisfaction when she asked, with only a hint of misgiving in her voice, if she could make another appointment for the same time next week.

Their session closed his evening.

After she had gone, he went upstairs to find Bill absent and the message light blinking on the answering machine. There were a few words from Bill, saying he was at a movie with a friend and would be home around eleven—and then an odder message, like something that had found its way accidentally across the phone lines to this extension. It was full of static and distortion, full of whispers and white noise.

From its depths, a voice spiraled out: "—just see, see if you can catch him, catch him in 'Catch a Can.' His mother was in 'Catch a Can,' so maybe he'll be—or she'll be. She always liked me. . . ." The voice was shredded, raw, like the parody of something. "—keep trying. Maybe they'll *both* be—"

This was interrupted by a voice that was clearer, calmer, chiding and sensible, coming closer and closer: "No you don't. Put the phone down. Who is it now? Who are you calling? Put it down. Hang up. There's a good boy—"

Plume listened to this message again in puzzlement, then erased it, shrugging it off. He poured himself a drink and had just begun to relax when the meaning of it hit him: "Catch a Can" . . . Ketchikan . . . Alaska . . . *Campbell*.

He hadn't heard from him for months.

He tried his number but got no answer. This wasn't unusual. Campbell was out most nights, and of course there was no machine. He always said he didn't hold with them: "Come on, sweetheart, why would I need one? If I'm here, I'm here—and if I'm not, I'm not. . . ."

Well he wasn't.

Traffic was heavy, and the lines at the supermarket longer than usual. By the time she pulled into the driveway, the shadows of fir trees—under skies pressing low—made it feel close to midnight.

At least the house was lit. Each window spoke its own shape; was glowing from within. From bedtime till morning she left a nightlight on in her room to keep her safe. And every day before she left for work, she turned on the living-room lights and the light on the porch so when she came home she would have somewhere bright to take refuge. It wasted electricity, but in this gloom-season it was the only way she could make herself enter the house.

Sometimes she forgot to leave them on and, confronted with the place's dark outline, she would end up on her sister's or Eleanor's doorstep, getting one or the other of them to come back

home with her and see her in. Eleanor would stay overnight.
Celia never did.

It wasn't a matter of asking. It was a matter of allowing whatever
happened to happen. Eleanor always stepped forward, volunteer-
ing, whereas Celia stayed back—and consoled. Susan felt too
proud to ask her sister for anything closer. Frozen as she was,
she could only accept unsolicited offers, never ask for offers to
be made—and that meant choosing Eleanor.

In the kitchen, she switched on more lights. Slender birches
outside the dining-nook windows did a leafless, spooky dance
as if to shake off the glare that reached them through plate glass.

She set the groceries down on the table and went to fetch the
mail: mostly bills, except for a thick envelope with a cover note
taped to the front of it. This note was so formal that at first she
had no idea who it was from:

Jan. 30, 1992

Dear Susan,

Please forgive my not writing or telephoning up to
now, but it's taken close to three months to progress
from a feeling of desperation to one of being simply
dispirited. I didn't want to saddle you with my despair,
since your own must be considerable. But can you
handle some lingering depression?

Winter is being its usual icy self, so I'm staying
indoors a good deal of the time. Being semi-
housebound has prompted housecleaning, and
housekeeping has turned up mementos that might be
better left untouched. Somehow I seem to be in possession of a whole archive. . . .

Susan dropped the note, opened the stuffed envelope and saw it
contained dozens of smaller envelopes, all addressed in Walker's
handwriting.

Choosing a letter at random, she began to read—urgently, hungrily, hopefully.

Aug. 25, 1990

Dear kid,

Yeah, you're right—I guess that makes me the swinging divorcé, racking up the wives like nobody's business.

Seriously, though, it's just Fate with a capital "F" and I can't control it. Everything seems settled or unchangeable for twenty years, then suddenly the changes all happen at once. But it's not capricious or on the rebound, as you suggest. It's the real thing. Even Eleanor's happy for me, so I don't see why you can't be.

It surprises me you feel so strongly about this. I really was hoping you'd come to the wedding. Can't help thinking your sense of loyalty is a little misplaced. After all, it was Eleanor who left me. Susan is quiet—not the ongoing melodrama that Eleanor is. She may not be as entertaining, but you'd like her I'm sure.

You asked me for a physical description or a photo of her. Why is this so important? She doesn't photograph well—she seems to evade the camera—and my drawing skills aren't really up to the task. (*Hers* are, but I feel funny asking her to do a self-portrait when you could easily come out here and see her for yourself.)

She's very sweet; teases me; treats me kindly. She doesn't have much more in the way of looks than I have, at least not in the conventional sense, and frankly that's a relief. Walking down the street with her isn't quite the floor show it was with Eleanor. This

will not be an "open relationship." And you don't
need to worry. We've both taken the test (negative—
as is, miracle of miracles, Eleanor). I intend to maintain unswerving marital fidelity. Am maintaining unswerving premarital fidelity now.

I guess I still haven't really described her. She has
sort of mousy hair that hangs straight down, some
might say "limp." A pale, rounded face, but with a
bit of square in the jaw. She's not fat, but softly shaped.
Medium height. Just average. (You can see why this
is difficult.) Her teeth are slightly crooked—

A cold spoon stirred in her brain, in a place where nothing had
been cold before. This was followed by a prickling sensation all
over her body, a blossoming numbness up and down her spine.
The feeling was of shock—as physical as a slap in the face; the
emotional equivalent of being sideswiped.

Who was this person? Why was he describing her as if she
were a horse?

Somehow the ineptness of his portrait of her undermined any
note of affection his words might contain. Where was love in
this? He made the marriage sound like a compromise—rational,
just possible to live with. Was it chivalry or condescension on
his part to have lied to her about his sister's reasons for not
attending the wedding? And why was it a "miracle" that Eleanor
had not contracted HIV? Did Mary know what she was sending
to Susan, or had she only looked at the envelopes, seen her
brother's handwriting, and decided his widow should have these?

Susan held the letter away from her, her hand trembling. She
wanted to get rid of it. She tucked it in its envelope and returned
it to its packet—from which, unable to resist, she selected another.

Again it was written to Mary, but dated from much longer ago.

                                                    March 6, 1971

Hey Poppins!

    Yeah, I know that annoys the hell out of you.

    This is just a note to say I got your birthday card
and the Jacqueline Susann, and I promise to get to it
as soon as I reach some kind of break in my school-
work. Right now we're having to read *Ulysses*, which
is really good too. You want to try it? My guess is they
won't have a copy in Havre, but I can send you mine
after I'm done with it: another one you'll have to hide
from Mom.

    I asked around but no one seems to know the scien-
tific names for those pills. All we've got here is marijuana. Eleanor says long-distance truck drivers take
them to keep awake, so it's not just actresses. But we
don't know any long-distance truck drivers. And even
if we did, they probably wouldn't be versed in Latin.
Sorry.

    Yes, you picked up the hint. Your brother now
swings both ways. We had a pretty wild night with
this guy from the French department (pun intended).
How about you? Are there happenings in Havre? Do
they have dope in the high school yet? Do you like
boys or do you like girls? Either one's fine with me—
I've decided to take the egalitarian approach. More
opportunities that way. But I like myself most of all,
and no one in books ever seems to talk about that. Is
there anything about it in *Valley of the Dolls* . . .?

Who *was* this person? Eleanor's creature?—or had he all the time
been Mary's?

    She did a quick calibration of birth and calendar dates, then
wondered what kind of college sophomore would write a letter
like this to a fourteen-year-old. Or had Mary always been the

way she was now?—straight, stiff, unshockable; intent upon gathering all the facts, no matter how sordid or unpleasant they were.

But Mary did not always gather facts. Sometimes she refused them.

She had refused to accept the fact of Walker's second marriage.

Susan turned back to Mary's cover letter. In the final paragraphs, she announced she was coming out West in two weeks' time for her parents' fiftieth anniversary. And she had given herself a weekend layover in Seattle instead of going via Minneapolis: "—because I'm hoping to see you. If this is inconvenient, let me know. I have a friend in Ballard I can stay with. But it's you I want to talk to, be with."

There was something rather touching about this.

There was also something mildly portentous.

Instructions followed on the best time to reach her. Ten p.m. to midnight, Boston time, was her "window of availability," as she put it. A consultation of flight dates, postal cancellations and the wall calendar revealed that she was talking about arriving at the end of the week.

In haste, Susan picked up the phone, dialed the number. And immediately she was back on more familiar ground. All the verbs and articles that Mary had mysteriously employed in her letter were still absent from her speech: "Glad you called. Knew you'd take time to think about it."

Susan assured her there was no need to think about it, but the package had been slow to reach her. Maybe there weren't enough stamps on it? Trying to keep any note of accusation out of her voice, she asked about the enclosed letters. Had Mary read them before forwarding them?

"Couldn't bear to. Why I sent them to you. Iffy business: reliving the past. Figured that since you *hadn't* lived it—"

"But they're all addressed to you."

"You had so little of him—" Mary's voice went thinner on the line, "—thought maybe you'd be wanting more . . .?"

. . .

Yes, more.

After ending her conversation with her sister-in-law, she called Eleanor, apologized for the last-minute notice and asked if she would come over and spend the night. Her pride, as was lately the case in her dealings with Eleanor, had slipped another notch.

"You need someone there with you?"

"I need someone," she conceded.

"What happened?"

"Oh . . . just the crevasse opening a little wider than usual, is all."

"Not to worry. Help is on the way."

By the time she arrived twenty minutes later Susan had downed half a bottle of wine from Walker's cellar. She had also taken a thick red Magic Marker and written MARY across the third weekend in February below a scenic wintertime shot of a snow-drenched Mount Rainier.

When Eleanor came in, Susan walked straight into her embrace and was clasped there, held there—but this was not enough. Her lips wanted skin; her nose wanted smells. She buried her face in Eleanor's neck, nuzzled and nestled in Eleanor's hair—but these were not enough.

She found Eleanor's mouth, grazed Eleanor's lips, and tasted there a lipstick flavor.

Taste was not enough.

She *pressed* herself into Eleanor.

Pressure was not enough.

Who was she? What did she want?

She didn't have any idea. She didn't know what to do.

Eleanor responded to this as efficiently as if she were a nurse hired for the purpose. They retreated to the bedroom . . . and except for their more prominent nipples, Eleanor's breasts were as slender as Walker's—as soft and as pouted. Her eyes were calm, too. And her nectar was as salty.

There was glory in this. There was order.

Sex—a tonguing and buckling, a finger-wet stroking—led straight past Walker, into sleep and into a dream where Eleanor was saying: "Unusual, the skeleton that can dance like that. . . ."

And there he was.

Not Walker but this other one. Right in the room with her.

Without his clothes he was thinner than ever: ill-fleshed, adolescent-looking. A certain toneless laxness in the way his skin fit his bones showed he might be in his thirties rather than his twenties.

He surged up towards her. His wife was nowhere to be seen. The bed where they lay was too small for him. His neck was at odd angles to the headboard. There was a milky warmth behind his ears, a tipsy smell in the depth of his armpits. She tasted him as you would a delectable fountain. Pleasure sprang from his thighs as he threw a loop towards ecstasy. And did he have a slight oniony flavor?

Yes, he did.

The movement of his loins kept spiraling toward her, opening her out to a place in the sea where the sky falls through. She could feel his shuddering. She could sense his finish—then saw he was terrified of her, turning his head to avoid her eyes. Reluctantly she let him go.

A bowl of fog, newly sprung from its basin, occluded his shape, whorled its radiance across him. . . .

She came to, sat up.

A creature was perched at the foot of her bed: the nightlight illumined it, the darkness expanded it. Its pelt was tawny and its ears were long. There was something not right about its squatting position, however. It had too many legs. Or perhaps its limbs were longer than necessary?

It took her a moment to think to look for Eleanor. It took another moment for her to see this *was* Eleanor—sitting in semishadow, her shape resembling an Afghan hound's. Her long blond tresses were its droopy canine ears. Her soft, supple skin was as smooth as smooth fur. She sat like a hybrid invention. She appeared to be a dog-woman—faithful, but to what? She called to mind those photographs where an animal's face and a human model's are airbrushed into one. She stared at Susan from a place where skin breathed and heat slid into random couplings. She looked pert and amicable and ready for more love to eat. The bedroom blinds gave her adequate stripes. Her eyes were a jungle predator's.

Susan asked: "What are you looking at?"

"You."

"Why are you looking at me?"

"I was wondering."

"What were you wondering?"

"I was wondering who you are."

"And what was the answer?"

No answer came.

She fell back asleep. She looked for the dream, but couldn't find it. Her man-boy had vanished.

When she woke once more, she found a note—"Had to get to work early"—left by Eleanor, who appeared to have leafed through Walker's letters to Mary, now scattered with the other mail on the kitchen table. Toward one in particular, she had drawn an arrow and scribbled, "Interesting!"

Susan crumpled the note, gathered the letters back into their envelope, then readied herself for a day at the office, trying not to think of what had happened and at the same time unable to deny how her body now hummed with the glow of Eleanor's attentions, the dream's caresses.

Even her coworkers commented on this: her skin flushed and roseate, her eyes not so nervous.

"Whatever it was," one of them said half enviously, "you look like you could use another night of it. . . ."

The ascent to SeaTac Airport, four days later, was like the scaling of a low plateau of freeway exits and entrances encroached upon by wisps of mist from nearby Puget Sound: mists that fitfully dissolved as they attained their runway. A more general haze to the west obscured the Olympics, while here on Highway 99 the bright but scratchy air would soon chill into fog.

In the meantime Mount Rainier loomed to the south like a vision emerging through TV snow. In the late-afternoon sunlight, its settled layers of milky turquoise were each shot through with filaments of gold.

Susan checked the arrivals board to see when Mary's flight was due: four o'clock. It was right on time.

Past airline counters was a shallow arena of marble floors, silver escalators and goods behind glass. Along its length, tourists exchanged currency, consumed fast food or purchased Tlingit carvings and Space Needle souvenirs. Gossamer string arrangements of ancient *Billboard* hits served as an anodyne to passengers' preflight nerves. But in Susan's case "Light My Fire," diluted to a seraphic lilt, induced only quiet sadness. Walker had been a fan of the original. He would have made some comment. Who would make that comment now?

Mary's plane was docking at a terminal reached by an underground rail shuttle. Susan, following signs, rode an escalator down to basement level and stood by three pneumatic doors which looked as if they gained admittance to a trio of elevators, but which, when they opened, revealed a train carriage filled with orange and yellow plastic seating. She moved with the crowd into this starkly lit capsule. The route was a circuit of only three stops, completed in a matter of minutes.

At the first stop, the doors parted like stage curtains and revealed Dr. Plume with a companion similar to him in height and build, but younger in appearance. They were escorting an old man, who steadied himself with a cane as he moved with them cautiously toward a departure gate. Plume and his friend fussed worriedly over this departee—who, she now noticed, wasn't old after all, but Walker's age or even her own. It was just that the life barely burned in him. A look of sweet befuddlement played over his haggard features. His smile was ghostly.

The doors closed and announcements were made in alternating Japanese and English, offering safety precautions and deboarding information. A bevy of Buddhist monks—some Asian, some white—appeared across the aisle from her, their saffron robes erupting like flames from the seats' plastic orange.

The train jerked. She grabbed the aluminum pole in front of her. Her contact with it was humid and dissolving. It drew her eye to a cast-iron fence that barred all riffraff from the formal gardens of an eighteenth-century square. To the north of the square was a French cathedral. Between square and cathedral

was a vast and patiolike brick expanse. And in the midst of this
expanse a purple-skinned jazz band was playing. The sound they
made was of jubilant, brass-warm darkness. The piano was at an
angle, like a stranded boat on a beach. The singer was a swastika
of prowling arms and legs, gawky in her minidress, with bangles
on her wrists. Her voice was all husk and cigarette-rasp, occasionally finagled toward glorious shout. She flourished a hand, then
made a fist as if to grasp the point of the lyric. She pandered and
disdained, squeezed a private joy from her public sound. Her
listeners recorded this with their cameras, but caught nothing.
Her voice had an ache; her man had an ache; their bed had an
ache—a noisy one. And in that bed, that man was a bad taste
longing to be soaked up and to have her do the soaking.

The song ended.

Between numbers, there was banter: "You there, honey—
yeah, you over there. Thank you for your contribution! You sure
you don't need it yourself? Looks serious, don't it folks?"

The crowd laughed.

"Tell you what, you come see me later and I'll rub it down
for you . . . I'll rub it *all* right down. You ain't married, is you?"

Susan could see who the singer was addressing, and what she
was talking about. She could also see his wife rejoining him,
tapping his shoulder, letting him know she was ready to move
on.

And then it was the plastic seats again: no longer occupied by
monks, or jazz bands, or anyone else.

Next stop.

Another crowd came aboard, lugging shoulder bags emblazoned with airline logos. At the far end of the car were Plume
and his pal, but no sign of their ailing friend. How much time
had passed? Surely they wouldn't have left him to board by
himself. He looked too far gone.

She disembarked where everyone else did—and realized she
was back in the main terminal. She searched for a clock: four

forty-five. Panicky now, she reboarded the train, concentrated on seeing it as a train and only a train, and managed, this time, to exit at the right stop. She found Mary sitting primly by the terminal's glass windows. Immediately she launched into apologies for being late, telling flustered lies about a traffic jam, then asking her how her flight had been.

Mary, standing up, grinned at her: "Bumpy. Drinks went flying. But captain stayed calm. Said it was the time of year."

She had with her one carry-on bag and her umbrella.

"That's all you brought with you?"

"This is it."

When they stepped aboard the rail shuttle, Susan, remembering the Boston T, explained, "This is *our* subway: it has three stops."

"Looks a little like New York's."

"It does?"

"The newer trains. Might be the same manufacturer."

The doors closed. An American voice spoke. A Japanese voice spoke. Within a minute they were at the main terminal. The doors slid open and Susan stood up.

But when she stepped out she was walking down Decatur Street, her dream-lover just ahead of her, his wife at his side. She could feel the constriction of the neckbrace he was wearing, sense how it impeded him, keeping him from staring anywhere but straight ahead, while trickles of sweat coursed down his bony back.

His wife was the one who hurried, the one who could more easily look around her. She glanced back toward Jackson Square, as if sensing some danger there—and, eyeing Susan directly, determinedly warned her off.

On the glass-enclosed skybridge from terminal to car park, Mary grabbed Susan's arm just as she was about to collide with a wandering toddler; and Susan, once rescued in this fashion from her New Orleans of jazzy clamor and humid heat, seemed to have no choice but to stick with the here-and-now.

Mary was a bracing breeze, a persuasive astringent tightening the air around her sister-in-law until it fitted reality's shape. Susan still intuited her couple's presence nearby—in the labyrinthine lair of the car park's Level 4; in the silhouettes of drivers alongside her on the freeway. But she also sensed that they could wait; that she would get another chance to convey her message to them, whatever it might be. In the meantime it was enough just to picture them in her rearview mirror or sense their image growing brighter in memory.

Over the next few days Mary took charge. Upon entering Walker's house—full as it was of sharp, glass-enclosed angles— she turned to Susan and announced: "Got to get you out of here. I mean *all* the way out."

From her handbag she extracted a map of Washington purchased especially for this trip. She unfolded and spread it on the kitchen table. Then, with her finger making a vague circumference around the state, she instructed: "Along the coast here. Or in these mountains, maybe. Anywhere you like. Name a place you want to go. Somewhere you've never been before. Doesn't matter where. As long as it's new—and nothing to do with Walker."

Susan scanned the map meekly; took in its maze of islands and waterways, verdant valleys and glacier-topped peaks, before alighting on the town of La Conner, just off Skagit Bay.

Mary met her eyes: "There, eh?"

"It's supposed to be touristy," she apologized, "but maybe this time of year it won't be so bad . . .? It used to be a hippie hangout. I've always been curious about it. My mom loves it— but somehow I've managed to miss all our family trips there."

Mary, approving the choice, commandeered Walker's Honda the following day and did the driving. The sky was overcast—

and the wooded suburbs on either side of I-5 were a gauntlet to be run before certain pressure points could find release.

At the King County line, an eye-ache that had been plaguing Susan for weeks was suddenly alleviated. Near Everett, as the highway arched up into turnoffs and overpasses, the whole of the Snohomish River valley came into view and a tangled feeling in her gut gave way to smooth tickle. To the east, icy mountain-tops were lost in the cloud cover, but blue-green slopes were visible.

At Conway, they turned onto a two-lane road and crossed a humpback bridge into farmland as flat as polders: Fir Island, where floods had been fierce in November and there were signs of damage still. The recent ruin of a humble manmade order—levees, drainage canals, tidy rows of plantings—was like the landscape's echo of her own loss.

La Conner was New Englandy, perched on a ragged piece of geography, less seasoned than its East Coast counterparts, not as storm-battered or as fragrant with bygone ages. But it also wasn't as crowded.

Along one side of its single main street, buildings backed directly onto a harbor. Along the other, a bluff rose with a stairway leading up to a residential district. The two women climbed this and took in views across rooftops, over water. Clouds imposed a limit on what could be seen, as the morning's overcast dissolved into torn sheets of rain.

Back down on the main thoroughfare, a restaurant offered them shelter just as a downpour began.

They ordered their meal. They were in a strange place. Mary was *out* of place. A type of person whom Susan didn't usually see was seated at other tables in this dining room: aging women who were idle. She wondered if any of them was a widow. She also wondered where one went to find clothes like theirs. And what about those hairstyles?

But it somehow felt dangerous to ask them about it. What if their answers dragged her down, made her more like them?

Instead, looking across the harbor to houses and treetops on the other side, she asked aloud, "What do you suppose is over there?"

Mary consulted her map: "Appears to be an Indian reservation."

Hearing this and thinking about it, she saw her life, if only for a moment, as part of a general sad state of human affairs where waves of existence, communal or individual, rose up and were destroyed; flourished—and then, inevitably, withered.

With this thought of withering, Walker's death came at her all over again, unbidden, from every direction, encompassing and overpowering her. She found herself crying—wide-eyed, hollow, not necessarily miserable, but succumbing to her own ongoing sorrow the way one might submit to a change of climate, from arid to dank. Hardly any point in trying to stay dry.

She managed a flimsy smile across the table at Mary and excused herself: "This just keeps happening. I think I'm over the worst of it, getting better, and then—"

"Don't worry. No need."

The words were gentle, unfussy. They made questions seem possible.

"Those letters you sent. You didn't read them again, did you? . . . but you knew what was in them?"

Mary reached across the table, took Susan's hand: "The things he put in writing—more flippant than he was. Maybe self-protective? Not that way face to face. But you know. . . ."

"I'm beginning not to know."

Mary released her grip, tapped the tabletop with her finger.

"No," she said. "Stick to it—what you see in your mind. Absence is as much a shape as presence is."

This struck a chord with Susan. This was what it felt like. But she refrained from saying how the *content* of that shape was changing, growing more alien to her all the time, in a kind of passive intrusion—refusing to disclose itself, but impossible to ignore.

"So the healthy thing," she murmured, "would be to smash that shape . . .?"

Mary's look was disapproving.

"No, no. Learn to live with it."

Her tone implied she had managed to do this herself. But her hands told another story—looked empty, at loose ends. They were lacking something.

It became clear what when she inquired: "You think I can smoke here?"

Susan supposed she could. There was an ashtray at the next table. Passing it to Mary, she changed the topic: "I was wondering—about your research. It's to do with drugs and memory? And emotion, too? Emotion and memory?"

With cigarette in hand and a wreath of fumes obscuring her face, Mary looked more complete. But she was cautious in her answer: "Emotion and memory? How do you mean?"

"Certain emotions—they're almost physical! They pull you in as if they're nothing to do with you. As if they're conquering you. Like—"

She had her doubts about mentioning the word, but saw no way around it.

"Like bereavement," she continued. "This dizziness at the loss. It really is physical. Whenever I think of him, it seems to trigger certain chemicals in the brain, almost like a drug rush—which leads to perceptual differences, aberrations. That's what it feels like anyway—"

"Yes, I see."

"So is that what you're researching?"

"Afraid not. Emphasis is more specific. Emotion and memory,

drugs and emotion: bigger subjects. Too big for my purposes. Important, I agree. Just not my field."

"Can a person reshape a memory—"

"Reshape?"

"—in accordance with an emotional need?"

Mary granted this with a cigarette flourish: "Imagine so. Probably often the case."

"—or *construct* a memory from scratch?"

Here Mary was hesitant: "More unusual. But certainly not unheard of."

"Can a person, an ordinary person, invent a whole existence for two people? Their faces, say; their manners, too. The way a novelist might."

"For what reason?"

"They just appear!"

"You're talking about yourself?"

Susan held back from affirming this.

"And you're saying you're ordinary?" Mary prodded.

Susan didn't respond to this either.

A small fishing boat chugged down the length of the harbor, and the two women watched it go by. It gave off vibrations, made the windows of the restaurant buzz and throb in motor-sympathy.

When it had gone, Susan asked: "What about Rwanda? You invented it?"

"No, no. It's a real place."

"I know that. But you hadn't been there?"

"Studied it," Mary said, as if correcting her.

"Why?"

Walker's sister, before answering the question, suggested: "Perhaps if we order drinks. Might help."

They tracked down the waitress, selected a bottle from the wine list. Then Mary, her lips and nostrils issuing curlicues of smoke, made a statement.

"An excuse," she said, "for when we met. You and I. Walker knew, of course. But was chivalrous. Didn't expose me, did he?" she said proudly.

"Actually, he did," Susan informed her, "later, on the train."

"But not while you were still there. He wouldn't have," she said confidently. "Too kind. Too considerate."

Susan didn't point out that even on the train he had not disclosed Mary's real reasons for boycotting their wedding. It was Mary's own surrendering of his letters which did that.

"Anyway, Rwanda: an experiment," she continued. "That was the main point. Randomly choose a spot in the world. Concentrate on it. Get to know it thoroughly, but strictly at second hand. Never go near it. Now: what seeps into you? Must be something. Can't be nothing. Say 'Rwanda' and here come images, here come memories. Whose?"

She flicked her ash into the ashtray and continued: "Most people wouldn't choose Rwanda, of course. Most go for some sort of Afterlife." She waved her cigarette at this, her smoke trail suggesting clouds filled with seraphim. "Convince themselves of it! Then act as if it's a condition of their existence. Been doing it for centuries. Guide themselves by it. I almost convinced myself!—'Not a bad place: Rwanda. Actually kind of pleasant.' People *choose* their truths."

Susan took a moment to absorb this notion of "truth" as a chosen option: arbitrary at first, then rooted into place.

It was strange to suppose that things which felt permanent and unshakable must once have felt new and unprecedented. Did people just fill themselves with whatever came to hand and then cling to it, consciously or unconsciously? Was that what she was doing now with her consultation of Plume and her evenings with Eleanor—trying to choose a new and less vulnerable version of herself?

She had no interest in abstracts—in afterlives or deities, credos or superstitions—but she did have an interest in the edge of personality: the possibility of controlling yourself, expanding yourself, doing damage to yourself. If control, expansion and damage were all options of behavior, then what, exactly, *was* personality? A hidden essence? A raw material waiting to be alchemized or excavated? A mass of impulses, only a fraction of which were acted upon?

Or maybe it was just an ongoing "interaction"—that word again!—of mind with mind, nothing more: a shifting back and forth, a chance-filled colloquy of behavioral broadcast and reception.

She didn't know, she wasn't able to say—although she felt the question had urgent bearing on her widowhood.

Suppose personality existed only in the space *between* mind and mind, in a maze of perceptions continually subject to change. And every time you met someone new, a new facet of it emerged—just as every time a person disappeared, a portion of it vanished: *She's a different person since she got married/her mother died/her son started school/her husband left her.*

She had read that in cities bombed flat, surviving citizens suffered a sense of amputation, grew listless and numb: *Truncated personality.*

She had also heard that, in the longest-lived of a group of friends, the lack of familiar response from long-familiar companions had damaging results apart from simple sorrow: *I'm not my old self, no.*

And of course with the loss of a spouse, it could hardly be expected that no transformation would take place, or that the components of personality shouldn't rearrange themselves, change accent and configuration. Was that why she had this ongoing sense of fooling people?—deceiving them into thinking she was still close to them, when really she was not?

She felt almost like a double agent, but with no idea of what the two sides were, let alone which side she was on. Was there viciousness in keeping these thoughts to herself? But there wasn't anyone, really, she could offer them to. With Walker gone, no one knew her. And she sensed that in Walker's absence something was coming loose within her, growing more reckless than before, moving closer to the surface all the time and not conforming at all to her idea of her better self.

There was a contradiction in her that needed resolution. Walker, she liked to think, had seen this contradiction and encouraged it in her, as the place she should go next, before his efforts were abruptly cut short. But she needed to reach him to verify this—she longed for the opportunity.

Maybe this couple in her waking "dreams" were leading her toward him. Maybe the woman from their train trip had been trying to do the same—while he was still alive, while it still mattered.

She thought these thoughts and then knew how weak she was, being so ready to settle for an easy answer, for spirits leading the way, giving guided tours of the truth and making it safely schematic.

She let no one know which way her thoughts were tending. She would have preferred not to think, or be thought about, at all. But people kept inquiring into her: Celia, her parents, Eleanor, Plume. Even Mary, now.

The situation was clear enough. She was being haunted by Walker—whatever form the haunting might take—and the thing to do was to face the questions this raised. If she was going to choose a truth, as Mary playfully had, she wanted to know precisely what her options were.

The wine helped ease the anxiety these ruminations induced in her, so she downed some more of it, gathered courage and asked: "What about ghosts, then . . .?"

"Ghosts?"

"You know—poltergeists, phantoms, specters, spooks. . . ."

Her tone was flippant, and she wasn't sure what she was after. But she felt all her bases ought to be covered.

Mary, catching sight of their meals approaching, extinguished her cigarette and hazarded an answer.

"Wishful memory? Or maybe guilty memory?" She gave examples: "Aunt Dora banging the silver around because she's no longer on hand to polish it and her niece doesn't bother to. Cousin Jimmy calling to say it was you he loved after all, when all he did before he died was cheat on you!"

"And what about ex-wives . . .?"

"What about them?"

Mary was suddenly less hypothetical, more alert.

Susan began, "It's just that Eleanor—"

The waitress placed two steaming plates before them and asked if they needed anything else.

Mary said, "Not right now thank you," and turned straight back to Susan: "Eleanor's been bothering you?"

The alacrity of the accusation signaled a switching of allegiance from first wife to second that struck Susan as exaggerated, inappropriate.

"No, no, Eleanor's been—"

"Helpful" would have sounded condescending. "Indispensable" was melodramatic. "With me all the way" made it seem as though she and Eleanor were on a sports team together.

"—there when I needed her," she finished weakly.

All the attendant complications—her bedding down with Eleanor, her dream of her neckbrace man before he was in his neckbrace—felt too charged a topic to introduce into the conversation. She didn't know how Mary would take them. She wasn't sure how she felt about them herself.

"She's been as good to me as my family," she added, wanting to do Eleanor justice.

Mary stayed tight-lipped at this, her disapproval unmistakable. Walker's ex-wife, it appeared, was off limits.

They returned to Mary's research.

"Edgar Allan has grandchildren?" Susan asked. "How many?"

"Over twenty—and all turning out to be great swimmers . . . !"

After coffee, they headed back for Seattle, Mary smoking every mile of the way while craning her head forward to catch the views. The monotone sky had broken up. Some sun was slicing through. Rainbows sprang from meadows green as Astroturf. From a confusion of squalls, Mount Baker rose too: a huge and pallid triangle above raggedy forest ridges.

"Thought he was being persnickety," Mary remarked after long silence, "but maybe he wasn't."

"Walker? About what?" Susan asked.

"In the restaurant," she explained, "the day we went to Cape Ann. Saying the landscape was dull. Disagreed, then. But in comparison with this—"

She gestured out toward Mount Baker, being eclipsed within a turbulent raft of clouds—as a scrim of rain from closer by spattered the windshield, and scattered sun made the fresh drops glisten.

"The weather," Mary continued. "Being able to see it. For miles and miles. In Boston, not so many vantage points. Maybe Walker was right."

The thought of him, and Mary's belated acceptance of his opinion, induced a quiet mood between them. Tires on the highway made a whir and a hiss, stretching each moment out. It would have taken effort to speak above the racket.

Past the Edmonds exit where the road surface grew drier and quieter, their mood seemed to lighten and Susan teasingly inquired: "So was there really a Cousin Jimmy?"

"Oh sure. Several of them."

"And an Aunt Dora too?"

"Absolutely."

Susan had to smile at this. Without Walker on hand to confirm or deny it, what way was there of knowing for sure?

None, she decided. Mary was Mary. And once you knew her, you accepted her for what she was. You even valued her for it.

They spent their remaining time together reminiscing about Walker and exchanging confidences, opening up to an unprecedented degree.

Still, there were things Susan kept to herself: like this sense of being haunted by a wandering dream-couple—or, just as unnerving, this feeling of haunting *them* as well. . . .

With Plume she was franker: "He's in a neckbrace now!"

"Who?"

"The guy in the dream, or—whatever it is. And they *are* in New Orleans! They're following our route almost exactly. Only he's hurt himself. Maybe on that ride in Disneyland, that Wild West thing. . . ."

Plume gave her a quizzical look.

"Or it might have been in bed," she continued. "The mattress was too short or something—threw his back out."

He gently challenged her: "Isn't this . . . a little elaborate? A little too logical for a dream?"

"I know, I know. It's like I see it, then I report it. But that's the way it feels! That's what's happening."

"Maybe if we start at the beginning. If you could tell me what else has happened this week so we can put this in some context, see what might have provoked it—"

"Well, Walker's sister came out for a visit. I guess that's one thing."

"Really? You didn't mention it last time. Something you were keeping back?"

"I didn't even know about it last time. It was kind of unexpected."

"I see. And how did it go? Any tension?"

"It went fine. I met her at the airport. That was where I saw him, in his neckbrace. I saw you there, too."

"You saw me?"

Plume looked uncomfortable at being brought into the picture.

"You were with a friend. Actually, two friends. One of them looked in pretty bad shape . . . ?"

His voice grew formal: "Yes, he asked us to help him."

She said more quietly, "He looked like he might be in the final stages."

"Yes, he is."

"We had someone at work—"

"I heard about it."

They kept a silence, both curt and sympathetic, for a moment— as if mourning, these days, had to be done efficiently if everyone was to get a fair share.

Then Plume pushed his inquiry forward, coaxed Susan into revelations about the packet of letters forwarded by Mary. This might be only their second visit together, but as he jotted the information down, he felt it represented a breakthrough of sorts. She was telling him everything that came to mind, it seemed. She wasn't holding back—which meant the question he needed to address now was of how much *he* should tell *her*, and when.

He continued: "So could your anxiety over the letters have triggered what you saw at the airport, do you suppose?"

"Oh no, I don't think so. I think they're two separate things."

"But the letters upset you."

"Well, sure they did!"

"In what way?"

"I guess because I only want to think of him the way I remember him. And it just never occurred to me that he'd keep on changing like this, almost turn into a different person."

"Just as your neckbrace victim seems to be changing—"

"It's not the same! With these letters, it's—it's like Walker got right into me when he was alive, you know? And now he can't get out. So he keeps twisting and turning and changing shape to escape. He keeps on being indefinite, unpredictable. Or that's the way it feels in my mind. I'm happy with him just the way he is, I don't *want* to find out anything more. But then I keep discovering this new thing about him and that new thing about him—"

Plume waited for more.

"This other business," she said, "this New Orleans thing—it's different. It's like it's from another dimension or something. It's just totally make-believe in some ways. Except I'm feeling guilty about it."

"How so?"

"Because it's like I'm really bothering them or have some kind of power over them—as if I'm in charge, even though I don't want to be, because I can make her look at me the same way the woman on our train trip made me look at *her*. I don't like it. It makes me nervous. And it makes me think I'm sick. I mean, really sick: in the head."

"There's nothing wrong with your head." His confidence as to this surprised her. "But what we've got to do now is explore these various elements—what you saw on your train trip, what you're seeing now—and find what links them together."

"All right—sure. But how?"

He folded his hands in a gesture of prayer and raised them to his lips. With his steady gaze, white hair and darker mustache, he seemed like some alien species of creature deriving strange nourishment from her, feeding on her benignly in ways she didn't understand.

"Perhaps by gathering any evidence we can," he offered, "and working our way through it."

"You mean the letters?"

"I mean everything: things he wrote, letters he received—"

She took this in but didn't volunteer anything. And with her lack of response, Plume found himself thinking his *own* way back toward images—both auditory and visual—of Walker. Not just memories, but a more general collage where distinctions between recollection and invention became uncertain: a matter, it seemed, of "creative editing."

Would the real Walker Popman please stand up?

Plume sensed that his moment for disclosure had come. He was about to spill the beans, such as they were. But as he did so—in the instant between one word and the next—another kind of image came to mind: a pitiful one of himself as a twig or branch or some feathery piece of debris floating on a powerful stream, a stream that ended in a waterfall. Closer and closer he floated, on currents ever more intricate. He had no control over his destination. He had no navigational skills, though he was gifted with an ability to imagine what having them might be like, as he bobbed and swirled and surged forth, nearer and nearer the brink. He had forfeited his right to control because he was about to lose control, break faith, betray a confidence.

And over he went.

"Your husband—"

"Yes?"

"Your husband spoke of something similar . . . similar to some of the things you've been describing."

"I'm sorry, what?"

This was a voicing of incomprehension, not a question.

Plume explained, "I'm saying your husband mentioned something about 'visions' or a 'vision'—"

She looked at him blankly.

"—although he was vague about it."

"I—I'd rather—"

She mumbled something which he couldn't make out. This was not the response he had anticipated. Her tone was one of collapse. He leaned forward, as if to grasp the end of her sentence, but was unable to reach it.

She raised her voice: "It's just that I'm not sure you should be telling me this. Maybe I'm not *supposed* to know. After all, I didn't know he was seeing you." She heard a martyrish vein emerging in her words and despised it: "What if he wanted to keep these things private?"

"Well he didn't tell me much, believe me. And what he said didn't always make sense. He was very much up and down in mood after Eleanor left."

She didn't exactly flinch; it was more that she contracted—not wanting to listen to this description of Walker. She was as doubtful of hearing it as she was of hearing secret things Walker had said. It was hateful to think of him in this light: subject to mood swing, erratic with sorrow.

"The thing is," Plume went on, "Walker did talk about this 'vision' he had—that was the word he used—right around the time he must first have met you. I thought maybe you were aware of it . . . ?"

There was no response. He couldn't tell whether she was listening to him or not. She had pulled herself so far back, she seemed miles away.

He tried again: "It isn't anything he mentioned to you, then."

She was slow to answer: "No, it wasn't."

"Because, you know, with the power of the mind to suggest,

if he thought he saw something, and then talked to you about it, then *you* might see—"

"No, he didn't. And I'm just really, really unsure we should be—"

"But what did you hope to get from coming here? Wasn't it some kind of information?"

She was looking away from him, absent to such a degree that he wondered if she could be having another of her "episodes." What if—while he sat in his basement office looking at her— she was mysteriously present in another city or some anonymous railroad compartment, looking upon her "dream-couple"?

The thought made him feel he was a stranger to her, utterly removed from her burdens, her concerns.

"Susan? Mrs. Popman?"

He didn't even know what to call her. And she seemed not to know how to answer him.

"Information *was* what you wanted, wasn't it?" he asked again.

When she finally did look back at him, she was blinking away tears and her voice was tight: "I thought it was. But maybe it isn't. Maybe I'm better off not finding out whatever it is—about him, about anything. Maybe I don't really want to know."

"I think you do," he said. "I think it's difficult for you, and you worry it will do you damage. But you do want—" he chose his words carefully, "—a revelation of some kind."

"But if it's a dream, if it's all only a dream—"

"If what's a dream?"

"This couple . . . Walker . . . everything."

"You're saying Walker feels like a dream to you now?"

"I only wanted to know why he was seeing you—why he *kept on* seeing you. After he met me, I mean. And never told me. I thought he was happy."

"I'm sure he was."

"Then why?"

"Well, it's not always just about happiness—therapy, I mean. It can be about curiosity. And in Walker's case I'm sure it was as much the latter as the former."

She voiced her objections to Plume directly: "Telling me things that he never told me himself. That can't be right, can it? And it can't be therapy, either."

"Well, that's true, it isn't exactly therapy. And it's a little more problematic than I'd anticipated: difficult to say where the boundaries are. But it might be something else, I hope. Something that could be useful to you, something that could help get you back on track. All I can say is that I'm interested—I'm concerned about—"

He heard himself digging himself in deeper and deeper—his voice sounding unctuous, his sympathy canned—until the false notes, involuntary though they were and as strenuously as he tried to correct them, gathered critical mass and provoked her.

"But this is all nonsense," she said helplessly.

"Nonsense?"

"It's just some kind of jargon—"

"I don't mean it to be—"

"It's all just pointless. Nothing can be done about the facts."

"And what are the facts?"

"That he's gone, that he's dead. And this is all nonsense."

"Not nonsense, I think—"

But he couldn't express the thought that was needling him: that he was making the same mistake twice; that he had been inept in his dealings with Walker, distracted as he was by his feelings for him, and that now—for different reasons but to an equal degree—he was being thoroughly inept in his handling of Walker's wife, who seemed to be readying herself for escape. Her mind might not know it yet, but her body was rising as if to quit the premises.

"Maybe we should get back to the evidence," he said.

"What evidence?"

"These letters you've mentioned, and anything else—"

"There isn't anything else."

"Drawings? Photographs?"

"The house is full of photographs. We're talking cartons full."

"—scrapbooks, souvenirs. Maybe Eleanor can help out with older items. She'd understand? My impression of her from Walker was that she has no trouble handling the unusual. It's the ordinary that's more of a stumbling block for her."

"All there are," Susan repeated, "are the photographs."

He blinked at her.

She felt she was letting him down; letting herself down.

"You never know," he elaborated. "They might be useful. Jog your memory—"

Her eyes reacted dully to this . . . and then opened wider: "The photographs—"

"Yes?"

"If it's in the photographs—"

"But not just the photographs," he advised her. "Letters as well."

"—the ones we took on vacation—" a note of panic entering her voice, "—I've got to find them!"

"What? Are they lost?"

"Not 'lost' but—We sent them all home, Walker kept mailing them. And everything was so crazy, I never even asked."

"Asked what?"

"Asked Eleanor about them. She took care of the mail, paid the bills when I was out of it. And she must have found the photographs, as well."

"Eleanor has all the photographs?"

"Not all of them. Just the ones from the trip. But if *they're* in them—Or if *she's* in them—I have to get them, show you—"

"If who? Eleanor? Your couple?"

But she didn't elaborate. She was in too much of hurry. Cutting their session short, she left as quickly as possible.

■ ■ ■

He saw two more clients before calling it a night—the first, a good-humored but discouraged middle-aged woman whose heroin-addict son made her life a misery, a problem with no solution that Plume could see, other than escape: sell her house, change her name, get out of town and start over again. But she didn't buy this: "Oh, he'd track me down, down to my last dollar. I'm telling you, drugs make people supernatural. I'm stuck with him for life." An unexpected smile curved along the lower part of her face, though her eyes stayed serious: "Some nights, you know, I think my only hope is that he'll overdose—and then I feel like a murderer, I feel like a monster. But he's the monster."

Plume had been told of the boy's police record—breaking and entering, disturbing the peace, one count of assault . . . it seemed he *was* a monster: in the making, if not yet full-fledged. Really, there was little to discuss. But the mother needed someone to talk to and was surprisingly good company, had a wry eye and lively mind: "When you're that close to someone hopeless, inter-locked with him, then you know exactly how *broken* the situation is: to what depth and in what detail. Outsiders don't get it. They've seen too many sitcoms. They think things can be fixed—but nothing can be fixed. Once that stuff gets hold of you, it doesn't let go, it *becomes* you. Or you become it. . . ."

His second client was a gay man in his early forties who appeared to have no identifiable affliction—"except I keep want-ing to be punished; I feel this deep need to be punished." This was only their second session together, but Plume by the end of it got the distinct feeling that this client didn't want to fight his masochistic appetites but to appease them—and had high hopes of being punished by *him*.

Then it was nine o'clock on a moonless, wind-blown evening, with a tumult in the trees wiping out all city sounds and making it seem like the middle of the night—with everyone sleeping, everyone dreaming.

He went upstairs, where it was dark and quiet. He assumed Bill was not home yet. But as he rounded the corner into the dining room he was met with the flickering dimness and ratcheting din of some antique mechanism.

It took him a while to place it: Campbell's old Super-8 projector.

On the wall were squares of light—liquid and evanescent—and sitting behind the projector, silhouetted by its lamp, with a bottle in hand, was Bill. He was staring at the images—floating on their sequence, it seemed. He had not heard Plume come in.

"What's all this?"

Bill turned to face him in shadow, the outline of a grin—or some other looser look—on his face: "That's what I was going to ask you, sweetie. Is that really your juvenile self?"

Plume turned on the overhead light: "No, it's not."

"Hey, I can't see as well this way."

"You don't need to see."

"Who took these? I mean, where is this? It looks like Woodstock!"

"It's not. Where did you find them?"

"Oh, some charity is collecting everyone's old stuff again, and I already emptied out my closets last month. So I thought I'd have a look through yours—and look what I found!"

"Please, turn it off."

"But why? That *is* you, isn't it? It's almost all you."

"It's not all me."

"I mean—like—right. It's not like you right now—"

Plume looked with concern at the nearly empty bottle.

"I just mean it's fun seeing you, at that age, in those clothes . . . and, hey, that haircut!—"

Plume made a move toward the projector. Bill made a move

to protect it. This left Plume uncertain. He looked toward the squares of light.

Not me, not me—that long-ago self who didn't know how to dress, didn't know how to move, didn't even know how to accept the attentions being lavished upon him . . . and a good thing, too, given the fickleness of their source.

"Hey!" Bill called out, pointing at the wall. "Was that Campbell? Did *you* take that?"

"Please, please, please—I'm asking you. I just really can't stand to look, I just really can't stomach it—"

Bill fumbled toward him: "But you're cute there! You're—"

Plume moved in closer: "I will break it. I will break the projector."

Bill stepped back toward the table and switched it off: "Okay, okay. Shit. Okay." He started to pack up the films, put the projector back in its case.

Plume in firm but unyielding apology said, "Don't worry about that. I'll take care of it."

"Why? What are you going to do with them?"

"I'm going to put them away, that's all."

"Well, you should. You should hang on to them. You might want them someday."

"You're right. I may. Are these all of them?"

"They're all I found. . . ."

The little reels of film looked toylike on their yellow plastic spools. Plume gathered them awkwardly in his hands.

"You're stressed, aren't you?"

"I am not 'stressed.' "

Bill indicated the projector: "Are you stressed because of this?"

"I am—I am not—How was your day?"

Bill would not be put off: "It was boring. You don't want to hear about it." He nodded toward where the film images had been: "This was much more exciting."

"But I could do with a little boredom."

"I couldn't. I'm already bored—" He breathed heavily. "No boredom, thank you, had enough of it. . . ." He said cajolingly, "There was a shot of you, you know, with your shirt off? How old were you then? Eighteen? Nineteen? Skinny as a whippet. So, who took all these? Campbell?"

Plume continued to pack up: "Yes, Campbell took them."

"Well, I can see why he went for you. I would've too. You look so fresh. You look so—I don't know—"

"I look like a fool."

"So? So did everyone! Those clothes? They all looked a little goofy. But no more so than now."

Plume had piled the films neatly back into their box, was clicking the projector case shut.

"Crazy day?" Bill asked.

Plume didn't answer.

"Your hours are getting . . . a little out of hand, you know? You didn't *use* to have eight-o'clock appointments. And last week you had that nine-o'clock one . . . ?"

"That was an emergency."

"What? Hysteria? Isn't that normal? It's the calm ones who worry me. What if they go psycho on you—?"

Again Plume didn't answer.

"Who's the craziest you've ever had? You told me, but I've forgotten. When was the time you felt most in danger?"

"I've told you, no, I can't talk about it this way—"

"So talk about what, then? I'm bored. I've been stuck here all evening. Can't make a sound—"

"You could go out to a movie, or . . . I don't know . . . a show—"

"I've seen all the movies I want to see. And I can't afford any 'shows.' And besides—" he straightened up enough to make it an invitation more than a plea, "—I'd rather do it with you, you know, if you weren't so busy."

This got no comment.

Bill went on, "What about a dinner party, then?" He mentioned some possible guests and a possible date: Saturday. "I looked at your calendar. You don't have anything down that I can see. . . ."

"I may have scheduled a client on Saturday."

"On Saturday? You've started scheduling them on Saturday?"

"There was no other time available. What about a breakfast instead of a dinner party? On Sunday. Maybe earlyish: eight o'clock."

"Sweetheart, you're the only person I know who actually enjoys being awake at that hour, let alone socializing. I can't put two words together—"

"Well, let's think about it," he said, and then excused himself, saying he'd forgotten something downstairs and would be right back. He left the dining room, taking the films and projector with him.

When he came back up, Bill was in a different mood: more melancholy, more wistful. . . .

"You wouldn't want to go to San Francisco, would you?"

"San Francisco? When?"

"Just for the weekend. Fly down. Fly back up."

"Where would we stay?"

This annoyed Bill: "Oh, hell, there's lots of places to stay."

"But would we stay with Donald?"

"Not if you don't want to. But I'd like to see him while he's still in reasonably good shape. He seems to be doing okay right now."

"I don't know. Maybe when there's nicer weather—?"

"You think the weather will be crummy . . . ?"

In typical fashion, they left it at that. Plume went to the kitchen in search of something to snack on. When he came back out, Bill remembered, "By the way, Campbell's dad called—says he hasn't heard from him for a while. He wondered if you had."

"I haven't."

"I didn't think so. That's what I told him. He says he's been getting strange messages lately on his machine. Can't tell if they're from Campbell or not. He's been trying him in Brooklyn, but doesn't get an answer."

"Neither could I the other week."

He didn't mention the telephone message that had prompted him to try.

"Well, if you hear from him," Bill said, "you should give the good doctor a call. . . ."

Back at the house, Susan made her own search first before contacting Eleanor. But the vacation photographs weren't in Walker's basement archive, which was meticuously dated and complete up to the weekend before their train trip, nor were they in the desk drawers in his study, which held all his essential documents: the deed to his house, his passport and health insurance forms, his birth certificate.

She considered the house itself. It gave an impression of clean lines and spatial transparency, but this was deceptive. More and more it struck her as the work of an architect who had gone a little crazy. Closets and cupboards, fitted under slanting roofs, were open to each other, linking various rooms in secret child-sized passageways. She had always been dimly aware of these backdoor connections, but had never fully explored them.

From the guest bedroom upstairs she entered them now, crawling with a flashlight into a cubbyhole where a ton of stuff—magazines and camera equipment, old clothes and camping gear—was heaped. Past this pile was a metal grille which offered a ceiling-to-floor view of the front hallway. She wriggled toward it and looked down, thinking that she might, with effort, hear old conversations between herself and Walker echoing on in another dimension—of time, of space.

A few yards further on, she found herself at the back end of the master bedroom's bureau, which was built directly into the wall. While pointing her flashlight up ahead, she placed her hand on something slippery in the dark beneath her: a long-forgotten Baggie half full of marijuana. There were photographs, too, that had spilled from the back of the bureau's drawers, but they weren't the right ones: ancient arty nudes of a very young Eleanor and an even younger lad whose erection Eleanor pointed to as if in an audiovisual lecture.

She moved on—ran a course of cobwebs, splintery wood and fiberglass insulation, until she found herself emerging from the bathroom's linen closet. She had brought the marijuana with her but left the photographs behind. She didn't want to know.

She did, however, gather the nerve to call Eleanor and ask her the necessary question—to which she got a hedging answer: "I put them aside for you, yes. But shouldn't you wait until more time has passed? Anyway they're safe. I have them."

"Can I come get them?"

"Is that really a good idea?"

"Or could you bring them here?"

"I'm not sure you should be left alone with them."

"You wouldn't be here with me?"

"You're asking me to come over?"

There was a moment's hesitation, followed by: "Yes."

She had the feeling of being used, manipulated—but she didn't care. While waiting, she sat down and perused the evening paper, turning first, as she always did these days, to the weather-and-obituaries page.

Half an hour later Eleanor arrived, package in hand, saying, "Maybe you'd better tell me what's going on."

"Going on?"

"The whole story. From the beginning."

Eleanor's voice was low, but commanding.

Susan asked, "You know about Plume?"

She did.

"Well now *I'm* seeing him."

She gave a brief account of her two visits to him and of her sightings of the dream-couple, omitting only the previous week's erotic dream of the "neckbrace boy" before he was in his neckbrace. She also spoke of Plume's hunger for evidence.

Eleanor demanded these disclosures before she would hand over the photographs. And she drew attention to evidence of another sort that might be of use, if evidence was what they were after—Susan's portfolio; the endless sketches she had made of Walker in the course of their sixteen months together.

Susan moved to get these, to have them on hand as a corollary to the vacation photographs, but Eleanor reached out and stayed her.

"Not yet. You asked me to come, remember?"

"Oh . . . yes."

They drew closer.

Susan had hoped it would be easier the second time around. But without Walker's wine buoying her up, she had trouble relaxing in Eleanor's arms. Breaking out of their embrace, she looked over at the living-room coffee table.

Eleanor's eyes followed hers: "What's that?"

It was the marijuana stash, looking smaller in the living room's brightness than it had by a flashlight's fragile beam in the dark.

Eleanor inquired, "Where did you find it?"

Susan told her, then watched her roll a sizable joint and light it. As they smoked, she marveled at how its toxins surmounted her objections to the closeness that Eleanor was intent upon and the comfort that she herself desired. . . .

There was a sliding of skins together. There was also, it occurred to her, an eerie absence of flashlamp explosions.

Her thoughts grew more abstract, more conical.

Each detail in a photograph, she decided, was a witness against the future; each smile could reveal an incipient betrayal, an unexpected absence. And by the same token, every pose could acquire a layer of helplessness, a retrospective irony, an odd note of bravado in the face of oblivion.

The drug made this make sense as it enveloped her. And it made caresses seem delectably nonspecific.

"Walker . . . ?"

"Not here, hon. I'm afraid it's me you're stuck with."

She peered and saw a shadow that resembled her own; a shadow that, on second glance and with deliberate vagueness, also resembled something else, a more deadly force, another brand of experience altogether.

But she didn't, as she reached for shoulders and breasts and belly, mention this to Eleanor.

Instead she played the game at hand; settled as deeply as she could into kisses, soft lickings, tender fingerings—and brought Walker with her as she came.

With Celia, she held back nothing at all.

"So which do you think is worse: consulting your dead husband's shrink in hope of finding out what made him tick—or smoking some really strong dope and then sleeping with his ex-wife?"

"What?"

"Given that you're hallucinating on a regular basis," Susan continued, "and nothing about your marriage is making much sense anymore."

"Wait a minute, wait a minute. You're sleeping with Eleanor? Or is it the shrink's ex-wife?"

"I'm sleeping with Eleanor," she sighed. "The shrink, I'm pretty sure, is gay."

"And you're really sleeping with her? I mean: having sex?"

Susan nodded nervously.

Celia leaned closer: "What kind of sex?"

"I just—My tongue—I just want my tongue to—Well, to be wherever Walker's has been."

Celia sat back: "That sounds like sex, all right—" she narrowed her eyes, "—but are you even attracted to her?"

"I don't know. It just sort of happened. It almost feels inevitable."

"And it's your first time with a woman?"

Susan shrugged yes.

"This is a regular thing? How many times—"

"Twice so far. But she's coming over again tonight."

"And what about these hallucinations? Have there been more of them?"

Susan told her everything.

Celia's tone was one of pity: "It all seems—well, kind of humiliating to me."

"In what way?"

"Like the whole experience has ground you down to nothing. You were really that wrapped up in him, huh?"

"You mean Walker?"

"Who else?"

"Aren't you, about Martha?"

"Oh, I like her all right. But I still need a break from her now and then. Lots of breaks, actually. And I'm always drawn to other women—which of course is a big no-no, a real betrayal of the sisterly thing . . . feminist solidarity and all that. But I'm hopeless. I'm even worse at the alternative conformity than I was at the mainstream one. I keep wishing they'd look less like Billie Jean King and more like the young Djuna Barnes. You know: jet-black hair, lots of heavy eyeliner. And why can't we rendezvous in opium dens off Jackson Street?"

Susan smiled at this.

They were in a Mexican restaurant in Madison Beach. From their table they could look at passersby on the sidewalks of Madi-

son Street where it broadened from arterial thoroughfare to asphalt piazza, before narrowing to boat-ramp width and
descending straight into Lake Washington. A small park, tiny
beach and series of compact bungalows were nearby, along with
several high-rise apartments whose elderly tenants hoped against
hope for a nonmenacing street scene. An occasional seismic
thump, however, announced that teenagers with their boom
boxes had taken a shine to this place and made it their turf.

The restaurant waiter was a dusky-skinned kid himself, nineteen or twenty maybe, and floating in a smiling dream. There
was reluctance in the way he set their luncheon plates down, as
if he needed plates' warmth in his hands and food's aroma in
his nostrils to be sure that this job and these surroundings weren't
the product of his own imagination.

Celia, the bolder of the two, asked where he was from and he
told her Guatemala. When she asked how long he had been
here, he said two months, then explained in halting English all
the advantages of living in Seattle: how nice the people were,
how great the opportunities, how striking the success that was
his already. He had his own apartment, right on Madison, and
could take the bus.

She asked him what he missed most about his country.

He said, "My mother and sisters. But I bring them here soon,
I hope."

They ordered a dessert to split, had coffee, left a large tip, then
went for a walk along the waterfront. Again the weather belied
the time of year. It was sunny, in the upper fifties, and two hardy,
bikini-clad souls were doing some mid-February sunbathing. Celia's eyes dwelled on them, then roamed the rest of the beach
in hope of finding other similar treats.

Susan, in the meantime, was absorbing sights that only she
could see; took her sister's arm and let herself be steered by it.
They walked from one end of the park to the other—a stroll of
no more than ten minutes. A chilling cloud appeared overhead,

and they headed back. The sunbathers, in the interim, had called it quits, prompting Celia to comment wistfully:

"Too bad—they're gone."

"Who?"

"The two in their swimsuits. You didn't notice?"

"No, I didn't."

"Now that, to me, is a sign as far as this Eleanor thing goes. A sign that you're having experiences that don't properly belong to you."

Susan vaguely agreed: "I was having another."

Celia looked at her sharply: "Another what?"

"Like when we went to Discovery Park. I was here—and then I was . . . somewhere else?" Rapid doubt played on her face. "How long has it been?"

"How long has what been?"

"We started into the park—and now we're back here. How long?"

"On our walk, you mean?"

"Yes."

"Five, ten minutes?"

"It felt longer than that."

"You had another . . . episode?"

"Yes, another one."

"Should you sit down, do you think?"

"I'm fine, I'm fine."

"But you were with them? That couple, again?"

"Yes. It was them."

"In . . . any specific place?"

"It—It looked pretty much like Boston, I guess."

Celia frowned: "You're sure you shouldn't sit down?"

"Let's sit in the car."

They passed the restaurant. The Guatemalan waiter waved at them, and they waved back. Then, from Susan's front seat, they looked through her dirty windshield at an impeccably tidy city street lined with brick and stucco houses, trim laurel hedges, early flowering cherries and freshly blossoming daffodils, all lit by intermittent puffballs of sunlight.

"No wonder you're hallucinating," Celia joked. "These bird droppings—they could serve as a kind of Rorschach test: make you see what you want to see. When did you have this washed last?"

"Not since I got back. Walker always used to take it in."

"Three whole months?"

Susan nodded: "A little more than that now."

"I could come with you if you like. Car washes can be fun, you know."

"They can?"

"If you're with the right person. . . ."

Celia's voice mimicked seduction—then grew more serious as they discussed her sister's phantom couple in greater detail.

Susan went from being in a daze to being panicky.

"I'm losing it. I really am. I keep hoping it's getting better, that it's going away—and then it comes back again. It just gets worse."

Celia approached the matter more as a mystery to be solved: "What if it's something you want to tell yourself but can't? I mean, these two don't exist, right? They're no one you ever saw. It's all just in your head?"

"But the places exist."

"That might not mean much. You could just be using them as a background, an excuse to invent something like what happened to you. And maybe the reason is: you're trying to change it."

"Change what?"

"The outcome. Give yourself a second chance."

"A second chance?"

"Sure."

Susan considered this, then rephrased it: "So I'm only seeing

what I want to see, even though I have no conscious desire to
see it, because I want to change the past?"

She looked at the windshield's chaos of bird droppings, embarrassed to admit, even to herself, that this was the first time she
had noticed them.

"Well, it's a possibility," Celia said, less sure of herself now.

"In that case, Chicago is coming up soon," Susan reminded
her. "It's practically the only place left."

This put a chill on them both.

"Better not to think about it," Celia advised her, losing all
confidence in her theory.

Susan nodded at this, then wondered aloud, "So what about
Aunt Ginny?"

"Aunt Ginny? What about her?"

"What does *she* see—?"

Celia looked at her sister worriedly: "I'm not sure it makes
any difference. Why do you ask? I mean, she's the one who's
crazy, if anyone is. Definitely neurotic."

"—or does she make a point of *not* seeing what's around her?
Imposing her own version of events instead, as a kind of defense
mechanism. Never exploring anyone else's angle. Maybe I
should be more like her! Maybe that's what makes her so strong."

"You think Ginny's strong? I think she's a wreck. If she didn't
have Dad. . . . She's always calling him, you know," Celia argued, "always wanting something from him. She's clingy. She's
dependent. She's nothing like you."

"But she gets what she wants."

"Not always."

"She thinks she can change the main facts of her life at will.
That's amazing!"

"No, it's not. It's deluded behavior."

"Not entirely deluded. She'll get that annulment, you know,
if she really tries for it."

"I doubt it. She's up against the whole judiciary system."

"She'll get the name change, then."

"That's possible. That's been Dad's tactic. He's almost talked her into it. He might even wind up paying for it, just to cool her down."

"See? She gets what she wants."

"In a wheedling, despicable fashion."

"Maybe that's what power is."

"But that kind of power can backfire. It's like crying wolf. Do it too many times and everyone washes their hands of you. You can see it happening with Dad and Ginny."

"Maybe every kind of power backfires."

"What are we talking about here?"

"The power to see? The power to change? I'm not sure."

"The last thing I would call Aunt Ginny," Celia declared, "is a viable role model."

"Oh, no, not that," Susan agreed. "Just a force of nature— and a slightly terrifying one."

"Well, I guess so."

Celia wasn't happy making the concession.

"And what about Martha?" Susan asked. "You're really thinking of leaving her?"

"Not leaving her."

This was said as if there were an accommodating middle ground between leaving and staying.

"What, then? Stay and make her miserable?"

"Naw," Celia grinned. "Just keep her on her toes. And make her wear Djuna Barnes eyeliner."

Both sisters laughed.

"Speaking of Martha, I ought to get back."

"Me, too."

"You want me to drive? You're not 'seeing' things now?"

"I'm fine. Really I am."

"Could you drop me off on Fifteenth? I need to get some groceries."

"No problem."

"Or what about a car wash first?" Celia suggested. "To cheer you up."

"Oh . . . not today. Maybe next week?"

Now that she'd noticed the bird droppings, she wanted to study them more closely.

"Well, as long as you can see where you're going."

"Hey, I never said that!"

They took off.

In the Safeway parking lot, as she got out of the car, Celia asked Susan if she would be going to Issaquah that weekend.

"I guess so. I told Mom yes. I'm not sure I'll feel like it, though."

"What if you brought Eleanor along?"

"Oh, I couldn't do that. It wouldn't be comfortable."

"I'm bringing Martha."

"It's not the same."

"It could be."

"No, really—it's not even a relationship."

As she spoke the words, they startled her with their clarity.

They also startled Celia: "It's not?"

"It's more of an . . . event?" she explained. "A way of correcting an imbalance? Like in a war or something. It's hard to describe."

Celia stared at her.

"Or maybe I'm just not used to it yet," Susan consoled her. "If you could give me a little more time. . . ."

Celia made a face but agreed to drop the subject for now, adding: "And don't forget. For our next date—car wash!"

They kissed and parted.

Celia's arm had stayed a reference point . . . but distant, oh so distant. The lapping of water merged with a fountain's splash. And the grass in the lakeside park became a quiet piazza—of brick this time, not asphalt.

She knew she was gone again: out of her mind, out of her body. But she took it calmly, inspecting, with an eye to their origin, the winding streets, the unfamiliar faces, the elevated highway streaked with rust, its traffic roaring overhead. . . .

Some buildings changed shape. An alleyway appeared. The sky was a colorless drizzle. And there they were! Her deepest pleasure came with drifting to the rhythm at which they sauntered, husband and wife. This was jazz-smooth. In a way, it was coming home.

The alley gave onto a street. The street curved around to openness. She was caught in a procession where children lined the sidewalks and old folks leaned out windows. The local fire department was a source of neighborhood pride. Every fireman was mustached, with sad eyes and a sallow complexion. A brass band played anthems, its wonky notes bouncing off housefronts. The swaying skirts of altar boys were a silence of bells. And a row of solemn gentlemen bore their load with seriousness—as if they were pallbearers, or porters hoisting royalty.

The source of the hoopla, the object of veneration, was a plaster saint gaudily dressed, its robes festooned with dollar bills. It bobbed in its finery down the odd-angled pavement. It worked like a puppet uniting its worshipers. Where were they going? Where *could* they go? This appeared to be a small world, easily escapable.

Her couple were across the street from her, on the far side of the saint's float. An unfamiliar language was being spoken—and then a familiar one, unfamiliarly cadenced. Her couple smiled condescendingly. She looked above their heads. In an open window, a palsied old man and his nervously assisting wife wielded an enormous black garbage bag filled with something heavy. They were waiting for the festooned saint to pass below them.

The whole procession idled for a moment. The old man teetered anxiously. And then, as soon as saint and brass band took a measured step forward, he started emptying. The contents of the bag got stuck. His wife hurried to help him, ferocious claws at work. And out it came: a blizzard of shredded newspaper.

Her couple felt it, looked up, saw what it was—and ducked away laughing, the paper clinging to them. They turned to follow the saint. Susan paralleled their path, thinking, "So am I in *his* photographs? If so, to what degree?" There seemed no earthly way of finding out.

The street unfolded and the dollars fluttered. Torn newsprint danced knee-high. A corner of a page went swirling past, and gave a date from just a week ago.

The language was Italian, and the firemen were swarthy and compact. Their job was to look for infernos—but there were none just now. The saint's float stopped at a Catholic school playground, beyond which lay the expressway that sealed the boundaries of the neighborhood.

A figure of local power stepped up to give a speech. . . .

But it was Celia's voice that came through, like a sudden trick on a stereo system:

"Too bad—they're gone."

Susan, recovering herself, asked who. But what she was thinking was: Where?

As if she hadn't guessed already.

She had talked it over in a limited way with her sister; and then, after dropping Celia off, stopped at a newsstand and bought a paper to confirm her suspicions. She turned to the back page and checked the national weather report. In Boston it was cloudy with a chance of light rain. But maybe she had read that the night before? Lately, she liked to see what the forecasts were across the country, comparing city with city, as a break from the obituaries.

She tried to recall her stroll in the North End, Boston's Little Italy, where she and Walker had gone for drinks with Mary. They'd even had a meal there. But had she really seen enough of the place to summon all the detail she was getting of it now?

At home, hoping for a clue from another source, she dug out the packet of Walker's letters and selected one he had sent his sister shortly before their visit to her. She browsed it, stopping at a particular paragraph:

> . . . still as smitten as ever, I'm afraid. When I look into her eyes, I can't help smiling. My heart races. It actually hurts!—especially when I'm teasing her, trying to get her riled. I didn't know your heart could hurt just from love. . . .

She felt the tears rising in her throat. And then an anger took hold of her, extinguishing the tears as fast as they came. It was as if she held a murder weapon in her hands; as if she had become the instrument itself.

Why hadn't she picked up on it? He ought to have seen a doctor. Night after night of "indigestion"? They both should have known better.

This hindsight did no good. It gave her a power of knowledge when she least needed it. And with power came dread, not just for Walker—who hadn't had a clue, not even about his own heart—but for her couple.

What was she overlooking in them?

She tried to formulate her fear for her neckbrace boy and his wife. Was it trepidation at a world where every intimacy might be a death in the making? They looked so young! How could they know what they were doing? Had they really kept faith with each other? A slipup could be fatal.

The more she saw, the less she trusted. Her fear for them was a complex thing, linking them to her. It wasn't just a worry at sexual contamination, although that was part of it. (Plume's ailing friend at the airport haunted her.) It was also dismay at the thought of a world where flesh—in the interest of quarantine—couldn't be fully explored; had to sever itself from the tumble and guts of life.

Between eros in the head and the threat of the physical, what were the options? A life-term imprisonment in the language of one's body? An endless solo dithering and isolated gumminess?

On the nights when Eleanor failed to show, she resorted to this herself before falling asleep, *so as* to fall asleep.

She resorted to it now . . . and promptly dozed off.

At least in sleep there were dreams to turn to. And in dreams nothing was forbidden, nothing was taboo.

She dreamt of a radiant Eleanor, an Eleanor who shimmied, an Eleanor who said, "The beautiful flowers are the ones that

are venomous—the plain ones haven't been buzzed much yet,"
then unjacketed herself to show her own fine poisons.

Susan had always counted herself among the plain, but sometimes wondered how it felt to be beautiful. Now, in the dream,
she wondered how it felt to shape slow deaths within you—to
yield those deaths elsewhere with a gentle probing, a blood-deep
kiss, an anxious drinking of sliding salts.

The dream stayed ominous. Bright hair was garbled into a
witch's frizz, a spreading taste in the dreamer's mouth. She and
Eleanor were a double self-portrait—loving themselves, leaving
themselves. Their minds and bodies bled to become identical.
A mirrored striptease commenced, with each of them discarding
an item at a time: mute smiles, a challenging flare of nostrils.

There was a fluttery feeling at hand as a two-way nakedness
took hold between reflections. Conjunctions at the hips showed
how viruses traveled. A vaginal exploration was gingerly initiated. Thumbs curled over pinkie and ring finger. Middle and
index fingers were the barrel of a gun. They did some problem-
solving: *Up me—and into me.*

The ruins of women walked down burgundy-carpeted corridors.

Upon waking, she felt marginally safer; remembered more
clearly what she and Eleanor had done together, and that they
had done it only twice. The rest had been innocuous caresses.
Surely she hadn't passed a barrier. Surely she hadn't strayed into
forbidden territory. It was a matter, next time—if there was a
next time—of taking appropriate safety measures.

She remembered with even greater relief Walker's mention, in
his letter to Mary, of Eleanor's blood status. But that was almost
two years ago. A lot could happen in two years. It was best to
be cautious. A man was a weapon, no matter how friendly. A
woman was a veil of concealment.

She thought again of her couple—the husband oblivious of
her visitations to him, except in her one dream of him; his wife

always keeping an eye out, a little more aware of what was happening—and felt her fears for them well up once more.

She wasn't just trembling at their peril, which was the ordinary peril threatening anyone who found mortal refuge in a lover's tenderness or a spouse's power. She wasn't even thinking of Walker's heart condition, too late to remedy, or this new and more exhaustive disease which her airport sighting of Plume and his friend brought into focus. She had gotten beyond that. What undermined her now was everything that had ever happened, everything that was *about* to happen. She could sense it coming, even if she couldn't see it. It was like riding the crest of a wave about to break. She wanted to be rescued; she wanted to be lifted out of it.

She had been safe, and now she wasn't safe—or the world wasn't. Or rather, she had had the illusion of safety, and that illusion was gone now. She could control the impulse of her flesh. She could say, "Fingers only," to Eleanor. But she couldn't control the past, not even her own. And she couldn't control her senses: her mind, her visions. . . .

Her young couple idly stared at her. They were going on an airplane ride. White clouds bubbled up below them. They had taken her advice and skipped Chicago. The wife read a magazine. Her husband peered out the window. They seemed to be luring her beyond the limits of herself; to be showing her things that, by all rights, she had no business seeing.

And then they left her; abandoned her.

At a loss, she stepped outside of Walker's house, circling its reflective plate glass. As she slipped from its shadowy side to its southern exposure, she was surprised to see the photinia sprouting new shoots. Vertical red spikes swayed out of rounded, waxy green: a spurt of bright inches after a dormancy of months.

Nature was a little too alive, a little too voracious. Treetop crows made derogatory comments. The fir trees flickered some depths at her.

And there seemed to be no city. There seemed only to be roads which led through woods from Walker's house to her desk at work, or from Walker's driveway to Dr. Plume's basement office—and then, by circuitous routes, back into Eleanor's embrace.

When she next saw Plume—bringing the photographs, as he'd requested, and her sketches of Walker, too, at Eleanor's suggestion—there was more than enough to talk about.

part four

punching through
mirrors

"So what you're telling me is I have no personality?"

They had been interrupted twice during this third visit—once when Plume, through the window, saw a squirrel interfering where it shouldn't have been interfering and went out to throw a stick at it; and now a second time with this telephone call from upstairs.

The caller, Susan could tell, was prefacing his message with a "brace yourself" remark—which gave Plume the chance he needed to decline to hear it: "I'm with a client. I'll be up as soon as we're done. Fifteen minutes."

He put down the receiver, turned to Susan, and said, "No, no, what I'm suggesting is almost the opposite—that perhaps you're exploring the possibility of moving *beyond* your own personality."

"And why would I be doing that?"

Plume's eyes swam uncertainly behind the lenses of his tortoiseshell glasses.

"Because of grief?" he ventured. "Because it may actually have liberated you in some ways . . .?"

She gave him a distrustful look: "In what ways?"

"Death makes us—can sometimes make us . . . appreciate what we have? By putting a limit or an outline on things?"

"But I already appreciated what I had. I'd never had anything like it."

"—or maybe just by knocking some sense into us, separating minor concerns from major concerns, giving us a chance to reorder our lives—"

"But I didn't want that chance."

She knew he was trying to be helpful—but he seemed only painfully inept, determined as he was to impose something abstract and theoretical on a situation that, for her, was quivering with a dozen layers of life.

She stopped listening to him; withdrew into memories, into loss upon loss, of Walker—a Walker whose sex poked up mischievously; a Walker who had no rough edges, no place where his personality jarred with hers. This edgelessness, this lack of friction, had been a comfort to her at the time, a sign of how well suited they were. But now it seemed to leave her stranded, with no sharp moments to cling to. Their very ease together appeared to make her all the more vulnerable to any and all revelations about him: in his letters to Mary, in Eleanor's occasional remarks about him, even in Plume's off-the-wall theories.

She wanted to tell someone, as she had half told Eleanor, "I guess we were misfits, the two of us—so happy that we didn't even know it. Or else we were the blandest, most ordinary people in the world, and I'll never find anyone that bland again, so what's the use?"

But she no longer entirely believed that she was so bland, or that Walker ever had been.

Far away in the distance Plume's diagnoses went increasingly off-track, and she found herself responding to them guardedly while keeping her more private thoughts—on the mysteries of intimacy without danger, of closeness without invasion or defeat—to herself. When he suggested she was avoiding the topic at hand, she confessed she wasn't even aware there *was* a topic at hand.

The reflection of his lenses grew surprisingly forlorn.

"Maybe if we examine the 'evidence' you spoke of last week," he said. "You brought them with you, the photographs?"

She told him she had—only they weren't what she had supposed them to be.

"Of your vacation, yes?"

"But not what I thought was in them, exactly."

Even the Lake Pontchartrain shots, which she had looked at with a magnifying glass last night, were a disappointment. The focus was poor. And the light in Walker's house was different from the light in Washington, D.C. Somehow it revealed less. It seemed to be revealing less all the time.

Eleanor's reaction, as they went through them together, had confirmed this: "That, over there—it *could* be a person . . . or maybe just a tree stump. Was it some kind of monument?"

Susan had no answer, couldn't remember if the park had monuments in it or not. It seemed, in memory, to be furnished only with wind and light and the oddly contorted shapes of the trees themselves. . . .

Plume repeated, "Let's have a look at them, shall we?"

She was willing to hand them over. But there was a question she wanted to ask first—about Walker. She'd had a certain change of heart.

"My husband—" she began.

He raised his eyebrows.

"—this vision of his. What did it consist of exactly?"

Again there were professional ethics to be considered, and he lingered over these, though without the ticklish nervousness he had experienced last week when trying to volunteer the information unasked.

He measured out his words: "It was of a woman, Walker said."

"What sort of woman?"

Plume explained, "He was in some confusion about this. First she was one thing, then another—"

"And he thought she was following us?"

" 'Us'? You mean the two of you?"

She nodded.

"No, I don't believe so. You weren't in the picture. He hadn't met you yet."

She tried not to react to this. But her silence indicated, more plainly than she wished, a connection she was making, one she preferred not to spell out until she better understood it, to do with her neckbrace man before he had his neckbrace; her only one-to-one contact with him—in their "tryst," as she thought of it, the dream encounter which had led to sudden panic and flight on his part. . . .

Plume, one step behind her, inquired: "You're thinking what you saw on your train trip has something to do with what Walker saw earlier—and with these two you're seeing now?"

"I don't know, I don't know."

"But you suspect it."

She told him she didn't know what she suspected.

"But you have a theory?"

Sighing, and feeling a need to distract his attention elsewhere, keep him at bay, she mentioned the neckbrace man's camera to him for the first time: how it was always pointing at her, how she tried to elude it but was unable to do so, how it was only his wife she "spoke" to in these waking dreams—giving "waking" a certain scrupulous emphasis—and never the husband.

"—which is what makes it a pattern," she went on, "and what makes it so predictable, too, kind of ridiculous."

"This business with the cameras, you mean."

"Yes, and it being such a woman-to-woman thing."

"You say you *did* tell Walker about this woman you saw on your train trip—"

"Or thought I saw."

"You mentioned her to Walker, and he just humored you? He didn't believe you?"

"That's what it felt like. It's hard to say. Even with the photographs. When I showed them to Walker, he always seemed to be seeing something else."

"And what about when you look at them now?"

"They're just—not quite what I thought they were. So many of them are out of focus. Especially the ones I took: the Polaroids."

"They aren't obvious, then? They aren't conclusive?"

"No they aren't. And even back then—I don't know . . . I can't really say anymore. I thought I could, but—"

She deliberately held back any mention of Walker's own panic that night on the train, before they reached Chicago, or the parallel fears she had induced in her dream-man months later. Let *Plume* be the one to make the connections—if, indeed, they existed. . . .

"And what about your dream-couple?" he asked.

"What about them?"

"Are they in the photographs?"

"Oh, no. I've looked: they're not."

"You're sure of that? Shouldn't we at least double-check?"

She held her purse firmly: "First I want to know what Walker told you—about this woman, the one in his vision."

He slid back, mildly frustrated: "As I said, his account of her was confused, there wasn't all that much to it. . . ."

She was wary of his words—and intent upon them, too, determined to hear them out.

". . . there was something he said, about her being closest to his heart," Plume remembered. "He mentioned it once, but never again. . . ."

Still, it was enough for her to extract the meaning she needed from it: *So he knew. He saw what was coming, and didn't want to admit it to her ("You'll just think I'm paranoid—") or even to himself. . . .*

"And afterwards—" Plume began.

"Yes?"

"Well, *you* came along. You seemed to shove it all aside."

"Oh."

Recalling Walker's words more precisely, he asked, "This woman on your train trip, the one you say Walker couldn't see, or wouldn't see—how would you describe her? Would you say she had a 'blank' face?"

Here it was, then, the corroboration she was after. It was all beginning to fit. But not in time to do Walker any good.

"Not blank," she said slowly, "so much as clear . . . or *muted*," she emphasized, "and a little desperate. Especially when she came up close."

"Came up close?" he echoed. "Where was that again?"

"In Boston. In the art museum there. The basement cafeteria."

He waited for more.

With a certain shyness, Susan added: "She was smoking a cigarette. I could draw her if you like."

"Perhaps if we look at the photographs first—"

She finally agreed to this; opened her purse. She had made her selection beforehand—and included only a few sexual ones that were unavoidable. The rest were of New Orleans: Lake Pontchartrain, the St. Charles streetcar, Halloween in the French Quarter.

She went through them with him, providing a running commentary.

"This was in San Francisco. The room was five flights up, and there was only an airshaft, no fire escape. The fire exit was across the hall. See this window here? I looked, but I didn't see how anyone could get up that high."

He squinted at the snapshot; saw darkness, radiance, strong sculpted flesh—and two small reflections, close together, which resembled a wild animal's dazed reflective eyes. But they could have been anything. The flashlamp had scattered light everywhere.

There were other shots which showed Walker frankly straining toward his climax. Plume was spellbound, embarrassed—and also alarmed. For the first time he thought she might be breaking down with grief, dissolving under a guilt that couldn't be named. How could she be showing him these? Didn't she see what was in them?

"These are the ones of New Orleans," she continued. "This one on the streetcar? It's not as clear as I thought. But see? That's her across the aisle. And these at night—there, in the window, behind the guy in the leather mask: that isn't my reflection. I'm not sure what it is, but that's not what I was wearing . . . ! These are by the water the next day. But they're all much blurrier than I remember. Or maybe I saw something in them—?"

She paused, marshaled her thoughts, speculated aloud: "Maybe a part of me knew what was going to happen."

She wanted to mention again, in more detail, the business of the gypsy-face on television in Los Angeles, transmitted from Dubrovnik—the experience of drawing her first and *then* seeing her. This type of thing weighed more heavily on her mind, lately. But she felt shy about admitting to it, as reluctant to dwell on it as on her dream-tryst with her neckbrace man. She said only, "Maybe we catch glimpses of things? Before we actually encounter them?"

She gave him time to react to this.

When he didn't react, when he simply sat there thinking his thoughts, she recollected herself and went back to describing the photographs: "These are all double exposures. Walker said something was wrong with the camera. . . ."

Plume picked among the images she offered, focusing not on the versions of them she was advocating, but more on what he chose to see: the three holiday-makers in the streets of New Orleans, for instance, who were leering at him from what appeared to be a curbside orgy. In Plume's mind, the visage of Walker strained toward them from his San Francisco hotel room, about to join them in their costumed revelries.

He pulled back, folded up, afraid she would sense his sexual arousal. He was so distracted by the flesh in the photographs that he failed at first to deliver a verdict on them.

But she made it clear she was waiting for one.

"Well," he said at last, "there's room for interpretation."

She smiled at him crazily. With his tepid response, something in her snapped. Her outer veneer stayed coherent, but just barely. She could see the images had affected him in some way. She could also see he was reluctant to admit this.

It was a conspiracy: a cover-up of truths that the snapshots revealed. She had been wavering before, but now she was right off-balance. She could feel it; she could sense it. And she succumbed to it, letting go. It was a liberating feeling! She was swept with relief and a strange surge of pride, too, as she saw herself go farther than Plume could ever go, deeper and deeper, to a place where nothing was guarded, where everything hooked right under the skin. She felt ruthless. She closed herself off.

Her shutting him out like this surprised him as much as it did her. She now had the air of a disturbed person: that clarity of lunacy or mania you can immediately discern when confronted with lost souls, out of their wits, in the supermarket or on the street. He asked as tactfully as he could if she would like him to write her a prescription, and she was amenable to this. He also wondered aloud if she would let him keep the photographs for further study. But she grabbed them back and stuffed them in her purse.

He went through the formalities of arranging another appointment for her, which she agreed to almost giddily. As he escorted her out, she grew less comprehensible with every step she took—almost traipsing as she slipped into the pleasant riddle of late-February evening gloom.

She disappeared from sight—and then returned. She had noticed something: "What's happened to your grass over there?"

She was pointing up ahead to a bare patch of lawn.

"That's a bitter corner—nothing grows there," he said, and had the feeling of revealing something . . . something he had never admitted before.

This got an unexpected smile out of her, a look of sympathy. And then she was gone, leaving him standing on his threshold.

His office phone rang. Closing the door onto the garden, he stepped in to answer it. On the line he heard a hoarse and crusty voice say, "Not Ketchikan. Juneau. I was trying to call Juneau."

A background voice said, "Okay, okay, whatever, just give me—"

The connection was cut, and a dial tone sounded.

Plume stared at the phone for the longest of moments. Then, for the third time this week, he tried Campbell's number.

No answer.

He placed the receiver back on its cradle. A fear crept over him. The shiny black instrument contained a world within it. He did not want to enter that world. He wanted to put its possibilities on hold for as long as possible.

Before his next client arrived, he went upstairs—where Bill was awaiting him with the news they had anticipated, the news about their airport friend, their friend who had gone home to die. And Bill was chafing, Bill was angry with him. He even had an angry smell about him. If the life of the house, the essence of their domestic routine together, was discipline, order and containment, then what it contained now was low-fevered resentment.

Bill had standing instructions not to make excessive noise when consultations were going on downstairs and never to interrupt except in an emergency. He had deemed the death of a close friend, however long expected, just such an emergency, and felt he had acted with a sense of loyalty in calling down to Plume. After all, he had other friends he could turn to, many of them easier to talk to than his lover had been of late.

Now he felt he was getting no thanks for that loyalty. Plume, as promised, came up at the end of his consultation and absorbed the information quietly, but showed almost no reaction to it. His nerves didn't allow him to. The transformation he had witnessed in Susan, followed by the phone call that must be Campbell's, had left him too disoriented, too distracted, to react.

Before returning downstairs, he said: "I won't be free until ten o'clock. Can you get flowers, a card? Send them to—whoever was looking after him?"

Bill shook his head, a light and dangerous smile playing on his lips.

"His brother."

"His brother, then. And here's a check—" A sizable amount was written out, with the recipient left blank: "You know where he'd want this to go?"

This got a nod, but no answer.

Plume left the room.

Bill held the blank check in hand.

What if this were the end? What would have been accomplished?

Any lithe or glancing note seemed to have dwindled out of the relationship. This made for a weakening loneliness, an increased vulnerability, an emptiness within.

There were ways of putting a cordial face on emptiness. There were things you told yourself: "It may not be passion, but at least it's friendly."

With this death, however, that no longer seemed true. There had been no argument. But something had been extinguished.

After Plume returned downstairs, Bill stood as though without instructions on how to quit the room. His thoughts quietly hummed. They took him right out of his body and into memory. And memory had a turbulent, illicit appeal; was now, more than ever, a source of excitement. It led into another world. And the gulf it revealed between past and present was unyielding: it would never be spanned again.

There was the time seven years ago on a hiking trip in the mountains (Plume had stayed at home, naturally) when a look between friends and a yearning for company had led to an affable slipup. By chance they were alone together, after both their partners had begged off the expedition. A teasing glance between them had said, "Want to—?" The smile that had followed said, "Why not?"

How could you resist it?

You couldn't—and even if you did, would you really be living?

At any rate they hadn't.

He had this encounter fresh in his mind's eye. He guarded it closely as he went out and bought flowers and a card in which he enclosed Plume's check, inscribed to the appropriate charity to honor a secret lover's memory and that of his longtime partner, already dead. And of course these would serve as an offering of condolences to the dead man's family as well.

The brother he had met on only a few occasions. The parents and other relatives he hadn't met at all. The deceased partner he had known quite well—and never liked until he knew he was dying.

There seemed to be an irony in this, but none he could define exactly.

When he came back home, he was stranded once again in

the center of this house which wasn't his house, in a quietly furnished room which prompted him to ask what he would most like to smash.

Heedful of the bargain he had made, he decided to smash himself—and headed for the liquor cabinet.

By the time Plume came upstairs he was well gone. A requisite exchange of medical details—"Yeah, it was the PCP that got him . . . he couldn't hold out"—gave way to a dry-eyed, caustic valediction: "So, hey, goddamn, there goes another one. It's relentless. It's so fucking relentless."

"I'm sorry. Really I am."

To both of them this felt like a rote response—Plume sounding numbly disconnected from his words of sympathy. And it elicited a blind, inept fury: Bill flailing against his lover, Plume taking the blows. Dry eyes gave way to tears and vodka breath, and then came a hunger for lips, for salt—not just a desire to fill the void with familiar skin, but a skewering, on Bill's part, of the teasing smile that had skewered him; and a dallying, on Plume's part, with images of Walker in the throes of love as revealed in crumpled Polaroids.

They played their phantoms—animals who had once worked magnificently—over one another. They strained, they shimmied, they circled around. They were drawn toward the cock that could be anyone's; a sex that knew no boundaries. They fucked in the dark and used each other thoroughly, knowing that their thoughts, like these actions, were taboo.

And after it was over, and Plume, learning when the funeral would be, had prepared his excuse not to attend it ("A Saturday? . . . I'll have to check my schedule"), they lay in a shadow that seemed complete.

Plume had the ghost of Walker bobbing in his head. Bill contemplated a force of another kind, as quiet as contagion. There had, after all, been other occasions—every few weeks or so for a year or two, before the affair tailed off of its own accord.

They had grabbed the chance whenever they could, never too concerned about protection. They were friends, they were buddies, they *knew* each other. The risk had seemed so remote.

It was time for a confession.

Plume's breathing was regular, drowsily relaxed.

Bill asked: "You know—this death?"

The breathing stopped. The body came awake.

"It's a little closer than you think."

Her appointments with Plume had brought no real answers.

So her first stop, the next day at lunchtime, was a well-stocked map shop on First Avenue downtown. Any clue would do. Anything at all. State maps, city maps, geological surveys that went into every conceivable detail of topographical character—whatever could serve as a pointer.

For instance: Lancaster, California, where the nun on the train had been headed, was seven hundred feet above sea level and surrounded by mountains. It also appeared to be dead flat. This did not seem consistent with what the railway buff had said about it being "high desert." Surely "high" ought to mean the mountains themselves.

Then again, seven hundred feet was higher than Death Valley, which was fairly close by and well below sea level. . . .

Checking the map's legend, she realized the contours were given in meters, which put Lancaster at an altitude, roughly, of two thousand feet. She had the feeling this ought to clarify something. But it didn't.

Her map of San Francisco was no better. It was on too small a scale to indicate where the streets, confronted by impossible hillsides, turned into stairways—or disappeared altogether. There was plenty of up-and-down implicit in it, but precious little information.

As for lower Louisiana, on a road map it looked like a giant, tepid puddle where an oversized breed of creature had lifted its cypress-trunk legs and gone *splat!* The place was a mess of swamps, bayous and lagoons. Staring at its odd strands of freeway and back roads brought no satisfaction at all.

Back at the office she glanced at her purchases all afternoon, hoping that—in the interim between phone calls, chats with copy aides and greetings from editors—a detail would emerge: a flash of insight that would split the moment open and reveal its true nature. But even her Chicago city map, when she finally worked up the nerve to look at its inset of the downtown area, drew a blank, was simply a pattern of street grid disappearing in the slanting asymmetry of Lake Michigan.

When she got home, she placed all the maps in a drawer for safekeeping and decided on another approach.

Before going in to work the following morning, she called the Art Institute in Chicago and asked to be connected with the museum store. A series of clicks and beeps led into a dire snippet of Holst, and then a gruff male sales assistant greeted her.

"Can I help you?"

Her voice was weak and stuttery, on guard against whatever stretching signals might emerge from the place where her life had collapsed.

Without adequate introduction, she began to describe the painting in the only terms she could: "Puffy arms? And with these kind of swollen legs?"

"Excuse me?"

"Looking in the mirror," she explained, "but not minding the decay. Can't remember the name of it. But it's of a lady sitting in her . . . *boudoir*?"

It was Walker's word. It was Walker speaking through her.

"Modern? Impressionist? American? European? You're looking for a postcard or a book?"

"A book—if there's one with this lady in it."

"Who's the artist?"

"I don't know. I can't remember. But the lady's name is Ida. The artist's name . . .?"

She cast about for it.

"His first name is Ivan!" she recalled. "But I can't think of his last. He's American. And modern, I think—from the 'thirties."

"Let me ask around."

Canned waves of energy—a crowd's buzz, a distant siren, a guard's instructive holler—were all catapulted beyond their normal range. They came from a world parallel with hers but hidden. Its hidden aspect encouraged her. This must be the way to pursue her inquiry. If this particular world could be said to exist, then perhaps other worlds did too.

"Think we've got it," the voice came back, "but it's only a postcard."

"And it's of Ida?"

"Yeah, it's of Ida. Some sad-looking dame," he remarked.

She could picture him shaking his head as he said this.

"Can I charge it—?"

"You want to charge a postcard?"

"—and could you mail it to me?"

"You can't just come down and get it?"

"I'm in Seattle."

"Oh."

There was a pause.

"Look, ma'am, there's just no way we can charge a postcard. We got a minimum—fifteen dollars—and this is, like, fifty cents."

"What about Gauguin?"

"What about him?"

"You've got a book on him?"

"We've got several."

"A book that's got that one: 'Who are we, where are we, what are we going to do'—something like that? A big panel thing? If you've got a book with that one in it, I'll buy it too. And can you mail it? With the postcard? First-class?"

"Hang on. I'll see."

There were more signals, more murmurs of a distant city. And then an outburst of raucous laughter. One particular voice, female and black, rumbled dramatically: "You better believe it—it's cold out there! And that ice!"

Another world, yes: but one that stayed in its place. She wasn't about to be lured into it. And her dream-couple seemed to have escaped it altogether.

The sales clerk came back on the line, friendlier now that a sale was in the offing.

"Gauguin? Yeah, we've got a nice one. Only twenty bucks, remaindered. Has the picture you want—the whole thing in black and white, and then three pages of detail, in color."

"I'll take it."

He asked for her mailing address, charge card number and expiration date. She gave him these, but felt there was still something missing, something she needed to ask before ending the transaction.

"Do I—?" She hesitated. "Do I, like, sound a bit crazy to you? I'm serious. It's just that I—I suffered a personal loss recently, and I'm having trouble . . . getting my balance back? This postcard—I know it sounds weird, but I thought it might clear up something for me."

"Well, like they say, Art can help you get a handle on Life. Although, I don't know . . . a picture like this—"

There was a sound of a cash register being rung, an item being slapped down on the counter. And then: "Okay. We'll get this in the mail to you this afternoon. Should be there by the end of the week."

"Wait a minute! Like who says?"

But she was too slow. He had already hung up.

The book arrived, and the postcard with it. Both, when enhanced by the power of Plume's pills, felt strong and purposeful.

The reproduction of Ida stood on the kitchen table, propped against the pepper shaker, bathed in an ordinary light. When Susan looked up the name in Walker's dictionary, she found it was German and its meaning was "happy." Buoyed up by Plume's prescription into luminous realms, she toyed with this meaning and savored its simplicity.

Then the drugs wore off and her thoughts lost direction. The postcard had taken her as far as it could go—which wasn't very far. Strange-colored paintings of Tahiti didn't help much either. She was back to square one—only mapless, imageless.

A letter from Mary, now returned to Boston, came to her rescue. With a growing sense of excitement, she read one part of it over and over again:

> . . . not talking about haunted-house creatures, of course, but the ghosts one carries in one's life; ghosts who can appeal only to the people who knew them when they were alive.
>
> I think of him as living in me, in a very real sense— as if I were giving him the shelter he needs. It's a sad thing, but not entirely sad if you talk about him, if

> you share him a little with other people, as I'm sure
> youmust. . . .

Susan took a double dose of Plume's prescription and, in an
inspired, pulsating fog, wrote back:

> Yes, exactly, someone inside you, moving around,
> advising you, telling you what to do, reshaping your
> memories. Or maybe "memories" is too strong a
> word: "omens" perhaps? Or "intimations"—? Out of
> one body, so many characters emerge! My plan is to
> introduce them all to one another. . . .

She sent this off; could hardly remember what she had written
once she sealed the envelope—then was surprised when she
didn't get an answer right away. She felt she had communicated
something of consequence.

There were omens to be found almost everywhere.

That weekend, while browsing through a stack of Walker's
books, she came across a title that, to her mind, confirmed everything she suspected. It was all right there on the opening page,
which began:

> There was baby born named Ida. Its mother held it
> with her hands to keep Ida from being born but when
> the time came Ida came. And as Ida came, with her
> came her twin, so there she was Ida-Ida.

That was as far as she could read. Drugged as she was, it was
impossible to concentrate. But she had the marvelous feeling that
in those few lines she had intuited the gist of the whole book,
which she returned to its shelf with a sense of satisfaction. It
described her situation perfectly.

She did not tell Plume of this, however. Instead she canceled her weekly appointment with him and called in sick at work as well, wary of leaving a house in which she felt so bathed in revelations.

It wasn't until Celia came to visit a few days later that she had a chance to run these revelations by anyone. She was floating an inch or two off the ground, feeling destructively giddy. And she was consulting with Walker on a regular basis: "You want me to sit over here—or over there . . .? It's really okay if I wear this shirt again . . .? Let's see now, what should I have for breakfast . . . ?"

She asked these questions while pacing through various rooms, her sister trailing a step or two behind her.

"Hey, who are you talking to?" Celia asked, then consulted her watch. "Actually, you know, it's closer to lunchtime."

Susan looked at her unsteadily.

Celia, distracted by worries of her own, took a moment to assess the situation before roping her sister in gently.

"So," she said, sitting Susan down at the kitchen table, "what's happened? Is it getting worse?"

"Huh?"

"Your vision-thing. Your dream-couple."

"Oh, they're gone for the moment. It's been a while. I'm wondering if they'll ever come back."

"So things are better."

"Sort of. Not as desperate."

Celia waited for more—and was worried by what she got.

"If I went crazy," Susan asked timidly, "would you take care of me?"

"If you went crazy?"

"Uh-huh. Would you?"

Celia made a joke of it: "Of course I would. I'd even help you on with your straitjacket. Only you're not going crazy. You're just worn out."

"The thing is: I've been learning things lately."

"Like what?"

"Like—Like this, over here." She went to retrieve Gertrude Stein's *Ida* from Walker's bookshelf, then thought better of it. "Or wait—more like this. They sent it to me." She handed Celia the Albright postcard of Ida: "Worn out, but happy. That's okay, isn't it? That's like me." Tears were streaming down her cheeks. "And there's a Gauguin book too that Eleanor would like. She likes small breasts."

"Um, sweetheart, you're not—? You're not on something, are you?"

"On something?"

"You don't sound so good. And you're looking kind of woozy."

"Only what the doctor gave me. It's a subscription."

"*Pre*-scription."

"No, sub— Oh yeah . . . right. 'Pre—' "

"You might want to cut down."

"I can't come down."

"I said 'cut down.' Susan? Uh . . . Susan? Are you with us?"

No reply.

Celia made some coffee. This seemed to help. Susan grew sharper.

After a second cup she drew close and asked: "So where's Martha?"

"She's not coming."

The answer allowed no further inquiry. There was another topic Celia wanted to clear up first.

"These pills," she asked. "They're making you like this? You're driving around on them?"

"Only this week."

"What are they for?"

"They're for—I don't know. To keep me calm, help me see. . . ."

"And make you forget things, too?

"Forget?"

"You never made it to Mom and Dad's on Saturday. You didn't even call. We waited for you! Mom had your place set."

"Oh."

"Where *were* you?"

"I'm sorry. I was with Eleanor, I think."

She tried to recall: Was it a dream of Eleanor, or had there been an actual visit?

"You're not sure?"

"Why? Did I miss anything?"

"Well, yes, you did actually."

Celia looked both proud and a little sheepish.

"What happened?"

"Aunt Ginny was there."

"And—?"

"I got a bit rambunctious, is all."

"Rambunctious, how?"

Celia smiled down into her coffee cup, then looked back up: "Oh, I asked if she'd ever considered becoming a lesbian. And if she did become one, would she complain about her women as much as she complains about her men?"

"Her men?"

"Yes."

"Actually—*man*, isn't it? There's only been one?"

"You think so?"

"Well, probably."

Celia considered this and conceded, "I guess you're right."

"So what did she say?"

"She—just kind of spluttered. And then left the table."

"Oh, Celia."

"I know, I know. It was bad of me. I was feeling reckless. But I get so tired of her whining. If you hate something, then *do* something about it. Run away. Drink yourself silly. That's how I'd handle it."

"Why? What else has happened? What have you done?"

With every gulp of coffee, Susan realized something was missing from her sister's account. Celia's air of innocence wasn't convincing.

"I haven't 'done' anything. But Mom and Dad are sore at me about Ginny. Or maybe just Mom is. Dad's hoping it'll keep her out of his hair for a couple of weeks. Ginny's theory is that it took place at *his* dinner table so he should have said something; scolded me. I told him it was just an innocent question. He passed that on to her, and said that he agreed."

"He didn't!"

"He did." Celia smiled. "She must really be giving him a hard time."

"And what else?"

There had to be more.

Celia leaned back on her chair and added blandly: "Well, Martha left me. That's the other big news."

"Oh, Celia—"

"On Friday. Reason I was so obnoxious, probably."

"I'm so sorry."

"It's all right."

Susan came closer, embraced her sister, didn't quite know where to stop: "Oh, Celia. . . ."

"It's okay, it's okay."

"No, it's not."

"I was expecting it—"

Susan pulled back: "You were?"

"—only I thought *I'd* be the one doing the leaving!"

"That's what I thought too!"

"Well, we were both wrong."

The two women held on to their coffee cups as if they were anchors of support.

Celia said, "But I'm supposed to be the one checking up on you. Dad made me promise. You know, it's weird—they don't seem too surprised about Martha. . . ."

Susan gave a nod at this.

"You mean you're not either?"

"Well, you do have this track record. . . ."

This was said as unaccusingly as possible.

"Anyway," Celia announced, "we need to furnish them with a full report."

Her manner changed from confidante's to inquisitor's: "So what's with all this postcard business?"

Susan grew vague again: "Just something I got from a museum. . .?"

"What museum?"

"In Chicago." She almost swallowed the word. "The Art Institute."

Celia looked at her sharply.

"Where I bought this book on Gauguin, too—over the phone."

She fetched it from the living room to show her. But Celia failed to see it as a clue to her sister's behavior. She moved on to another concern.

"What about this doctor? This is still Walker's shrink?"

"Yes. I'm seeing him on Monday. I missed this week's appointment."

"And you really think you need this guy?"

"He needs me! I've shown him Walker's photographs. And I'm going to show him some of my sketches—"

"He needs you, but you're paying him?"

"The insurance pays. And I think that maybe it's Walker he needs. Anyway it's all a kind of exploration; it's not really therapy. I only have to see him one more time, get some more pills—"

"And then what?"

"Then I'll quit him, end the visits."

"What's his name? I'd like to have a talk with him."

"No, please. I've been figuring it out. It's almost over. And I'm perfectly all right."

Celia looked doubtful at this.

"Really I am," Susan assured her. "You can tell Mom and Dad."

"Tell them what? That you're all drugged up and consoling yourself with color plates of Gauguin?"

"Just that I'm doing fine; that I'm doing okay on my own."

Celia looked even more leery.

"And besides, I still have Eleanor."

Celia relented: "Well, I suppose I'm in no position to hold that against you."

Susan, taking this for encouragement, lowered her voice and asked in some embarrassment, "Look, there're some things I sort of need to know. I feel so out of it! Like what do I do when she moves her legs and spreads them to let me—?"

"You're really getting into this?"

"Well—"

The sisters exchanged a secret or two, then parted.

By the time she met with Plume again, in early March, their roles had been reversed.

At Celia's insistence she had cut down on the pills. And upon emerging from their haze she caught a glimpse of how things stood, began to see her situation in a more bleak but solidly grounded light—whereas Plume was in free fall, his thoughts in constant ricochet, his heart in an uproar over all he might lose. For the last twenty-four hours he had been wondering, "Does it show? Does it show?"

It did.

Susan, noticing his discomfort, asked straight out: "What happened? Your friend from the airport. Is he all right?"

"No. He died. Two weeks ago. That call that came while you were here."

The smile he wore was an agony of nerves. He took off his glasses, revealing a look of gaunt fatigue. The impact, if not the detail, of his loss was obvious.

She told him how sorry she was.

His smile froze tighter: "I can't say we weren't expecting it."

"No, I guess not."

"It's a part of the picture these days."

"It's getting that way. For a lot of people, yes, you're right—I suppose it is."

She thought of the dead man: leaning on his cane at SeaTac Airport, seeming to change his age before her eyes, growing younger and younger, and frailer and frailer. She did not like this picture.

"Well," Plume said at last, putting his glasses back on, "shall we pick up where we left off?"

Their conversation assumed an air of unreality, of information being withheld or an alternate universe being considered. Plume had pen in hand but wrote nothing down. Instead he dithered on one minor point after another until he threw in, not as casually as he hoped, "So why was Walker taking all these pictures?"

"He was a photographer. That was his job."

"Yes, but why was he taking *these* pictures? And so many? You were on vacation, weren't you?"

"That's what he did with his time off. It wasn't just his job—it was his hobby. His vocation, I guess."

"Would you say he ever learned to relax?"

Plume's hands were folding and unfolding in busy twisted prayer.

"But he was always sort of relaxed," she said guardedly. "And full of energy too. That's just the way he was."

Her words renewed the liveliness in images of Walker that Plume had dancing in his head—images which, with effort, he was able to set aside, repress.

"You're more at ease talking about him lately," he continued. "Our sessions together are helping, do you think?"

"Well, maybe."

The question felt as odd as a film actor turning toward his audience offscreen and inquiring, "The movie is going well, yes?"

"So what are your plans?" he asked.

This could be taken several ways. She didn't know how to answer it.

She told him that she had no particular plans.

"That might be just as well," he said.

"Really? Why?" She had trouble concealing her annoyance at the presumption in his voice.

"In this new situation," he explained, "where, with anyone you meet, you have to ask yourself: 'Am I interested enough in him to see him through bad times?'—"

"Yes?"

"—a situation where you might find yourself all too easily committed to someone to the bitter end, just out of simple decency—"

"But that's always been the case," she countered.

"It has?"

"With Walker I knew I was ready for everything, almost from the moment we met. That's what made it work. That's what love is."

She felt strongly about this, but tried to keep all eloquence out of her voice as she said it, thinking that any expression of these feelings was too much like showing off, flaunting a privilege.

He didn't take her up on this, instead leapt nervously ahead: "This thing with Eleanor—"

"What thing?"

"—even if it's not sexual—"

She started to speak, then let it pass.

"—it's nevertheless a closeness," he went on.

"But it's not casual," she replied.

"It happened so quickly!"

"Only because all the pieces were in place."

"Ah."

A question formed in her mind which she didn't want to ask. She had made an assumption—but now, observing him, she began to have her doubts about it. There was no way of continuing without being sure of her facts.

"Your friend who died," she forced herself to say, "the one you were helping at the airport. *He* wasn't your lover, was he?"

She had assumed the healthier man was.

"No, but we'd known him a long time."

She softened her manner, as if to share with him in both his bereavement and his presumable relief at a friend's lengthy suffering finally coming to an end. But her empathy, she could see after a moment, was misdirected. He was anything but relieved. In fact he seemed completely bewildered, disoriented.

"So he was a very close friend?"

He made no reply. He couldn't tell her about Bill, or Campbell—the news all arriving at once. That felt like too much bad luck; that felt like being surrounded and having to ask for assistance. And, besides, bad luck could spread, couldn't it? He was sure it could. You had to keep it to yourself. You mustn't breathe a word of it. You mustn't pass it on to anyone. In some deep part of him, superstition had taken over: *Don't tell, never tell.*

"Are you all right?" she asked.

He wasn't. If he let death get one step closer, he would have no advice to dispense to anyone. He would be adrift, stranded. And in the simplest pragmatic terms he would be without income.

He managed to focus sufficiently on his client to frame a question that might help him regain balance.

"Strength—you have it? It seems to be increasing?"

"A little. With time."

She was uneasy discussing this with him.

"Where does it come from?" he asked.

In his mind he saw his various losses, both past and impending, restricting his thoughts and activities to a point where he was paralyzed, each additional death consigning him to a place that was *exiled* from strength, devoid of human contact.

He looked at Susan in puzzlement. Despite her collapse at their last appointment, her experience seemed not to have imposed on her a similar exile—but then she was half his age and had suffered only the one loss, however great. And presumably she was under less of an active threat.

"I've had to borrow it, I guess," she offered.

"From what?"

"Well, from my family for a start. They've been good to me. Eleanor, my parents, my sister, Walker's sister—they've all been helping to see me through."

Plume, avoiding thoughts of his own lack of family, mused on this, then challenged her, "They help you, you say. But are they always truthful?"

"What do you mean?"

"With Eleanor, for instance. You've grown so close in a short period of time. But does she tell you everything? Do you trust her?"

She relaxed. He might assume this was tricky ground, but it wasn't. She had thoroughly accommodated herself to the kind of posthumous polygamy that linked her to Eleanor.

" 'Trust' doesn't seem the applicable word," she said. "It just feels like a natural process—like widows consoling each other. Or not even 'like.' That's what it is, really."

He looked dazed at this.

She smiled sadly: "We're both mourning him, you see. And I think he'd understand. On some level I was thinking it almost the minute we were out of Chicago."

She had never named the city so easily.

"So," he went on, tidying loose ends, "she already told you about the cards, then."

"What cards?"

"The tarot cards."

She waited for more.

There was the hint, ever so slight, of a smile on his face, a smile not of nerves but of relief at still having something to offer—information, advice—even when he was in such a bad way himself.

"Just that she gave Walker a reading," he continued as soberly as he could, "and saw what was going to happen. Apparently that was why she left him."

"You mean she saw he was going to die?"

"Well," he had to admit, "not in so many words."

"Then what, exactly?"

"I'm surprised she didn't tell you."

"She'll tell me if I ask her. What are you telling me?"

He spelled it out: "Her prediction—the cards' prediction—was that there would be three women in his life. And since she was only Number Two, that meant Number Three was on her way. And of course after Eleanor left, Number Three turned out to be you."

"And you took that seriously?"

"If he thought it worth mentioning, then yes I did take it seriously. Very seriously."

She didn't know what to say to this. Here they were, back on this business of the "occult" again. It disturbed her to think that Plume in some way was advocating it, saying it should be given credence. That wasn't what she wanted to hear. What she wanted, if anything, was to be talked *out* of any inclinations she had in that direction.

Plume, in the meantime, was incapacitated, teetering on the edge of some impossible abyss.

Playing his own biggest card, he told her: "I have Walker's tapes, you know. On cassette. Recordings of our sessions together. I could play them for you if you like. You could hear him for yourself."

She stared at him and realized that in his distress he was convinced he had a claim on Walker—certain rights to him, as it were. He seemed in the throes of a feeling, or not even a feeling but an *expertise*, that was both invasive and voyeuristic, all of it rationalized and made to seem clear-sighted. Just as she had broken down at the end of their last session, he was, in his equivalent way, breaking down now. And this necessitated a confrontation of sorts—to establish whose feelings were stronger, more genuine and durable; to sort out whose relationship, hers or Plume's with Walker, took primacy here.

The temptation, so powerful, to hear her husband's voice after not having heard it for so long—apart from his meaningless answering-machine greeting—came and went. She saw her alternatives with sudden clarity, and made her move.

"Right here, I think, would be a good place to end our sessions."

Plume, still caught up in his revelations, was saying, "I've got them on file. I could play them for you." His words came off as a strangely generous threat: "If you want to hear him, you only have to ask me."

"If I want to," she told him, "I will."

"When I see you—"

"I'll give you a call."

"—at our next appointment."

"There'll be no appointment."

"Next Monday?"

"No. This is it. This is final."

But even as she said this she wondered where the determination to act had come from and whether it was reliable or fleeting, a true decision or just a passing impulse unlikely to prevail.

Walker, in her mind, was a vivid engine, a generous fugue

topped off with a cockeyed grin—a grin that showed he took none of this seriously. He liked the substance of things to spin like a top, to gambol in midair like a trapeze act . . . or was she making this up?

She had no way of telling. Four months—it was close to four now—had put an analgesic distance between her husband and herself. She would like to have established the exact occasions when he had smiled whatever beneficent smile it was that had held them together, a smile that was fading on her now. She longed to have some tangible record of its every appearance— but she didn't want Plume getting wind of this.

Instead, she looked at him with concern and saw that for the moment he could no longer function in his role. His offer of Walker's tapes was a clear sign of this, and made clear too that the kindest thing for her to do would be to make a clean break from him. She had sought his assistance in a desperate moment, and he had given it to her. His inability to assist her now could not be held against him. He was hurting. She sympathized, but had no answers for him. And if she wasn't careful, he might succeed in including her in his hurt.

Suppressing any note of antagonism toward him, she said, "I really won't be coming back," then added with feeling, "And I am sorry, truly sorry—about you and your friend."

He was uncertain what she meant by this, what she might have guessed. Did she know about Bill, too? How could she? It wouldn't do to have the news circulating publicly. Would she keep it to herself?

But he didn't have the nerve to ask this favor of her.

"I'll call you," she repeated.

And then she went.

There was no sound from Bill upstairs—and no sign of his next client. This was the ten-minute interval he allowed himself between sessions: a chance to clear his mind, to meditate on answers.

Campbell's call had come last night, on top of everything else—not on the office line, but on the home phone after midnight, when Plume and Bill were already in bed, though not asleep. (With this latest news, they'd hardly slept all weekend. They had simply held on to each other.)

Bill answered on the first ring—but then, unable to cope with its confusion, passed the receiver over to Plume: "It's—I can't tell—some kind of collect call from Juneau . . .?"

Plume took the instrument in hand and heard a rasping tirade: "—if he says so, then I say so. If the Man from Juneau's got it, then I've got it. If the Man from Juneau is evaporating, then the whole world . . .?"

"Campbell?"

". . . Juneau . . ."

"Is that you?"

"You shouldn't go up there."

"What is it? What are you talking about?"

". . . ah oui, je know—"

"Is anyone else there? What's wrong?"

There were voices in the background, the sounds of people entering a room. And then a woman spoke sternly into the phone: "Hello, who is this?"

"I'm . . . I'm sorry, was that Campbell Bolter I was talking to just now?"

"Yes, that was Mr. Bolter."

"Is he sick? Is something wrong? We've been trying to reach him."

"You're a member of his family?"

"I'm—I know his father. His father's been trying to get in touch with him."

"Mr. Bolter said he notified his father, called him and no one called back, no one's been to see him. He called his mother, too, and spoke with her. He says she knows—"

"That's—That can't be true."

"Oh it is. Been here three weeks, and no one's telephoned, no one's come. It happens. It's not unusual."

"I mean he can't have called his mother—she's dead. And his father's been trying to reach him. His father called me. We've both been trying him. At his apartment. In Brooklyn. Where is he? Is this a hospital?"

"This is Long Island College Hospital. Who is this again?"

"I'm . . . his psychiatrist. Or was. I saw him for a number of years before he moved to New York."

"You're not local?"

"I'm in Seattle."

"You didn't call him? He called you?"

"He called me—"

"Then we got a problem. We can't have this patient calling long distance. He can't afford it. He's been doing this, always in the middle of the night. I mean, he just keeps on doing it. Can you call him back, sir?"

"Right away. What's the number? And who's his doctor?"

He turned on the light, scribbled down the information—doctor's name, hospital address, telephone numbers—and immediately called back.

The nurse's aide was helpful, transferred him to her station and explained Campbell's predicament. His landlady had found him. He had come down with the pneumonia—and let it go for too long: "There's treatments now, you know. But he left it too late." He also had the beginnings of KS, and what appeared to be mild dementia—though with so little background on him it was difficult to say how much. During his cogent episodes, he insisted he had notified his family, but that they didn't need to see him.

"But now you're telling me he hasn't called?"

"No one. He hasn't called anyone."

"Sure he has. He's been making crazy calls—some to Alaska, one to Montreal, these ones to Seattle. Or we thought they were crazy. How's he remember the numbers? He didn't say his family was from out of town."

"There's just his father—" Plume gave her Dr. Bolter's name and number, then asked to speak again to Campbell. "And can you tell him who it is? Can you say it's Jerry? Tell him it's Jerry Plume."

She transferred his call.

A gleeful croak, the mere outline of a voice, came on the line and asked: "Sweetheart, is that you?"

"It's me. It's Jerry."

"Can you see me? You should see me!"

"I'll come see you soon."

"You really should. You should come see. I'm like the leopard, changing my spots."

"But the leopard can't change its spots."

"Oh that's right. You know, sweetie—?"

But the thought, after a moment, evaporated in midsentence. "Know what?" Plume prompted him.

"That's right," the raggedy voice came back brightly, with reference to nothing at all.

A faltering conversation ensued. Plume would ask a question— "Do you still have your apartment?"—and would get no answer. He would ask it again—and Campbell would say, "But I'm telling you yes."

"I'm sorry—I couldn't hear you."

"I was nodding my head. I'm nodding my head when you want me to."

After ten minutes of this, and a few more words with the nurse's aide, Plume hung up and called Dr. Bolter. As they spoke, he had the pleasant sensation of solving a problem, helping to make connections. But when he got off the phone, he couldn't unwind. There was still no chance of sleep—not for him or Bill. They were too encircled, too tense with the threat.

He thought again of the calculation, the cold and necessary

calculation that applied to every encounter he could imagine now—not just man-to-man anymore, but everyone: man and woman, even mother and child.

The report on Bill had come late Friday afternoon and the results were positive—which meant it was his turn to be tested: "But you can die of other things. People do. . . ."

He said these words in this room where he spent so much of his time, alone or in the company of someone who paid him to listen. And he thought once more of Walker. He even crossed to his file cabinet, pulled out the tapes he had offered Susan and weighed them in his hands. Then he took out Campbell's Super-8 films, from a bottom desk drawer where he had hidden them from Bill, and considered these as well.

"People do," he murmured again. "Lots of people do."

"Oh, no," Eleanor protested, and the look in her eyes was of teasing mixed with threat, "I'm not getting caught with the cards again." As if the cards were merely a technicality—symptomatic of something that was undoubtedly true but rarely admitted.

"So you won't give me a reading?"

Susan was taking the matter more seriously than she had expected.

"Afraid not, hon—but you can ask for something else if you like."

She ignored the invitation in these words; wanted either confirmation or a categorical denial.

"You do know how to give one, don't you?"

They were sitting in Eleanor's apartment on the southwest corner of Queen Anne Hill, with Eleanor reclining on a couch and

Susan perched in the armchair next to it. Across the street, the land fell away in the ground-cover greenery and skeletal trees of Kinnear Park. Beyond the park—and a hundred or more feet below it—were the chilly waters of the Sound, skinned over in smooth metal surface, with snaky currents wrestling underneath. Two ferries, cheery and serene, slid over the water, their outlines merging and separating as one pulled into Elliott Bay and the other headed out to Winslow or Bremerton.

"Give what?" Eleanor asked. "A reading?"

Her voice was high and floating, a little enigmatic.

Susan nodded yes.

"But anyone could," she said. "All you have to do is study it. I could lend you a book to read tonight and you could come back tomorrow and give *me* one. It's a game, that's all. It's fun at parties."

"You used to give Walker readings."

"Just once, is all."

"And?"

" 'And'—? And what?"

"It must have said something."

"It said any number of things. That's not the point. It depends on how you look at it—on how you *choose* to look at it. There's an element of interpretation involved. No use taking it to heart."

"But it upset him. You upset him with it."

"There's a lot I used to do that got Walker upset."

By way of example—or so it seemed—she came forward, her fingers alighting not on Susan's shoulders but on a spot just lower down, sending a shiver across her breasts, along her arms . . . until Susan pulled back, persisted with her inquiry.

"There has to be something you told him," she insisted. "Something that hurt."

Eleanor gave her a look that said, *I see we'll have to go back to the basics—and here I thought we'd gotten past that.*

Out loud she declared, "I told him what I saw, and what I felt like telling him. No reason to hide it. No big mystery involved. Except insofar as any human exchange is a bit mysterious.''

"That's a pretty big 'insofar.' "

"Well, you're right about that, hon. You're onto something there.''

"So what you're telling me—''

"What I'm telling you is: Walker liked things simple. And he wanted limits. I knew that from the start. But I thought his limits encompassed more than they did. It took me a while to realize there were things he'd do only because he was doing them with me. He would never have done them on his own. And after I realized that, it took me a while to act on it.''

She explained this quickly as though eager to move on to other business. But Susan refused to be hurried. She looked around the apartment—at the prints on its wall, the track lighting, the low-slung furniture, the view out over avenues of water where glum freighter traffic made a slowly moving painting—as if to catch a clearer glimpse of how Eleanor might proceed; how she had proceeded in the past.

She asked, "You don't like limits?''

Eleanor leaned forward to confide: "Some, yes, of course. But not limits in behavior . . . not sexual behavior, anyway.'' She sat back. "It isn't even a matter of liking. More an inability to stay put.''

The apartment was furnished in a blond, Scandinavian manner and was spotlessly clean—cleaner than Susan's Capitol Hill apartment had ever been. But in spite of this, or perhaps because of it, it felt empty at the center. Susan shivered.

"You're chilly?'' Eleanor asked. "I could turn up the heat if you like.''

Susan admitted she wouldn't mind it warmer.

Eleanor vanished to fiddle with the thermostat.

Upon returning, she inquired, "So what's the latest on our friend Dr. Plume? Has he come up with any solutions?''

"No, not really."

"But you're enjoying your visits with him?"

" 'Enjoy' isn't exactly the word."

Eleanor's face composed itself into a semblance of sympathy: "I suppose it wouldn't have been Walker's either. But you're coming closer? To wherever it is he's taking you?"

"I don't think so. He's having a pretty bad time himself— which makes it awkward."

"What kind of bad time?"

Susan outlined what few facts she had been able to glean of Plume's recent loss.

Eleanor's expression was guarded. This was the kind of news item she never liked to hear: "How close a friend?"

"Not his lover—but close. Anyway, it's left him a wreck. He's out of it."

"So will you keep seeing him?"

"Probably not."

Eleanor waited for more.

"Actually," Susan confessed, "that's kind of why I'm here— to tell you I'm quitting with him."

Now that she had come to the point, however, it felt embarrassing . . . to be reporting every move she made to Eleanor almost as soon as she made it.

"What about your dream-couple?" Eleanor asked. "Aren't they still in the picture? Don't you need Plume's help with them?"

"Oh, I haven't seen them in a while. Two weeks, at least. I think they may be gone."

"And what does Plume say about that?"

"He seems to have forgotten about them. It's Walker he wants to talk about."

"Why's that?"

Susan debated this briefly within herself, then offered, "Do you know, I'm almost beginning to think he's in love with him."

"With Walker?"

Susan nodded tentatively. But Eleanor, sitting up straight, dismissed this possibility: "He never did Walker much good that I could see."

"And did you?"

"Did I what?"

"Do Walker much good?"

"Sweetheart—" The word contained as much impatience as endearment. "—when you're married it's never that simple. You ought to know that."

Susan didn't, but stayed quiet on this. The electric radiators made a buzzing sound. A scent of dusty heat began to rise from the baseboards. Eleanor slipped off the coarse-knit sweater she was wearing and revealed a blouse made from a material that Susan associated with the 1970s—a supple synthetic, with hidden highlights that emerged with each change of light. On Eleanor its blue verged on an indigo which glimmered either violet or a glassy turquoise-green when she altered her position, however slightly, on the couch. Beneath this slippery color-play, Eleanor shone with an invitation that expanded moment by moment, now that the question of Plume had been—to her way of thinking—put to rest. In the outline of her shoulders and her breasts was a shifting readiness, a willingness to experiment, that gave Susan a sensation of vertigo. And above this unstable surface, Eleanor's face was the same as ever: calm under pressure, serene with the implication that if there were any cessation in the flux of the world around her she would immediately become subject to restlessness, irritation, even willful hostility. Eleanor liked to keep things moving.

"Why don't I play the psychiatrist?" she suggested. "You'll save yourself some money. And we can talk about anything you like."

"Anything?"

She came close: "Anything at all. That's the best way, isn't it?"

She waited for a response; then intercepted the first word Susan offered: "Walker—"

"Would you like me to describe him when he was young?"

"Only—Only if—"

"And I'm allowed to be as frank as I like?"

"I don't know. If it's not too—"

"I want there to be no shyness between us," Eleanor pleaded. "And there isn't any, is there?"

Susan wasn't sure of this.

"If we can't talk straightforwardly about him, what can we talk about?"

Again, Susan didn't know: "You want to tell me about you and Walker?"

"To start with, anyway."

Susan looked dubious, but Eleanor held out her arms in a welcoming gesture: "Come sit by me."

Susan stayed where she was.

"What?" Eleanor laughed. "You think I'm going to bite?"

Susan frowned at the words.

"I won't," Eleanor smiled. "At least, not yet."

This was met with a glance which prompted Eleanor to comment: "You look like you're ready to attack."

"I'm ready—"

But she didn't know which it was: a readiness to launch an attack or to withstand one.

Eleanor gave her a look that encompassed both possibilities, then began to scale Susan's defenses. Her words filled the quiet room, dispersed like smoke through it, wreathing evanescently from place to place, with no single point being emphasized. They were like a path you follow in a dream toward a crossroads where time and distance begin to lose their meaning.

Susan listened. But it was a while before Eleanor's disquisition penetrated. There were sounds of hollering from the street outside. There was the low vibration of a ferry's announced departure.

". . . what parties were for," Eleanor was saying. "The way people fit together—socially, sexually. But maybe you never saw it like that? I remember it from high school: this boy I knew who touched me, touched my breasts . . . in summer, in June. I was only wearing jeans and a T-shirt, no bra underneath. And the T-shirt was thin. He was gay. I'm pretty sure I knew it at the time. No sense of threat in him, just curiosity. After all, we were alike in certain ways and he wanted to feel the ways in which we were *un*alike. I wanted to feel them too! I let him touch me. And later on . . ."

Susan glanced toward windows filled with soft spring evening light.

". . . these rumors about me and my best friend. Or not rumors exactly. How else do you learn to kiss? And there were some about him and a guy who was a senior. So we thought we'd better try it with each other, give them something else to talk about. We could have faked it, I guess, but we wanted the details to be convincing—and besides he was cute, I wanted to! It worked out just fine, he did okay with me. Boys that age, they're so skinny—well, some of them—it's like you can slip them in wherever you want. There're these others who are big all over: football players, wrestlers. But I wasn't interested in them. I was after the dropouts, the potheads, the art students, the ones who wore beads and listened to music. . . ."

Susan had her own experience of that, there in the family photograph album: herself as a baby, squawling in her mother's arms, a little string of love beads around her neck, while her parents went marching in an antiwar protest downtown.

". . . what a blast, just touching and triggering it, seeing the mess he made, and I was a mess too. His fingers tentative, you know?—as if he couldn't believe it. But then when I took his hand. . . . I think it was the display that excited him, the exhibitionism involved. It had to be. Or maybe the novelty of it, since he lost all interest in it later on. We got carried away. I can't believe how careless we were! Didn't listen to anyone, didn't take precautions. We were just lucky I guess. . . ."

Susan felt her throat go dry, her heart lift.

". . . kept in touch in college. He was out here, at the U.W. I ended up in Boulder. Georgia wasn't the place for either of us. Even Atlanta was a lot more dismal than it is now. . . ."

Bring him back. Bring him back if you can, why don't you? And if you can't, then just shut up. What else am I here for?

". . . to his funeral the week after Walker's. But I didn't want to say anything, didn't want to burden you with it. And, actually, having to help *you* helped me to stem off the panic. But I wish you could have met him. It was too late to introduce you. He was always so skinny. Sickly, really. No margin of resistance. But beautiful in his way. First love, I guess. . . ."

Not him.Walker.

". . . what drugs I took. Not that they made any difference: I was confident. Not many people are, you know. I don't know where I got it. My brothers don't have it. I mean, most people will allow you to seduce them just because they're not used to the attention. They're yours for the taking, the first time anyway, you ever notice that? So there he was, all lit up and pretty. Sunburned, he'd been out hiking. Quite the outdoorsman. But when I got him upstairs and pulled down his shorts, his ass was skinny and pale and cool to the touch, and his cock was hard and warm. I was surprised all over again—at the power, the helpless urgency of it. There's that interval—you know?—between your first time and your second, before you get used to it, before you become fluent in it, so to speak; that interim when you start thinking of flesh as this otherworldly realm, the farthest thing from matter-of-fact. Next to impossible to arrange getting there. There's this invisible border. And then you crash through and it feels so good, this time you *really* want it. And he gave it to me. And I found out for myself that they come in different sizes, maybe not as varied as breast-size, but still. . . ."

Susan looked down to where Walker was smiling at her, a smile that traveled up through time, through his changes of flesh, diminishing in vigor.

". . . only I wanted more. Back when you could sniff each other. Back when tongues could go wherever they want. . . ."

His smile was on Eleanor's lips. His gaze was in Eleanor's eyes—and reflected in her own.

". . . till you use yourselves up. Well, you know how men are—all full of this haste? Which I thought meant variety, wanting to do it with everyone. But not him: quick but, my goodness, so devoted! In love! Reliable and delicious and willing to put up with almost anything. Hardly any personality to him at all once he fell for me, except the voyeur—so that was what I cultivated, that was what I worked on. He was anything but casual. Any departures from our routine were better arranged as a game with certain rules: 'Within these bounds there *are* no bounds.' You want me telling you all this? Or maybe you'd like to see. . . ."

Eleanor stood up, went to the bookshelves, searched for something, returned with a photograph album. Images were falling out of place. Some were pasted into precise chronology. Others had nothing to hold them, were tucked between pages, loose, sliding out.

There was one of a Gallic-looking young man of thirty or so—tidy body, compact flesh—feasting (in profile) on the willowy shape of an impossibly young Walker. In another, shot head-on, Walker's partner was the one who stood, tawny-skinned, head thrust back, with arms lifted and clasped behind his neck, so flesh became a sculpted arc—while Walker knelt at his feet, back to the camera, long hair obscuring his precise activities in the region of his partner's sex but making clear a certain bobbing motion of his head as his hands held fast to his partner's hips.

Susan stared at the photograph in dismay.

"Now what you've got to understand," Eleanor counseled her, "is that this isn't Walker. It isn't him at all. Just like this—" She came in for a kiss, a lingering flick of the tongue, and then pulled back: "—isn't you. Is it?"

Susan wanted to say no. But if it wasn't her, what was it? It was definitely something, and not anything entirely objectionable. It wasn't nearly as distressing as these photographs were. But Eleanor was already moving on again, flipping pages, a few of which Susan wanted to stop and examine for the glimpses of Walker they offered, no matter what he was doing, no matter whom he was with.

Not that there were many of him. Most were of Eleanor. Walker, after a certain point, vanished altogether and was replaced by his wife engaged either in solo activity or in the company of one, sometimes two, even three young men . . . or, on rarer occasions, women. Eleanor lingered over one shot in particular, a black-and-white glossy, attractively composed, in which she was considerably older than her partner, who appeared to be still in his teens and had a stream of tattoos on his runner's body: skin so shiny and snug on the bone that it looked like an exoskeleton. He was wedging his hardness into Eleanor, who accommodated him on all sides, taking his knobbly shoulders into her hands to mold them, letting his skinny face and dead eyes approach her fluid mouth and luminous gaze. She guided him into limbs that eased open.

"Now that," she said, "is Walker—all over. That's him. And that, really, was him from the start."

And it was. Even if he was nowhere in sight.

Susan looked away. She couldn't stand to see him like this—again and again, pulled deeper into something he was driven to see, not be.

There had always been this need of Eleanor's for a varied

experience, an experiment among the sexes. That was obvious. But the thought that this might have been Walker's chief attraction to her was new and disturbing.

Eleanor was more than enough for him, a world unto herself. So what must he have felt when he discovered he was nowhere near enough for her, that increasingly he was the accessory and not the object of her desire? How could he have stood it?

He had his pride, and his vanity too. It wasn't in him to protest or show his disappointment. He would never have caused a scene. And yet he clearly had taken in each facet of his situation, faithfully documenting every stage of it. It occurred to Susan that by the time he got to *her*, he had succumbed to a kind of soul fatigue. His vigor with her seemed almost to be, in retrospect, a charade concealing exhausted resources, a patience worn to the point of literal heartbreak, prompting him to settle for something simpler and cozier, something a damaged heart could bear. He wanted only to be tethered—on film, in spirit, in the flesh; to have limits imposed on him that could never have been imposed by his first wife. He had yearned to be the sole object of Susan's attention. And he was glad to return that attention in kind. All his waywardness was in his mind. He had no need to act it out with other people.

But he must really have loved Eleanor to have met her on her own terms, to have endured her for as long as he had. At the very least, he must have been impressed by her. Or maybe it was just that he adhered to the idea of marriage—or, if not marriage itself, then the idea of devotion: that it was meant to last, that you were expected to find all your ardor and order within its confines and, to that end, search yourself for every possibility of flexible understanding, adaptive behavior.

Those would have been his expectations. Whereas Eleanor—

But there was no telling what, exactly, Eleanor's expectations had been; Eleanor, who was stepping up to Susan now and saying, "This feeling of having the dead inside you—it's no good, is it? I wanted something living. I mean *really* alive, with no repetitions, no chance of decay. I hate it when things drag out, lose shape. You want to know why I ended it with Walker? You're asking me why?" Her body, along with her voice, was yielding up an answer. "I'll tell you why. Because I could see other possibilities for myself. Who doesn't? Everyone needs to. But I had a hell of a time convincing Walker he had possibilities too. You, for instance. You were on your way. I think that we both must have known that on some level—and known that there wasn't much time."

Susan said nothing, pulled back, did not want to hear this.

"Everyone who loses someone," Eleanor continued, "learns to live for that loss. In expectation of it, I mean. Anyone who imagines the worst hopes for the worst—however secretly, however ashamedly. Everybody knows that only loss can put the drama in your life." She waved her hand airily. "No reason why you should be different. You would have gotten tired of him, you know." She put a finger on Susan's lips to stop her protest. "You think I shouldn't be talking to you like this? You think it's—what, irreverent? But we're women. We're strong. Stronger than you think. Stronger than Walker, anyway. We can take it. Everyone needs memories: as many as possible, or your life feels empty. But you've got to work for them. You don't want to pine for just one thing when it goes from your life. You don't want to regret a single missed opportunity. It's better to regret as much as possible! To have adventures. And once you start, you never want to stop. It's what I said: like being fluent in a language—such a pleasure to use it. Exhausting sometimes, but worthwhile, rewarding. Always so satisfying to put a talent to use."

Her smile was close to Susan's skin. A weaving of impulses filled the room. She steered Susan toward the softly lit window: "We're on display, you know—"

This was a continuation of their earlier intimacy—a reprise of it which, paradoxically, showed it to be nearing its end.

"—and I've got fifteen years on you," Eleanor reminded her. "Sometimes it doesn't feel like much. But it's enough."

Susan, still shivering, wondered where Walker was in all this. Would he, at Eleanor's instructions, have photographed this? Yes, she decided, he probably would—except she would never have come this far if it hadn't been for him leading her here. The air was flecked with visions, flashes of reverie: Walker, broadened from his skinny student self to a husky shape which was the only version of him she had ever known; Walker driving himself against her, looking in semi-amusement at her, with an easy trust that had probably escaped Eleanor entirely, even if she still thought of him as being, to some meaningful degree, her own.

Eleanor's caresses were a bypath, a detour. She was whispering again, "You would have tired of him, just like you're tiring of me. See? You're losing patience. And that's what always happens. Things can't help fading."

She went on to describe some people who would be arriving at her apartment later in the evening: "I think you'll like them. I think they'll make you complete. And they're anxious to hear about Walker from another angle, another point of view."

Some of these impending visitors were regulars, Eleanor explained, while others were newcomers. In Walker's time, they had appeared only occasionally, either solo or in couples. Now Eleanor was knitting them together, making them cohesive as a group. . . .

Susan thought: Soul fatigue? Or was this more like mental fatigue?—a constant ferment, an endless unpredictability, an appetite for piling up experience, skin upon skin and layer upon layer, that tore at the heart, wore on the nerves. It was something she wasn't built to withstand.

"We could begin now if you want," Eleanor was saying. "You could tell me about him. What he was like with you. With me, he tried so hard to be unusual! But I knew he wasn't. Affection is only true if you can turn it around, twist it inside out, into teasing or cruelty. You could let me see you again, let me sense him in you. I'd enjoy it. Really I would."

Susan was leery of this: "But I can't get close to someone who feels like that."

Her own fatigue was sharpening. Proximity was dangerous.

Eleanor said: "I'm not asking you to. . . ."

Apparently there was a choice here, as there had been with Plume: succumb to this influence and embrace both the ease and violation of being Eleanor's entirely—or withdraw from her, while she still could, into safe but more solitary self-possession.

Brooding on this choice, she grew alert to Walker's ex-wife smiling at her in tacit acknowledgment of the point of no return they had reached. And she realized Walker had been mistaken. No matter what he had thought (and part of her yearned for Eleanor to give her the same tarot reading he had been given so she could know precisely *what* he had thought), the cards were merely a convenience, an excuse, a way of breaking news to him that should have been obvious just from his own observations.

With this realization, some of the evening's spell and a little of the misery of the last four months were broken. Recovering herself, she announced her next move; suggested she was done with haunting or being haunted.

"Where's the phone?" she asked. "I've got to make a call. And then I'll be going."

"So soon?"

This was not a question but a sudden lament, surprised and forlorn. Eleanor was unused to being abandoned. Rejection— another person's decision to act and terminate, to be as swift and ruthless as she was herself—undermined her . . . and made her look years older.

Susan, ignoring her, keyed in Plume's number. On the second ring his recorded message began to play. As she listened to it, she pictured the route she had followed since leaving his office an hour or so ago—to Capitol Hill, where she parked in front of

Celia's building but didn't go in; down the ski-slope plunge of Denny Way and over the freeway; past the Space Needle and through the heavy traffic of lower Queen Anne; up to Eleanor's place, toward a sky that kept spinning conclusions out of itself, then taking them back again, thinking better of it. . . .

Plume's greeting ended and the beep sounded.

Susan said: "I asked her. Are you there? Do you want to hear about it?"

Clicking static on the line was followed by Plume's voice, live but hedging: "I'm expecting a client."

"This won't take long. And I won't be calling again."

"You won't?"

"No—I thought I told you. This is it."

His reluctance to believe this didn't stop him from inquiring: "So what did she say?"

She parceled her words out carefully: "Well . . . it may have been in the cards—but the cards didn't make it happen. They were just a convenience. Sort of a handy tool. A pointer."

She felt it wasn't a real person she was dealing with on the other end of the line but a creature of her imagination. It surprised her, then, to hear him reply, in a voice as alluring and threatening to her as Eleanor's: "And what about the photographs? Are there more of them?"

"Photographs?" she asked. "Of course. Hundreds. Maybe thousands."

"You know what you have to do, then, don't you?"

"No, what?"

She braced herself, silently phrasing her refusal to hand any of them over to him. But his plea, when it came, was not what she expected.

"Burn them," he said.

"What?"

"Destroy them."

"But why?"

"They shouldn't exist. When you're fighting off a chill. . . . Get rid of them."

The words were an echo from long ago, another life.

"That's the next step," he insisted. "I've destroyed all the tapes: I've destroyed everything." He seemed to be saying this to someone other than her. "The photographs are all that's left. It's for the best."

"What is?"

"Burning them. You have to burn them."

He repeated the words with the fervor of a mantra or an article of faith.

There was nothing she could say to this. She couldn't tell him that for the past week she had carried them with her all the time in the car; that when it came right down to it she couldn't bear to part with them.

"Where are you now?" he asked.

"At Eleanor's."

"And where is she?"

"She's right here."

"I'm expecting a client," he told her again.

"Then you should go," she advised him.

"Yes, I should. And you should too."

"That's it, then," she said lightly. "We're done."

"No, we're not. You still have to burn them."

She waited for more.

But the dial tone sounded.

He had broken their connection.

Unnerved, but trying to put a good face on it, she turned to Eleanor and approached her, enfolding her chastely as if across an agreed-upon abyss of mutual distrust or as though they had quarreled, made up and now were going back to the way things were before they ever met.

They made no date for the immediate future. There wasn't any need to.

As she stepped outside, the clamor of city and Sound grew louder. A railroad whistle wailed as a train passed below. A docking ferry loosed its multiphonic blast—melancholy and flatulent.

She got into the car and drove with intensifying purpose, all the time aware of the evidence she was carrying with her: the portfolio of photographs and sketches in the trunk.

On Aurora Avenue, she sped above the dark hollow of Lake Union and then up a steady incline of motels and ramshackle businesses that lined the thoroughfare. She passed adult book-stores, fast-food restaurants and faux-marble outlets, before glid-ing down through Woodland Park and along the shores of Green Lake.

The sunset was making silhouettes, black and cartoon-sharp, to the west. Spindly trees and inky rooftops lined the ridge to her left. A magenta grandeur reared up behind them. And the street she followed was a ramp ascending. It took slanted leave of the grid it emerged from. The light was fading and the lanes intertwined. Their direction was confusing as she saw her young couple—who came right up to her, passed by, overtook her, but in great agitation, as if they saw something she didn't. At least the woman did. Beyond them, as dim and spectral as figures seen through a thickness of time, was every combination imaginable: male/female, male/male, father and son, mother and daughter. Not even couples, necessarily, but any link which started in the heart and ended up as image or memory: something a lens of the mind could be trained upon.

There was a density of atmosphere. The air became burdened. A potion of toxins rasped at Susan's throat. Her own sense of loss was combined with a general sense of loss—or was she, as Mary might have said, "projecting"? She felt she was looking for a platform, lost in a maze, about to go under. Maybe she had been wrong. Maybe she *did* have what a rat had.

To the south, Mount Rainier was enormous in the sunset. A pollution-sparked haze crawled up its flanks like a lava flow in reverse: a red-and-ocher fireball in her rearview mirror. . . .

When she glanced back at the road, she had to brake sharply. This was the nightmare. This was too much. She pulled over, blocking someone's driveway, unable to tell what was real and what was imagined. And it took her some time to find out—to smell the gasoline, interpret the voices.

There was an accident up ahead, a disarray of vehicles on their sides.

The thought naturally occurred: *Was I the cause of this?*

But it seemed already to be done with, already to have happened.

She sat on its outskirts for a while; and then, with caution, pulled back into the traffic moving around the wrecked vehicles.

The road was peopled with figures who swam out of balance. Caught in her headlights, their much-too-bright heads were a new kind a photograph. And the wreck was hushed, ornately still, as if it had been freeze-framed. The crowd couldn't believe it was over yet. They were waiting for something more to happen—the body behind the wheel to rise and walk away, the vehicles to erupt into well-rehearsed flames.

As she drove past, the scene resembled a vision she might be having as much as a sight she was witnessing. But its reality was beyond question. It was what Chicago had been: ". . . too much in focus."

There was movement: of Susan's dream-woman, mysteriously uninjured, stepping away from the debris. In the mottled light, a crazy kind of river played across her face. Like Susan, she was alone. And like Susan, she was part of a procession.

Everything about her was slippery. Everything about her was ravaged. Her eyes were vivid with shock. Her face was aghast with coincidence. It was, Susan wanted to tell Plume, anything but a "blank" face. There were whole worlds to be explored in its panicked, detailed movement. There were losses pouring through her as though she had a limitless capacity for them.

Something about her demeanor, however, struck Susan as strange.

The grieving widow (for there was no denying she *was* a widow now, judging from the way her husband, still in his neckbrace, had the steering wheel and half the steering column jammed into his chest cavity) was looking not at her own car with her spouse in it but at Susan's vehicle passing slowly by. And her look, as Susan met her eyes, was one of recognition. . . .

Susan kept driving, navigating her way past the wreckage, trying to absent herself, accelerate away from it. Half a mile along, however, that wreckage's meaning overwhelmed her, connecting her to it as if by invisible and contracting threads. She pulled into a side street and parked, still gripping the steering wheel. Then she got out of the car and paced the sidewalk up and down, studying the houses on either side of her—squat bungalows with drawn curtains, heavy eaves, hidden lives.

She saw into what was hidden, had the sensation of being gathered into an embrace—into the arms of a congregation almost. She realized how easily she could be taken for the phantom she herself had seen on every stage of her and Walker's train journey, a phantom she now suspected Walker had seen as well, in one form or another: an envoy whose purpose was to hint at his end and warn her of her loss. And all of this was hidden. Or, if not hidden, too manifold to grasp.

What was it Walker had said in Boston? Something about wave action?

The meaning of wreckage wiped out her voice. The action of waves—erosion upon erosion, erasure upon erasure—made it just one link in a chain of voices, a general chorus whose notes were haphazard and whose message was rhythmic.

To Plume, she realized, this could only resemble a general

mayhem: too many deaths ripening at once, a plundering without instinct, a hand covering the eyes to take the sight from them, a fist fitting a mouth to take the breath from it. It must seem a sly, brute force—capricious and exact—that dragged you down muttering, "Is . . . Is . . ."

Until it muttered: "Isn't."

But there were ways of fighting it. Or, rather, there were ways of working with its downward spiral, as the living must.

She got back in her car. She felt she had been out wandering, moving to and fro in time, sifting through layer upon layer of it, and now was shrinking back inward, almost to a pinpoint, becoming someone small and pragmatic, with no need to see anything more, hardly a need even to affirm her own existence. By the time she pulled into her own driveway, she knew what she had to do.

On the answering machine was a message from Celia: "Yoo-hoo! You there, babe?" And in a singsong voice: "You're ignoring me again. . . ."

There was another from her mother, sounding strained and demure: "Since you weren't able to make it last Saturday, we were thinking that maybe this weekend—"

And, finally, there was one from Aunt Ginny, who was starting up her own interior decoration business and wondered if Susan would like to be her first client. She went on to give her rates, which were outrageous, and the discount she was offering her niece, which was minimal.

Susan listened to these and took quiet comfort from them, before digging out the machine's instruction manual. Quickly, like a gymnast whose stunt depends on speed as much as strength, she erased Walker's greeting and replaced it with one of her own: "I'm not here right now, but if you'd like to leave your name, number and the time that you called—"

She knew there was more to Plume's panic than the one friend's loss. She assumed he was worse off than she was at the moment. But at the same time she wondered if his fears, as all-encompassing as they were, weren't in some ways worse than the circumstances that gave rise to them.

What if fear of the matter was worse than fact of the matter?

"Come on, come on," she wanted to tell him, not knowing, exactly, whose words were surfacing in her. "Come over where there's no more fretting about the world, no more straining against what's right or wrong with it. See? There's only this sinking deeper into the way things happen. . . ."

But she couldn't quite follow this piece of advice.

All that night she wandered through the house, upstairs and downstairs, making it her own. Walker smiled his loopy smile at her, ready to welcome her among the mute annihilations, the mirrors that never speak. He wanted to punch her on through them, bring her over to the other side.

The notion of this pleased her, and her thoughts inclined toward him. Her eyes kept a lookout and her heart skipped a beat. Glancing down, however, she saw she hadn't moved an inch.

In an old familiar way he chided her, showed her something, made a suggestion. She willingly agreed to this—but the opportunity passed once more, and again she had failed to act.

He turned away from her.

She made a silent protest, beamed two faces toward him at once: one that was going, the other staying. A mistake, perhaps.

His smile vanished. He let her go. What were the proper procedures to follow under the circumstances? Imagining the "other side," it turned out, was only marginally like reaching it. Thinking your way past mirrors appeared to be less like punching through them than learning to straddle them lightly.

That left just one other item of business to dispose of. Her packet of "evidence"—the photographs she had carried around with her these last two weeks.

She fetched them from her car, dropped them in a Pendaflex folder and tucked them away for safekeeping in the basement files that held the record of Walker's life from the years before he met her and the short while after.

Her sketches of him, however, were hers—were *her*. She would keep them on hand, by her bedside perhaps, for the duration, she decided, or until she had lost all connection with them. . . .

Back upstairs, she adjusted the thermostat to shake off the cellar's chill. And as the house warmed up, she relaxed, at the same time growing more alert. She was aiming for the next wave, the approaching pulse, the tangible abyss of a life without Walker. This would mean growing older; she was aware of that. And it also meant succumbing to her loss . . . a kind of suicide, almost. Or maybe, as with marriage, just a further name change, but of a subtler variety: one with no outward symptom.

Whatever it was, she had resigned herself to it.

Everything else was in order. All coincidence had lapsed. A pattern was complete and a glory had faded. Walker had loosened her a little from his spell; was now sad nourishment for memory.

With a feeling of indulgence, she took one last look at her younger self, her unscathed self—in some ways, her best and weakest self—before moving ahead. . . .

And then she was gone.

Acknowledgments

Many friends, with their criticism and encouragement, helped this book along its way. I'd like to thank Sally Bowdoin, Sîan Ede, Janice Findley, Susan Golomb, Karl Holzheimer, my sisters Melissa Mayernik (for enthusiasm) and Dr. Margaret B. Upchurch (for tips on water mazes), Doug Nufer, Kathleen Skeels (for botanical advice), Karen Wardley and Alix Wilber. Special thanks to Peter Theroux for helping to make the connection, my editor Amy Cherry for drawing out the parts that weren't there and, last but not least, John Hartl for his genial companionship and remarkable patience.

The memories of others no longer here—Ron Snyder, Donald Kitch, Christopher Cox, Rajeeve Gupta, Tom Sprake—are in this novel.